YOU FIT
THE PATTERN

Books by Jane Haseldine

THE LAST TIME SHE SAW HIM

DUPLICITY

WORTH KILLING FOR

YOU FIT THE PATTERN

Published by Kensington Publishing Corporation

YOU FIT
THE PATTERN

JANE HASELDINE

KENSINGTON BOOKS
www.kensingtonbooks.com

KENSINGTON BOOKS are published by

Kensington Publishing Corp.
119 West 40th Street
New York, NY 10018

All Kensington titles, imprints, and distributed lines are available at special quantity discounts for bulk purchases for sales promotion, premiums, fund-raising, educational, or institutional use. Special book excerpts or customized printings can also be created to fit specific needs. For details, write or phone the office of the Kensington Special Sales Manager: Attn. Special Sales Department. Kensington Publishing Corp, 119 West 40th Street, New York, NY 10018. Phone: 1-800-221-2647.

Library of Congress Card Catalogue Number: 2018912507

Kensington and the K logo Reg. U.S. Pat. & TM Off.

ISBN-13: 978-1-4967-1098-7
ISBN-10: 1-4967-1098-3
First Kensington Hardcover Edition: April 2019

ISBN-13: 978-1-4967-1099-4 (e-book)
ISBN-10: 1-4967-1099-1 (e-book)

10 9 8 7 6 5 4 3 2 1

Printed in the United States of America

*To my agent, Priya Doraswamy, constant advocate,
pitchwoman extraordinaire, super cool soul sister, dispenser
of excellent parenting advice. And friend.*

YOU FIT
THE PATTERN

CHAPTER 1

Heather Burns coiled her perfectly highlighted blond hair into a tight bun and frowned as she gave her face a brutal inspection in the mirror of her parked yellow Range Rover.

Dissatisfied with her appearance, Heather pulled the skin back from the corners of her jawline and took in the wistful reminder of what she used to look like when age meant nothing because the onset of its ravages hadn't yet struck.

God, getting older really was the ultimate bitch, the thirty-nine-year-old thought, and scanned the empty parking lot of Mayberry State Park in Northville, a suburb of Detroit, where she and her teenage daughter, Carly, lived.

Heather gave up on her face momentarily and spun around to the backseat to make sure she remembered the four FIND YOUR NEW HOME HERE! signs dotted with cheerful red-house emojis for her nine AM open house, her day's next order of business after her early-morning run. Satisfied when she spotted the signs poking out from underneath her briefcase, Heather took to the rearview mirror to resume her search for any new wrinkles.

She needed new headshots for her latest batch of business cards and beat her French-manicured fingernails against the dashboard as she fretted over the stone-cold fact that a pretty face sold more houses and raked in bigger commissions. She had learned early on that looking good was a job requirement for a successful Realtor. And Heather had already bore catty witness to a younger crop of thinner and blonder girls already jockeying at her RE/MAX office for a chance to snag her clients.

Heather dug her hand deep inside her bag and retrieved a business card her friend had given her over drinks at a downtown Detroit bar during a recent girls' night out. Heather studied the phone number on the card and recalled how her friend swore to her with the enthusiasm of an infomercial host that if Heather just made an appointment, she'd feel so much better about herself. Presto chango, renewed self-esteem courtesy of a couple syringes of Botox and assorted fillers stuck in her face.

Heather tossed the card back in her bag and decided she'd stick with her crow's-feet. At least for now.

The sharp bite of the early-October Michigan morning hit Heather as she exited the Range Rover and she began to shiver. Heather worked through her usual series of stretches and felt a renewed pang of guilt for giving Carly a new phone. Her daughter had ultimately worn her down, complaining about the sheer humiliation of being the only person in her group that had a flip phone. Carly had hammered home the injustice that even elementary-school kids had iPhones, and there she was, a ninth grader, forced to use a relic.

Carly was a good girl, a straight-A student, and a solid athlete who excelled on her county-rec baseball and soccer league teams, despite the grenade Heather's dad had thrown into their lives after he walked out on his family to take up with a pharmaceutical sales rep he met at his physician's practice. After her ex had bailed on his latest weekend with Carly, Heather had caved on the phone as some sort of half-baked consolation prize to make her daughter feel better.

She was sure her good girl would never abuse the privilege of the phone. But three weeks later, Heather soon learned that phones with cameras, where images could be quickly snapped and texted to boys or girls who fluidly changed their allegiance of friendship in a teenage hormonal nanosecond, were dangerous toys, not modern-day commodities for kids to communicate.

One stupid slip of judgment and the selfie of Carly in her underwear had spread like wildfire around the school. But Heather would make it right. She hated confrontation and usually choked under pressure, her voice melting into a quaking stutter when she had to face down a hostile encounter. But this was for her little girl, so Heather had made an appointment to talk to the principal after the open house.

Moms would go to any length for their kids.

A cool gust of wind sent the fall leaves scattering like a swirl of bright copper pennies across the ground. Heather ignored her chattering teeth and took a quick glance at her watch: 6:00 AM. Her Range Rover was still the only car in the parking lot. But Heather wasn't worried about running alone. The park was an old friend, one that she had discovered during her sophomore year of high school when she first ran track. A sad smile played on her lips as she recalled the state record she set senior year for the eight-hundred-meter race, a crowning residual jewel she sometimes pulled out as a reminder of a time when she believed the world was brimming with endless possibilities just waiting for her with a beckoning hand.

Glory days, baby.

Heather's feet found their pace as she started her run. She

completed her first loop around the lake, the one-mile mark of her four-mile run, and pushed herself faster and harder for her second round.

Running for Heather was like meditation. Her mind was usually clear of any worries or regrets when she ran, and the sound of her sneakers slapping against the pavement was a soothing white noise, a temporary respite from memories of her last date with her ex-husband who announced over a plate of shared pasta puttanesca that he wanted a divorce.

She discovered later that his new lady was at the restaurant waiting for him, watching the scene unfold from a seat at the bar.

Heather felt the tears come, but she forced herself not to cry. She was fine. Just fine.

The sun crested its way up to the top of the tree line and Heather checked her watch again: 6:45. Time to head home for a quick shower and to make Carly lunch before she went to school. Heather slowed her pace to a fast walk and made her way back to the empty parking lot, where she spotted another vehicle cutting around the corner, breaking her solitude.

As the car got closer, Heather could see that it was an older-model tan Buick driven by a gray-haired woman, who gave Heather a quick, friendly wave with a mittened hand as she passed. The Buick stopped at the other end of the park by the duck pond, where Heather frequently saw a group of people from the senior center do tai chi.

Heather did her usual routine and headed to the public restroom before she left the park. She always downed a large bottle of water before she ran, so the women's room was her final stop before her twenty-minute car ride home.

The door to the women's room creaked as she opened it. Heather hurried inside, grabbed a handful of brown paper towels from a dispenser near the sink so she wouldn't have to touch the icky bathroom door handle, and entered the stall closest to the door.

Heather began to come up with her strategy on how she could steady her nerves during her meeting with Carly's principal, when the bathroom door opened, the rough *screak, screak, screak* of its hinges sounding like a rusty nail being dragged across the floor.

Plodding footsteps thumped past Heather and then a stall door banged shut on the far side of the room.

Heather flushed the toilet with the toe of her sneaker and approached the sink. She did a quick look in the mirror and saw the reflection of someone's feet planted underneath a stall. The wearer had on a set of black orthopedic shoes and tan pantyhose that poked out from the elastic bottom of a pair of gray sweatpants, the outfit likely belonging to the older lady in the Buick, Heather figured.

Heather finished washing her hands and decided to slip a note in Carly's lunch box before she left for work, letting her daughter know she loved her and that everything was going to be all right. Something along the lines of, "I know this all seems terrible now, but it will be okay. I promise."

"Oh no," a woman's voice creaked. Heather turned to see a roll of toilet paper drop onto the floor from inside the occupied stall and then make a slow crawl in her direction, the tissue unwinding in a wide strip until it abruptly stopped and landed on its side next to the garbage can.

Heather started to move to the door, thinking she had to hurry if she was going to get Carly to school on time, but stopped when she realized she needed to do the right thing.

"Are you okay?" Heather asked.

"Just old age," the woman answered with a dry laugh. "I have arthritis and my hands don't work as well as they used to. Can you hand me the roll if it's not a bother?"

"Sure," Heather said. Something in the woman's voice

niggled in the back of Heather's head, but she quickly moved on to the upcoming open house, hoping to God she'd get some actual prospects instead of the neighborhood looky-loos who usually showed up.

She carefully picked up the toilet paper, thinking how gross the outer layer was, since it rolled its way across God knows what was teeming on the gray cement floor. She wound a few loops of tissue off until the spots of wetness and dirt were gone and then shoved the wad of soiled tissue into the garbage.

"Here you go," Heather said. She bent down and reached her hand up under the woman's stall.

"Thanks so much, Miss Burns."

The thin chime of a warning bell went off inside Heather over the sound of her name being spoken so intimately by the stranger.

Heather tried to quickly retract her arm from under the stall door, but the vise grip of an unseen hand latched itself around her wrist.

"Hey! What is this?" Heather cried out. "Let go!"

The lady was senile, she had to be, Heather reasoned as she fought to keep her balance from her crouched position and free her hand, figuring the old woman inside the stall would be no match for her. Heather reared backward to try and break away, but her arm was pulled forward with such force, Heather was sure it would rip out of the socket.

"Help! Please! Somebody help me!"

Heather felt a second hand wrap around her forearm and she pitched forward, slamming her face into the gray stall door.

A sharp pain pulsed like a jackhammer from her nose as Heather's thoughts screamed out to her, *Don't give up, can't give up!* She started to cry and wondered how this old woman could be so strong.

"Please, I have money in my car. And my credit cards. You can have them. Just let me go."

An unexpected surge of hope spread through Heather as her attacker released their grip and Heather's arm slipped free.

This was her chance. She knew she needed to run, to get out of the confined space as fast as she could. But Heather Burns, the queen of choking under pressure, kept her title and froze in place as the stall door banged open.

Her attacker ran a large hand across their mouth, leaving a smeared trail of bright pink lipstick down their chin. Heather slowly crabbed her body toward the door and spotted the tendrils of a gray wig spilling out from a small trash can in the back of the stall.

Two minutes too late, Heather realized she made a critical mistake by ignoring the off-sound of the woman's voice as a tall, well-built man with sandy-blond, short-cropped hair and a smile so wide, it almost split his face, exited the stall and loomed over her.

"Don't fight," the man said. "It's going to be much easier if you just give up."

"Please, I'll give you my money. You can have everything. I swear."

"I don't want money," the man said. He pulled out a folding knife from underneath a bulky dark blue sweatshirt and snapped open its six-inch blade. "On your stomach. Now."

Heather felt a sickly panic move through her as she stared at the weapon, which had a green-fatigue, military-like handle and a black blade with an inch of serrated teeth by its base.

The man was going to rape her. She was sure of it. She closed her eyes and wondered if it would be better if he just killed her instead.

"On your stomach, I said."

Heather thought of her daughter, who would be waking up for school about now and wondering where her mother was. She mustered a reticent nod, knowing she needed to do anything to get back home, and flipped over on her stomach in a prone position.

She shook as she waited for the man to pull off her running shorts. But he reached for her hands instead, roughly pulling them behind her back and then binding her wrists together with something that felt to Heather like hard plastic that bit into her skin.

"Let's go," the man said, and pulled her up. "We're going to take a ride."

Heather had stopped trying to find the emergency release latch in the trunk of the Buick, where the man had stuffed her. After realizing the car was an older model and didn't have a release pull, she had resorted to pounding her feet against the top of the trunk in a futile effort to get it open.

During the beginning of what Heather thought was so far a thirty-minute ride, she could hear what she decided was city traffic. But for the past ten minutes, the honks and revved engines of aggressive Detroit commuters had ebbed and all Heather heard now was the Buick's wheels humming underneath her as she sat, crammed in a fetal position in complete blackness.

The Buick came to a sharp stop and Heather tried to scramble to come up with a flight plan. She cursed herself for not leaving Carly a note to tell her where she was jogging, so her daughter could call the police with a location when Heather didn't come home.

Daylight flooded the Buick as the trunk swung open, and Heather squinted to see her attacker looming over her.

"If you try to run, I'll kill you," her abductor said, and flashed his ugly black and camouflage-green knife from the

pocket of his sweatshirt, as if Heather really needed a reminder.

Heather could smell the sour musk of the man's sweat not
quite masked under his cologne when he pulled her out of the
trunk. He wrapped his arm around her waist, and Heather
felt the dampness of his sweatshirt on her back.

Heather took a quick mental snapshot of her unfamiliar
surroundings to come up with an escape route if she could
get away. The Buick was parked on a desolate side street next
to an old brick church that looked like it was about to crum-
ble. A sliver of the remote Detroit skyline was visible from
the side of the church, which meant the man had likely driven
them to one of the city's run-down, left-for-dead neighborhoods that skirted Detroit. What that meant to Heather was,
the likelihood of anyone stumbling by to help her was going
to be as likely as her winning the lottery or getting crowned
Miss America.

"Move," the man whispered in her ear.

In lockstep, the two entered the abandoned church. The
depressing, cavernous space was littered with a few ruined
leftovers of the church's likely golden era when parishioners
filled its now-gutted pews. A splintered, keyless organ lay
hangdog on its side in the middle of the aisle, and what was
left of a broken stained-glass image of Jesus on the cross
framed the rear wall of the church.

Heather shivered when she reached the end of the aisle,
where someone had tagged *I love weed* in black graffiti letters, and she turned slowly around. She did a quick mental
picture of the man's face so she could describe him to the
cops if she was able to get free, and was struck by the odd realization that the man who abducted her was good-looking.

"Please. I have a daughter."

"No, you don't. You have two sons."

"You're wrong! This is some kind of mistake."

"No mistake. But you're not right yet. I need to fix you."

The man pulled out his knife, reached behind Heather, and sliced apart the twist ties. He then dug into a green-fatigue duffel bag and pulled out a long, dark wig and a piece of blue clothing.

"Put these on."

"Jesus, what is this?" Heather cried.

The man looked through Heather as if she weren't there. "I'll dress you."

Heather screamed and her voice echoed through the lonely belly of the church, a haunted cry to no one, as the man carefully arranged the dark wig over her blond hair. He took his time and teased out a few long strands so they cascaded down to the tops of her breasts.

"Better. But still not right. Put the dress on."

"Will you let me go if I do?"

The man continued to look through Heather and slid his tongue over his lips.

Heather grabbed the dress from his hands. She'd play along. He had to be a freak is all. If she just did what she was told, maybe he'd let her go. If he was going to kill her, he would've done it by now, Heather convinced herself. She looked at the piece of clothing she was supposed to wear. It was a bright blue dress, which was sleeveless, with a scooped neck, a fitted high waist, and an A-line skirt.

"Take off your shorts and shirt. It needs to be perfect," the man said. He turned around as if to give Heather privacy so he wouldn't see her in her underwear.

"Don't look," Heather said. She undressed and then pulled the garment over her head. "Okay. It's on."

The man cocked his head to the side as he took in his creation. He rearranged a few locks of the long, dark wig so they framed Heather's face, and, seemingly pleased with himself, smiled.

"Size two. It fits you perfectly, just like I knew it would."

"You've been watching me?"

"I've seen you running. You fit the dress, just like I thought."

Heather shivered and tried to move backward and away from the man, but fumbled and tripped on a step that led up to the altar.

"She would've never done that," the man said. "Don't ruin it."

"Who are you talking about? I don't understand."

The man grabbed Heather by the waist and drew her against his chest. Unable to hold it together anymore, Heather sobbed as her attacker began to sway with her in his arms.

" 'Hold me close and hold me fast . . . The magic spell you cast . . .' "

The man sang softly and tenderly in her ear. His voice hung on the last word, triggering a memory for Heather, something long ago and familiar. She worked it through her head, and caught an image of her eight-year-old self rummaging through the contents of her family's garage and discovering her mother's old jazz albums.

The name of the song and singer was on the tip of her memory when her attacker spun her around and then slit her throat in a single fast, deep cut.

Heather's hand shot up to her neck in surprise. She tried to stop the bleeding, but there was so much of it and the laser-sharp pain was such that she had never felt before.

A strange wheeze came from her throat, like a child blowing a whistle, and she collapsed in front of the altar. She stared up at the splintered image of Jesus in the stained glass and was no longer able to fight off the truth.

She was dying.

Something warm and wet trickled from Heather's mouth.

She pictured Carly from a long-ago memory when her daughter was just two, her Carly laughing as her plump little legs poked out of a striped onesie, her little girl racing down the hallway of their house, with Heather trying to keep up from behind.

She tried to hang on to the image and block out the horror around her, but was still vaguely aware of her killer, huddled on the floor over a piece of paper, drawing while he hummed.

The man stood above her now, smiling and holding up the picture he had drawn, strange and intricate symbols in turquoise and red.

"Do you like it?" he asked, and beamed like he was showing her his masterpiece.

He then lifted up Heather's left hand, slipped something inside it, and folded her fingers closed against her palm.

Heather struggled to take her last breaths as the man brushed his lips against her ear.

"We are one and the same, my Julia," he whispered. "For now, write everything for me. Every single little detail."

CHAPTER 2

Julia Gooden eased up on the killer pace from her ten-mile dawn run when she reached her place of reprieve. The graveyard.

Julia pushed her way through the wrought-iron gates of the Sunset Hills Cemetery, the five-mile mark to her Rochester Hills home, and kept pounding forward. Her breath came hard and fast as she ran past the somber, neat rows of gravestones. The sun pierced through a nettle of trees in the distance and her sneakers left behind a tattooed dent in the dewy grass until she reached her destination in the back of the cemetery lot, away from the road and close to the peaceful solitude of the woods.

It was still there.

Julia smiled as she picked up the baseball she had left behind during her last visit. While most people brought the traditional bouquet of flowers or wreaths to remember their loved ones who had been laid to rest, Julia had carefully selected a ball with a New York Yankees insignia for her older brother, Ben.

Julia had been the only thing Ben had loved more than the Yankees during his nine short years spent on this earth. And he had tried to protect her until the very end.

Julia looked up to the gray sky and felt the familiar ache of loss and pain as a vivid image of Ben flashed through her memory like a bittersweet postcard from the little boy who promised he'd never leave her, not in a million years.

Three decades had passed, but sometimes when Julia was alone, she felt like her brother was still right beside her, with his jet-black hair, crooked smile, and red shirt, grabbing her hand as the two ran down the boardwalk to snatch a rare moment of happiness in their desperate young lives.

Julia bit the side of her mouth to keep herself from crying. She knew crying never did anyone any good or gave back what was taken.

Benjamin Gooden Jr.

Julia ran her finger over Ben's name on his gravestone and shivered as she thought about the one truth that had stayed with her: Nine-year-old boys should always find their way home.

Julia had finally turned off her front porch light three months earlier when Ben's case had been solved. The lifelong ritual started when Julia was seven, the night Ben was taken from the room they shared. When she had returned from the police station, she hoped the light would help her brother find his way back home.

A tiny beacon in a tempest, like the hope that had somehow remained inside her. Even the cruel answer of what happened to her brother couldn't snuff that out.

Ben would've wanted it that way.

Julia ran her fingers over the baseball's red stitching and took hollow comfort in the fact that at least she now had the answers that she had chased for the majority of her life. She knew from her experience as a crime reporter that many families never found out what happened to their kidnapped child. Some nights, after she put her children to sleep, Julia felt selfish when she wondered which outcome was less agonizing for those who were left behind.

A dozen dry, scattered leaves blew across Ben's marker as a gust of a cool October wind kicked up. Julia swept the fall leaves away and then set the baseball back in its rightful place.

She did a quick look at her phone to check the time. Julia didn't want to leave just yet, but she knew she'd need to hustle back home for a call with her New York book editor and her return to the newsroom following a three-month sabbatical to write a book about Ben's abduction and how she was able to find his killer after thirty years.

Julia gripped Ben's gravestone with a gloved hand and sprinted out of the cemetery to the road that would take her home. She ran past her oldest son Logan's elementary school and wondered if anyone ever really got closure, especially when the hard-won answers were stuff of monsters and howling nightmares that no little child should ever have to endure.

The warmth and familiar smells of her home wrapped around Julia when she went inside. She knew she had to get moving, but still paused in front of her little boys' bedroom, taking in the peaceful sight of her sleeping sons. Her three-year-old, Will, had migrated to Logan's bed since she had first checked on them before her run. Logan, who had just celebrated his ninth birthday, lay cocooned in a ball, with his shiny black hair standing out against his Pokémon pillowcase. Her towheaded Will wore his favorite Captain America pajamas and was sprawled out at the foot of Logan's bed.

Julia beat a quick path to her home office where she pulled up her manuscript in preparation for her seven AM call with her book editor. She then clicked on her newspaper's website to see if there were any updates on the story that she couldn't let go.

Julia snapped the tip of her pink-and-gold *Make It Happen* pen against her desk in an inpatient rhythm as she tried to sift out the missing details on the dead woman. Julia dropped the pen and put her head closer to her computer screen, as if the proximity to the newspaper story about the single mother, April Young, age thirty-four, who was last seen jogging along the Detroit RiverWalk, would help her figure out what the cops didn't tell the reporter who was playing babysitter on her beat.

Julia's eyes ticked off the story's bare-bones facts. April was a first-grade teacher and a mother of a six-year-old boy. Her body was discovered by a homeless man in an abandoned Catholic church in one of Detroit's still-struggling neighborhoods. The coroner estimated the missing woman had been dead for several days before her remains were found.

It was a twelve-inch "just the facts, ma'am" kind of follow-up story, with no new details about the murder, no mention of possible suspects, or, at the very least, any color elements about April Young. Based on the scant facts, which were really nothing more than a rehashing of the first article that went live the day before, Julia figured the general assignment reporter didn't have good sources to work in the cop shop. Either that, or the guy was too lazy to call the school where April worked or to track down any relatives to get quotes about April to include in the article. That was a no-brainer on a day-two story, even if the new reporter with the unfamiliar byline was fresh out of journalism school.

Julia could admit that she was as proprietary as a jealous lover about her beat of twelve years. But she had to concede on one point, that the article had a hell of a land mine that the reporter, and subsequent editors, buried at the bottom when it should have been the lead: Police would not give specific details about the cause of April's death, but they did confirm the crime appeared to be "ritualistic in nature."

Julia studied the picture of the abandoned church that had run along with the photo of a smiling April from her elementary school's yearbook. From her years on the beat, Julia knew what was on the other side of the yellow crime-scene tape that the police wouldn't comment on could speak volumes about the killer. If he was ritualistic, as the cops indicated, the person who murdered April would be an organized planner who likely left his signature behind as a perverse clue, or a braggart's calling card.

Julia envisioned a mental rolodex of the killers she had covered who fit easily into that category, including the Holly Hobby murderer, who had slaughtered six nurses during a three-month spree across the city one summer after the victims got off their swing shift. The police came up with the Holly Hobby nickname, since the killer wrote the initials *HH* on the dead nurses' stomachs after he raped and then strangled them.

Julia clicked out of the story about the murdered runner and vowed she'd get answers from the police and would doggedly investigate what happened. April Young and her family deserved at least that.

Julia's home phone rang on her desk, and she felt a flip-flop of nerves in her stomach when she saw the call was from a New York City 212 area code.

"Okay. It's all good," Julia said, trying to convince herself, and answered the call from her book editor.

"Hey, Julia. It's Tom Shea," her editor said in a rapid-fire, time-is-of-the-essence, New York City sprint. "Look, I had a chance to read through your manuscript."

"What did you think?" Julia interrupted. "You can be honest."

"I will. Here's the thing. It's a heart-wrenching story.

That's why we wanted you to write it. There's no one better to tell the story about what happened to your brother. But after reading the manuscript over the weekend, it kept coming up short. I couldn't put my finger on it at first, but then I realized what was missing."

The nerves in Julia's stomach over her first book critique and the one story that mattered to her the most were replaced by a plummeting free fall.

"I know I didn't leave out a single detail. The story is beyond thorough . . . ," Julia started, but backed down when she heard the defensiveness in her voice. Julia was never afraid of a fight when it came to disagreeing with her editors at the paper, and she figured she had a pretty thick skin. But this story was personal. It was hers.

"Don't get me wrong. You did a great job on the reporting. But you got into everyone's head, but your own. You need to take the readers on an emotional ride with you. You lost the one good thing in your life when Ben was abducted. Your dad was in and out of jail, and your mother was an alcoholic. And then your parents took off and abandoned you after Ben went missing. You didn't say once how that made you feel."

"I don't need people to feel sorry for me. How I feel doesn't matter."

"Yes, it does. Readers want to know. How did Ben's abduction change you? Did it affect how you raise your own kids? Is it the reason you became a reporter, to help give people answers you couldn't find for yourself? You see where I'm going with this?"

"I do. But in all due respect, I think you're wrong. I'm not the story here."

"You're part of it. But more important, you're the narrator, the little sister left behind to deal with the aftermath and your relentless pursuit to solve the case. Right now, you've written a flat account of the facts. Anyone could've done that."

"That was grade-A reporting I did. I even spoke to my brother's killer in a jailhouse interview. I don't know anyone else who would've had the balls to do that."

"Point taken. But let me ask you something. Why did you want to write this book in the first place?"

"Because I wanted to tell Ben's story. I didn't want him to be forgotten. He was everything to me growing up."

"That's the soul of the story. And that's what you need to write. Like I said, it's a good start, but send me a revise with more of you in it. Take your time. And feel free to run anything by me. Just shoot me an e-mail if you have any questions. Don't get me wrong. What you wrote is really good. But I know you can make it great."

Julia hung up and stared at her *Make It Happen* pen, now wanting to chuck the thing with the inspirational quote across the room.

The aroma of freshly brewed coffee wafted down the hallway from the kitchen, meaning Julia's live-in housekeeper and self-appointed den mother, Helen Jankowski, was already up.

Julia headed to the shower and put the water to the coldest temperature, wondering if she'd be able to deliver on her editor's demands. Pushing herself was nothing new. Digging into her true feelings about what happened to Ben was treading on sacred ground.

A blast of ice-cold water pelted against Julia's skin. She stayed under the spray until she couldn't take it anymore and exited the shower, shivering. She dried her long, dark hair and pulled on a blue-and-white–striped dress over her lean size-two runner's frame. Julia always figured blue was a good choice for her, since it matched her eyes, the same piercing bright azure hue she had inherited from her con man father, Duke Gooden, who was currently on the lam, God knows where, from the FBI.

Julia grabbed her briefcase and old-school reporter's notebook, where she jotted down a reminder to call her Realtor to check on the status of the closing of their house, which had recently gone into escrow, since Julia was ready to make an offer on a home she had her eye on in the Palmer Park neighborhood of Detroit.

Julia slipped her heels on with one hand and gave one more glance to her still-sleeping boys. She then went down the hallway to the kitchen, where Helen, a whisper-thin older woman with a thick Polish accent and a killer pierogi recipe, was busy making lunch for Logan.

"Thanks, Helen. I was going to do that."

"I figured after your phone call this morning, you could use the extra help."

"How do you know about my phone call?"

"I heard a snippet of it when I was heading to the bathroom. Your story was excellent. Don't let the bastards get you down. You give me the word, and I'll set him straight. Saying your story wasn't good enough . . ."

"So you overheard my phone conversation in the hallway when the office door was closed?" Julia asked, and gestured to the other house landline next to the coffee machine.

"You are a very suspicious woman," Helen said, and put a mug of coffee down in front of Julia. "It seems that you are in the right line of work."

"Thanks for the support, but my editor was right. I should've known better. I didn't follow my own rules."

Julia patted Helen's hand and jotted down a note for Logan and slipped it in his lunch box, letting him know she loved him, and although everything seemed really hard right now, the move to the new house was going to work out just fine.

"Tell the boys I love them," Julia said. "And remind Logan he's got basketball practice on his new team tonight."

"I don't think the boy wants to do that."

"I know. But it will give him a chance to meet some kids ahead of time from his new school before he starts. I just want him to be okay. He's had to deal with a lot of changes already. Both boys have, with the loss of their dad."

Julia took a look out the window of the kitchen to the rear yard and had a sudden image of her former, estranged husband, David Tanner, building Logan's tree house. Their marriage was already on irreparably damaged ground when he was killed. There were too many ghosts of bad memories of the man she spent nearly ten years with in this house, and it was time for Julia, her boys, and Helen to make a fresh start.

"The boy will be fine. Logan is strong. As for me, as long as I have my six-burner stove in the new house, I'll be happy. Take this," Helen said, and put her hand inside the pocket of her apron. She came out with a piece of sturdy red string from one of her many sewing projects, which was tied in a slipknot, and handed it to Julia.

"Thanks, but what is this?" Julia asked.

"A Polish tradition. When I was a little girl, before my parents got my brother and me out of the country to protect us from the Nazis, my grandma, my *babcia*, warned me about the evil eye. The day I said good-bye to her, she attached a piece of red string like this one with a slipknot on my suitcase to protect me. I know you think I'm a superstitious old woman, but I believe it saved us. My brother and I made the journey safely. My grandma and my parents didn't make it out. My grandma sent all the luck with me and my brother."

"That's a beautiful thought. I don't believe in the evil eye or superstitions, but if it's important to you, I'll take it," Julia said, and tied the piece of string around the loop to her purse. "Do you want me to avoid walking under ladders and black cats, too?"

"You joke around all you want, but I believe in these things. I woke up this morning with a bad feeling about you. I see a dark cloud over your head, my Julia Gooden. Be careful out there."

"Always," Julia said, and headed out to April Young's school, her starting point to unearth some answers about what happened to the slain teacher.

CHAPTER 3

Two weeks earlier

April Young felt a searing burn in her lungs, but made herself keep running even though she was pretty sure she was going to puke a couple of times already during her thirty-minute jog.

April panted heavily and decided to give herself a break. She slowed her pace to what was slightly more than a fast walk, even though she wanted to get out of the creepy section of the RiverWalk Trail as fast as possible.

She had made the unwise decision that morning to explore the Dequindre Cut half-mile path, parts of which took her past vacant warehouses, confined dark spaces, and graffiti-strewn concrete walls, including one classy message that read, *Bite me,* above a spray-painted picture of an engorged male organ.

Not a great place to be running alone at six-thirty in the morning, she now realized. But April had taken the recommendation about the Dequindre Cut from the good-looking guy she had met last weekend while she was jogging along the much more scenic and populated Gabriel Richard Park section of the trail.

April knew one thing for sure: She hated running. She'd been at it for three months, starting out with her friend Gwen, the principal at her school. But running didn't get any easier for her, no matter how many times she did it. And some days, she barely clocked in over a mile.

But she kept at it. April had never given up on anything in her life. And she wasn't going to let a two-mile run break her.

After her husband Jack's death in Afghanistan, April knew she had to do something, anything, to make sure she kept moving. The daily runs, as painful as they were, made her feel like she was pushing forward. Otherwise, she was afraid she would atrophy to the point that she would give up and stay in bed, hugging Jack's Marine T-shirt, the one that had been returned to her, along with his other belongings from his final tour.

April pushed ahead on the empty path and admitted to herself that although she'd never likely sign up for a marathon, the fact that she was out here at the crack of dawn was an accomplishment. And it had helped get her A game back. April needed to be her best for her son, Kyle, and for her first-grade students, who relied on her to show up every day with her usual greeting, "Good morning, my sweethearts."

April's thoughts turned to a little boy she was tutoring, Pedro, who had yesterday offered her one of his gloriously sweet, shy smiles while the two of them listened to Rosetta Stone tapes in April's attempt to help her struggling student learn English.

"Buenos días, *Señora Young,*" Pedro said as he stood outside April's classroom, waiting for them to start their lesson. He handed her a picture of a flower he had drawn and a bollo, *a sweet roll his mother had made fresh for her that morning.*

April spotted a concrete enclosed part of the trail in the distance, where a section of the path cut underneath a bridge. She flashed to a horror novel she had read recently, the genre not really her style. She was more of a romance, chick-lit fan, but the book was in Jack's trunk of items that came home without him. So she read it to feel close to him again.

April looked up to the top of the bridge that ran above the tunnel section of the trail and saw a car pass by, likely an early-morning commuter, she figured, and felt a hollow reassurance that there were other signs of life around her.

If she could just book it as fast as she could through the tunnel, she figured she'd be okay. April told her students they just had to jump when they felt scared. She guaranteed them the water wouldn't be as cold as they thought.

Time to walk the talk.

"Stop being such a friggin' pansy," April said. She picked up her pace and tried to take her mind off the pain in her calves by thinking about the cute guy she had met on the trail last weekend.

She hadn't been with anyone since Jack's death a year ago, and never once considered it. Until now. She felt guilty about betraying her husband's memory, but there was something about the fellow jogger she met—his easy, friendly appeal—and it definitely didn't hurt that he was pretty great to look at. April put the guy somewhere in his forties, older than she was, but she didn't care. He was tall, with a tightly muscled, strong build, sandy-blond hair, and green eyes. But what really grabbed her was his intensity. When he looked at her, he made her feel like she was special.

April started humming the Rihanna song "Only Girl (In the World)" and her dormant fantasies that she had shelved since Jack's death came to life. She pictured the fellow jogger's lips and found herself smiling when she thought how it would feel to run her tongue over them while he was on top of her.

April steeled her nerves as she approached the tunnel, but then stopped short when she saw a figure inside, running in her direction.

April had a rule that she would never get into an elevator alone with a stranger, and it held true now. There was no way she was going to be trapped inside the dark tunnel with God knows what kind of freak of nature that could be in there.

April backed up from the mouth of the tunnel and calculated she'd be able to run up the embankment if the person shuttling fast toward her was a mugger. But she felt a welcome surge of relief, coupled by a nervous excitement in her stomach, when the person emerged and gave her a wide, surprised smile.

God, she couldn't believe her crazy luck.

April wiped a trickle of sweat from her brow and ran a hand over her shoulder-length, light brown hair that she realized likely looked a hot mess.

"Twice in one week," April said to the man she had met the weekend before.

"This is my lucky day," he said. "Okay, full disclosure here. You mentioned you usually ran at this time, so I got up early in case I might bump into you."

"Really?" April asked, and then felt ridiculous for sounding like a high-school girl with an obvious crush she wasn't sure she should reveal yet.

"Absolutely. I really enjoyed talking to you and kicked myself for not asking for your number. I see you took my suggestion about the Dequindre Cut. It's a little more urban. But I like a little Detroit grit sometimes."

"Me too, but I've got to say, a couple spots along this route are a little . . . how should I say it?"

"Like you're running through the 'hood?" he asked. He

smiled and his greens eyes stayed on April. She turned away so he wouldn't see her blush over the attention.

"I couldn't have put it better. I caught some interesting graffiti along the way."

"Oh, right. I forgot about a couple of those tags. Definitely not for the eyes of a classy lady like yourself."

"You're sweet. I'm glad we ran into each other again, too. I remember what you said about your son."

"Ben."

"I'm so sorry. I can't imagine losing a child."

"It's okay. I don't want you to feel bad about it, Julia."

"Julia? No. My name is April."

The man smacked an open palm against his forehead. "Oh, God, I'm an idiot."

"Please don't worry about it," April said. "It's okay. Most people I know are bad at names. As a teacher, I have to make it a point to remember all my students' names on the first day of class. Otherwise the kids will eat you alive."

"I bet you're the best teacher at Collington."

April smiled, but wracked her brain to try and remember whether she had told the man where she worked. April was sure she had mentioned she taught first grade. But had she mentioned Collington?

"I'm so sorry. It's a stupid habit I haven't broken yet."

"Julia is your wife's name," April said.

"Yes. She and my son, Ben, they died in a car crash about a year ago. I wanted to make a good impression if I saw you again, but I'm thinking I just blew it."

April reached out and gave the man a friendly pat on his hand.

"It's okay. I've done that before," April said, and remembered the times she accidentally called a male teacher her husband Jack's name. "I'm sorry to hear about your wife and son. Do you have any other kids?"

"No. They were all I had. It's been tough, but I'm starting

to rebuild things. Listen to me going on about my problems. It must be hard bringing up two boys all by yourself."

"It has its challenges, but I only have one son."

The man looked up to the embankment and an older-model Buick that was parked on the side of the road on the far end of the bridge.

"Someone's got car trouble," he said. "I should probably help. I always try to be a Good Samaritan when I can. Can I ask you something?"

"Sure," April said, and wondered if he was going to see if she wanted to grab a coffee.

"I hope I'm not being too forward, but did your husband die from a roadside bomb? You should be really proud of him, a Marine dying in the line of duty."

"I'm sorry?"

April felt a knot tie itself tightly in the middle of her chest as she looked back at the handsome man standing in front of her. She couldn't remember everything they had shared when they ran into each other before, but she was positive she hadn't mentioned Jack was a Marine, let alone the fact that he had died while serving his country. And she was certain she had only given him her first name, so there was no way he could've found Jack's obituary if he tried to research her on the Internet.

"How do you know about that?" April said as a raw edge of defensiveness rose in her voice.

"I apologize. I shouldn't have brought that up. My mistake. You wear a size two, right?" he said, and inched in closer. He did a quick inspection of her face and then frowned. "You have freckles. I didn't notice them before. There's always a work-around, though. A little foundation should fix you up just fine. Just as long as you fit the dress. I'll make you look like her, no problem."

"I don't know what this is all about, but I'm leaving."

April took a hasty step back and reached into her waist pack as her hand searched for her phone. Her eyes darted up the embankment and she wondered if she could outrun the man who was now only a few feet away from her. She snatched out her phone, and with a shaking hand, she began to punch in 911, but the man grabbed her wrist and squeezed until she felt something crack and her phone fell to the concrete.

"What the hell is this?" April cried. "You're hurting me! Let go!"

The man extracted a camouflage green-handled, black-bladed knife from underneath his T-shirt and pressed the blade against her stomach.

"Time to fix you up," he said.

CHAPTER 4

Collington Elementary School in Hamtramck, fifteen minutes north of Detroit, was a tall, distressed redbrick building, with an American flag waving out front and a bright yellow sign next to the main door that read: DETROIT SCHOOL OF EXCELLENCE.

A bus pulled away from the curb, and Julia felt a pang of guilt that Helen had to drive Logan to school instead of her, a mother-son ritual Julia had enjoyed during her brief sabbatical.

Julia exited her SUV when the first bell rang and walked against the tide of parents that were flooding out of the gates to the parking lot.

Inside the school office, Julia worked to get the attention of an attractive, fifty-something woman with short brown hair, round glasses, and a flowered sweater set, who was on a call, repeating over and over, "Well, that's school policy."

The assistant, whose nametag read *Janet*, hung up and addressed Julia with an all-business "Can I help you?"

"Yes. I'm looking for your principal, Gwen Holiday,"

Julia answered, pulling the name out of her memory, since she looked it up on her phone before she went into the school. "My name is Julia Gooden. I'm a reporter. I'm working on a follow-up story about one of your teachers, April Young. I'm sorry about what happened to her."

The assistant, Janet, dropped her head back in the direction of her computer, dismissing Julia. "Principal Holiday has appointments all day. We've already talked to the press."

"I realize that, and I know the principal must be very busy, but this is important."

"Everything is important," Janet said. She sighed heavily and made her way to a closed principal's door. Julia waited for a sum total of thirty seconds when Janet came back with her answer.

"Like I said, the principal is tied up all morning, and we won't be making any further comments to the press."

The office assistant returned to her desk without looking at Julia and began to tap her pink acrylic fingernails against her computer's keyboard. Julia tried to come up with a Plan B when the side door to the interior of the school opened and a little boy came in with a freshly bloodied knee.

"Hold on, Aiden," the assistant said.

Julia made a move to the door leading to the parking lot as the office assistant escorted the child inside the adjoining nurse's office, giving Julia the opening she needed. Julia reversed course, made a beeline to the principal's door, and went inside, not bothering to knock.

The principal, Gwen Holiday, was sitting at her desk, signing paperwork. She stood up when Julia barged inside. The principal was thin, with a blond bob, and wore a tan-colored pantsuit, with a gold-and-green elephant brooch pinned to her lapel.

"Can I help you?" the principal asked in a polite but defensive tone.

"I'm sorry to come in like this. I didn't think you'd talk to me otherwise. I'm Julia Gooden, the reporter your assistant told you about."

"You need to leave. I've already talked to the media. This is a tragedy for our school."

"I have no doubt. I'm very sorry about what happened to Ms. Young. I have a son in third grade, and I can't imagine if something happened to one of his teachers. If you'll give me a minute to explain, and if you still want me to leave, then I promise, I'll go."

The principal sized up Julia and sat back down in her chair. "Go ahead."

"I realize this is a terrible tragedy . . . ," Julia said.

"April was my friend."

"I'm sorry for your loss. I want to find out who killed April. I've followed the coverage about her, and I don't think the stories have shown what kind of person April was, and how much she meant to her family and the people at this school. April was a single mom?"

"That's right. She has a son, Kyle, who goes to school here. Kyle's grandmother told him April died in a car accident, because she couldn't tell him the truth."

"Can you tell me more about April? I want to be sure my stories memorialize her the right way."

Gwen gestured with her head for Julia to sit down in the chair on the other side of her desk and Julia complied, realizing she was in. At least for a few minutes, and that's all she needed.

"April showed up here every morning an hour early to help her kids who were falling behind. A good percentage of our students are below the poverty level and they're not getting help with their studies at home. April was there for them."

"She was divorced, taking care of her son by herself?"

Julia asked, guiding the conversation where it needed to go, since she knew husbands, boyfriends, and exes were generally the first people the cops would look at in a case like this.

"No, her husband died overseas. He was a Marine."

"I'm sorry. I imagine her death is going to be even harder for her son then. Did April have a boyfriend or anyone else she was seeing? Or maybe an issue with a parent at school?"

"No. April's husband died last year. She couldn't bring herself to date anyone since. As far as parents, I can't say this about many of my other teachers, but all the parents loved April. She was that kind of person."

"April was a runner. Did she always run on the RiverWalk Trail?"

Gwen ran a nervous hand across her desk. "Yes, and I feel terrible about it. I was the one who convinced her to start running with me last year. After her husband died, I figured it would be a good outlet. The Detroit RiverWalk was always her route when she started running alone. She only ran about a mile or two every morning, but she did it six days a week, usually at the crack of dawn before she had to go to work. She lived with her parents after her husband died, so they were home with Kyle when she ran. I always told her not to run by herself, especially so early in the morning when there weren't as many people around. She never listened."

"When you ran with April, did you ever see anyone who made you think twice? Maybe another jogger or someone who was hanging around who approached April?"

"April got plenty of looks from guys. She was pretty and fit. She definitely got second looks when we ran together, but nothing untoward. I'm divorced. I know creeps when I see them."

"April didn't say anything to you about someone who might have approached her when she went running alone?"

"I mentioned this to the police. April told me about a man she met at the RiverWalk, and she really liked him. April ran later on the weekends, since she didn't have to be at school, so there were more people on the jogging trail. I took it the man she ran into was a fellow runner. She said he was really nice. I got the impression she was hoping he'd ask her out if she saw him again. We were having coffee before school when she mentioned it. It was a couple of days before she died."

"Did April tell you his name?"

"I'm pretty sure she didn't. If she did, I don't remember. April did say he was older, maybe in his forties. April was thirty-four. It didn't bother her, though, because she thought he was really cute. She told me she'd 'met a hot guy.' I remember thinking it was a big deal for April to say that, because she hadn't expressed any interest in dating since her husband died."

"So, no name, but if she thought he was attractive, maybe she told you what he looked like."

"She didn't give specifics. April had a big heart and I think what really got to her was the story about his son. Being a teacher, that had to hit home."

"What was the story?"

"His son died recently. April told me the boy's name. It was Ben. I can't remember if April told me the man's name, but I do remember his son's, because it was the same name as my dad. Ben."

"That's a coincidence. My older brother, his name was Ben. He died when he was nine."

"A child. I'm sorry to hear that," Gwen said. "There was one more thing I told the police. Granted, I'm not implying this man April mentioned is the person who killed her."

"Of course. I understand. You're doing the right thing, sharing every bit of information you know."

"April said the man she met, he told her that he volunteered at the Michigan branch of the National Center for Missing and Exploited Children. She told me she thought he might be a social worker or something along those lines. I got the impression April thought she finally met a decent guy. But these days, you never know. I just wish I could remember his name. Stupid that I remember his son's name, but not his."

"If anything else comes to mind, please give me a call."

"I will. Can you do me a favor? The press keeps running the same picture of April. It's her yearbook picture from last year and she absolutely hated it. Her mom and I were talking about that this morning. If you run another story, could you use a different picture of her? I know her mom would appreciate it."

"Of course. If you speak to April's mother, please give her my condolences. I'd like to talk to her as well, if she's willing."

Gwen grabbed her phone, scrolled through her camera icon, and then pushed her cell across her desk toward Julia.

"April loved this picture. That's her and her late husband, Jack," Gwen said. "If you give me your number, I'll send it to you."

Julia took in the image of a pretty, trim woman with shoulder-length, light brown hair and blue eyes. In the picture, April Young was tan and smiling in a white dress standing next to her husband in his Marine uniform.

Julia slid her business card across the desk to the principal. "I appreciate your time. I promise, I'll do my best to find out what happened to your friend. My cell phone number is on my card. Please text me the picture of April, and I'll make sure the paper runs it with all future stories."

Julia left the school office, and by the time she reached her car, the principal had already texted the photo. Julia studied the picture of the happy young couple in the prime of their lives and considered the grief April must have felt as a widow left alone after a tragedy to raise a young son. The teacher had already endured so much.

"Who did this to you?" Julia asked as she took in the image of April. "I'll find out. I promise."

Julia swung her SUV onto Chrysler Avenue and then hooked onto the on-ramp for I-75 South into downtown Detroit and her newspaper. She made a mental point to call April Young's mother later that morning. Julia would normally hunt down her address and ring her doorbell, showing up without warning, since it's easier to say no to an interview over the phone than in person. But in case April's son was home, Julia would call first. She didn't want to upset the little boy any more than he obviously was.

The Detroit RiverWalk, Julia knew from running it herself, was a popular jogging spot along the east riverfront, a relatively short three-and-a-half-mile loop that spanned from the Joe Louis Arena to Gabriel Richard Park. It opened as early as six, a time when April likely took her run, and a time when it was least populated. The route would've taken April through parks and pathways and open space, where someone who knew her routine could easily lay in wait in the predawn darkness. Although April could have been snatched up randomly, the fact that the cops had referred to her killing as "ritualistic" made Julia's gut tell her April's killer handpicked her.

Julia thought about the man the principal had mentioned, the one who told April Young his son had died and that he volunteered at the Michigan Chapter of the National Center for Missing and Exploited Children, an organization Julia knew well.

Julia called out to her Siri to find the number for the nonprofit and waited until a receptionist answered. Julia was then patched through to the agency's director, Guy Peterson.

"Hey, Julia," Guy answered. "How are things going with your book on Ben? You've got to promise me that I'll get a signed copy."

"I hit a bit of a roadblock. I've got some revisions to do. My editor wants me to put more of my feelings into the story."

"That would be a good thing for you to do. I tell families all the time that sharing memories or letting people into their grief helps with the healing process. Holding everything inside isn't good. I know your brother meant everything to you. You won't be betraying his memory if you share your story with others."

Julia ignored Peterson's good advice and redirected the conversation to the real reason she was calling.

"I'm working a story I was hoping you could help me with."

"Cold case or current?"

"Neither. I'm trying to find someone who may volunteer for you."

"If you're asking in a professional capacity, I can't give out private information about one of our volunteers."

"This person may be a suspect in a murder case."

"Are you talking a murdered kid here? All our volunteers undergo extensive background checks."

"No, not a child. The person I'm looking for is a man, an adult in his forties. Apparently, he told the victim he had a son named Ben who had died. I'm not sure how the child passed."

"If it's an abduction case, the only Ben in our database would be your brother."

"I don't have a name for this man, but he might be a social worker. I know that's not much to go on, but I thought it would be worth checking out."

"That doesn't ring a bell. Let me ask around, though. I'll

call over to my counterpart at the Michigan Chapter of the National Children's Alliance as well. Maybe the man you're looking for volunteered over there. Some people get our organizations mixed up."

Julia ended the call with Peterson and passed the five-mile sign to her exit when her cell phone rang on the dashboard. She hit hands free and answered.

"Hey, Gooden. It's Navarro. This didn't come from me, but you should head down to McCray Street past Seven Mile. There's an abandoned Baptist church at the end of the street. Russell and I just arrived at the scene."

"A church. Is there a second victim?"

"You got it. Same setup as the first vic."

"April Young."

"There was a waist pack that was left behind with a license in it. I'll give you the name if you promise to keep it under wraps until I tell you otherwise."

"I promise."

"The latest victim's name is Heather Burns."

"A waist pack. Was Heather a runner?"

"We don't know yet. Are you close?"

"Five minutes out."

"Dispatch wasn't specific on the church, just the address, otherwise the press would be swarming, so you should be able to get a head start."

"I owe you, Navarro."

"I know it. Got to go, Gooden."

Julia hung up and waved an apology as she cut off another driver in order to make the unexpected exit she'd need to take to get to McCray Street. She was familiar with the neighborhood from her beat and took a slow cruise down a side street that paralleled McCray to get a view of the church before making herself visible. Although she knew almost everyone on the Detroit PD, and they, in turn, knew her by face and reputation, there were always a few new rookies or transfers who would take a blanket approach to the media as being the enemy, so she wanted to get into the scene through the back door first, to be sure her access wouldn't be blocked by an unfamiliar officer.

Julia parked two blocks down from the back entrance of the church. She grabbed her tape recorder, phone, reporter's notebook, and pencil, and picked her way through an over-grown thicket of weeds until she reached the rear lot of the Baptist church.

"Julia Gooden," a male voice called from behind her. "Big surprise seeing you here, trying to sneak into the scene."

Julia turned to see Branch LaBeau, a forty-something cop who had been working patrol since Julia could remember. LaBeau was of medium build, with a thick head of light brown hair and a cleft in his chin. Julia vaguely re-called him telling her that his first name was actually Scott, Branch being a childhood nickname. The conversation oc-curred as reporter and officer killed time, waiting for the excavation of a body, or at least some of its bones that con-nected to a skull discovered in a landfill on the outskirts of the city.

"Are you the official crime scene babysitter?" Julia asked.

"That's right. I'm here to keep people like you out," he said.

"Come on, LaBeau. You know me. I won't touch any-thing. I just want to find out what happened to this woman. If you think about it, we both want the same thing here."

LaBeau shook his head but smiled.

"You want to sell papers. I want to protect the public from assholes like the one who sliced up that woman inside there," LaBeau said and jerked his thumb in the direction of the building. "Whoever killed the victim is into some freaky shit."

LaBeau narrowed his gaze at a couple of teenagers who cut around the corner of a neighboring house in the direction of the church. The two teenage boys wore hoodies and each carried a brown paper bag. The two were distracted, both trying to outman each other with tales of their recent sexual hookups, but abruptly stopped when they looked up and caught LaBeau in his blue patrol uniform.

"What do you have in the bag, boys? Spray paint or a forty-ounce?" LaBeau asked, his deep voice seeming to split the air.

From inside the hoods of their gray sweatshirts, Julia saw two sets of eyes go wide. The brown paper bag one of the boys was clutching slipped through his hands and made a sharp shattering sound when it connected with the pavement.

"Shit," the thinner of the two boys yelled, and took off running with his friend close behind him, the teenagers looking like scared jackrabbits trying to escape the snapping jaws of a hungry fox while they fled.

"You're not going after them?" Julia asked.

"Nah, they're small-time. Hopefully, I gave them a scare at least, so maybe the next time they cut school, they'll find a different place to get buzzed instead of inside a church. That's a sacrilege."

"I never took you for a religious type."

"There's a lot you don't know about me, Gooden. You just need to take the time to ask," LaBeau said.

"Give me two minutes inside the church. I'm guessing the victim is another female runner."

"I like you, Julia. I always have. But I don't want to be your leak. You want answers, Navarro and Russell are inside. Come back later and they'll probably talk."

"There's no later. I need to talk to them now. Come on, LaBeau. Can't you make a round of the building? There might be someone out front trying to get in. It wouldn't be your fault if I slipped inside when you weren't here because you were doing your job keeping the crime scene contained. Just one question to Navarro and Russell and I'm out. It will be like I was never here."

LaBeau rolled his eyes. "I'm going to my car. You owe me a coffee, Gooden," LaBeau said. "The guys inside kick you out, that's on you."

"Is it just Navarro and Russell?"

"No, there are a couple more cops, including a new guy from Chicago. He's heavy on the cologne."

LaBeau stopped guarding the door and walked toward the front of the church, giving Julia a wave with the back of his hand without turning around.

She waited until he was out of sight and then hurried up three broken cement steps to the rear door. She opened it slowly and peered inside.

She immediately spotted Detective Raymond Navarro, a big man at six-three and 220 pounds. Navarro had a thick shock of dark hair and was the same age as Julia, thirty-seven. He had on his usual unofficial uniform of motorcycle boots, jeans, and a fitted black T-shirt underneath his leather jacket. Next to Navarro was his partner, Leroy Russell, who was in his early fifties and wore his trademark bald Mr. Clean look, which he'd had since Julia first met him. Next to Navarro and Russell were two other officers, one she knew well, a veteran, Corporal Gary Smith, who was a whisper away from retirement, and a younger officer dressed up in a suit.

Julia quietly slipped through the open door into the church. She knew she would likely get kicked out, but if she were lucky, she'd be able to get in a few questions before she was escorted out. But more important, Julia wanted to see Heather Burns. Julia's mantra had always been, if she got to see the body, it would make her work harder to find the victim's killer.

"Hey, what's she doing here?" the unfamiliar police officer in the suit said as he spun around after catching Julia's movement out of the corner of his eye.

Navarro glanced up and nodded at Julia. "She's good, Esposito. She's a reporter. We know her."

"You Detroit cops need to smarten up," Esposito answered.

"We're plenty smart. Julia, this is Carlo Esposito," Russell said.

Esposito walked toward Julia purposely with hooded eyes in an intimidation pose, but Julia kept walking forward in his direction, not backing down.

"How long do you think she's been dead?" Julia asked.

"The coroner's office will have to confirm, but I'm guessing maybe a few hours. A couple of teenagers cutting school found the body," Navarro said.

"Yeah, the idiots came in here to smoke weed," Russell said.

"You think because you're cute you can come in here?" Esposito asked Julia. "I'm from Chicago. That shit doesn't work with me."

"She's dressed just like the other one," Navarro said. He bent over the body of Heather Burns and studied the dead woman's face. "Looks like a wig this time, too."

Russell got down on his haunches next to his partner and took a closer look. "Poor kid. The killer slashed her throat deep, down to the bone. Hey, Julia, this is weird, but the dress the victim is wearing—I think you've got the same one.

You wore it to the police awards banquet, I think. Not that I was looking at you or anything."

The new cop, Esposito, temporarily halted his pursuit, turned around to take another look at Heather Burns's body, and then turned back around to Julia.

"Weird coincidence, reporter girl," Esposito said. "The victim looks a hell of a lot like you."

CHAPTER 5

Navarro rose up from his squatted position next to the body of Heather Burns and pointed in the direction of the church's organ that was turned on its side.

"Right by where Julia's standing, I see something," Navarro said. "It's pink."

Navarro brushed past Esposito and bent down next to the organ. "It looks like a woman's exercise outfit, shorts and a matching pink T-shirt. Get some pictures of this, Russell."

"Excuse me, Julia," Russell said, and moved past her to get to the newly discovered piece of evidence. "Looks like someone took the time to fold the clothes up, nice and neat."

"'Excuse me, Julia'? What's with this polite crap? She needs to get her ass out of here," Esposito said.

"You think the killer grabbed the victim while she was running, brought her here, and then made her change into the blue dress?" Julia asked, ignoring Esposito and getting in a question before the inevitable happened and she got booted from the scene.

"Aren't you the smart one? Time for you to go, sweetheart," Esposito said. He latched onto Julia's arm and pulled her in the direction of the front door and to the street.

"I'll go, but don't ever touch me again. And my name is Julia. Julia Gooden. Not *sweetheart*," Julia told Esposito, and tried to work her arm free. "I mean it. Let go of me."

Navarro shot Esposito a hard look, and the new cop released his grip.

Julia felt the burn of frustration, not being able to get any of the cops to confirm her theory, and started for the exit. Unable to let it go, she turned around one more time to try and get a better look at Heather Burns, whose body was still mostly obstructed by the cops hovering around it.

"Ms. Gooden, I'd ask what you're doing here, but that would be a silly question, now wouldn't it?" a female voice said.

The acting chief of police, Beth Washington, stood in the open doorway. Washington was in her early forties, with smooth black skin, a short, stylish pixie haircut, and a curvy build.

Julia had known Washington since her first day on the job at the paper. Both were new to their positions at the time. Washington had just started as a new detective, having worked her way up from patrol, and Julia was new to her cop beat, having returned to her home state of Michigan after her first newspaper position in New Orleans. Julia had also frequently run into Washington socially, since her youngest son had played Little League with Logan.

"Sorry, Chief. Not trying to cause a problem. I'm going to leave, but can I ask you something, just to make sure I've got it right?"

"You've got one question," Washington said as she kept moving. "Make it fast."

"If I write that Heather Burns is the second victim found in an abandoned church wearing the same blue dress and wig as April Young, would I be correct?" Julia asked, basing her assumption on what she had just overheard.

"I'm not going to ask how you know all that, especially the victim's name and how the crime scenes are duplicates," Washington said, and gave Navarro and Russell a knowing glare.

"I don't want to get the story wrong."

"All right. Your facts are correct. We're going to release a statement this afternoon that will include the same information. If you want to break it before we issue the release, I'm okay with it. But I will ask that you not release the name of the victim until we contact her next of kin."

"Of course. You have my word. Can I attribute everything to you?"

"No. I don't feel like dealing with a ration of grief from the rest of the media for letting you get this first. Just say it came from a high-ranking source in the department and leave it at that," Washington said. "No names."

"Sorry, Chief. I was just kicking her out," Esposito said. "The media are scum."

"Not all of them. Gooden is okay. But you need to get out of here, Julia. If you want to call Navarro or me later for more details or to confirm anything, that's fine. I've got work to do."

Washington turned her back to Julia and proceeded to the front of the church and the victim.

Corporal Smith rose from his bent position in front of the altar to give his boss a better view, and, in turn, offered Julia her first chance to see a complete picture of Heather Burns in her death pose.

Julia knew she had to make it quick. She moved closer and noticed Heather's eyes were wide open and her throat was sliced clean across. Julia then focused in on a hand-drawn picture resting on Heather's stomach. In the center of the paper was a large symbol that struck a familiar chord, an intricate red-and-turquoise heart with a vertical line cutting through the center, creating two mirror halves.

In the four corners of the paper, the killer had also drawn a single circle flanked by two crescents that were flipped in opposite directions, like reverse bookends.

"That damn picture again," Washington said.

"The killer left something in her hand this time, too," Navarro said to his boss. "You got any more thoughts on the picture?"

"It's a heart, so maybe a lover who left him, and he's dressing the victims up to look like the woman who broke his heart," Washington said.

"Beth, I think I've seen that picture before," Julia called out to the chief.

Washington turned around and shook her head. "You're still here. You've got twenty seconds to tell me what you think this thing is before Esposito walks you out."

"I'm not sure about the four symbols in the corners of the picture, but I've seen the one in the center before. The heart. I know a cop who could probably confirm it."

The deep crease in Washington's forehead eased a bit and she gave Julia her full attention.

"Who's the cop?" Washington asked.

"Douglas Prejean. He's a sergeant from New Orleans. He was a source when I worked at the paper there before I came back to Detroit. Can I take a picture and send it to him?"

"Not a chance. What do you think the symbol means?" Washington asked.

"Prejean is the expert. But I saw something like this on a story I worked with Prejean at the *Times-Picayune*. If that's what I think it is, the heart, it's an occult symbol, possibly tied to voodoo."

"Okay, Julia. Call your source. But outside. You need to

get out of here. Navarro, follow her and let me know if I need to talk to Sergeant Prejean any further."

Julia obeyed orders this time and followed Navarro out to the crumbling front steps of the church, where she began to search for Prejean's number on her phone.

"What do you think you're doing, Gooden?" Navarro asked. "You can't just waltz into a crime scene like that."

"You gave me the address," Julia said. "What did you think I was going to do?"

"Wait outside and ask Washington and me questions when we were done with our initial investigation. You know the rules."

"I do, and I wouldn't be doing my job if I followed them. But you know I won't burn you or Washington. I promise," Julia answered.

LaBeau surfaced from his patrol car that was parked on the curb and looked between Julia and Navarro.

"Everything okay here, Ray? I see you've got reporters creeping around. Julia must've snuck in the back door while I was checking the front."

"Do me a favor and keep an eye on the back of the building. I think that's the main entrance for drug dealers and kids skipping school looking for a hangout."

"You got it," LaBeau answered.

Julia waited until the patrol officer was gone to apologize.

"Hey, sorry. I wasn't trying to make you look bad with Washington."

"I know you weren't, but you push it to the limit sometimes, Gooden. Tell me more about the Louisiana cop."

"His name is Doug Prejean. He's been with the NOLA PD for at least twenty years and he's good. Prejean's worked all over the city, Algiers, the French Quarter, and I think he's stationed in Treme these days. He's investigated occult cases in the past, so he should be able to help."

"You keep in touch with this guy?"

"I saw Prejean a few months ago. He's got Michigan connections. His wife is originally from Ann Arbor. He met her when she was in school at Tulane. They inherited her mom and dad's house when her parents died. They were here this summer, and Prejean and I met up for lunch to catch up."

"Make the call and put it on speaker."

Julia scrolled through her contacts until she tapped on Prejean's number. On the third ring, Prejean answered, his voice heavy with equal parts Cajun and Deep Southern Bayou drawl.

"Hey, Julia. This is a nice surprise. What's going on?" Prejean asked, his voice sounding like thick, sticky molasses falling from a spoon. "Everything okay with your boys? It was real nice to see you in August when me and Claudette were out your way."

"Hey, Prejean. We're all fine. I'm actually calling on business. I don't mean to put you on the spot, but I've got you on speaker with a Detroit police detective, Ray Navarro. He's a great cop and a close friend of mine."

"How you doing, Sergeant?" Navarro asked. "We've got a case we're working that Julia seems to think you might be able to help us with. We've got two victims, both females. The women were both runners. We think the killer snatched them up while they were jogging and took them into separate abandoned churches in the city. The guy dressed them up the same in a blue dress and black wig."

"I appreciate Julia's endorsement, but I don't see how I can add anything to what you-all are probably doing already," Prejean said. "But if you want my cheap two cents, it sounds like you've got a serial killer on your hands. The guy is likely organized. A planner. I'm betting he scouted out the victims ahead of time, knew the routes they ran and when they'd be there. Once the guy chooses his next victim, he could've picked them up by playing some kind of game, a ploy to gain their sympathy, and then he takes them to another location to commit the murder."

"Thanks, but we've already established that. Julia wanted to ask you about a picture the killer drew and left on his victims," Navarro said. "We think he killed the women and then placed the picture on both the victims' stomachs."

"Okay, Julia. What you got, girl?" Prejean asked.

"I think what the killer drew is some kind of occult symbol. When you were working that case in the French Quarter, the killer who was murdering tourists, you showed me some of the pictures he had in his apartment. The picture the killer left behind at the crime scenes, it reminded me of those."

"Right, the Papa Legba killer, at least that's who he thought he was. The guy would get high out of his mind on crack and then he believed he was the guardian of the crossroads. He'd pull drunk tourists from the gutters of Bourbon Street so he could try and connect them to the other world right before he killed them with a hammer. Stand-up guy. Tell me about your picture, Julia."

"It looks hand-drawn, very neat, and structured. In the center is a picture of a heart with an intricate design. Granted, I wasn't up close."

"Can you fill in the blanks, Detective?" Prejean asked.

"Sure. The pictures left behind with both victims were the same. There's a line drawn down the middle of the heart, and an identical pattern of lines on either side. There's a set of two crosses and asterisks inside the heart, and then more on the top and bottom."

"Sound familiar?" Julia asked.

"Can someone send me a picture? I'm guessing the cops are smart up there in Detroit and won't run the risk of letting a reporter snap a picture from a fresh crime scene."

"Something like that," Julia answered.

"Okay. I can picture what you described. Granted, I'd still have to see it, but going from what you're saying, I'd say it's a sketch of a *veve.*"

"That's what I thought," Julia answered.

"You've lost me," Navarro answered.

"A *veve* is a religious symbol used in voodoo. If it's a heart, it's got to be Erzulie," Prejean said.

"I'm still lost in the weeds here," Navarro said.

"Erzulie is a popular voodoo goddess. She's well known in these parts. We got a voodoo store on Royal Street in the French Quarter named after her. If you believe in that type of thing, Erzulie represents love, sexuality, and passion. Her Catholic counterpart is the Virgin Mary. Were these two women you mentioned sexually assaulted?"

"We don't know about the second one yet, but the first victim wasn't," Navarro said. He grabbed his phone from his leather jacket and began to search the name Prejean had mentioned.

"Then I'd say, and this is just a guess, he's offering up these women as sacrifices. He's dressing the women up to look like the woman he wants."

Navarro shot Julia a look and then went back to his phone.

"Bingo," Navarro said, and put the screen in front of Julia to see. On it was the same heart image the killer had drawn. "That's it. I looked up Erzulie and *veve* and got a bunch of hits. The pictures I'm seeing match the ones the killer drew."

"You said the picture the killer drew had some other symbols?" Prejean asked.

"Right. A circle with crescents on either side."

"That's not voodoo. Seems more like a pagan type of thing. Maybe he plans his killings around the stages of the moon."

"I'm betting this guy doesn't have plans to stop anytime soon. I've been a cop for fifteen years, and I've never seen anything like this," Navarro said.

"I've worked my fair share of occult cases. You need my expertise on this one, give me the word. I've got some time coming to me."

"Thanks for the offer. I don't think we'd refuse the help. If you could hang on the line with Julia for a minute, I'm going to get my chief, Beth Washington. She's going to want to talk to you," Navarro said. "One more thing. You mentioned voodoo and the occult. Just so I'm straight here, what do you think this guy is into exactly?"

"Sounds like your boy is freestyling in the art of black magic, mixing a little bit of this and that. One thing I can say for sure—whoever this person is, you-all got some big problems in the city of Detroit."

CHAPTER 6

The man who killed April Young and Heather Burns looked at the sign his wife made for him that was hand-painted in red letters—MAN CAVE, NO GIRLS ALLOWED—that hung on his work shed door.

What a joke.

The wife finally gave him permission to purchase the shed after two years of him asking. It was set up in the backyard of their brick ranch home with the well-tended garden in front. And despite Wifey's complaining about wasting their hard-earned money on something "so unnecessary," once they bought it, she actually seemed to like him spending time in there so she could vacuum in peace or post updates on Facebook and Instagram.

He figured his wife probably thought he busied himself in the shed doing woodwork projects or reading one of his books. He had crazy, fat stacks of books—mostly occult, true crime, and horror classics—that were so high, the wife threatened to donate them all to the library. Or burn them. So the shed was a good compromise as a place where he could stash his reads and take care of personal business.

Once inside, he locked the door and wallowed in the darkness. He'd put the light on when it was time to do his work, but right now, he wanted the freedom to drop the mask he was forced to wear in the real world, one that he had carefully cultivated and edited through the years to fit into his current scene. Everyone felt comfortable around the persona he came up with after years of shaping and molding: a good-looking, easygoing man with a big, happy grin. Who wouldn't love that guy?

He ran his tongue across his front teeth as the memory of the runner from Mayberry State Park, Heather Burns, came to mind, and the shocked, whimpering sound she made when the blade of his knife made a clean slice across her neck, going down deep, deep, deeper, until it reached the bone. He briefly cupped his hand over the erection in his pants and pictured the woman in the long, dark wig and blue dress he had snared after weeks of meticulous planning. She had so easily acquiesced to his demands, just like the first woman had.

His latest victim hadn't turned him on. What he had done to her did.

The man dropped his hand away from the throbbing in his pants. Time to get to work.

He reached for his earbuds, plugged them into his phone so the wife wouldn't hear if she was snooping around the yard, and hit play.

A wave of nostalgia moved through him as the first haunted strains of Louis Armstrong's trumpet and then the jazz singer's throaty bass began to play: " 'Hold me close and hold me fast . . . The magic spell you cast . . .' "

A sentimental lump formed in his throat as "La Vie en Rose" continued, bringing him back to his childhood in Louisiana. He had grown up in Iberville Parish's Plaquemine, the town tucked between the swamps of the Atchafalaya Basin and the highbrow state capital of Baton Rouge.

His time in Plaquemine had been filled with zydeco and jazz music that his uncles always seemed to have playing in their cars or when he and his grandmother came over for a visit to one of their trailers. Grandma Leticia's favorite had always been New Orleans's own Louis Armstrong.

The uncles, really his grandma Leticia's brothers, took him hunting for squirrels, deer, and rabbits in the dense, sticky woods that were thick in his parish. He had even once shot an alligator in the tail before it slipped back into the bayou east of the Atchafalaya Basin Levee. And, of course, there was the food: rich, glorious, and drippingly succulent. He breathed in deeply. The smells of his grandma's étouffées simmering on the front burner of their old two-story house behind the family's Sunoco gas station felt as real and familiar as if she were working her magic on a portable burner right in front of him.

It wasn't a particularly idyllic childhood, though, if you looked at the big picture, like he often did. His mother had told him hundreds of times that he had ruined her life. That's what she had said for most of his first six years, like she could be out partying and having the greatest time of her life if it weren't for his sheer existence.

But that never bothered him much.

His mother got pregnant at fifteen, had him at sixteen, and was killed while she worked the register at the family Sunoco when she was twenty-two. He had been sitting on the dirt in front of their house, looking at the pictures in the *Alice's Adventures in Wonderland* book his grandma had given him, when he heard two gunshots.

Pop, pop!

It was the third of July, so he figured his uncles were lighting off early fireworks, a couple of big rockets that would have gone off over the house. He had shielded a hand over his eyes to look for the explosion of colors in the sky, but then diverted his gaze to a black pickup truck tearing up the gravel on its hasty getaway dash from the Sunoco.

His mother's killer had left with a sum total of 148 dollars from the cash drawer and ten cartons of cigarettes.

He was the one who had found his mother's body before his grandma could get to him.

No big deal.

He had walked calmly to the Sunoco, crept behind the counter, and stood placidly, taking in his twenty-two-year-old mother who had been shot in the eye and torso. Her killer had popped off two slugs at close range with a shotgun, leaving half of his mother's head blown clean away.

Even at the age of six, he knew he should feel something. Anything. Sorrow, horror, disgust, relief that she was out of his life. But he just stood there, stock-still, with his hands at his sides, taking in the sight of his now-dead mother.

He couldn't feel a thing.

At that moment, his emotion over the sight of the fresh kill that was his mother was pretty much how he would've felt if his grandmother put a plate of meat loaf and mashed potatoes down in front of him at the dinner table.

His grandmother held him tightly afterward, and for the first time, she let him wash the mud off the crawdads in her giant silver strainer in her sink later that night. She probably figured he was in shock because he seemed so excited to wash the dirt off the mudbugs, rinsing them over and over in the cool water and picking out the dead ones from the squirming batch. His grandma even let him drop the little crawdads into the pot of boiling water. His grandma started to fuss and then stopped herself when he insisted on dropping them in a small handful at a time. He couldn't tell her, but he wanted to elongate the experience of watching something die at his own hand.

He had learned something about himself that day. Seeing a dead person didn't move him much. But killing something with his own hands, now that was cool.

He opened the closet in the shed and pulled out one of the size-two blue dresses that hung neatly inside. The lucky girl would get plucked from a running trail if she fit the part, just like one of those desperate women on the show *The Bachelor*, humiliating herself just to get a rose.

Louis Armstrong's raspy baritone continued to play privately in his head and he swayed back and forth to the music. He ran his hand down the smooth fabric of the blue dress and pictured Julia Gooden wearing it, just like she had the first time he had laid eyes on her.

He shimmied the blue dress off the hanger, pressing it to his body, and recalled how there had been five blue dresses when he started.

Two down, three to go. Five was a potent number to him, representing the manifestation. A four-corner-marked square with the number in the center, bringing protection, luck, and power from the five elements: earth, air, water, fire, and ether, which would allow him the freedom to pursue his heart's desire. The dot in the middle of the number-5 dice: Julia Gooden.

He killed the women as sacrifices to get her, dressing the other women up in Julia's likeness for Erzulie to recognize what he truly wanted. And she'd give him Julia in the end.

He put the dress back on its hanger and moved to a table in the corner, where he found his pad of paper and two pens, one red and one turquoise, and began to draw his devotion. He had gone to St. John the Evangelist Catholic Church in Plaquemine every Sunday with his grandma while he was growing up and celebrated his First Communion in a little powder-blue suit when he was in second grade. But the real religion, what stuck, was what his grandma did in the pole barn in the woods in the back of their house.

He knew his grandma was Creole and proud of it. Although he was white in appearance, his grandma was mixed, with light brown skin and pale green eyes. Her daddy had been purebred black and had taught her what he had seen his own father do, passing on the mantle from his own daddy before him.

Some called it voodoo, others called it black magic. But never was it to be confused with hoodoo, which had Haitian roots. His family was New Orleans through and through. His great-grandfather's ancestors came from Benin in Africa, the source of what would become voodoo in New Orleans.

Whatever people wanted to call the secret fringe religion he had discovered growing up, the man who had killed April Young and Heather Burns simply called it one word: "beautiful."

On Sunday nights while growing up, he would creep down to the woods when his grandmother thought he was sleeping. He'd run down to the pole barn and watch his grandma standing in front of a crowded room, holding a snake over her head and chanting. She caught him once, staring in awe and wonder behind the pole barn door, and then chased him back to the house. She gave him an extra-hard spanking with a belt, but then soothed his tears as he lay in bed. His grandma explained what she was doing was as spiritual as what he was learning at St. John the Evangelist. She patted his hand and shared that there was only one God. But she also believed there were other spirits under Him, helpers who would carry the message between themselves and the God she believed in. And sometimes, if you gave sacrifices and special prayers to these spirits, the message would be put on fast track.

Through the years, he mixed the voodoo, a heavy dose of Catholicism that was already a voodoo staple, and his own later interest in black magic and paganism, the latter he picked up from a goth chick he dated in college. He melded all of them together until he found something perfect.

He went back to the closet and reached down to the second shelf and stroked the remaining long, dark wigs on the Styrofoam mannequin heads, thinking how Julia's hair would feel even softer, so much more luxurious.

God, his erection was so enormous now, it hurt.

He pulled out a binder from the last shelf and sat down on the floor, thumbing through its contents that he spread out between his legs. The majority were stories Julia Gooden had written from her crime beat. Her line of work intrigued him. She obviously gravitated to the dark and violent. That had been their first connection he had recognized, a deviant common ground.

He picked up the last article on the floor and held it between his hands. This was the story that changed everything. The clipping was a picture of Julia and her son Logan accompanied by an article detailing how Julia Gooden had helped solve the case of her missing brother.

Even before that revelation, he liked Julia the moment he set eyes on her. She was striking in an exotic kind of way, with her thick, dark hair, large blue eyes, and an olive complexion. She was very pretty, but definitely not the most beautiful woman he had ever seen. The most beautiful had been the reason he and his grandmother had left Plaquemine and moved to Michigan, where they had relatives.

His uncles had covered it up for him. The woman, a girl really, was only nineteen. On the night he had followed her to her car after her shift working the counter at CVS, the girl's fair, peaches-and-cream skin had blushed crimson in anger when she threatened she'd go to the police if he didn't stop following her wherever she went, the library, the mall, outside her house, anyplace he could find her.

He was in his first year of college and couldn't have that kind of spot on his record.

So he killed her. Slit her throat clean across with a hunting knife one of his uncles had given him for his sixteenth birthday.

The first time was always the most memorable. She'd always be his girl.

Still, there was something primal in Julia he connected with, making her his sole focus now. His first kill was becoming more and more of a distant memory. And then when he and Julia spoke, it was magic.

But the story about her brother revealed her secrets and resolve. Julia was the perfect woman, who had sacrificed so much.

And she was going to make him famous with her stories.

He scooped up the articles and shoved them back in the binder, which he carefully slid into its place in the closet. He then sat down on a folding chair in the corner of the shed and slid a DVD into a small TV and watched the recording of Julia talking to a news anchor from CNN about her brother. He was transfixed on Julia's demeanor. She was composed and professional, never once breaking down or crying when she spoke about her brother. She looked ahead at the camera calmly and recounted the facts without a sappy display of weakness, just like he would've done at the age of six if someone from the TV news had bothered to interview him about his mother.

He and Julia were two peas in an odd pod. He reached down for the throbbing thing in his pants and began to touch himself. He closed his eyes and imagined Julia in the blue dress while the two danced to their song, the way her hair would smell, how she would whisper that she loved him, and then the look of shock and betrayal on her face when he slit her throat.

He'd tell her he loved her when she took her last breath. And then he'd take his own life, their paths finally unblocked in this world so they could be together in the next.

The up-and-down motion of his hand gave an electric jolt to every delicate nerve in his groin and his mind fixated on how he was going to get Julia's attention. Not to mention the fact he was going to be a bona fide celebrity soon, up there with the likes of Ted Bundy, a pretty boy like himself whom he had long admired.

He'd worked so hard for this moment. None of the other bona fide celebrity killers had even come close to what he'd done. All the planning, the intricate steps, the pictures he drew, his disguises, and the clues he left behind that the stupid cops hadn't figured out yet. He knew he'd need to reach out to Julia directly, because she was smart enough to play his game, where the cops were struggling to keep up. Julia would pay attention to him, and her stories would detail their black dance, until he killed her.

He was going to get his girl. And she was going to make him a household name for the ages.

Everything was coming full circle. And it was about time.

Normal life was so goddamn boring.

He closed his eyes and remembered the feeling of the blade of his knife severing the women's throats, a hard tug across their flesh until the sharp metal sank in and worked its way down to the bone.

He liked the sound it made and the feeling of the women going limp against him after they shot their hands up to their necks in disbelief over what he'd done.

Stupid girls.

He was so close to climaxing when a loud knock sounded on the door.

"Are you still in there?" his wife called out, ruining the perfect moment. "You need to get moving or you're going to be late."

"Just finishing up some work. I'll be right out," the man said.

He cleared his mind and concentrated on his breathing until he felt his erection go down.

He then walked over to the closet and reached in for his uniform.

Time to be normal again.

CHAPTER 7

An adrenaline rush surged through Julia when she walked into the newsroom. Having stalked the stories on her beat hourly during her sabbatical, Julia felt a strong pull of anticipation as she took in the familiar hub of activity and sounds that were a newsroom: Reporters firing off questions in an intermingled chorus doing phone interviews; a 911 dispatcher coming over the scanner above Julia's desk reporting a possible domestic in the Woodbridge neighborhood; the voice of a CNN anchor cutting through the noise from a TV mounted on the wall; and one of the copy editors and the City Hall reporter going at it in a heated debate because someone had changed the reporter's lead and ran the story without telling him first.

Julia followed her familiar path to her desk, passed the sparse features department, half of which was gutted due to layoffs, and nodded a greeting to the sports desk editor, Scott Baylor, a sixty-year-old newsroom veteran a blink away from retirement. He had started out as a young reporter covering the Tigers long before the team moved to Comerica Park.

Baylor let out a low whistle as Julia walked by.

"Hey, Hollywood. Now that you're a big-time author, I'm surprised you came back to us peons," Baylor said with a friendly smile.

"Nothing could keep me away from you. How's Betty doing?"

"The wife's making me crazy, now that she's retired. Too much time on her hands. The only way I'll ever leave this place is if they take me out on a stretcher."

"That could be arranged. I know a couple of guys who could take care of that for you," Julia answered, and gave Baylor a wink. "Just give me the word."

"Still a ballbuster. Glad to have you back, Gooden."

Julia shoved a three-month pile of mostly junk mail off her desk and then filed a summary of her story for the editors' daily ten AM meeting. Julia opened her notebook and took in what she had jotted down from her talk with April Young's principal and the Heather Burns crime scene. She then blocked out the sounds around her and got in the zone.

Julia got as far as knocking out her byline when her city editor, Virginia Remi, approached her desk.

"Welcome back," Virginia said. Virginia was in her late forties, with red hair and the loudest laugh in the newsroom. Virginia had gained Julia's respect when her now–city editor covered the Oakland County beat and wrote an exposé that sank the former county treasurer for embezzlement.

"I'm not going to bother to ask if you've been following the news about the dead jogger in the church, because knowing you, you've been obsessing over it," Virginia said. "For today, Robert Friedrich will take the lead, since he's been covering the story in your absence. How about you make some calls to your cop sources, and you can feed him anything you get."

Julia felt a blaze of heat move up her neck and she jumped up from her chair. "No way. This is my story. And in all due respect, the coverage on April Young has been terrible, and that's being nice."

"Is that right?" Virginia answered. She folded her arms across her chest in a defensive mode. "This is not a debate, Julia."

"There's been another murder. I was just at the scene. The woman was a jogger and she was found in an abandoned Baptist church, off Seven Mile."

"No shit?" Virginia said, the interest of the new victim resonating in her voice. "You have an ID?"

"I have more than that. But I'm not passing it along to your new reporter. This story is mine," Julia said.

Virginia took a look across the newsroom, likely at her new, poorly paid, recent college grad, Robert Friedrich.

"Okay. I'll move Robert over to general assignment. What's the latest victim's name?"

"It was told to me off the record. We can't go with it until the cops notify next of kin. She's thirty-nine."

"I want to go with the name. I don't want to get beat by the *Freep*," Virginia answered, using the nickname of the *Detroit Free Press.*

"No one else has the story yet. I know that as a fact," Julia said. "I gave the cops my word we wouldn't go with the name, and they promised I'd get it first."

"Fine then, at least for now. What else do you have?"

"Both victims were runners, in their thirties, and the killer dressed them up the same way, with a long, dark-haired wig and a blue dress."

"It sounds like a demented serial killer to me. That's horrible, but I love it. What else?"

"The killer left behind a drawing at both scenes. The pictures were the same, an intricate hand-drawn red-and-turquoise heart."

"This is good, really, good, Julia. The devil is always in the details."

"I called an old source of mine back in New Orleans to verify something about the picture."

"Right. I forgot you worked the cop beat in New Orleans before you came here. But why are you calling a New Orleans cop for a Detroit story?"

"My source, Doug Prejean, he's a sergeant in the NOLA PD. He's a great cop and he's worked a bunch of these types of cases before. Prejean thinks the picture is an occult symbol, likely voodoo-related, and the killings could be some kind of sacrifice. Prejean talked with Chief Washington and he's going to consult on the case. He's got Michigan connections, and he's flying in tomorrow to help the Detroit cops."

"Human sacrifices, voodoo, blue dresses, wigs, and the occult. That's a damn good story. Two bodies. We're calling him the Blue Dress Serial Killer, you got that, Frank?" Virginia called out to a copy desk editor, who waved a jaded hand of acknowledgment in response without looking up from his computer.

"You want to label him a serial killer already?" Julia asked.

"You want to tell me you don't think the killer is going to strike again? Two is all it takes. He's got a pattern, and the FBI will likely be brought in. So 'serial killer' it is. Okay, Julia, go with what you have. Do your best to work your sources to give us the latest victim's name on the record. I don't want to get beat on that. And, Julia?"

"Yes?"

"It's damn good to have you back."

* * *

Julia spent the rest of the afternoon hustling down details about the two dead women and returned to the newsroom at five to file the story. When she was done, she pulled out a yellow legal pad from her top desk drawer and wrote down the names of both victims side by side. Heather Burns and April Young were both single mothers in their thirties and they were runners with the same lean-body type. Julia drummed the end of her pencil against the legal pad and tried to piece together other commonalities between the two women that connected them to their killer.

Julia's thoughts turned to her boys and she hoped their transition to her going back to work went smoothly. She took a quick glance at a framed photo on her desk of Logan and Will taken two summers earlier. Logan's arm was looped around Will's shoulder, always the big brother and the protector, just like Ben had been to her. Logan flashed his trademark crooked smile in the photo, the exact same one Julia's brother Ben had so easily offered up to her like a reward so many years ago. At times, Julia thought Logan's resemblance to Ben was uncanny. Both her brother and oldest son had jet-black hair, high cheekbones, and dark eyes that tilted up on the ends.

Julia's cell phone rang and she instantly recognized the number. It belonged to a now-sober, but still recovering, addict who had done a couple stints in prison, stole Julia's credit card information nine years earlier, and threatened to come after a then-infant Logan if Julia went to the police.

"Hey, sis," Julia answered.

"Wow, you actually answered," Julia's older sister, Sarah, said. "I figured you'd be out chasing down criminals."

"I am. I'm working on a big story right now about two dead women. Both had kids, so it's a real tragedy."

"It sounds like you're busy. I have an invitation for you, but if you can't make it, that's cool."

Julia could hear her sister taking a deep puff on a cigarette, and she figured Sarah had snuck out in the alleyway for a quick smoke at the substance abuse treatment center where she was a counselor.

"Let me guess. A Marlboro Light break and you're working the late shift. What's the invitation?"

"Yeah, I'm just getting off work," Sarah answered. "I have this thing coming up at the center. It's a cheesy ceremony here where they recognize people who have sobriety anniversaries. Mine is eighteen months. I've been seeing a guy who's going to be there, but I'd like you to come if you can. If you don't want to or have other plans, I get it. Say no now so we can get this over with."

"I'd love to. When's the ceremony?"

"Really? Okay, well, thanks. It's in two weeks. I'll text you the details. There's something else I've been meaning to talk to you about. I'm hoping you're going to be cool with it."

"I've got to go, Sarah," Julia said, reacting to a new e-mail alert from Virginia that popped up on her computer screen. "Let's catch up later."

Julia hung up and clicked on the e-mail. In the message, Virginia cc'd the managing editor and the editor in chief, and gave Julia kudos for her story. Julia took a quick look at the article in the news queue that Virginia had edited and saw that Virginia had no follow-up questions.

Surprisingly, it was going to be an early night.

Julia shoved her personal belongings in her bag when her cell phone rang from somewhere inside her cavernous purse. Julia scooped her phone up and answered after seeing the familiar number.

"Gooden, I thought you should know, there's going to be a press conference in about twenty minutes," Navarro said.

"On the dead runners? Don't do that to me. If you've got

more information, you have to tell me now. Where's the press conference? At the station?" Julia said while her mind scrambled to plot out the shortest route to the police station in rush-hour traffic.

"No. The address is 100 Riverfront Drive, eleventh floor."

"I just filed my story. I'll see you in twenty."

Julia parked her SUV on the street across from the address Navarro had given her. She took the elevator up to the eleventh floor and rang the buzzer of her destination.

"Glad you could make it, come on in," Navarro said. His black leather jacket was off and the barbed-wire tattoo etched on his muscular bicep from logging daily hours at the gym was visible from beneath the fold of his black T-shirt.

"This is an unorthodox place for a press conference, don't you think?" Julia asked, and followed Navarro down the hallway. "Is this someone's apartment?"

"It's mine."

"This is your place?" Julia asked. "I'm not sure I'm comfortable with this setup. Am I the only member of the press here?"

Navarro ended the tour in his living room that had more gym equipment than furniture, leaned back against his sole couch, and let his deep-set hazel eyes settle on Julia's face with an intense gaze. "You got the only invitation."

"Okay then. I appreciate the exclusive. Do you mind if I record this?"

Navarro raised an eyebrow. "If that's what you want to do, I'm game."

Julia dug into her purse for her tape recorder but came up empty-handed.

"I must have left the recorder in my car," Julia said, and pulled out her reporter's notebook and pen and posed her first question. "Have you found any further connections between the two dead women?" Julia asked.

Navarro moved toward Julia and she retreated until she was backed against the wall.

"What do you think you're doing? And you didn't answer my question," Julia said.

"Sorry, but the dress you have on is very distracting," Navarro answered. He closed the space between them and trapped Julia by putting both his hands against the wall by her sides, boxing her in.

"I don't think this is appropriate," Julia answered. "Do you do this with all the female reporters, Detective?"

"Just you. Hold on a second. I think it's about to get pretty loud in here. Don't move."

Navarro put the Kings of Leon on his stereo and turned up the volume.

"I missed you," Navarro said. He pinned Julia back against the wall and then slid his hand underneath her dress.

Julia let her notebook and pen fall to the floor as Navarro slipped his tongue down the length of her neck and to the point of the V in her dress. She arched her back as she felt Navarro's mouth on hers, and his hand worked its way up her thigh.

"I don't think we're going to make it to the bedroom," Julia said.

"We don't have to."

Navarro easily lifted Julia up and she wrapped her legs around him.

"Gooden . . ."

"Yes, Ray?" Julia asked as she tried to catch her breath.

"I love you, baby."

Julia lay on top of Navarro, the two of them naked in his bed, her blue-and-white–striped dress lost somewhere back in the hallway forty minutes earlier. She traced her finger against the scar on Navarro's shoulder from a bullet he took for her at the Packard Plant a year earlier.

Julia laid her head against Navarro's chest and breathed in deeply, savoring his smell, something that had always been virile and intoxicating to her. The two had first lived together as a couple in a studio apartment in Mexicantown when they were both twenty-five. But their relationship ended after Julia turned down Navarro's marriage proposal because she thought they were too young. Navarro took the rejection hard, but their friendship and close bond remained intact, even after Julia married someone else, David Tanner, the former assistant district attorney. Out of respect to Julia, Navarro didn't pursue her, even after her messy separation and infidelity on David's part. But when David was killed due to transgressions Julia would have never been able to forgive, even if he were still alive, Navarro and Julia rekindled their relationship, one that Julia now knew she should have never left in the first place.

Navarro stared out his bedroom window to his view of the Detroit River, and Julia knew exactly what he was thinking.

"You're going to catch the guy," Julia said.

"I have to. Heather Burns has a daughter. Her name is Carly. Russell and I spoke to her today. Jesus, the poor kid was a mess. She and her mom were really close. We found Heather Burns's Range Rover in Mayberry State Park in Northville. We figure that's where she was jogging when the killer picked her up. Carly said her mom always jogged at dawn, since she tried to get a run in before work."

"Just like April Young."

"Yeah, and just like you."

"I'm always careful when I run alone," Julia answered.

"One thing I can't get out of my head is that whoever killed these women, he made them look like you."

"There are thousands of women with long, dark hair in the city."

"Come on, Julia. You have the same blue dress the killer made the victims wear. Same designer, same size. You wore it when I took you to the police awards banquet."

"It's got to be a coincidence is all," Julia said, but she felt a cool shiver move through her that cut her to the bone when she pictured the body of Heather Burns lying slumped on the floor in the blue satin A-line dress, and her own exact version that hung in her bedroom closet.

"Neither one of us believes in coincidences. And you fit the pattern. You're in your thirties and a single mother who runs. Both women had the same body type as you."

"I'm already paranoid enough as it is, Ray. I've been working hard not to be that way anymore."

"I know you have, and I'm not trying to scare you. I just want you to be careful. Have you ever run in Mayberry State Park?"

"No. But you and I have run the RiverWalk Trail plenty of times."

"Until we pick up this guy, no running without me. I'm serious, Julia."

"I called the wig shops in the city to see if anyone remembered selling two long, dark-haired wigs to the same person, but I came up empty."

"We checked that angle, too. The killer could've ordered them online. We found another wig in Mayberry State Park."

"The killer's got a thing for wigs. The latest one is dark-haired, too, I'm guessing."

"No. It was short and gray," Navarro said. "It was stuffed in a garbage can inside a stall in the women's bathroom where we found Heather's water bottle by one of the sinks. We think the killer left the wig behind on purpose, just like the heart pictures he drew."

"Why the gray wig this time?"

"We think the killer wore it," Navarro said. "He probably dressed up like an old woman to make Heather Burns let down her guard and then he grabbed her in the bathroom. Unless he's dressing up to role-play."

"Like we just did," Julia said.

"No, ours was nothing like that, beautiful."

"So you're saying the killer likes to dress up in women's clothing?"

"Not necessarily. He might like to take on different roles to present himself to his victims. The way April Young and Heathers Burns were both dressed up, he's making them look like the person he fantasizes about. Whoever the killer is, maybe he's trying to look like someone who would please her or that she would feel comfortable around."

"So what he wears could be symbolic?" Julia asked.

"Nothing is off the table," Navarro said.

"Did you find the man with the dead son who allegedly volunteered at the local chapter of Missing and Exploited Children? You know, the one April Young ran into on the RiverWalk Trail."

"How do you know about that?" Navarro asked.

"I talked to the principal at April's school."

"Of course you did. Why did I bother to ask?"

"I put a call into Guy Peterson. He said the description of the man didn't ring a bell, but he was going to ask around," Julia said.

"We haven't found him, either. Did the principal happen to mention the name of the man's dead son?" Navarro asked.

"Ben," Julia answered. "I see where you're going with

this. But I don't want to think someone is killing innocent women because of some kind of twisted link to me. All right. I do see the connections, though."

"So humor me. I'm going to ask you some questions."

"Are we role-playing again? I'm ready if you are."

"This is serious. Have you noticed anyone following you, or maybe someone who keeps showing up, like an unfamiliar face in the crowd who's making a habit of being where you are?"

"Not to my knowledge."

"Okay, how about anyone on your beat who's coming on to you, or a guy who knows something personal about you that you didn't tell him? You know a stalker's drill. Or maybe someone sent you an anonymous gift?"

"No to all of the above."

"Just be careful and be smart, like I know you will. But I promise you one thing."

"What's that?" Julia asked.

"If anyone ever tries to hurt you, I'll kill them."

"I know you would. But I can protect myself. Stop worrying so much."

"Taking care of you and your boys is my job," Navarro said. "How did the call with your book editor go today? I'm betting you nailed it. I'm so proud of you, babe."

Julia groaned, pulled herself off Navarro's body and sat up next to him in bed. "It didn't go so well. My editor said what I wrote was a 'flat account of the facts.'"

"That's bullshit. Your story was great. What's this guy's number?"

"Jesus, you sound like Helen. No, my editor was right. I should've known better. He wants me to include more emotional insight on how Ben's abduction impacted me as a kid and now as an adult."

Navarro ran his finger down the length of Julia's arm until he reached her hand. "Are you okay with that?"

"The way I feel about Ben and what happened to him, that's mine. I'll share how I feel with you, but that's it. I've never been comfortable talking about my brother with anyone else, especially strangers. Putting up walls keeps you safe."

"You're safe right here," Navarro answered. He pulled Julia against his chest and kissed the top of her forehead. "I want to ask you something. Are you satisfied?"

"Are you kidding me? Did I sound like I wasn't satisfied a few minutes ago?"

"No, not sexually. I mean, are you happy with us? I'd hoped after you found out what happened to your brother, you'd feel more settled. But you still seem restless. It's okay if you feel that way. But if there's something I can do to make you feel better . . . I just want to make everything good for you."

Julia pushed Navarro down on the bed and leaned over him so their faces were inches apart. "I swear, you've made me happier than I've ever been in my life. Got it?"

Navarro offered up one of his perfect smiles. "I've got it, Gooden."

"I was thinking, how'd you like to spend the weekend with us? If you don't have plans already."

"You mean overnight? I thought you wanted to hold off on that with the kids."

"The boys are crazy about you. They talk about you all the time. They'd be so excited, and I'd get you for the whole weekend. I was thinking, I'd love to make this a permanent situation. You could stay with us every weekend, I mean, if you wanted to. But don't feel obligated to say yes. I realize you have a life of your own, so if that would cut into your bachelor time, it's completely okay."

"If I had my way, it would be permanent, but that's something you'd have to tell me you wanted first."

"So that's a yes for the weekend idea?"

"A definite yes. I'll take the guest room."

"I think the boys will be okay with you staying in my room."

"Really?"

"We'd need to turn the volume down to zero, though. No wild sexual episodes like what just unfolded here."

"I wasn't thinking about sex, I swear. It's been a long time since I woke up next to you."

"Detective Ray Navarro, my hopeless romantic. I won't let it slip to your cop buddies."

"It's all for you, babe. Maybe you'd let me take the boys to a Lions game some weekend?"

"Just a guy thing? I'm okay with that. Logan and Will would be thrilled," Julia said. "I'm going to invite Prejean over for dinner tomorrow after I pick him up at the airport. It was a good move to have him consult on the case. Prejean knows his stuff. I'll invite Russell to dinner, too."

"Russell told me he started seeing someone, so he may want to bring her."

"That works for me," Julia said. "Who's the mystery lady?"

"He won't say."

"Russell usually likes to brag about his latest conquests. He must really like her if he's keeping her ID under wraps."

Julia got up from the bed and started to search for her clothes. "Logan has a basketball game on a new team in the city tonight through the Wayne County Parks Youth League. I can't be late."

"That's a hell of a view, Gooden," Navarro said as Julia walked with her back to him, naked down the hallway to find her dress. "Remember what I said about running alone. Do me a favor and listen to me for once in your life. I mean it this time, Julia."

"I promise. I'm committed to changing my stubborn ways. I really am. I don't plan on putting myself in harm's way."

"Sure. I still think you're beautiful, Gooden, even when I know you're lying."

CHAPTER 8

Julia made a pit stop in Midtown at Avalon Café and Bakery on Woodward to pick up a treat for Logan, a s'more whoopie pie, his favorite and a reward for starting on a new team amidst a flood of nerves Julia knew her son was sorting out.

The restaurant was already filled with an early dinner crowd and Julia took her place in line to order from the counter, all the while turning the seemingly disconnected pieces of the murdered joggers' case over in her head like a Rubik's Cube puzzle.

"Julia. Julia Gooden?"

Julia took in the man belonging to the voice who was departing from the dining room with a refined swagger of a pretty boy who was keenly aware of his looks. The man was in his early forties, five-ten in stature, just three inches taller than Julia, with short light brown, carefully styled hair, a trim build, and was dressed professionally in a dark blue suit and a lavender dress shirt opened at the collar.

Julia knew that if you live in a city long enough, no matter if it's jam-packed with hundreds of thousands of people, you could still wind up running into familiar faces. And the ones you'd prefer never to see again seemed to somehow show up anyway.

Alex Tillerman, a doctor Julia had dated in her early twenties before she was with Navarro the first time, held his hand out, but Julia ignored the gesture, giving him a slight nod of recognition instead.

Julia had met Tillerman when she covered a story about his receiving the Physician of the Year Award from the local medical society when she was interning for the *Detroit News*. Julia had called things off when she realized Tillerman was an arrogant womanizer who had a weekend cocaine habit. Tillerman had also become increasingly possessive and jealous during their six-month relationship. After the breakup, Tillerman continued to pester Julia, not giving up and calling her nonstop, mostly late at night when she figured he was high, but she ignored his persistence. Julia figured it wasn't that he honestly still cared about her. Tillerman just wasn't used to being dumped. He wanted to get her back so he could do the deed himself.

"Hey, Julia. It is you. How've you been?" Tillerman asked, and gave an attractive blond waitress a discreet once-over as she passed. "I'm still at Harper University Hospital. I haven't seen you around there in a while, not since that drug dealer was shot up and paralyzed. What was his name? Tyce something, right? I remember you were there at the hospital to interview him. A couple medical staff said you were worse than one of those ambulance-chasing lawyers, but I set them straight."

"You're talking about Tyce Jones. He's a friend of mine."

"You're friends with a drug dealer?"

"Tyce isn't into that life anymore. How about you?"

"Ah, Julia. Still a tease."

Tillerman did a quick glance at Julia's empty ring finger and tried to hand her his card.

"I take it you're not married anymore. My cell phone is on my card. I'd give you my home number, but I'm staying at a hotel right now. I'm going through a divorce. We should grab a coffee sometime to catch up. It's a coincidence that we ran into each other. I was thinking about calling you, now that I'm single again."

"I'm seeing someone."

"Who's saying I was asking you on a date? Just a friendly cup of coffee between old friends." Not taking no for an answer, Tillerman dropped his business card into Julia's open purse. "You've got my number now. See you around, Julia."

"No, you won't," Julia said. But Tillerman had already gone.

The Wayne County parks-and-rec gym in the Bricktown District, where Logan was playing his game, was located across the street from the Saints Peter and Paul Church, the oldest existing church in Detroit.

Julia didn't consider herself religious. Not by a long shot. The last time she had prayed was when she was seven. Julia had sat alone in the police interview room the night Ben was taken, her mother having been hauled off to the drunk tank to sober up. In that moment, Julia had prayed with all her might, figuring her sheer desperation would surely get God's attention. But God never answered, so Julia had simply stopped praying.

An old Chrysler sputtered to a stop across the street, further connecting a stark memory of her past, as if the old junker had appeared on purpose, the universe putting it in her path as a painful reminder.

During his short nine years, Ben had always tried to make everything right for Julia when nothing was. Julia looked on at the old Chrysler and its occupants getting out, a mother and a baby, likely heading into the church in hopes of getting money, food, or a voucher for a safe place to sleep for the night.

Julia looked through the scene across the street and instead saw her brother Ben, huddled next to her in the backseat of their father's run-down Chrysler that had become their temporary home. Ben tried as hard as he could to make the desperate situation seem okay and told her a bedtime story about a magical wizard named Mr. Moto.

"Will you tell me that story every night?" Julia asked, and snuggled up against Ben to try and get warm.

"Sure. Get some sleep. I'll stay up for a while to make sure everything is all right," Ben said. "We're going to get out of this. I promise."

Helen's Volvo was already parked in the lot and Julia hurried to catch up. Her arrival clocked in ten minutes before the game's onset, but the gym was already packed with parents who had spilled over from the stands onto the sidelines.

Julia spotted Logan on the periphery of a group of a dozen boys on the far end of the basketball court, his dark, shiny hair standing out against his new team's red jersey. Logan dribbled the basketball, keeping his distance from the other boys, who were huddled together in a tight pack, talking and practicing shots from the foul line.

Most of the other boys' attempts were complete air balls, nowhere near reaching the net. Julia felt a swell of pride, knowing her Logan, who practiced shooting hoops in their backyard every day after school, could make the shot from the free throw line, no problem.

A skinny bald man with a beard, who wore a red team jersey, put his arm around Logan's shoulder and walked him over to the other boys. The man, who Julia figured for the coach, then moved Logan to the head of the line for his turn.

"You can do it, baby," Julia said under her breath, recognizing Logan's nerves thinly disguised underneath his attempt at a cool demeanor.

A mother always knew her son.

Logan bent his knees, the ball resting on his fingertips. He then extended his right arm and released, just as Julia had watched him do hundreds of times before when he shot around in their backyard. Julia's smile spread across her face as she watched the slow backspin of the ball and its perfect arc as it came down and swooshed through the net.

"Way to go, Logan!" Julia yelled as loud as she could, and let out a piercing whistle through her front teeth, getting more attention from the curious mothers and other strangers in the stand than her son, who looked back at Julia and gave her a shy wave before he rejoined his teammates.

Julia turned back to the stands and spotted Helen and Will approaching in her direction. Her younger son then broke from Helen and came barreling toward her, causing Julia to almost lose her footing when Will grabbed her in one of his fierce little-boy hugs.

"Did you see that? The boy is a protégé," Helen said of Logan. "How was your first day back at work?"

"Good, but I missed everyone," Julia said. She lifted Will up in her arms and gave him a kiss on his forehead. "How was preschool?"

"Lennox has bugs in his hair," Will answered.

"Ooh. Head lice," Julia said.

"I checked Will already. He's fine. But he's getting a cold. The preschool called and I picked him up early. We were just waiting for you to get here. I'm going to take him home to rest and I'll make dinner so it will be ready when you and Logan get in."

"Why didn't you call me about Will? I would've left work."

"That's exactly why I didn't call. It was your first day back. The boy doesn't have a fever, just a runny nose. He will live," Helen said. "Logan needs you here. He pretended to have a stomachache on the way over."

"He's nervous," Julia said, and pressed her wrist against the side of Will's forehead to see if he felt warm. "He doesn't feel hot. Are you okay, sweetheart?"

Will sniffled and rested his head against Julia's shoulder. "Too loud here. I want to go home."

"I'll take Will home. Can you stay for Logan's game?" Julia asked.

"No. I go home with the boy," Helen said, and pulled Will from Julia's arms. "Your Logan, he needs you. I can manage a child with a runny nose."

"Bye-bye, Mamma. It's okay," Will said as if sensing her guilt.

Julia watched the two leave, feeling torn as she tried keeping all the balls she was juggling in the air from falling.

The loud grating sound of the buzzer announcing the start of the game blasted overhead and Julia eyed the stands, finding a coveted vacant seat in the third row, next to a group of women Julia estimated were about her age.

Julia navigated her way through the throng of spectators until she reached a woman with long blond hair and a full face of carefully applied makeup. The blonde was sitting next to the empty spot. The woman was well dressed in a pair of black designer jeans, a loose jade-colored silk shirt, and a pair of killer black high heels, which seemed insane to Julia to wear to a kids' basketball game.

"Is anyone sitting here?" Julia asked.

The woman gave Julia a quick up-and-down glance, clearly sizing Julia up as the potentially unwanted new competition. The woman then barely nodded her consent and began to reach inside her extra-large Michael Kors purse that contained a small terrier dog inside.

"Tell you what, never mind," Julia said, not wanting to deal with the drama. "I'd rather stand and be closer to the action."

"No, please join us," said a dark-haired woman, who gave Julia a welcoming smile. She was sitting next to the blonde who thought it was somehow chic to have a live animal in her pocketbook, stealing Paris Hilton's eye-rolling trend from nearly twenty years earlier. "I'm Charlotte. Charlotte Fisher. I think our kids are on the same team. My son is Steven. He's the kid with the crazy mop of curly hair."

"I'm Julia Gooden, and this place is packed. Is it always like this? My son Logan's old team, we'd be lucky to get the first three rows filled during a game."

"Parents here take the games pretty seriously," Charlotte said.

"Does your son go to Pierson Academy or Avalon Elementary? Everyone here, their kids pretty much go to one or the other," Charlotte said.

"Neither yet," Julia answered. "But Logan will likely be going to Avalon. We're thinking of moving to the area soon. I'm a big fan of public schools, so we didn't look at Pierson."

The blonde with the dog turned and gave Julia a disapproving glance. "Pierson is the best private school in Wayne County. They have a higher rate of Ivy League college acceptances than any other school, private or public, in the state."

"I toured Avalon and I really liked it," Julia said. "The principal was fantastic. He grew up in the Brewster Projects with an incarcerated dad and single mom and managed to graduate from Harvard. I'm guessing he didn't attend Pierson, and he did pretty well for himself."

Julia ignored the chilly stare from the blonde and jumped

to her feet as Logan stole the ball from a player on the opposing team and dribbled it down the court toward his team's basket, nailing a two-point layup.

Julia let out another whistle and clapped her hands, causing Logan to look up to the stands and give her a small smile.

The boys ran back down the court, and Julia watched as a serious-looking boy on Logan's team threw an elbow into the stomach of another kid on the rival team who had the ball.

"Foul!" the referee called.

The blonde got to her feet in her staggering high heels and cupped her hands around her mouth. "That's a stupid call! Are you blind, or what?"

"I'm taking it that's your son who the ref just called a foul on," Julia said. "He threw an elbow to the other kid."

"No, he didn't. That referee is a low-class moron. The other boy tripped and Jared ran into him. It wasn't a foul."

"Look, it's just a game. The kids are having fun. And I'm betting that ref you just yelled at is probably barely earning enough to cover the cost of gas to get here for working the game," Julia said.

"Your son is the dark-haired boy?" the blonde asked coolly.

"Right. Logan."

"Who does he train with?" she asked.

"This is Sophiah, by the way," Charlotte said, introducing her blond friend, who hadn't bothered to do so herself yet.

"There's a silent *h* at the end of my name," Sophiah answered. "I added the *h* myself a few years ago. I always tell my son that it's okay to be different. Different is special."

Julia held her tongue from telling the woman she probably should tell her son it isn't so special to elbow a kid in the stomach on the basketball court. Julia knew she needed to play nice for Logan, even if it was killing her not to speak her mind.

"You didn't answer my question. Who is your son's basketball trainer?" Sophiah asked. "Another mom has a retired point guard from the 1998 Pistons training her son. It costs her two hundred dollars per half hour, but I'm telling you, it's worth it. Look at Ethan's technique."

"Two hundred dollars to train a kid for junior rec league? That's crazy," Julia said. "My son doesn't train with anyone. He just shoots around in our backyard after school."

"Jared doesn't have time to 'just shoot around' after school," the blonde answered. "His schedule is full. Mandarin lessons Mondays, Wednesdays, and Fridays, and then he goes straight to basketball training before he comes here. Tuesdays and Thursdays are his light days. He's only got lacrosse and violin after school, so he gets home by seven. It's really not a lot, because his weekends are free now, since he doesn't have to study for Pierson's gifted-and-talented program anymore."

Julia looked away from Sophiah's giant, gloating grin before she said something she regretted or flat-out slugged her.

"I'm not trying to brag, but Jared's English teacher told me he got one of the highest scores on the GATE test in the school's history. I asked that they test Jared's IQ to see if he's a genius. Gifted and talented is one thing. Genius is different. Genius is special."

"How old is your son?" Julia asked.

"He's nine. He'll be ten next month," the blonde answered.

"You're putting some seriously high expectation on your son, and he's just a child. People can parent the way they want, but it's good to let a child just be a kid sometimes," Julia said. "If there's that much pressure early on, it can screw kids up when they get older. Rebellion, drugs, eating disorders, you can fill in the blanks."

"I guess it's a good thing your son isn't trying to get into Pierson then. They expect discipline and training from their students."

Julia felt like she was in a sequel to the movie *Mean Girls*, this one entitled *Mean Girls 2: All Grown-Up and Still Bitchy*, when she caught an aroma of something powerful coming from the blonde's purse.

"You may want to check that. I think your dog may be the one who needs the discipline and training," Julia said.

"Oh, shit," the blonde said as she inspected her bag with her furry accessory inside and picked her way out of the stands in her skyscraper-high heels.

"You were amazing," Charlotte said with a laugh. "Most people don't stand up to her. She's a little, what should I say, high-maintenance? I guess that's the best way to describe her."

"I think you're being way too generous," Julia answered. "I could come up with a few other words for her."

"You're blunt. I like that. Are you a lawyer? You strike me as the type who doesn't mind confrontation."

"No, I'm a newspaper reporter. I cover the crime beat in Detroit."

"No kidding? No wonder you wouldn't take Sophiah's shit. You being new in town, why don't you join us for a girls' night out? We're going to the Sugar House in Corktown tomorrow night. It's always packed and there are plenty of single guys. I don't see a ring, so I'm guessing you're not married."

"No, but I'm seeing someone."

"Come with us anyway. We always go dancing afterward," Charlotte said.

"Dancing?" Julia asked, trying to go back to the recesses of her memory to the last time she went to a nightclub, but she came up empty. "Thanks, but that's not my style. When I'm not working, I'm home with my kids."

"Then you definitely need to join us. What do you do for fun? You can't be all work and then in mommy mode. Every woman needs some 'me' time."

"I run. Every morning."

"I'm a runner, too. If you won't do a girls' night out, how about we go running together? I'm free this Friday, if you can make it. Let's plan on setting up a play date with our kids, too. That way, your son will have a friend before he starts school."

"That's really nice of you. I'll take you up on both offers. I'm guessing your son doesn't go to Pierson Academy then?" Julia asked.

"That pretentious place? Not a chance."

"I knew I liked you."

Julia gave Charlotte her contact information and then watched as the blonde, Sophiah with a silent *h* at the end of her name, returned empty-handed, having likely dumped her soiled purse and her dog accessory in her car, Julia figured.

Sophiah nabbed a vacant seat in the front row and called out to her boy, "Come on, Jared. You need to hustle!"

Jared spun his head in the direction of his mother's voice just as he attempted to jump and snag a rebound.

Julia winced as the boy, distracted by his mother, came down at an awkward angle and crumpled down on the gym floor when he landed.

"That doesn't look good," Charlotte said.

"Time-out!" the coach from Logan's team called, and the gym filled with the sound of a referee's shrill whistle.

When the boy didn't get up, Julia's motherly instincts kicked in. She made her way down from the bleachers until she reached the gym floor, where the coach for Logan's team crouched down by his injured player. The coach looked uncomfortable to Julia, as if he didn't quite know what to do, and continued to pat Jared on the back, like that would somehow help.

"Mind if I take a look?" the referee, who blew the whistle, asked Logan's coach.

The referee was about her age, Julia estimated, and he had the name *Jeremiah Landry* sewn into a label on his Wayne County Parks and Recreation shirt.

"My ankle hurts really bad!" Jared cried.

"You're okay, Jared. Walk it off, buddy," Sophiah said. Instead of getting up to check on her son, she remained seated in the stands. "There's just two minutes left on the clock. Hey, ref, make him go back in the game. He's fine."

Landry ignored the blonde's directive and bent down next to the boy. "You're going to be okay, son. Can you move your foot for me?"

"I can move it, but it doesn't feel good. I don't want to play anymore."

"You don't have to," Landry said. He gently gripped the boy's ankle between his two hands and made small, circular movements with the child's foot and then nodded to the coach. "There's an ice pack in the gym office. I don't think anything's broken, but he could have a sprain. For now, he needs to ice it. My recommendation is for you to stay off it for now, Jared, and have your mom take you to the doctor tomorrow to get it checked. You're going to be okay, I promise. You'll be back playing before you know it."

"He can play," Sophiah said. "You can do it, baby."

"You're going to be good as new," Jeremiah said, continuing to keep his focus on the hurt player instead of his mom, but Julia noticed the ref raised his voice so the mother would be sure to hear his advice. "But if you play on a sprain or another injury, your ankle might not heal right. The play-offs are coming up, and if your team makes it, I know you wouldn't want to miss the big game. You take care of yourself first and don't worry about sitting out this time."

The mention of "the play-offs" made Sophiah's eyes burn bright.

"Come on, Jared. It's okay. Your team is going to need you when it counts," Sophiah said, and patted the empty seat next to her.

"Don't put any weight on your foot. I'm going to get you to your mom," Landry said. He pulled the boy up carefully, looped one of Jared's arms around his waist, and nodded for the coach to do the same on the other side.

When Jared was safely eased to his seat in the front row, Landry gave the boy a fist pound. "We'll get you iced up, and that ankle's going to start to feel better. I promise," Landry said, and jogged back to center court.

Julia began to return to her seat, but changed her route when her cell phone rang and Navarro's number came up.

"Hold on one second," Julia said to Navarro as she picked up. She beat a quick path out of the gym and found a corner in the hallway of the building far enough away from the din of the crowd.

"I'm at Logan's game. Can you hear me?"

"Barely. I wanted to give you a heads-up. The *Freep* reporter has been digging around, so I want you to get this first."

"You're a lifesaver, Ray."

"The killer left behind something with each of the victims."

"I know about the picture."

"There's something else. With April Young, the first vic, the killer left a Monopoly game piece in the palm of her hand. It was a red plastic house."

"What does that mean?" Julia asked.

"Heather Burns was a Realtor."

"He was leaving a clue about the next victim."

"The killer likes to play games. Heather Burns had something in her hand, too. It was a charm of some kind of blackbird. We dusted it for prints, but nothing came back. This guy must've been gloved. He knew what he was doing. There was also no DNA to work with underneath either of the women's fingernails, so it looks like neither of them tried to fight off their attacker."

"Maybe they were too scared to fight. Or he killed them before they could. Thanks for this. I'm going to call the copy desk and have them update the story I wrote that's already up online so we won't get beat. Are you okay with that?"

"I ran it by the chief. She knows the *Freep* was likely going to get it from a source they have in the coroner's office, so she's fine with it. Just don't name us directly as a source."

"That's a deal. I should get going. The game is about to end. I'll be seeing you tomorrow night, right?"

"My bag's already packed. See you soon, beautiful."

Julia quickly tapped the update on her phone and called the copy desk, letting them know she was about to send the updated story to them.

She barely hung up when the gym doors opened and a sea of parents and their players herded out.

"Damn," Julia said, and worked her way against the tide and back inside, where Logan was sitting alone on the newly vacated stands.

"Sorry I missed the last few minutes of your game. I had to take a work call. You were fantastic," Julia said.

"Thanks. You don't have to cheer so loud the next time," Logan said. "Being new and everything, I don't want to stand out."

"Are you kidding me? You couldn't shut me up if you tried. Did you meet any of the other kids on your team?"

"Not really. No one really talked to me. All the kids know each other already."

Julia sat down next to Logan and grabbed her little boy's hand.

"I'm so proud of you. You played great today because you worked hard and practiced. And you tried something new. I know it wasn't easy. I got you a s'more whoopie pie to celebrate. Let me just grab my briefcase. I left it in the stand, and we'll get out of here."

"Man, people here sure don't know how to clean up. If kids in my school left all this garbage behind in the gym, they'd have to go to the principal's office."

Strewn across the bleachers were dozens of empty water bottles, half-eaten bags of chips, and other debris. Julia looked back at the ref, Jeremiah Landry, who helped the obnoxious blonde's son. He was whistling the Gipsy Kings' "Bamboléo" cheerfully as he swept the gym floor.

"The ref seems like a nice guy. Let's help him out," Julia said, and the two began to pick up as many empty water bottles as they could and dumped them in the recycling bin.

"Thanks, but you don't need to do that," Jeremiah said.

"We don't mind. They make the referees sweep, too?" Julia asked.

"I get paid extra to clean up after the games. I don't mind."

"You should get paid extra when you get harassed by obnoxious parents, too," Julia said. "You made good calls today. Don't let those jerks get to you."

"I never do." Jeremiah offered up a slow, easy smile, reached out his hand, and introduced himself. "Your boy here has a heck of a good shot. I can tell you've been practicing, son. Way to hustle out there."

Jeremiah slid down so he was at eye level with Logan. "My only piece of advice, bend your knees when you're playing defense. That'll help you move faster. If I'm already in defensive stance, with my knees bent, and I see the ball being passed to the guy I'm guarding, I only have to make one move to steal it instead of two. Does that make sense?"

"What do you say, Logan?" Julia asked.

"Yes, thank you, sir," Logan said.

"We appreciate the tip. I guess the rude parents you deal with are an unfortunate perk of the job," Julia said.

"I love being a ref, and the kids for the most part are great, so I just let the other stuff roll off my back."

"That's good, but I'm betting you have some war stories," Julia said.

"More than a few. I had an irate dad one time who, I'm pretty sure, was going to punch me in the face for a couple of fouls I called on his kid. The boy was totally out of line and tripped another kid he was guarding. I saw the dad and his boy at a restaurant an hour later, and neither of them recognized me. So I guess when I'm in the gym, I'm the bad guy, but when I'm out in public, I'm invisible. It works for me."

"I'm Julia, by the way, and this is my son Logan. You were great tonight with that boy who got hurt. Seriously, stepping in like you did when his mom was trying to force him to play was admirable."

"Some of the parents get way too wired during games. They forget about the welfare of their children, and all they can think about is winning."

"You're really good with kids. I'm guessing you're a parent," Julia said.

"Actually, I'm not," Landry said. "My wife and I wanted a big family, but she couldn't have children, so we settled for dogs. Mainly rescues. It's not anywhere near the same as kids, but at least we don't have to pay for college."

"Good point," Julia said.

"Are you guys ready to leave? I'd be happy to walk you

out. The gym is always packed during the games, but the parking lot clears out pretty quickly when they're over. The church across the street, it does a lot of good. My wife and I are members. But they run a men's shelter, and there can be some, how should I say it without sounding judgmental . . . 'unsavory types' hanging around sometimes after-hours. The parks-and-rec department doesn't want it getting around, but there were a few car break-ins in the parking lot last week."

"I can protect my mom," Logan said.

"Of course you can. I can see that you're a brave young man."

"Thanks for the offer, but we'll be fine," Julia said.

"My mom, she's tough, and her boyfriend is a cop," Logan said with a streak of unfiltered pride in his voice.

"Police are the good guys, true heroes among us. Have a good night then. Once I lock up, my wife and I are off to catch a show at Cinema Detroit."

"What movie are you going to watch?" Logan asked.

"East of Eden."

"A James Dean classic," Julia said. "Cinema Detroit is a great spot."

"Believe it or not, I proposed to my wife there during a showing of Franco Zeffirelli's *Romeo and Juliet.* My wife and I, we're total movie buffs."

"It was nice to meet you," Julia said. She put her arm around Logan's shoulder and the two of them walked out of the empty gym to the parking lot.

"Hop in, bud. S'more whoopie pie or bust," Julia said.

Julia's ringtone sounded in her bag just as Logan climbed into the backseat.

"If it's Uncle Ray, ask him if he can come to my next game. I want him to see me play," Logan said, and shut the car door.

Julia fished out her phone and decided to roll the dice and answer, even though the caller ID came up as unknown.

"Julia Gooden," she answered.

"At last."

"Who is this?"

"I'd tell you it's the Blue Dress Killer, but that title disgusts me. You were there today, right? I figure with all the details you had, you were inside the church. I just read your story. It was masterful. I already know that you're clever, so I'm guessing you're not the one who came up with that ridiculous name for me. Other serial killers, and thank you for calling me that, have much better titles. The Grim Sleeper, Son of Sam, the Green River Killer, the Boston Strangler, BTK, now those names are memorable."

Julia dug into her briefcase for her reporter's notebook, pencil, and cassette recorder. She put her phone on speaker, hit the play button on the recorder, and then instinctively started scribbling down the caller's comments as quickly as she could.

The man's voice sounded unfamiliar, emotionless, and almost robotic in tone.

"How do I know you're the killer?" Julia asked, feeling the familiar surge of energy she got on her beat when a story was clicking in place, mixed in with revulsion that she was likely talking to the person who had killed Heather Burns and April Young. She took a quick glance at Logan inside the car and raised a finger, letting him know she'd be a minute. "For all I know, you're just a jerk who's trying to screw with me or a crazy wanting to take credit for a crime he didn't commit."

"Good move. You're trying to rattle me, make me think you don't believe me so I'll slip up and give you some hints about who I am. Not going to happen. You want proof? Okay. Both the women I killed, I left behind drawings that I

placed on their stomachs. Staging is so important. Your story
didn't include the details about what I drew. I'm guessing
the police asked you to leave that out, to see if the real killer
could fill in the details if I came forward."

"What's the picture you drew?" Julia asked.

"Not a picture, but a devotion. It's a heart, turquoise and
red. I drew it pretty. It's a religious symbol."

"To Erzulie. You've got some ties to voodoo. But those
moon drawings, those were different. Those were Wiccan."

Julia heard the person on the other end of the phone gasp
with pleasure. "You never cease to impress me. That's correct. I didn't think anyone would put that together. Erzulie,
the goddess of sexuality, love, and desire. Our own Virgin
Mary. The other symbol you mentioned, it's the Lunar
Triple Goddess, a staple of pagan witchcraft, the original
Holy Trinity from the three stages of womankind. You get
an A on your first test, but now I need something from you.
Give me a name."

"What are you talking about?"

"A name. Something better than the Blue Dress Killer. It's
not good enough. Give me a better name or I'm going to kill
again. Tomorrow morning, bright and early."

"I'm not playing your game."

"Your choice. I've already got the woman picked out. I've
been watching her for weeks. April Young, Heather Burns, I
already know the names of victims three, four, and five. I'm
even willing to give you a tiny bit of information about my
next girl. I'm only doing this because it's you, Julia, and I'm
willing to buy you some time. But you need to give me a
better name first, or my offer comes off the table. I've got
my uniform and knife prepped and ready. It's important to
dress the part."

"Hold on . . . ," Julia answered as her mind spun to come
up with something. "Magic Man."

Julia felt disgusted with herself as soon as she said it, having allowed herself to get sucked into the caller's manipulation.

"*Ahhhh*, the Magic Man Killer. I like that. A lot. Good girl. I'm really enjoying how we're doing this together. It's special, don't you think?"

"No, I think you're disgusting. How do you know me? From my stories?" Julia asked. "How did you get my number?"

"So many questions. The game is going to change now, since you figured out the first puzzle with the drawings. Let's see if you can figure out something else before it's too late. Look for the dark magic in Detroit. I wish you could see me right now. I've got a smile as big as the Cheshire cat's. If you find the place, there'll be something waiting there for you."

"You like to play games. What does the blackbird charm mean?"

"Very good. You're smarter than the cops. I'm betting you'll figure it out before they do. It's all connected. The charm, the black magic. I'm not giving you anything more. But I do need to ask you something."

"What?" Julia answered in disgust.

"Have I gone *mad*?" he said, his voice coming to life and suddenly switching from monotone to theatrics as he strung out the last word.

"'Gone'? I think you've been that way for a long time. Did you dress up those women to look like me?"

"I'm doing all this for you. We're exactly alike."

"I'm nothing like you."

"No? I know who you are. You'll see. How do you really feel about your dead brother? You compose yourself very well, considering the tragedy. Or maybe you're just a hollow shell. Are you capable of love, Julia Gooden? Did you love your brother, who was murdered?"

"Stop trying to play me," Julia said. "I'm going to find you, asshole."

"Such bad language for a lady. I have one small request. Things are going to get a lot worse, unless you agree."

She gripped the phone in silence, refusing to let him goad her this time.

"Write everything I do. Every single little detail."

CHAPTER 9

The early-morning sun blinded Julia when she looked into her rearview mirror at Navarro's Chevy Tahoe pulling up behind her. Navarro and his partner, Russell, had followed Julia from her house in Rochester Hills to a business on Bagley Street in downtown Detroit.

Julia had briefed the police the night before after her call with the newly minted Magic Man Killer, and Navarro had insisted on staying at her house, keeping a watchful eye over her and her family while he stood guard on the couch.

Her destination was directly across the street from Hello Records, an indie emporium where patrons could buy, sell, and trade their music. The funky vinyl and shellac record store had a bright yellow sign out front that promised: SOUL, JAZZ, BLUES, FUNK, GOSPEL.

"We're heading to Highland Park," Navarro said, and leaned into Julia's open car window. "There's a guy there who might look good for this. His name is Jeb Wilson. He just got out of Carson City Correctional on a rape conviction. His probation officer told me he was involved in Satanism and cut up a girl as some kind of sacrifice when he attacked her. Poor kid is lucky she got out alive."

"Jeb Wilson. His name doesn't ring any bells," Julia said.

"Even if he's not our man, he may have information that can help us."

"It's not even nine and my day is already sucking," Russell said. He stood on the sidewalk and cupped his hands near his mouth to warm them. "If nothing comes out of grilling freaky rape boy, we get to hang out with a couple of Wiccan meet-up groups later. I kid you not. At noon, we've got a sit-down with a pagan coffee klatch that meets once a week at the Starbucks on St. Antoine to talk about God knows what, probably some hocus-pocus shit. I blame Starbucks for this. A black coffee at Dunkin' Donuts is all anyone needs. Skinny, half-caf latte, my ass. You sit around and drink that shit, it makes you crazy."

"There's nothing wrong with being different, as long as you're not hurting anybody," Julia said.

"Whatever," Russell said. "Get a load of this. Our cybercrimes guy found a real winner who calls himself Rowan. Old Rowan's website says he's a voodoo priest right here in our very own Detroit. For a C-note, Rowan claims he can reverse a voodoo curse or concoct some kind of love spell that can make the chick you've got the hots for lose her panties with just one look. Our cybercrimes guy found out Rowan's real name is Myron Bruce, and he's based out of Seattle. The prick has sites set up in every major city. Voodoo priest, my ass."

"Russell, could you give us a minute?" Navarro asked his partner.

"Sure. Hey, Gooden?" Russell asked. "Speaking of asses, watch yours today."

"Thanks. I'll be fine."

Russell started whistling Stevie Wonder's "Superstition" and headed back to Navarro's vehicle.

"I don't like you being out here alone like this. What time do you pick Prejean up?" Navarro asked.

"Ten. I'm going to the airport right after I finish talking to Tyce."

"You don't think you're wasting your time with him?" Navarro asked.

"No, if anyone can help me, he can."

"Okay then. But make me a promise. Be careful. I'm serious, Julia. Don't be overconfident on this. The killer is playing some kind of game, and you're at the center of it. You know how to take care of yourself, but I don't like this. We've got your cell and house phone tapped in case the killer calls you again."

"I'll be all right, Ray. I promise."

Navarro sighed and ran his fingers in frustration through his thick shock of dark hair.

"You need to do something for me. I'm not going to let you and your boys hang solo with all this going down. I checked with my apartment manager. He has a vacant unit next to mine. They use it as an executive rental and it's fully furnished. He agreed to let you move in short-term. There's plenty of room for all of you, including Helen. And I'll be right there. I'm not going to discount that the killer knows where you live. We can get you into the place tomorrow. I know you're going to say no, but please think about it."

"Okay. We'll do it. "

"Just like that? I don't have to fight you on this?"

"Not this time. The Magic Man Killer has got a direct line to me. I don't know how close it is, but I need to make sure he doesn't get anywhere near my family."

Navarro, the once-little boy whose nana took him to Mass every Sunday growing up, did the sign of the cross over his chest.

"I didn't realize I was that much trouble that you're turning to God for favors on my behalf," Julia said.

"Just pulling out all the stops to make sure you and your family are okay. But promise me you'll be careful and call me as soon as you leave here."

"Has anyone ever mentioned you look even more handsome when you're worried?" Julia said.

Navarro offered Julia his perfect smile and then rapped his knuckles hard against the roof of her SUV.

"Got to go, babe," he said. He leaned farther into the car, gave her a lingering kiss, and then returned to his Tahoe, all the while keeping his focus on Julia to make sure she arrived safely inside her destination.

Julia gave two hard knocks on the front door of the building that was owned by one of her best sources, Tyce Jones, a former major drug dealer in Detroit who was now an entrepreneur. Despite his legit transformation, Tyce was still Charlie Hustle, working all the angles to make a mark in the music scene.

A giant man with lustrous ebony skin and a Rasta tam hat opened the door and stared way down at Julia. "What you want?"

"Hello, Rufus. So nice to see you, too. I need to see Tyce, please."

"He's sleeping. He had a late night at the club."

"It's an emergency. Tyce is expecting me."

Rufus slammed the door, his usual welcome to Julia.

Navarro, who was still on the lookout, started to get out of his car, but Julia waved her hand, letting him know she was okay.

The door opened up again and Rufus popped his head out. "You carrying?" he asked.

"As always, no. I don't own a gun."

"Just let her in, for Christ's sake."

Rufus moved out of the way of his boss, who was making a slow roll toward Julia in his wheelchair. Tyce Jones wore a Detroit Pistons cap that sat backward on his head, a red leather jacket, white pants, and a pair of red lace-up Jimmy Choo sneakers. He pulled off a pair of large gold DITA Grandmaster sunglasses and rubbed his eyes.

"I've got a killer hangover. You got anything in your bag?"

"Yes, special delivery from Helen," Julia said, and pulled out a carefully wrapped brown paper bag with fresh pierogies. "Eat them quick. They're still warm."

"They better be, making a man wake up so early. I was out late last night dancing."

"Dancing?"

"Come on, Gooden. My legs might not work, but I can still move in this chair. Lots of pretty mammas want to sit on my lap when I get moving," Tyce said, and slapped his hands on the arms of his wheelchair. "If you're done talking trash about the disabled, follow me."

Tyce led the way up his wheelchair ramp to his office on the second floor, which was complete with two gaudy red leather couches that matched his sneakers.

The bigger, the louder, the better. Tyce Jones's style.

Tyce let out a cavernous yawn, showing off his two gold front teeth.

"I didn't mean to sound like a jerk about the dancing thing."

"I was just playing with you. I know you, Gooden. We're cool," Tyce said. "If you came during business hours, I'd show you the crazy mix-up we're creating downstairs in my music studio."

"Last time I was here, you were mixing up speed metal and gospel."

"You remembered. The heaven-and-hell mix-up. People

weren't ready for that. I wait for people to catch up to me because I'm so far ahead. But now I'm working a slick new sound. I'm going back to my roots, straight-up reggae with a mix, but not rap, too many mainstream guys into that now and watering down that shit. We're getting down to some homegrown reggae roots with a zydeco backtrack this time. I'm talking a couple of white-ass nerds playing fiddles and accordions in bow ties and square little glasses and my smooth Jamaican brothers bringing it on home."

"That's right. Your mom's from Jamaica," Julia said.

"She still remembers when you came to visit me in the hospital after I got shot and wound up in this thing. That's when I knew you were a friend, not a person you'd twist for information. You hung by me, paying your respects, and didn't ask any questions," Tyce said, and pressed a button on his intercom system. "Hey, Animal, get your ass up here. Julia Gooden wants to hear you sing."

"No, I don't. Really. No offense, but I don't have time."

"It's gonna be worth it."

Animal, aka Tyce's cousin, who Julia had recently learned was actually named Rufus, stood on the other side of Tyce's desk like a mammoth statue that could only be moved by some kind of ultrapowered heavy machinery.

"Jimmy Cliff's 'Many Rivers to Cross.' Hit it, cuz. I want you to blow her mind until there's nothing left in that big reporter's brain of hers," Tyce said. He leaned back in his chair, with his laced hands resting on the back of his head.

"Come on, Tyce," Julia started, but Rufus closed the door tight and planted his massive, and probably gun-packing, frame a foot away from Julia.

Rufus closed his eyes, tilted his giant head toward the heavens, and began singing the first few strains of the reggae song in a perfect, heartbreaking pitch.

"That's beautiful. Honestly," Julia interrupted. "But a woman is about to get killed if I don't help her."

"Another day in the 'hood," Tyce said. "All right. You heard the lady. Haul your ass out of here, Animal. Makes me want to cry every time I hear your voice, though."

Julia waited until the door closed and then dove in.

"Who do you know that does black magic or voodoo in the city? Probably someone on the fringe."

"Damn, girl, you always come to me with some crazy shit. This about the stories I seen about those women being killed in the churches?"

"That's right. The killer called me last night. He told me he'd give me a clue about the next victim. He said I needed to look for dark magic in the city."

"Mmmm. You think 'cause I'm a black man I should be some kind of authority on this subject? First you knock the disabled and now you're trying to take down a brother."

"I'd never do that. You know what's happening on the street more than anyone I know, even most of the cops."

"All right, Gooden. I'm just yanking your chain. You're so damn serious all the time," Tyce said. "I got the pulse of the streets better than the cops, huh? Flattery will get you in a little bit, sugar. Sure, I know something about that. We got black magic in Jamaica, you know. We call it Obeah. It's closer to Haitian voodoo. It's serious stuff where my mom comes from. I've been there before, middle of nowhere in the hills of St. Mary in Jamaica. You can still get your ass whipped by the cops or sent to jail if you get caught messing with it. Granted, the people who practice Obeah these days live in the sticks. Bunch of uneducated dudes with two teeth, if they're lucky, running around in the country, believing in that crazy business."

"You know people who practice black magic in Detroit?"

Tyce leaned back in his chair, clasped his hands together behind the back of his neck, and looked up at the ceiling.

"There's a sister, she got a place down on Broadway. She has a business, on the down low. It's not because she's doing anything bad. This lady, she's shrewd. She just doesn't want to pay no taxes. She's from Haiti. Her name is Roseline Alcy. She knows my mamma."

"She's got a shop?"

"Nah, it's a home business. Roseline does readings and blessings. She sells stuff, too, cemetery dust, herbs, oils, shit people use for potions. She'll make one up special for you or she'll sell you the goods to do it yourself. She also got gris-gris, you know, voodoo dolls and mojo bags. She has a full-service shop. For the right price, she'll serve up a blessing or a curse, depending on your individual needs. I thought about using her once when I first got in this chair, but you wound up taking care of that for me with your stories."

"How do you know about gris-gris and voodoo?"

"Like I said, my mamma taught me about it. What I've found, through the years, a lot of that hocus-pocus stuff gets tangled up together. Obeah, witchcraft, black magic, voodoo—people just looking for something to make their lives better, just like when they go to church in their Sunday best to take Communion. Gris-gris is like a rabbit's foot or a four-leaf clover, if you ask me. I don't know if the Roseline chick believes in that kind of stuff or if she's just doing it to make bank. From what I hear, she does a good business in town."

"You got an address for this Roseline?"

"I got an address for everyone, whether I've met them or not. I am the unofficial badass prince of Detroit."

Tyce busied himself on his phone until he found what he was looking for. "She's on Broadway. 1306. She lives in an apartment complex. Eight-G."

"The 1300 block of Broadway," Julia repeated. "That's a decent area of the city."

"You sound surprised. What, you expect her to be living in the projects? Girl is a money-making entrepreneur. Got to love that. If my reggae-zydeco mix-up doesn't get me to the Billboard Music Awards, maybe I'll look her up. A scrappy businessman like myself, I'm always looking for a new angle."

"Charlie Hustle. That's you."

"Damn straight. So you say the killer called you personally? Sounds like he's a cat and wants you to be the mouse he can bat around. Watch yourself. The cat, he always wins, and the mouse gets eaten."

"Don't worry about me. I'll be the one who catches the cat first."

"That's you. Small, but deadly. You go then, you crazy mother."

"One last favor. Call this Roseline and let her know I'm on my way to see her."

"It's always one last favor with you. Fine. But if you need anything else, don't call me until the sun goes down. Thank Helen for the eats. I'm hauling my ass back to bed."

CHAPTER 10

Navarro pulled his Chevy Tahoe into a trailer park on the outskirts of Highland Park and stopped across from the address Jeb Wilson's probation officer had given him.

Navarro knew he needed to stay focused on the case of the two murdered runners, and the recently released convict inside the trailer, who had brutally raped a nineteen-year-old woman. Navarro had read Wilson's file over and over until he memorized it. He was never a skimmer on the details.

The scene of how Wilson had abducted his victim played in Navarro's head. Wilson had ambushed the girl in the back lot of the Dunkin' Donuts where she worked. The victim had a routine and took out the trash in the back of the store at exactly three PM, the end of her shift, the time Wilson had snatched her up.

Like the Magic Man Killer, Wilson planned to precision.

A slow burn grew inside Navarro as he realized the teen who Wilson tortured and raped would never be the same.

Clean and simple: Jeb Wilson was a bad man. Navarro woke up every morning with the same sense of purpose. He needed to make sure he kept the bad men like Jeb Wilson away from the innocents, and especially away from the people he loved.

At thirty-seven, Navarro was still relatively young, but a veteran on the force with fifteen years on the job. In that time, he'd learned some valuable lessons, including that a cop should always keep their personal business at home and as far away from the job as possible. You let your emotions slip or you allow your mind to drift to your own problems when you were working a case, it was a real possibility that you would wind up dead. Or worse, your partner would be killed because you lacked discipline, and their death would be your fault.

But the Magic Man Killer was different. The woman Navarro loved more than anything he ever had was in trouble.

Nothing new for Julia Gooden.

Still, Navarro had a bad feeling about this one. His *abuela*, his grandma Christina, had given him a piece of advice he thought was just an old wives' tale, yet one he never forgot. One Sunday as they walked hand in hand back home from church, his grandma had told him the little voice inside a person's head, instinct, your gut, whatever you wanted to call it, was a warning from God. That worry that wouldn't let go was a voice from heaven to look out for the *mal de ojo*.

The evil eye.

Navarro's father was from Spain, and his mother had been second-generation Mexican American. In his maternal grandmother's Mexican culture, the evil eye was a big deal. If someone possessed a malignant internal power that was strong enough, they could drain or completely flick out another person's soul. If you believed in that sort of thing.

Navarro didn't think the evil eye was necessarily real, but he did believe in God. His early faith had cemented that, from his First Communion to his years as an altar boy. He even still went to services every once in a while, especially when he was working a tough case. Navarro had seen true evil in men during his time on the force, but he believed in the idea that angels always beat demons. Light continued to shine in the darkness. And good guys always won in the end. In Navarro's world, they had to.

Or at least the good guys had to put up a hell of a fight.

Navarro studied Wilson's place and thought about his grandma, who had raised him after his father went to serve a life sentence for killing his mother when Navarro was eleven. Navarro had watched on helplessly, hidden underneath the family's kitchen table, while he cried silent tears as his drunken dad choked his mother to death.

He looked through Wilson's trailer and saw a childhood memory. His mamma, so lovely with her dark hair and always ready smile for her "beautiful boy," danced with him in their tiny apartment's kitchen before she went to work as a hotel maid, the two of them laughing as salsa music played on a small radio.

In the dark, when he was alone some nights, Navarro felt the familiar hammering ache of shame that he should've done more to help his mother, that he should've saved her from his dad's beatings that led up to her death. It didn't matter that he was just a kid. You protect the ones you love and do the right thing, no matter the circumstance. And if you don't, you're nothing more than a coward.

There were moments before his mother's murder, flickers of memories of his physically imposing father, Alejandro, who had earned the nickname *el Toro*, or the Bull, a salute to his Spanish birthplace, but more so from his large, imposing frame and epic, almost-urban-legend takedowns of his opponents in his neighborhood boxing ring. What Navarro had left of his father was his inherited build, the handwritten letters from jail that kept coming for the past twenty-five years that Navarro threw into the garbage unopened, and a few tiny strands of undead, tender memories that came to Navarro sometimes just before waking. The one that surfaced the most was when he was six and experiencing a moment of pure joy on top of his father's mighty shoulders while father and son spent the afternoon in the neighborhood park.

"Just hold on to the kite. Don't worry, mi hijo, I've got you," Navarro's father said to his little boy.

Navarro looked up at cloudless blue sky and to the main event, the orange-and-brown tiger kite, with its long tail flicking in the wind. Navarro held the string tightly between his small fingers and closed his eyes, feeling his father's strong hands on his little legs, and knew this was the best, most wonderful day of his life.

This time, he didn't need to crave. His father was paying attention to him.

"I'm sorry about what happened at the house before. I made a promise to your mom, I'll never raise my voice again, little Ray."

Navarro had since learned that real men always kept their promises.

And right now, Navarro knew he had to pull out all the stops to save Julia.

He had failed his mother. He couldn't fail Julia, too.

"Hey, earth to Navarro," Russell said and gave his partner a light punch on the shoulder. "Big surprise. Wilson's place is a dump. How do you want to play this?"

"We go in and push him hard. If he's not our guy, I'm betting he knows something."

"I can read you, Ray. I know you're worried about Julia, but she's tough. And smart. Don't do anything stupid here or lose your cool. You get thrown off the case for letting your emotions get the best of you, you're not going to be able to help Julia if you get shoved to the sidelines."

"I'd never let that happen. I'm worried about Julia, but I'll make sure she's safe."

Navarro looked toward the trailer as the front door opened and a man came out. "Let's go."

Navarro did a quick assessment of Jeb Wilson. Even from a distance, Wilson looked far more ragged than his original mug shot picture, since the usual grind of prison had obviously worn him down. Wilson was skinny, with paper-white skin that looked even paler against his jet-black, spiked hair. He had a long, braided black beard that hung halfway down his stomach and a tattoo of a pentacle, a star enclosed inside a circle, etched on the side of his left temple.

"He looks cheerful," Russell muttered as he exited the car.

Wilson was busy locking the door to his trailer, but turned around abruptly when he caught Navarro and Russell heading up his path.

"You Jeb Wilson?" Navarro asked.

"Who are you?" Wilson said. "I don't like your energy, man. It's hostile."

Navarro pulled out his badge. "Detective Raymond Navarro, Detroit PD."

"Shit. You two come here to jam me up? I've done nothing wrong. I got a job, and if I'm late, I'll get sacked. I can't violate my probation. If I lose this job, I'm screwed."

"I know all about it. Your probation officer is a buddy of mine," Navarro answered. "My partner, Russell, and I need to ask you a few questions."

"Sure, whatever you say," Wilson said. He made a move like he was going back inside his place, but then pivoted at the last second and took off, skimming past the right side of his trailer and the back of his property.

"Runner!" Navarro yelled to his partner, and bolted in Wilson's direction, while Russell took the opposite route in case the suspect tried to escape by circling around to the other side of his property.

Navarro surfaced to the rear of the lot and spotted Wilson trying to scramble up a chain-link fence that had a stretch of I-75 on the other side. He caught up to Wilson before the suspect was even a quarter of the way up the fence, grabbed him roughly by the shoulders, and threw him down to the ground.

"You got nothing to hide? Why are you running then?" Navarro asked. He pinned Wilson against the fence, patted him down, and then handcuffed his hands behind his back.

Navarro spun Wilson around as Russell appeared from the other side of the trailer.

"Wow, dirtbag. What's that stench on you? Marijuana and patchouli oil?" Russell asked.

"You're slow, old man," Wilson said. He offered up a nasty, sharp-toothed grin to Russell and then spit in his face.

"Oh, friggin' disgusting," Russell said, and ran his hand over his cheeks, trying to wipe off Wilson's stream of saliva.

"Screw you, man. You're violating my rights."

"You spit on me again, I'll be violating a lot more than your rights."

"Walk," Navarro said. "We're going into your trailer for a little talk."

"I don't have to say shit. You just want to get me out of sight so you can beat on me. That's how all you cops work."

"Your choice. I've got your probation officer's number on my cell. One call about how you tried to run from two Detroit PD officers, your life is going to get even worse than it is," Navarro said.

"Fine. You guys are assholes. I'm going to make up a real good satanic curse for you."

Wilson began to chant something, but Navarro stopped him short with a hard shove.

"Keep moving. The only curse coming anyone's way is yours when I send you back to Carson City Correctional."

"You believe in the Devil?" Wilson asked. His voice seemed to deepen as he plodded forward along the side of his trailer.

"The Devil was an angel who was kicked out of heaven because he was weak. He let his pride get to him. Big mistake," Navarro said.

"You're one of the weak ones."

"The way I see it, you're the guy with the handcuffs on."

"The Devil knows who you are," Wilson said. "If he doesn't, I'll make sure of it."

"The Devil doesn't scare me, and you, little man, surely don't, either," Navarro said.

Navarro motioned to Russell and then to Wilson's back pocket and the set of keys that was poking out from his jeans.

Russell grabbed the key chain, which had a black circle and *Pagan* stitched in cheap gold thread across it.

"Which key to open the door?" Navarro asked.

"The biggest one of the chain."

Russell worked the key in the lock. As soon as the door to the trailer opened, a rancid combination of mildew, dead air, and marijuana slipped out. Navarro pushed Wilson forward to a scuffed metal table in the middle of his kitchen. On the table was an ashtray jammed to capacity with spent Camel cigarette butts.

"Stand still," Navarro instructed, and removed the cuffs from Wilson's wrists.

"Now sit."

"I'm not a dog," Wilson said. He sat, sighing heavily over the effort, and pushed the long sleeves of his plaid shirt up, exposing a giant tattoo of a man's bearded face that was made up of a maze of connected leaves and vines.

"What's your tat, the boogeyman?" Russell asked.

"No, the green man. It's a pagan symbol. The green man is tied to the earth. The girl I cut up and raped in the circle in the woods, her blood was a sacrifice to him," Wilson said.

"The green man isn't real," Navarro said. "The heinous stuff you did to that girl is."

Wilson shrugged. "It's not like I killed her."

"You mind if I look around while you and my partner have a little chat?" Russell asked.

"Not if you don't have a warrant," Wilson answered.

"Let me ask you something," Navarro said. "You're obviously a planner. The girl you tortured and raped, you planned the whole thing out patiently ahead of time, didn't you?"

"I already did my time for that one, but yeah, so what."

"You went to the Dunkin' Donuts where she worked and got coffee there once a week for a month. You got to know her schedule, her patterns, and then you forced her into that shit-kicking car you got in the front of your property," Navarro said.

"The car belongs to my ex-wife," Wilson answered.

"I bet you two had a wonderful marriage," Russell said.

"The two joggers who were killed, we know that was you," Navarro said.

"What are you talking about, man? I don't know nothin' about no dead joggers."

"Sure you do. I did the math," Navarro said. "The first woman you killed, you picked her up on the RiverWalk Trail a month after you got popped loose from prison. You must have been pissed off in jail, serving all that time, pent-up, going crazy. It pushed you over the edge and you went looking for another victim as soon as you got out."

"You're crazy."

Navarro bent down and got in Wilson's face, giving the ex-con an intimidating stare-down.

"You like to cut women. You slit her throat," Navarro said, and pushed a picture of April Young across the beat-up table.

Wilson took a two-second, disinterested glance at the image and shrugged. "Never seen her before."

Navarro pulled out a second picture from inside his leather jacket.

"How about her?" Navarro asked, and held a picture of Heather Burns in front of Wilson's face.

"If I was going to sacrifice another woman, and I say, 'if,' these chicks aren't my type. They're basic. They're real nice-looking, but I don't get any energy vibe off them. That's what I care about. You can have the hottest chick, buck naked and begging me to give her some, but if she doesn't have good energy, I'm not interested. Maybe I don't get a read on those two women in the pictures because they're dead. The girl I took from Dunkin' Donuts, her aura glowed bright yellow. It was beautiful. I had to take it from her."

"You say one more sick thing, I promise, I won't hold back," Navarro warned, and slammed his fist down on the table, causing Wilson to jump back in his chair. "We know about your phone call last night."

"I called plenty of people last night. What are you talking about?"

Navarro pulled out his cell phone and found the picture of Julia he wanted. He had taken the shot of Julia in the blue dress when she accompanied him to the police awards banquet.

"You killed those two female joggers as some twisted sacrifice to her," Navarro said, and held up his phone for Wilson to see. "Then you made them put on that blue dress, the same one in the picture."

Wilson took his time looking at the picture of Julia and reached his hand out to touch it, but Navarro pulled his phone out of Wilson's reach.

"You do know her," Navarro said. He had trained himself years ago to keep his cool, to not let his anger make him get physical when he was working a suspect, even being tested on many occasions when the case involved a child. Intimidation was one thing, but actually hitting a suspect crossed a line you could never recover from. But right now, Navarro had to dig deep not to give in to his baser instincts and beat Wilson into a bloody stump. "Answer me."

"I'd remember her. This one, she's got interesting energy, it's bright green and blue, almost turquoise, but there's something dark around her aura trying to get in," Wilson said. "Blue eyes like the sky, black hair like midnight."

"Your poetry sucks," Russell said.

"I'd like to cut her."

Navarro spun around and slammed his motorcycle boot against Wilson's chair, which flipped over on its side with Wilson in it.

"Easy there, Ray," Russell said.

Wilson scrambled back up on his feet and took a nervous glance at the door, but Navarro pulled up the chair and planted Wilson back into the seat.

"You're never going to cut anyone ever again. We know you killed those women."

"No way, man. You better back off. I don't know anything about that. I've been working straight doing construction since I got out. I got to, for probation and all. I get to work at six-thirty every morning."

"You're lying. It's nine o'clock, and you're just hauling yourself out of the house," Russell said.

"It was supposed to be my day off. The foreman called me a half hour ago. He said one of his guys went home sick and asked if I wanted to pick up a shift. You call him and he'll vouch for me. I was working on the mornings those women were taken on the jogging trails."

"How did you know the victims were picked up in the morning?" Navarro asked.

"I saw it in the news. I've been watching that shit nonstop. They're calling the guy the Magic Man Killer. That's freakin' cool."

"Get up. We're taking you in. I'd rather grill you at the station. You know why?" Navarro asked.

"I don't care."

"Because I don't know if I'll be able to hold back from hitting you if I stay here much longer. Those two women who were killed, they had kids. They were innocent. They didn't deserve what happened to them," Navarro said.

"Ray. Over here," Russell said. He was looking at something inside a dark jar on the kitchen shelf.

"Hey, that's my stuff!" Wilson said, and jumped up from the chair.

"Stay where you are," Navarro warned. He went into the narrow kitchen and looked where Russell was pointing. Inside the jar was a bag of weed and a crack pipe that was lined with brown residue inside its bowl.

"This looks fresh. Better call Stoner Boy's probation officer now. Time to go to the station, loser," Russell said.

"Okay, okay, hold on. Listen, I didn't do nothin' to those two joggers. I'm telling you the truth. You call my foreman. He'll vouch for me. You keep this between us, I'll give you something."

"I'm not agreeing to anything. What've you got?" Navarro said.

"I met a guy who was deep in Satanism and the black arts. He could be the one who killed those chicks."

"You don't get to slide by offering up one of those weekend pagan warriors who draw circles in a field and dance around naked with flowers in their hair," Russell said.

"No. Not an amateur," Wilson said. "I know a couple of people who were into some real dark shit like me."

"Who are they? You got names?" Navarro asked.

"Billy Lincoln, but he died of a meth overdose about a year ago. And Randy Thomas, he went real dark. But Randy met some chick and she turned him on to Christianity. The dude teaches Sunday-school classes down at Mars Hill Church in Grand Rapids now. When he turned like he did, I stopped talking to him. That was a year ago, so I don't know what he's up to these days."

Navarro pulled out a notebook from his leather jacket and wrote down Randy Thomas's name. "You got a number for him?"

"Yeah, sure," Wilson said. He reached for his phone and showed Navarro the number from his contacts' page.

"That's all you got? You don't know how to deal very well," Russell said.

"Come on, man," Wilson said, and stroked his hand down the length of his braided beard. "Okay, I got one more thing, but I didn't know the guy personally. He was a friend of Billy's. He's the one who was real deep into the dark stuff I mentioned. I met him just one time. We all got together at a property that had some real nice woods at a place Billy knew in Dearborn Heights. The guy Billy brought, he was a freak. He started talking about books and stuff. Everyone got stoned except for him. He said he needed clarity to do his work."

"Books? What kind are we talking here?" Navarro asked.

"Horror, true crime, occult shit. I don't read if I don't have to, but the stuff he was talking about sounded kind of cool. He mentioned some story about a carnival run by a demon. This guy, he was real smart. I thought he might've been a nerd with the books. But then he brought out a big old snake from his backpack and it started wrapping around his arm. He ran his tongue down its belly. That was some freaky shit. I thought it was his pet or something, but then he cut off the snake's head. He slices what's left of it down the middle and lets a couple of drops of the snake's blood drip on his face."

"Lovely," Russell said.

"So then the guy, he throws what's left of the snake into the bonfire we built, and, I swear, the flames rose like ten feet or something and turned crimson. I saw the Devil's face in the flames. It was beautiful, man."

"People see strange things when they're high. You got a name for this person?" Navarro asked.

"Just his nickname. Billy referred to him as the Voodoo King, but he was into way more than that. Black magic, Satanism, Wiccan, it was all mixed up, the stuff he believed. Usually, people go one way or the other, they fixate on just one practice. Billy, though, he acted like this dude was a legend or something, that he could tap into the dark power like no one else he'd ever met."

"The Voodoo King, huh?" Russell asked. "What did he look like?"

"I couldn't tell you. It was dark and I was real high. I don't remember. We had candles around the circle we made and we had the bonfire going, but the guy had a hoodie on."

"Did he say anything else to you, maybe where he's from?" Navarro asked.

"We got into a conversation, and he said something about the place where he came from originally, he could do some real fine work there, better than in Michigan, I guess. He talked about voodoo in Louisiana, stuff he learned there, so I took it he might have spent some time down in the South."

"Did he have a Southern accent?" Navarro asked.

"No. I'd remember that. Southerners sound dumb as shit. This guy, his voice sounded regular."

"You got anything else on him?" Navarro asked.

"Look, I was stoned pretty bad, but I got the feeling he might be in the military or something. He had that kind of disciplined intensity. He could've been law enforcement. It was just a vibe, you know. I study people's energy. He was focused, man."

"You're telling me you think this guy's a cop?" Navarro asked.

"Yeah, could've been."

CHAPTER 11

Julia circled the Delta Arrivals Terminal and tried to spot her former source, NOLA sergeant Doug Prejean, amidst the crowd. Prejean was older than Julia, early forties, but when she met him for lunch in Detroit a few months prior, Julia realized Prejean had hardly aged since she first met him fifteen years earlier.

At the time, Julia was just twenty-two, overly ambitious, but still green with inexperience during her first days on the job at the *Times-Picayune*. Prejean had taken pity on her. He and his wife, Claudette, had her over for dinner a few Sundays during her first month in New Orleans to help her feel at home in her new city. Julia had wondered if Prejean's generosity would turn into a sexual play, but he never once hit on her, and Julia chalked his kindness up to Southern hospitality and simply being a good guy.

Julia had been keenly aware that the majority of female reporters at her former paper nursed major crushes on Prejean, most of them swooning over the fact that he looked like a young Kevin Costner. But Julia never thought a thing about him in a romantic sense. Prejean was a source, a relationship line she refused to cross, until she met Navarro and couldn't help herself. But more important, Prejean was married. For Julia, a couple's union had always been sacred ground.

An airport bus pulled away from the curb, giving Julia a tight opening that she wasn't going to lose. She swerved her SUV in front of an outgoing taxi and snagged a spot next to Prejean, who was standing underneath the ARRIVALS sign.

The New Orleans officer was tall and trim, with sandy-blond hair. His skin was tan with a residual bronze glow from the hot Deep South sun, and he had the makings of a mustache and goatee that were new since Julia last saw him. Prejean wore a pair of khaki pants, a dark brown, distressed, leather bomber jacket, and aviator sunglasses, looking Southern cool and effortlessly easy against a backdrop of a gray sky in "hustle for everything you've got" Detroit.

The cab driver Julia cut off blared his horn and pulled up in a hurry next to Julia, ready for a fight. Prejean moved in to take care of the situation, but Julia had it under control. She offered up a sharp, conciliatory wave, making zero eye contact, and then popped the trunk for Prejean's suitcase.

"I see your driving style hasn't changed. How you doing, Julia?" Prejean asked, and gave her a hug. "You want me to drive? I know Detroit pretty well."

"Thanks. But there's no way I'm letting you or anyone else drive my car in my city," Julia said.

"I see you haven't changed either."

Prejean slid into the passenger-side seat. As soon as he clicked his seat belt in place, Julia hit the gas pedal hard.

"Where's the first stop?" Prejean asked. "You better watch your speed, girl. I'm not sure my badge can work its magic in Detroit."

"Sorry, I'm in a hurry. I can drop you off at the station or you can go with me. The killer called me last night. He's playing games, trying to give me clues about the identity of his next victim. I'm going to meet someone a source hooked me up with who could have information."

"Then I'm riding with you. Tell me what you've got."

Julia took the I-94 East exit toward the city and debriefed Prejean about her call with the Magic Man Killer.

"Did his voice sound familiar?" Prejean asked.

"No. I recorded the call and replayed the tape over a million times. His voice sounded flat, but then he got theatrical at one point, like he was putting on a show. I'm sure I haven't spoken to him before."

"He could've used a voice changer. We do that all the time. There are plenty of apps and gadgets out there that can change a person's voice. Or he could've disguised it without technology if he knew how. I have a Southern accent, right?"

"Are you kidding me? A wicked one," Julia answered.

"I'll take that as a compliment. But listen up. I'm going to change my voice. Ready?"

"If you want to set yourself up to fail, go ahead."

"Think about the conversation you had with the killer. Maybe he left you some hidden land mines that you don't think are important," Prejean said in a perfect, flat Midwestern tone.

"That's really good there, NOLA cop. I told the Detroit PD all this already. The killer said I should look for black magic in Detroit."

"It sounds like you've got a good lead on that already. What else?"

"One thing I keep coming back to, the killer said he had his uniform and knife ready. If he wears a uniform for his job, he could be anything from an airline pilot to a sanitation worker. That's a tough one to narrow down."

"Unless he wears a special outfit for each of his murders."

"Navarro mentioned that, too. Maybe the killer is role-playing."

"Navarro's the cop who was on the phone when you called me?" Prejean asked.

"That's him. He's a great detective and has been a friend for a long time. We're seeing each other."

"A cop? No go, Julia. I don't think that's a good choice for you. Most cops get divorced, at least twice. The job gets to them and that's a relationship killer. It doesn't matter what gender you are."

"You're not that way," Julia said.

"About me and Claudette, things haven't been going great for a while. We got married so young. People change and grow apart."

"I don't like where this is going."

"We're still friends, but we're more like roommates now. Claudette and I decided we're going to separate. It was a mutual decision. We're still living together, but we're going our separate ways."

Julia pictured pretty blond Claudette sitting with her on the front porch of her home on Royal Street in New Orleans. The two women drank sweet tea as Claudette patted Julia's hand and reassured her she was going to be okay in her new city.

"I'm sorry to hear that. I figured you two would be the exception," Julia said.

"It's okay. I'll always have the greatest respect for Claudette. It's a good time for a change for both of us. Our son is graduating from high school this year. It's hard to believe, but Claudette had him when we were both just twenty-four."

"You want my two cents?"

"I don't think I'd be able to stop you, even if I didn't."

"You're forty-three?" Julia asked.

"Don't be adding on another year. I'm forty-two."

"If you're having a midlife crisis, buy a convertible. You and Claudette were really good together."

"It's not like that, Julia. People change. Claudette is thinking about moving to Florida and selling the place in Ann Arbor. Depending on how things go with the Detroit PD on this case, I'm keeping my options open about moving to Michigan. I've already got a friend here," Prejean said, and gave Julia's shoulder a light, friendly jab.

"You're thinking about a transfer?" Julia asked.

"Twenty years working New Orleans, I'm ready for something new. I don't want you to feel bad for me. I feel more alive than I have in years."

"I'm not exactly thinking I should say congratulations somehow."

"If you're done grilling me about Claudette, I have some questions for you."

"I've told you everything I know about the Magic Man Killer, but go ahead."

"It's not about the case. This one's personal. You never told me about what happened to your brother. Claudette had on CNN one morning over the summer, and I almost fell out of my chair when I saw you talking about how you helped find your brother's killer after thirty years. How come you never told me?"

"That story is mine. It isn't a good one to tell."

"You're going cold on me, girl. I feel it. You always kept what was important to you close to the vest," Prejean said. "You don't want to talk about your brother, I'm fine with that. But this cop you're dating. You need to be careful."

"As far as Navarro goes, that's a battle you're never going to win."

"Down, girl. You and this cop are serious?"

"Very."

"I'll let you know what I think of him."

"No, you won't. Navarro doesn't need your endorsement," Julia said.

"I don't want to get off on a bad foot with you here. You've always been like a little sister to me. I just don't want to see you hurt. I know cops."

"So do I. I'm not twenty-two anymore, Prejean."

The two drove on in silence for a few minutes, Julia not wanting to hear any more of Prejean's unsolicited advice, and Prejean likely getting the message loud and clear that he better not go there with Navarro, as he busied himself with his phone.

"You can't be mad at me anymore when you hear this," Prejean said. He put his phone on the SUV console and the first few mixed strains of accordion, Cajun fiddle, guitar, and drums intertwined into a lively pulse of zydeco music that filled the car.

"'Good-bye, Joe, me gotta go, me oh my oh,'" Prejean sang in a smooth tenor.

Julia kept her focus on the highway in front of her, trying her best to ignore Prejean, but Prejean grabbed her right hand from the steering wheel and moved it to the tempo of the music.

"Come on, *bébé*, you know you want to sing along. Remember this song?" Prejean asked.

"It's been a long time. But, sure, I remember."

"*Laissez les bon temps rouler,*" Prejean said. "Let the good times roll, darlin'."

Julia smiled, but took her hand back from Prejean, since the only people she let hold her hand these days were two little boys and a six-foot-three Detroit detective.

"Sorry about before. We got off on a bad start. I realize I was giving you a hard time about your new man. But you've got to admit, you haven't always made the best decisions in that area. The guy you married certainly didn't turn out to be a prize."

"Thanks for the reminder."

"What was the name of the doctor you were dating when I first met you? The one I had to send packing back to Detroit?"

"A bad penny that keeps showing up. Alex Tillerman. I ran into him recently. I could tell he's still a jerk."

"The doctor. I remember. Claudette told me he traced you down to New Orleans after you left Detroit and was giving you a hard time."

"You met him at the airport."

"Let's just say, I scared him straight. Our soil in New Orleans is too pure to have a loser like him set foot on it. He got on a plane back home to Michigan real quick after I made him see the light. He was a jealous, possessive ass, as I recall."

"Your memory is correct. I don't think he cared about me. He just wasn't used to a woman breaking up with him," Julia said. "Do me a favor? Turn up the music. That way I won't have to hear you roasting me. But you don't have to worry about me now. Navarro is a good man, the best I've ever met."

"It sounds like the girl's in love," Prejean said.

"I am."

Prejean gave Julia a smile and turned up "Jambalaya," rapping his hands to the rhythm of the music on the dashboard, while Julia turned the conversation she had with the Magic Man Killer over in her head, until she grabbed Prejean's cell and tossed it in his lap.

"Turn that down for a second. There's something else the killer said that I keep coming back to."

"Yes, ma'am," Prejean said. "What you got?"

"The killer told me he had a smile as wide as the Cheshire cat's," Julia said.

"*Alice in Wonderland*. Are there any connections to the book and Detroit?"

"I already looked into that angle. The only links to the city I could find were an *Alice in Wonderland* performance at the Bonstelle Theatre last summer, and a Mad Hatter Tea Party at the Detroit Institute of Arts a few years ago."

"You held that back. What else?"

"The killer said he and I were alike."

"He's messing with you, trying to get into your head, to make you unsure of yourself so you're vulnerable," Prejean said.

"He said something else that I thought was off. The killer asked me if he'd gone mad. Maybe he was looking for me to validate it."

"I know that line. It's from the Mad Hatter. He says it to Alice and she answers something to the extent that he's nuts, but all the best people are. The killer wants your acceptance for his actions and his warped state of mind."

"You can quote passages from *Alice in Wonderland*?" Julia asked.

"Almost every word of that story is embedded in my brain. My kid, Brian, he was in a school production of it last year. He played the Mad Hatter. He's not into theater anymore, but I heard him and Claudette rehearsing his lines around the house so many times, I've never been able to get them out of my head, God help me. Hey, girl, that's your block," Prejean said, and pointed to a quickly approaching street.

Julia swung her vehicle onto the 1300 block of Broadway and snagged a parking spot across from the apartment building Tyce had told her about.

On the street, Julia dug through her purse for any stray quarters to plug into the meter. Prejean stood next to her, still humming the "Jambalaya" song, but then abruptly stopped and grabbed Julia by the wrist.

"We're in the right place," Prejean said. He slid his aviator sunglasses down to the bridge of his nose and pointed overhead. "Check out the sign."

" 'Henry the Hatter,' " Julia said.

" 'Detroit's exclusive hatter since 1893,' " Prejean read. "The Mad Hatter. You found the place, baby girl."

CHAPTER 12

Julia hurried across the street to the Broadway address and shoved her cell phone in her pocket, having just debriefed Navarro in under a minute flat about Tyce Jones and the woman she and Prejean were about to visit.

"Navarro's ten minutes out. He's going to meet us," Julia said. "His partner will catch up with us later. Russell is trying to track down a potential suspect in Grand Rapids."

"Score one for you, but the Detroit cops should've gotten this first."

"No, Navarro and Russell are the best. They interviewed someone who might have met the Magic Man Killer," Julia said. "I just got lucky I had a source who knew about this woman."

"What's her name?" Prejean asked.

"Roseline Alcy. She's from Haiti."

"Haitian and New Orleans voodoo are two different things. Granted, there's some crossover, but if the killer is linked to Louisiana voodoo, I'm wondering why he brought you here."

"Like you said before, he's probably mixed up with more than that. That triple-goddess moon symbol he drew on the pictures he left with the victims, you said that was pagan, not voodoo."

"Doesn't matter. With that Hatter business across the street, we're in the right place."

The Broadway apartment building was a stately brick high-rise. Julia buzzed apartment 8-G in the glass entryway and waited as static crackled from the intercom, followed by a woman's voice with a silky Caribbean accent.

"You have an appointment?" the woman asked.

"No. I'm Julia Gooden. Tyce Jones called you about me."

A single, long blast from the buzzer sounded and Julia opened the door to the complex, quickly, before Roseline could change her mind. Julia and Prejean then snagged the elevator to the eighth floor.

Prejean took the lead down the hallway when they arrived, but Julia pushed ahead and gave three hard raps on Roseline's door.

"I know it's your instinct to want to be the alpha dog here, but my source referred me to Roseline, not you. I want us to win her trust so she'll talk," Julia said.

"Got it. It's good to see you've grown."

A tall, regal-looking woman with lustrous ebony skin opened the door partway. Julia estimated Roseline was somewhere in her midsixties. Her lips were painted crimson and she wore a red-and-turquoise head wrap and a matching satin turquoise dress.

"Thank you for meeting me. I'm Julia Gooden. Tyce Jones is a mutual friend. I'm a reporter, but I'm not here about a story. I'm looking for information about two women who were killed, and I think the person who murdered them has a connection to you."

Roseline stayed planted, blocking the entrance, and kept

an unblinking, tethered stare on Julia. "Tyce didn't tell me about any dead women. He said you wanted information for a story. I don't like this."

Roseline started to close the door, but Prejean put his arm in front of it.

"Who's this man? I don't want any trouble, and that's what I see you bring to my home."

Prejean started to answer, but Julia swept in quickly.

"I'm not trying to cause you any problems. I'm just looking for answers. I swear. This is New Orleans detective Doug Prejean. He's an old friend and he came here to help out with the case. Please. A woman's life is at stake."

Roseline narrowed her eyes, continuing to assess Julia, as if she were doing an inventory of her soul.

"Okay then. You can come in. I take your word that nothing is going to come back to me. I run a clean business here."

"Thank you. Just so there aren't any surprises, another friend, a Detroit police officer who's running the case, will also be coming by to ask you a few questions. The person who killed the women, we think he has ties to voodoo, and possibly Satanism and black magic."

"Those are very different things, each precise in its own study and beliefs. Satanism isn't welcome here."

"I understand. For full transparency, the killer gave me clues about his next victim and one led me to you. We don't think you're at risk in any way, but you may have information that can help us find the woman."

"Then I better clear my name. It's best to face bad luck when it's in your path. Follow me," Roseline said, and led Julia and Prejean down a hallway with dark cherry hardwood floors and soft yellow walls, until she reached the bright and open main living area.

Julia was surprised at the modern appearance of the place,

figuring Roseline's home would be dark with candlelit shrines and walls lined with potions, voodoo dolls, possibly live snakes, and God knows what else. Instead, Roseline's apartment looked more like a page from a Pottery Barn catalogue.

"You from New Orleans?" Roseline asked Prejean. "Then you know a little bit about what I do."

"I know a lot about Louisiana voodoo. But Haitian is different."

"That's right. But both are spiritual in their nature."

"But sometimes those spirits are dark, aren't they? We need to ask you about your customers," Prejean said. "You got anyone who walked through your door, a male looking for a love spell? Maybe he told you he was obsessed with a woman he couldn't have. He came to you for help and believed what you sold him—a gris-gris, a mojo bag, a dark spell—gave him the power to kill those girls as a sacrifice to get the woman he wants."

"No, no, no. That's not how I play. I don't go into the black arts, and I'd never take money to help kill a person, no matter how much someone offered. I don't like where you're going with this."

"We're not saying you helped the killer," Julia interrupted, and shot Prejean a look. "No one is suspecting you of anything right now. All we know for sure is the killer led us to you. We need to figure out why."

Three sharp knocks sounded down the hallway and Roseline retreated back to her front door and peeped through the keyhole. "Your Detroit cop a big guy?" she called out. "Handsome boy with dark hair?"

"That's him," Julia answered.

Roseline opened, but still did her "hover at the door" routine, like she had done to Julia and Prejean, and assessed Navarro before she let him through.

"How'd you get up here?" Roseline asked.

"One of your neighbors buzzed me through the front. I'm Detective Ray Navarro of the Detroit Police Department. Pleased to meet you," Navarro said, and shook Roseline's hand. "May I come in?"

"Sure. You have better manners than that other boy. Come on now," Roseline said, and returned to the living room with Navarro.

"Ray, this is Doug Prejean," Julia said, making the introductions.

"Pleased to meet you. Julia speaks very highly of you," Navarro said.

"Likewise," Prejean said in a friendly tone, but Julia could tell he was sizing Navarro up. "Let's get down to business."

"I was just telling Roseline one of her customers may be the killer," Julia said.

"You keep a list of people you do business with?" Navarro asked.

"It's confidential. Just like our conversation is going to be."

"I'm not here to get you in a jam," Navarro said. "But this is a murder investigation, and we'd like your help. The person we're looking for is male. We believe he's somewhere between the age of thirty to midforties. And we think he has ties to New Orleans voodoo and possibly some darker elements. The women he killed, he dressed them up in a black wig and blue dress. Both victims had a hand-drawn picture the killer left behind on their stomachs. The pictures had a symbol of a voodoo goddess in the center."

"Erzulie," Julia said.

"The goddess of love, sexuality, and passion," Roseline said. "Most of my clients, they're women. I do love spells for them, sure. Most people who come through my door are looking for love, money, or success. A few look for retribution. I don't guarantee it, but I clean their energy and help them tap into what they need."

"Your male clients, are any of them in the military or law enforcement?" Navarro asked.

"A cop?" Julia asked in surprise, but Navarro kept his attention on Roseline.

"I don't know what kind of jobs my customers do. Could be military. Could be teachers. Could be doctors. Could be anybody. What they do for a living makes no mind to me. I'm here to help them have a better, more spiritual life. I use my gift to help people who need a breakthrough to the other side."

"Do you have any customers who like books?" Navarro asked. "Maybe you have someone who reads a lot and mentioned it to you. Horror or occult novels maybe."

"No. I don't run a book club here."

"How about anyone who gave you pause? Maybe a client who told you about wanting to kill or hurt women?" Navarro asked.

"No, nothing like that. Most of my business, I do blessings for love and financial success. I also do house cleansings and revenge spells sometimes, too. There's nothing wrong with wanting payback from the people who've done you wrong, as long as the revenge isn't greater than what the person suffered. That way, the energy is clean. I supply what the customer needs, incense, candles, mojo bags, voodoo dolls, and herbs, depending on the situation. No one ever came here about wanting to kill no one. If they did, I boot their bottom to the street."

"You keep records, Roseline?" Navarro asked.

"I'm a successful businesswoman. Of course. But I'm not going to turn them over to you."

"Like I said, I'm not trying to jam you up. But I need you to write down a list of all the men who came to your store recently and anyone who hired you for a revenge curse or mentioned that love goddess."

"Erzulie. Okay, I'll do it, as long as it doesn't hurt my business. You know a little about voodoo, Detective Navarro?"

"Honestly, no, just what I've been able to find out in the last few days. I grew up Catholic. You're the expert."

"Since you're a nice boy, I give you a crash course. Erzulie you talk about, she's a goddess, a *loa*. You find her in Haitian and New Orleans voodoo. There's some overlap there. New Orleans, it's intertwined with Catholicism heavy. You a good Catholic. I can tell," Roseline said. "I see an image of the Virgin Mary prayer card and a pretty, dark-haired woman standing next to you. That lady, she passed. Her prayers been keeping you safe when you had no business being so. You'd be long dead if it weren't for her."

Navarro kept an even stare back at Roseline, but he rubbed his index finger over one eyebrow, a subliminal habit Julia knew Navarro did when he was uncomfortable or taken by surprise.

"In voodoo, people believe in one God and the search for a better understanding of the spiritual aspects of life. People who practice voodoo believe God is first, followed by the spirits that oversee everything on the earth. Ancestors play a heavy role, too. They're called on for wisdom and protection. The stuff you see in the movies about devil worship, zombies, or human sacrifice, that's not voodoo. That's Hollywood, baby. Voodoo pure and spiritual. People capitalize on it though, and that's wrong. Most of the voodoo dolls you can buy, they're not real. They made in China."

"Those books you keep of your clients, I need a copy for my eyes only. Men and women. Can you do that? Unless you're hiding something, you won't be in trouble, I promise," Navarro said, and flashed Roseline a smile.

"You ask small first and then you slip in a bigger request. I see how you work. I bet that dimple in your left cheek helps you get your way every time."

In the corner of her eye, Julia saw Prejean give a discreet eye roll.

"Sure, honey. I do that for you. I can tell you a good man, but good men sometimes do wrong things. Don't screw me, *chéri*. You wouldn't want me to be mad at you. Now come on. I told you what I can from the physical world, but let me see what I can find out from the spiritual."

"That's not necessary," Julia said, but Roseline was already making a beeline to the rear of the apartment.

"Don't worry," Roseline said without turning around. "I don't plan on sacrificing any goats."

"I'm not a fan of this," Julia whispered to Navarro and Prejean. "If she wants to talk about the case, fine. We'll see if there's something there. But if she starts talking about anything personal, I'm going to shut it down."

"She's not going to read your palm, if that's what you're worried about. There's nothing to be afraid of," Prejean said. "I can't tell if she's legit yet. We're either going to get a big show from a bullshit artist, or just maybe, and I'm not betting on it, she'll have something that can help the case. How about you, Detective? Are you spooked?"

"No. Sometimes you work a case and it leads you into some weird territory," Navarro said, and turned his attention on Julia. "I know you don't like this type of thing. If Roseline says anything personal that makes you feel uncomfortable, I'll be right here."

"Okay, Dudley Do-Right and Chicken Little, let's go," Prejean said. He gave a big wink to Navarro and Julia, and the trio followed Roseline's path through a doorway that was covered with a bamboo-string makeshift curtain that thrummed with a light rattle as they passed.

Inside, Roseline sat in the middle of a round table with a row of seven lit black candles lined up in front of her.

Julia did a quick pan of the room that was unlike the other parts of the apartment she had seen. A heavy black curtain hung across the window, and one wall was filled with jars and vials of what looked like an assortment of oils and herbs, necklaces and voodoo dolls. In the corner was a lit shrine with prayer cards to the Virgin Mary and St. Peter.

"This is a place of peace and spiritual enlightenment," Roseline said. "There is nothing to fear here. I ask the help of our ancestors and spirits to bring clarity to me as an earthly conduit."

Roseline leaned down, blew out the first candle, and closed her eyes. She began to hum in a low, guttural tone and rocked back and forth in her chair until her eyes slowly opened.

"Mmm, mmm, mmm. Your killer, he spent some time down South. I see swampland. It's the bayou. There's a body of a girl in white who's floating down there. Her eyes wide open and she's looking straight at me. Poor baby. She was his first kill. She been dead a long time and wants to be found. College girl."

Roseline shivered. She did the sign of the cross, blew out a second candle, and closed her eyes again. She then continued on, with what appeared to be her ritual, rocking back and forth and humming, until she opened her eyes and this time looked straight at Julia.

"I see five blue dresses. They laid out all in a row. I'm told these represent the victims he's already killed or picked out. Two down, three to go. That's what I hear. Two got a chance to be saved. One, I already see, her body in a trunk. She close to death."

"Do you know their names?" Julia asked.

"It don't work like that. No questions. I need to concentrate," Roseline said. "The last three victims, I see a raven, a spider, and a little boy. The last one, that child, protecting you something fierce."

"Hold on. Who's the 'you' you're talking about here?" Navarro asked.

"The lady right there," Roseline said, and pointed her finger at Julia. "The killer, he wants things from you, Julia. A lot of things."

"What's his motive? Are we talking sex?" Prejean asked.

"No, that's not what motivates this boy. He wants Julia to make him famous. But he likes her, too. A whole lot. He thinks you two are the same, but he wrong. I can see that. That boy who's protecting you, the killer knows about him. He feelin' like some kind of reaction you had to the boy make you just like him."

Navarro reached over to Julia and rested his hand on the small of her back, sensing her discomfort.

"Ah. I see now. Reporter and cop. You two together. There's a deep connection between the two of you. You're soul mates."

Roseline closed her eyes and blew out another candle.

"I see your pasts. You two been doing this dance together through many, many lives. This one, you finally getting close to perfecting it. You broke up when you were younger, went your separate ways, right?"

"We're here to talk about the case. Our personal stories aren't important," Navarro said.

"That's where you're wrong. It's all connected. The past, the present, the future. One tiny little step in the wrong direction, you throw off the whole cycle," Roseline said. "You, handsome, wonder what your life would've been like if you stayed together. I see your younger selves, a very strong love, but something happened and you parted ways. It was the right outcome. Spirits looking out for you, even back then. If you two stayed a couple, you, Detective, would've been dead at twenty-five. I see a little apartment. You're sleeping alone. Your girl isn't there. Someone came in for her, killed you instead. Same thing happened in your last life. You left that girl a widow. But you two got it right this time around. You're going to be okay."

"My friends here aren't looking for a consultation from

the Psychic Network," Prejean said. "Easy pickup you did, though. The cop grabs the girl, you figure they're a couple and make up a story. He's a cop working a dangerous job. You make up a tall tale to distract from what you don't know."

"I know what I know. You, sir, I see trouble in your past right behind you. Some things you left behind in New Orleans coming back. You know it, too," Roseline said. "What your partner say about that, boy?"

"I don't know what you're talking about. I've got no problems here or at home. If this is all you've got, I think we're about done," Prejean said. "What do you say, Navarro?"

"Not yet," Roseline said, and blew out another candle. "Your last name is Gooden, right?"

"I don't want to talk about me."

"Maybe you don't, but I need to. I see two children. One tied to you. The other tied to both you and your partner. The first boy, he passed. He's glued to your side and won't leave. His presence is very powerful for a child. In voodoo, ancestors come strong, and this boy, he come the strongest I ever seen. The boy, he's small with black hair and he's wearing a red shirt. He should pass to the other side, but he won't. He's staying here to protect you, just like he promised. But you need to set him free. This boy should've moved on, but he can't. You need to give him permission to go."

"You looked me up when Tyce called. You knew my name."

"You're not that important I'm going to be spending my time Googling your name on the computer. This boy standing right next to you, he came to this world with one purpose, to save you. Let him do that, and then he can move on. He'll still look out for you after he goes. Part of him is in another boy I see. Those two boys look alike. That part is not going anywhere. This boy your brother? He die a violent death?"

"I don't want to talk about my brother," Julia said. She

felt pinpricks move down her arms as she pictured two almost identical pictures in her mind, like two mirror images:
her brother, Ben. And her son Logan.

"Thank you for your time. If the detectives have any more
questions, they can stay, but I need to leave," Julia said. She
backed up quickly without looking behind her, her eyes
fixed on the black candles and the thin wisps of smoke that
rose from them in front of Roseline.

"Hold on, Julia," Navarro said.

Julia continued to back out of the room and through the
bamboo curtains. As she turned around, her hip clipped hard
against a long wooden hallway table, knocking a stack of mail
to the floor.

Julia wanted to get out of the apartment as fast as possible,
but stopped when she spotted a manila envelope amidst the
strewn white pieces of mail that were scattered at her feet.

"Navarro, Prejean. I see something," Julia called out. She
bent down and picked up the manila envelope. Roseline's
name was written across the front, but there was no return
address or sender's name. On the upper left-hand side of the
envelope was a hand-drawn picture of a perfect circle, with
two crescent moons on either side.

"What do you have?" Navarro asked.

"Triple Goddess symbol," Prejean said. "When did you
get this?"

The bamboo string curtains chimed again as Roseline
came through into the hallway.

"Yesterday. All that was in my mail slot. I haven't had a
chance to go through it yet. I got no hurries. It's usually junk
mail and bills."

"This one isn't. Okay, from the stamp, it was mailed two
days ago from somewhere in the city," Navarro said. "It's
going to be tough to get a print on the envelope, but we may
have a shot with what's inside."

Navarro reached into the pocket of his leather jacket and pulled out a pair of plastic gloves. He snapped them into place over his hands and extracted a folded single piece of white lined paper from inside the envelope.

"It's to you," Navarro said, and held the paper up so Julia could see it.

At the top of the paper was a drawn turquoise-and-red heart and then a handwritten note:

Julia,
If you found this letter, you're as smart as I thought
you were. So here's a reward.
Mr. Dark.
901 W. Lafayette Blvd.

Julia dove her hand inside the pocket of her dress for her phone and plugged in the address.

"901 West Lafayette Boulevard, it's a bookstore. I've been there before. It's John K. King Used and Rare Books," Julia said.

"I'll check out the Mr. Dark reference," Prejean said. He worked his finger across the keypad of his phone, studied the results, and then held up his cell for Navarro and Julia to see.

"I'm not sure if it's the fit, but Mr. Dark is a character in some horror novel written by Ray Bradbury."

"I know that book. It's about a carnival that comes to town run by a demonic force. *Something Wicked This Way Comes,*" Julia said. "It has to be."

Julia followed behind Navarro and pulled into the parking lot of John K. King Used & Rare Books, a giant, blue-gray, four-story building that was once a glove factory. It had a large picture of a hand and its pointed index finger painted along the corner of the building.

"This place looks pretty beat," Prejean said as he got out of the car, his voice almost getting lost amidst the sound of the expressway.

"This store is classic Detroit. It's got character," Julia said. "The killer led us to a bookstore. We need to look beyond the occult angle. With the *Alice in Wonderland* mention and now the Ray Bradbury novel, the killer is tied to books somehow. Maybe he's a writer. Or an English teacher."

"Or a librarian. Or just a freak."

"He could be a customer here," Navarro said as he approached. "This is how we should play it. Prejean and I will talk to the owner. Julia, you look for the book."

"Maybe the killer works here," Prejean said.

"This guy's smart. I can't imagine he'd bring us to the place where he works," Navarro said. "But still, you never know. Let's go."

John K. King Used & Rare Books was a massive space with tall, cavernously deep rows of books. The sections had paper and cardboard signs taped up on their ends, with handwritten descriptions of the genres that could be found inside the towering racks.

A skinny, short employee with a red apron and a scraggly beard poked out from behind a giant stack of books. He was having a conversation over a walkie-talkie and gave the trio a friendly wave, but lost his smile when Navarro flashed his badge.

"I need to talk to the owner," Navarro said.

"He's out for lunch. Can I help you?"

"I need to find a Ray Bradbury book," Julia said in a rush. *"Something Wicked This Way Comes."*

"Hmmm. I don't think it's in our rare book room. That's appointment only, in our second building. But if we had it, I'd let you go right in, of course. Is this about a stolen book or something? If it is, you're going to need to come back to talk to the owner."

"No, it's nothing like that," Navarro said.

"Okay. Well, we don't have a computerized catalogue of our books, but I manage the first floor here," the employee said, and handed Julia a map. "On this floor, we've got our popular books. They sell pretty fast. We've got some classics. So look here first. If you don't find your book, check the third floor. We've got mystery, science fiction, and fantasy up there. A couple picture books, too. Our fourth floor is mostly obscure, hard-to-find books. I doubt it will be there. Our books are alphabetized by author, but I can help you look. I'm Jim, by the way."

"Julia can look for the book by herself. This other gentleman here, he's a cop, too. We want to talk to you about a possible customer who may be involved in a series of crimes."

Julia heard Navarro's voice trail behind her as she looked on at the daunting rows of books, dozens of deep, long, intimidating stacks that she was afraid would take hours to pore through.

She began to sprint, running by the rows of books and their hand-scribbled signs that listed travel, military, biography, metaphysical, and religion categories, anything other than what she needed, until she found a fiction section in the back.

Julia stepped on her tiptoes as she ran her fingers over the spines of the books, skimming the hodgepodge of genres. She passed by a Jackie Collins novel next to Chaucer's *The Canterbury Tales* and worked her way backward, up the alphabet, until she reached a row of books whose authors' last names began with the letter *B*.

The dust from the books stuck to her fingertips as she quickly traced over the titles of the works. Julia felt a nervous strum go off inside her when she found Ray Bradbury's *Fahrenheit 451* right next to a well-worn paperback of *Something Wicked This Way Comes*.

Julia snatched the novel from the shelf and fanned through its pages until a white index card fell and landed at her feet.

Julia scooped up the card and read the handwritten message: *Victim Number Three. Thirty-one. Raven's Poe. For your eyes only for now, Julia. You write about my work after I'm done. No news stories about the information I just gave you until it's over. You do, and I'll slit her throat before morning.*

CHAPTER 13

Julia stood her ground, parked in front of the circular cutout in the bulletproof glass partition in the reception area of the Detroit PD, waiting to get in to see the chief.

It had been radio silence from Navarro and Prejean in the past hour since the duo's retreat back to the station following Julia's hard-won breadcrumb of the Raven's Poe clue. And Julia wanted in on whatever the cops had after her personal searches on the possible identity of the killer's next victim came up short.

In this instance, there was no time to hurry up and wait.

"Sheila, can't you just let me in? The chief is expecting me," Julia asked the receptionist behind the glass. Sheila was in her midsixties, with a poof of blond hair and a sweep of light blue eye shadow over her lids. Sheila shot a look back inside the open door to the precinct and shook her head.

"Sorry, Julia, but since Washington took over as chief, she's been real tight about things, you press guys included. We kind of think of you as our own reporter around here, but I don't want to get in trouble. I can tell you one thing, though," Sheila said, and leaned in close to the cutout circle. "Washington's going to be meeting with an agent from the FBI pretty soon."

"So the Detroit PD is asking for help on a profile of the killer," Julia said.

"Maybe. That's above my pay grade."

"Incoming," Julia said, and gave a subtle nod of her head as Chief Washington walked past the open door behind Sheila on her way to the lobby.

Julia pivoted away from the glass partition, so as not to arouse the chief's suspicion meter, and pretended to look at something on her phone when the buzzer sounded and the door to the inner sanctum opened.

"Five minutes, Julia. I'm about to go into a meeting," Washington said. She held the door open for Julia, who hustled through it and kept pace behind the chief.

"I know. You've brought in a profiler from the FBI."

Julia watched as the back of Washington's head shook back and forth. "We should just have a direct hotline to call you with everything that happens in my department. You've got four minutes now. Come on in."

Washington led Julia into her office, a place Julia had been to many times before, including when it belonged to the former chief, John Linderman, who was currently an inmate at Carson City Correctional. When Washington was appointed to the position, Julia had noticed the chief didn't display any personal family photos of her sons. Even in the highest-ranking position in the department, Julia figured, Washington still felt like she had something to prove as a woman and single mother, which she likely thought could be leveraged as a vulnerability to try and drag her down even by members of her own team.

Washington took her jacket off and leaned up against the front of her desk with her arms folded across her chest and her weapon holstered at her hip.

"What do you want, Julia?"

"To be embedded in the investigation. The killer calls me directly, gives me clues, and then sends me on a scavenger hunt across the city. He's reaching out to me directly, Beth. I have an inside line on him."

"I can't do that."

"Yes, you can, and you should, if you're smart like I know you are. I'll make a deal with you."

"I don't deal," Washington said.

"Come on. You need me as much as I need you. I found Roseline on my own and that led us to the envelope the killer left for me. I got nothing in the past hour trying to chase down the Raven's Poe lead. You let me be part of this investigation, on the sidelines, and I'll give you my word on something I've never agreed to before. One stipulation I won't break on though, you don't get to see my stories ahead of time, but I'll run what I plan to write by you and Navarro before the articles go live. That way, you can be sure the timeline on when you want information released works for you and doesn't jeopardize the case. Look at me as a witness in real time and I'll give you everything I've got."

Washington's eyes ticked to the clock on the wall and her likely countdown to her meeting. "That's not the way my department works."

"You and I have known each other a long time. We may not have always agreed on everything, but at least from my end, I can say I always respected you. And, I hope, the one thing you could say about me is the same. I realize you may feel like you have more to prove as a woman in your role, but nobody in the entire department deserved getting promoted to chief more than you."

Washington went back to her desk and opened a drawer, pulled out a picture, and turned it around for Julia to see.

"That was me, my first week on patrol fifteen years ago. I volunteered for the night shifts so I could spend time with my sons. You want to act like we're sisters because we both can play the woman card? But I'm one thing you're not. I'm a woman, and I'm black. Don't pretend like you know what it's like to be me. You don't have a clue. A lot of my own people think I got promoted to chief because I'm a female and a minority and I ticked off the right boxes for the progressive mayor, but this is not necessarily a progressive department. Detroit has one of the highest violent crime and homicide rates in the country, and I made a commitment when I took this job to reduce violence in the city. And now, just three months in, I've got a serial killer plucking females from jogging trails, slitting their throats, and dumping their bodies in abandoned churches after he plays Barbie dress-up with them. You have no idea what kind of pressure I'm under."

"I'm sorry. I didn't mean to offend you, and you're right. I don't know what it's like to be you. But I remember when I first started on the cop beat, I had to work like hell to prove myself. Every single day, I had to show that I was smarter and tougher than the guys in the newsroom and the old guard who was still in charge of the paper. I'm good at what I do, and I'm proud of it. Let me help you catch the killer. I'm not going to stop asking."

Washington tucked the photo back into her desk's top drawer and looked back at the clock.

"You run everything by us first, and I'll let you be embedded in the investigation, but I get to tell you when you walk away. This isn't about me being a bitch. It's about me doing my job."

Julia felt the smile come and she jumped up from her chair and shook Washington's hand.

"Thank you, Chief. You won't regret it. What did you get on the Raven's Poe lead?"

"And so it starts. Navarro and Russell may have something. They got a tip about an English professor named Raven at Wayne State. They're going to interview her."

"I want to tag along."

"Not interviewing witnesses. The press has a way of intimidating people."

"So do cops."

"That's my rule. I have to go into a meeting now."

Washington reached the door of her office and turned around.

"Are you coming or what?"

"Absolutely. You won't regret this."

Julia followed Washington to the squad room where Navarro, Russell, Prejean, and Corporal Smith were standing in a semicircle around a man Julia had never seen before. Behind the group were three large white poster boards. One on the far left had a picture of Heather Burns pinned to it, with pertinent information known about her written in black marker underneath. The board on the far right had the same setup, but with a picture of April Young at the top. The center board had just a name at the top: *MMK*.

Navarro looked up from the huddle and raised an eyebrow of surprise when he saw Julia.

"Gentlemen, I'm guessing that everyone who's already here has been properly introduced," Washington said. "As you know, the Magic Man Killer, or MMK, as we're now calling him, has been making direct contact to Julia Gooden. We generally wouldn't let a reporter anywhere near an investigation, but since Julia is at the center of it and appears to be the focus of the killer's attention, I've given her a modified pass card into the case. Let me repeat, a modified pass card, with the understanding that Julia will be running anything and everything she plans to write by us first. Is this correct, Ms. Gooden?"

"Absolutely. You have my word."

"Then let me make the only other necessary introduction. Agent Jake Britton, this is Julia Gooden. Agent Britton is part of the FBI's Behavioral Analysis Unit, and I've had the pleasure of working with him on numerous occasions through the years."

Britton, who looked to be in his late forties, had a thick mane of salt-and-pepper hair. He was as tall as Navarro, but thin. He had a patchwork of scars down the right side of his face from his left temple to his jawline that Julia thought might have been caused by some kind of burn. He locked eyes with Julia and then looked back to Washington.

"Your call on the reporter. But this conversation is not on deep background. Whatever I discuss in this room is completely off the record, and I better not ever see it in print."

"Understood," Julia said.

"You can trust Julia," Navarro said. "Our department has worked with her for a long time, and she's respected around here by everyone."

"Thank you, Detective, but I'm not looking for an endorsement. Okay, let's get down to it," Britton said. He went over to the center of the three boards, picked up a black marker, and wrote down *organized* under the killer's moniker.

"A killer's behavior is a mirror to their personality," Britton continued. "In this case, MMK selected his victims carefully and struck at an exact time and location when he knew the female runners would be at the parks where he abducted them. Without forensic evidence, we need to rely on behavioral clues."

"The killer is a planner," Washington said.

"Exactly. He's patient and methodical," Britton said. "He likely spent weeks studying these women, picking them out ahead of time, studying their patterns and schedules, not to mention the abandoned churches he scouted out and the ritualistic methodology he used in the murders. MMK, I believe, displayed control at his crime scenes, but what he left behind was almost theater in his staging, the wigs, the dress, the hand-drawn pictures. And the location of the churches where he killed the women. These were not opportunistic crimes. Your killer is restrained and highly disciplined. But he likes the ornateness of the ritual. And I'm betting these aren't his first kills. Neither of the victims was sexually assaulted?"

"That's right," Navarro answered.

"Then I'm guessing the motivation is a thrill crime. But based on the voodoo and occult symbols left at the scene and the same images on the notes that were found, the killer is also motivated by religion. He could believe he is hearing voices or communication from gods or other beings who demand he commit murder."

"Like the Son of Sam," Julia said.

"Down where I'm from, we know a little bit about black magic," Prejean said. "Our killer here, he's into a hybrid voodoo, Satanism, and some off-shoot Wiccan practices. And he's got some ties to mainstream religion based on the fact that he killed both women in churches. The heart symbol, Erzulie, is the voodoo goddess of love and sexuality. He dressed up those women to look like Julia, I'm betting, as a sacrifice for Erzulie. Her Catholic counterpart is the Virgin Mary."

"To different halves of how he sees the perfect woman, the virgin mother, and a passionate, sensual lover," Britton said.

"The victims weren't sexually assaulted," Navarro said. "We don't think the two killings were motivated by that."

"I don't think it's sexual desire he has for the victims, or for Julia," Britton said. "But he wants your attention, Julia. That's why he reached out to you. You're the object of his fantasy. If we look at his postoffensive behavior, we see he's trying to inject himself into the investigation by calling you and leaving behind clues with your name on them. You give him power by writing stories about MMK and his work. He wants the attention because he feels powerless in his own life. His normal every day is probably mundane, and he may have an overbearing spouse. But I think his fixation on you is more than the fact that you can give him fame. He feels attached to you somehow. He thinks the two of you have some commonality."

"Why is he leaving behind clues? April Young had the game piece of a house in her hand, which was obviously a nod to the fact Heather Burns was a Realtor. And now he tried to tip me off about the next victim with the Raven's Poe reference," Julia said. "Is it a game to him?"

"A game where he's the one in control," Britton said. "But he likes the thrill of the chance of getting caught. He snatched the two joggers from public places. It was early in the morning when he took them, but someone could've easily seen him. He wants the excitement because he's bored and unhappy in his normal life. That's probably why he called you with the hints about his next victim."

"Just killing isn't enough to get his rocks off," Russell said.

"How do you think he knew the women?" Julia asked.

"I'll let you take that one, Beth," Britton said.

"We've tried to pinpoint any connections between April Young and Heather Burns," Washington said. "They didn't mingle in the same social circles, and their kids went to different schools. We're going through their computers, but we're pretty sure they got on the killer's radar when they were out for a run. That's where we figure he first saw them. He's probably watched you run, too, Julia."

Julia felt a bloom of anger grow and twine itself inside her as she pictured her private moments in the cemetery where she stopped during her early-morning runs to visit her brother's grave.

"The suspect Navarro and I interviewed referred to the man he met as the Voodoo King. He thought he might be a cop or ex-military," Russell said. "The blue dress that the victims were found in, Julia wore a similar one to the police awards banquet."

"You're thinking a Detroit cop is the killer?" Julia asked.

"Here's what I think. Your killer is male, in his thirties to midforties, college educated," Britton said. "He likely used a ruse to trick his victims into trusting him. They might have known him, but only as a casual acquaintance, and if so, a person in a position they would've let their guard down if they saw him. He likely leads a normal life and is married. You represent something to him, Julia, in the truest form of womanhood or the power he feels, based on what he thinks your connection is. In his deepest thoughts, and when he allows himself, he knows that he's strange. But as the woman who he respects and idolizes, you, Julia, give him reassurance that's okay. He's going to keep killing to please you, to get to you. The only thing that will extinguish this is his final conquest."

"What's that?" Julia asked.

"To kill you. That's the last, final, glorious end. My suggestion? Get a twenty-four-hour police tail around you and your family, if you haven't already."

CHAPTER 14

The Magic Man Killer eased his Buick to its familiar spot behind Hidden Hills Cemetery in Rochester Hills and parked on the other side of the woods where he had watched Julia so many times before. He found his man-made path of beaten-down grass and leaves, his habitual trail that led him to his previous hiding place, a huge maple where he had claimed a lookout on a high, sturdy branch. There he was camouflaged and hidden by the patchwork of leaves that had turned from vivid green to spikes of orange, rust, and yellow, having changed colors during the months that had slipped past while they kept his cover.

From his past perch, he had been able to see Julia first as a tiny speck running down the road until she was so close, standing over her dead brother's grave, he could see the rhythm of her chest, a rapid up-and-down, her body adjusting from the grueling full-tilt suicide runs she did every morning to immediate restive pose.

Julia pushed herself so hard, almost like a punishment, a retribution for a life gone wrong, he thought. Her guilt over being different, just like him.

He liked that. So very much.

There were times during his stakeouts when he had to wait for Julia or his other victims for hours. But that was no big deal. He had learned the philosophy and discipline of hunting through a stint in the military to help pay for college, but more so from his uncles. They taught him the odd juxtaposition of the macho yin and nature yang of being one with the woods, silent and still for hours until it was time to kill.

But he didn't care much about the carcass, the meat, or the conquest of the dead animal.

He preferred the pursuit, no matter how long it took. The slow hunt, studying his prey before the kill, was what he took the greatest pleasure in, more than the actual deed. He thought about this sometimes as he lay in bed, staring up at the ceiling, wishing to God his wife would go to sleep or using the memories to help make him hard if she was asking for some.

The Magic Man Killer moved past his usual lookout tree and continued on for the first time to the open space of the cemetery. He got close enough, seeing the back of Ben Gooden's gravestone now, and remembered a time when he was thirteen and had spotted a massive twelve-point buck, proud and majestic, locked in front of his doe and fawns.

The alpha male protector.

His younger self had studied the glorious animal from his rifle's scope, but he didn't take the shot. Had he told his uncles, they'd have called him crazy for not bagging such a magnificent prize. For five straight days, he came back to the same place, hidden behind the stump of a dead tree, and watched and waited, feeling the seductive tickle of his finger on the trigger of his .30-30 Winchester lever-action rifle with a side mount, when the buck came into sight. On the sixth day, MMK had heard his cue: the gentle swing of tree branches and the broken snap of leaves, nature parting a way for the massive animal. MMK didn't breathe when the buck entered the clearing in front of him. He was sure he could hear the buck's heart beating, his prey's muscular organ pumping its lifeblood through its body, until it was silenced by the thunder crack from his rifle's shot.

It was early evening now, and the graveyard was empty of visitors. MMK rested his hand on the Ben boy's grave and wondered why Julia stopped there every time after her dawn runs. She had shown no emotion about the little dead boy during the TV interview he had watched, so her ritual intrigued yet confused him. Maybe she felt guilty for not loving her brother, the boy she told the TV anchor had always protected her until his final breath.

He and Julia were more alike then she'd ever likely know.

Except for her habitual graveyard visits. When his grandma Leticia dragged him to the cemetery to visit his own mother's grave on the outskirts of Plaquemine, where they had once lived, it was like Chinese water torture for him. He could care less that his mother's body was rotting in the ground.

The bitch.

But he did like the succulent scenery around the place, especially the Spanish moss that dripped off the branches of the giant Bald Cyprus and the sumac shrubs' upward spiral of spiky flowers and leaves that looked like waist-high, exploding lanterns.

His grandma Leticia just loved the sumac and would bring a little pair of shears to snip off the red drupes which she would later crush and turn into a delicious spice that tasted like the most heavenly burst of citrusy lemon that she'd rub on her catfish before she popped them under the broiler.

A cool autumn breeze gusted through the graveyard, and MMK shivered in delight as he kicked away the leaves that covered the marker of Benjamin Gooden Jr., and found what he came for.

The baseball Julia had left behind.

During the TV interview, Julia had painted her brother in an unemotional tone as her great protector. The Magic Man Killer knew from his expertise in the dark arts and the occult that the dead were just the same as they were in the living, but sometimes their power and instincts grew stronger when they passed through to the spiritual world.

MMK couldn't run the risk of the dead boy coming between him and his Julia.

He carefully slid the ball into his pocket and replaced it with a small mojo bag filled with black magic herbs and rested it against Ben Gooden's marker.

Inside was a potent cocktail.

Asafoetida, the devil's incense, to ensure the child's spirit wouldn't try and protect his sister.

Ground blueberry, which caused strife to an enemy when left upon its door.

And knotweed, to paralyze the little boy on the other side of the crossroads, should he try and come for him.

MMK looked out to the road far away in the distance, where a sheriff's car appeared.

He tempered his breathing and turned around slowly, making a steady retreat back to the woods. Once he was inside the safety of the trees, he peered back out and saw the law enforcement vehicle pass by and then turn down Julia's street.

The Magic Man Killer cupped his hand around the cool roundness of the baseball in his pocket and returned to his Buick.

It was almost showtime for Raven's Poe.

CHAPTER 15

Julia scoured the scant hits on her computer screen as she tapped the end of her pink-and-gold *Make It Happen* pen back and forth on her home office desk in frustration. Her stable of sources hadn't shed any light on the elusive Raven's Poe reference, so Julia was scrambling as a last resort to Internet searches.

A rookie move, just like letting a source e-mail you responses to questions instead of a live interview, where you could follow up and drill them. But sometimes you're forced to work with what you've got.

She grabbed a set of headphones and put them on Will, who was snuggled on her lap, her youngest son playing learning games on his LeapPad. If she could track down a lead, Julia hoped to make calls about the newly minted MMK, and she didn't want her youngest son to hear any of it. Conversations about murder and death and slashed throats weren't good topics for three-year-olds. She dabbed a Kleenex under Will's runny nose and hoped Facebook would bring her luck, since Google was striking out for her in a big way.

Julia's cell phone rang and she immediately recognized the person she'd been ignoring for most of the day, her editor, Virginia. Julia realized she couldn't keep this up much longer, so she took the bullet and answered.

"Hey, Virg. Sorry I haven't checked in yet. I've been busy running some leads."

"Jesus Christ, Julia. I'm about to go into an editorial meeting. I have you down for writing the lead story for tomorrow's paper, and I have no updates on the website yet. You can't tell me you still don't have anything. I need something from you before I go into that meeting, or my ass is going to get handed to me. What are the cops telling you? We already ran a story that the killer called you directly. This has turned into a national story and our online subscriptions nearly doubled in a day."

"So glad I can help the paper make money," Julia said dryly.

"Come on, Julia. You know how this works. I had Thom Derry write a story to feed the beast about other killers who've reached out to the press. But your story is way more compelling. The Virginia Tech killer sent a video and statement to NBC after the attack. And the Zodiac Killer, he mailed letters to the *San Francisco Chronicle*. But the Magic Man Killer reached out to you directly. You actually spoke to the man who slit those women's throats. The cops think the killer is dressing up the women to look like you. This makes an already-big story explode, and you're at the center of it. This puts a big spotlight on us. What can you give me?"

Julia bit the side of her lip as she weighed her options. Her natural instinct as a reporter told her to jump on the story and tell Virginia about the clues left behind at Roseline's and the bookstore. Julia was hitting a wall trying to find the next victim, and if she wrote a story about the clues, it could help spread the word and possibly save the next woman in the killer's crosshairs. But he had given her a warning.

She was stuck. The only thing Julia knew she could do with the least amount of collateral damage was to try and buy some time.

"I don't have anything new. I'm working on it," Julia lied as her mind scrambled for a tidbit she could feed to Virginia to get her off her back. "I heard the Detroit cops are stepping up patrols in the parks with running trails in the city, especially during the early-morning hours. The cops told me they're getting grilled from the public and City Hall about not doing enough to catch the killer. I'm working another angle, but maybe one of your new reporters could do a ride-along when the cops are patrolling one of the parks. It would be a decent color piece for us and it might buy some good-will with the public for the Detroit PD."

"You think your sources would go for it?"

"If you pitch it right. Call Corporal Gary Smith and drop my name. Just be sure the reporter you pick isn't too green or pushy. I don't want it coming back to me. When you talk to him, Smith should be able to give you a statement on where the cops are in the investigation. Run that story online and in tomorrow's paper, and then you can have the ride-along story on the paper's website in the afternoon. That should cover you until I get something more."

"The ride-along isn't a bad idea. I'll have Thom call Corporal Smith. What's the angle you're working?"

"Got to go, Virginia. I've got another call I've been waiting for," Julia lied again as a knock sounded on her office door and Helen poked her head inside. "We'll talk later."

Julia hung up on Virginia and gave Helen a thumbs-up. "Your timing was perfect."

"How is the boy?" Helen asked.

"Runny nose, but still no fever."

"Good. Remind me, how many people will be here for dinner? I think eight, but maybe you said ten?"

"I forgot about dinner. Don't worry about it. I'll call everyone and cancel. Prejean should still be with the cops, so I'll call Navarro and let them know."

"You will do no such thing. I have been cooking for the past three hours preparing for this meal. You all eat. Then you work. I will put the boys to bed after dinner, so you can feel free to discuss your dead women. Such talk," Helen said and shook her head. "You'll all think better after you've had my food. We go to the apartment tomorrow?"

"Yes. Navarro is bringing by the keys tonight. I'll pack up a bag for the kids. I'm hoping we'll only be there for a few days. Navarro is staying over tonight, and he'll be staying with us in the apartment, too."

"For security reasons only, no? A man staying over at an unmarried woman's house, people will talk. Perhaps he should make you an honest woman."

"One step at a time, my friend."

The front doorbell rang and Julia looked at the time on her computer: 6:30 PM, and she was no further ahead on pinpointing the killer's next victim.

"I'll get it," Helen said. "You keep working."

"No. I'm done here. Take Will, please."

"You are worried."

"No, just cautious."

"Fine. If you need me, the boys and I will be in the kitchen making dinner."

Julia handed Will to Helen and was relieved when she saw the recently dispatched police detail still parked in front of her house and Prejean on her doorstep carrying a large bag in his hand.

"Did you bring dinner?" Julia asked, and welcomed her friend inside.

"No, something better. Toys. Where your kids at?"

Julia called for her children, who tore into the living room, but then became subdued when they saw the stranger.

"Boys, this is my old friend Doug Prejean. Mom knew him way before either of you were born. Prejean, the handsome kid with the dark hair, that's Logan. And the little boy hiding behind his brother with the blond hair is Will."

"Very nice to meet you, gentlemen," Prejean said. "Now, down South where I come from, you don't venture into a new place you've been cordially invited unless you bring a little something with you. You look into this bag and you'll find a present each. Go on. Don't be shy. Most kids I know would be tearing in to get their gift. Your mamma taught you good manners."

Logan looked to Julia for permission and she nodded her consent.

"Thank you, sir," Logan said. "Is this mine?"

Logan held up a black-and-purple box with a child on the cover who was wearing a large black hat and carrying a floppy-looking white rabbit. The box promised *One hundred spellbinding tricks inside!*

"A magic set?" Julia asked Prejean.

"Every little boy should have a magic set at least once in their lives," Prejean said. He then leaned into Julia and whispered, "I had no idea what to get Logan. The owner of the toy store recommended the magic kit and I didn't realize what a stupid idea it was, considering the investigation, until I was driving over here. My bad, okay?"

"The irony doesn't elude me, but thank you."

"And for the very smart little boy who's hiding behind his brother, I've got something for you, too. Someone told me you like superheroes. Is that right?"

Prejean dug into the bag and pulled out an Iron Man figure.

"For me?" Will asked.

"For you. Iron Man is my favorite Avenger."

"The boys and I will set the table and leave you two to talk," Helen said.

"You must be the lovely Helen I've been hearing so much about," Prejean said. He lifted up Helen's hand and gave it a kiss.

"Ah, another handsome and charming police officer in this house. Just what we need," Helen said, and rolled her eyes, but Julia could see the older woman's cheeks flush over the compliment.

Julia waited until Helen and her boys were out of sight before she launched into Prejean.

"Tell me you and the Detroit cops got something. I struck out."

"Don't be too hard on yourself. You beat the cops on finding Roseline. We just picked it up from there. We tracked down a woman whose name is Raven Jones. She teaches English lit classes at Wayne State."

"Washington mentioned her."

"She probably didn't tell you Miss Raven teaches a class on true crime and occult novels and how they fit into popular culture. You win a new car if you can guess the title of one of the books her students are assigned this semester."

"*Something Wicked This Way Comes.* Great work. How did you find her?"

"It was Russell's idea. I guess his ex-wife is a professor at the school, so he gave his ex a call and she told him about Miss Raven. We went down and talked to her on campus. She's divorced, but on good terms with her former husband, and she said no other male has given her any reason to think twice, except for one student, Taylor Aberdie, who was in the military, midthirties or so, who dropped out of school recently. She said the guy was a really good student, but intense to the point that it made her feel uncomfortable sometimes."

"Did you pick up the suspect?"

"That's the thing. Navarro talked to the school administrator, and it turns out Taylor Aberdie wasn't his real name."

"Don't students need to provide ID to register, like a driver's license?"

"Two forms of ID, to be exact. Taylor gave the school his license and a military ID. Both were bogus. So was the address Taylor gave as his place of residence. Navarro checked. It's matched to a Sunoco station somewhere downtown. A team coming in for the next shift is going to keep an eye on Ms. Jones, and the cops are trying to track down the real ID of the male student."

"Sounds promising. I'm guessing Raven Jones fits the profile?"

"Well, some. She's a single mom. But she's not a runner. And she's older than the other victims."

"How old?" Julia asked.

"Forty-five."

"I don't know, Prejean. The killer is methodical. How old are her kids?"

"She's got one son. He's twenty-two."

"Heather Burns and April Young had young kids. I get the name and the book reference to the English teacher, but the other connections aren't there. What's her body type?"

"She's a lot curvier than you. No offense."

"None taken."

The doorbell rang and Julia looked out to see Navarro on her doorstep.

"Your cop. He's a solid investigator, but he's too nice to people," Prejean said.

"He's not nice to the bad guys. That's all that matters."

Navarro leaned in and gave Julia a kiss on the cheek and then turned and nodded at Prejean.

"Did Prejean tell you about the professor?" Navarro asked.

"She's not the one," Julia said.

"Chief Washington likes her for the next victim."

"Well, the chief's wrong. We can't stop looking and we're running out of time," Julia answered.

A galloping of little boys' feet running as fast as they could resounded down the hallway and Logan appeared with his magic hat in hand, with Will just steps behind.

"Hey, Uncle Ray!" Logan said, and threw his arms around Navarro. "I'm learning magic."

"A gift from Prejean," Julia explained.

"If it's okay by you, Julia. I've been thinking. I can bunk here until the case is over, just to keep an eye on things," Prejean said.

"I've got it covered. I'm staying here tonight and then I'll be with Julia and her boys in the temporary place in the city," Navarro said.

"We'll just be staying there for a short time while we do some repairs on the house," Julia said, repeating the white lie she had told Logan and Will.

"Uncle Ray's sleeping over again? Awesome," Logan said. "Can I show you my magic set, Uncle Ray?"

Logan didn't wait for Navarro's response. Instead, he grabbed the detective by the hand and led him to the kitchen with Will close on their heels.

"I'm guessing I can't smoke in the house?" Prejean asked.

"I thought you gave up that nasty habit."

"I did. I only sneak in one when I'm working a tough case. I hear your front porch has a hell of a view. Want to join me?"

Prejean grabbed a jacket from Julia's coatrack and motioned toward the front door.

"You blow smoke in my face, you're done."

Prejean draped the jacket around Julia's shoulders and the two went outside into the crisp night air.

"I don't know if I'll ever get used to the cold if I move here. If it gets less than forty-five degrees in New Orleans, they start talking about closing the schools," Prejean said. He dug a Lucky Strike out from his coat pocket, sparked a match from a pack with *Barrel Proof Bar, Magazine Street, New Orleans* across its top, and then inhaled deeply.

"So you weren't kidding about moving here."

"It's a strong possibility. I talked to Washington about a transfer. Claudette is actually in Ann Arbor this weekend, getting the house in order to sell. We'll split half the money on the sale, and I could buy a condo in the city."

"It sounds like you've got it figured out."

"I'm getting there. And for the record, I've got doubts about the lady professor, too. The Detroit cops are going the other way, though."

"I'll talk to Navarro. That woman is out there, like a sitting duck. We have to do something. Did the cops get a print on the notes or on the Ray Bradbury book?"

"No. The killer's smart. But we know that already," Prejean said. "So Navarro is staying over?"

"Yes. Am I about to get another lecture?"

"Don't get me wrong. I like Navarro. He's a decent guy. Your kids seem to like him a whole lot. Logan's face sure lit up bright when he saw 'Uncle Ray,' didn't it? Your cop friend is getting deeper into your life. Just be careful."

"What's your point?"

"Most cops under the age of fifty are players, especially if they're good-looking."

"So Navarro's a player? What about you? Were you unfaithful to Claudette?" Julia asked. "Not a fair assumption to make on a man, is it?"

Prejean stubbed out his cigarette and focused on the lights of an approaching car. "I spent the afternoon with Navarro. I saw the way women looked at him, especially the female professor at the college. She gave him her card, and I'm sure she wanted him to call her for more than this case. I got a good sense about these things. I'd be fine with him as a cop partner, but not as a partner for one of my girls."

"Lay off Navarro. I'm not having this conversation with you again."

"I thought things were going to be different when I got here."

"Different how?"

"Different between you and me," Prejean said, and reached for Julia's hand, but she quickly took a step back.

"What are you doing?" Julia asked.

"Not what you're thinking. What I meant was, we haven't been getting along ever since I got off the plane. We've been buddies for a long time. You're happy with the cop, then I'm happy for you. And as cute as I think you are, *chérie,* you're not my type. It would be like dating my little cousin or something. I worry about you is all."

Prejean moved in front of Julia when the approaching car slowed to a crawl. "Looks like you've got company."

"Nothing to worry about. But thanks for being my human shield," Julia said.

A familiar blue sedan pulled to a stop in front of Julia's house. Russell got out, along with his passenger, a tall, attractive blonde with a trim build. The two walked up Julia's path, the blonde laughing as Russell looped his arm around her waist.

"Oh, God," Julia said. "I can't believe this."

"You know Russell's date?" Prejean asked.

"You could say that."

Russell and the blonde got halfway up the path when the two spotted the company on the porch. "Hey, Julia," Russell said. "Thanks for the invite. I'd make introductions, but they're obviously not necessary."

"This is unexpected. Russell said he was bringing a date, but he failed to mention it was you," Julia said to the blonde.

"Am I missing something here?" Prejean asked. He reached his hand out to Russell's companion. "I'm Doug Prejean. I'm an old friend of Julia's."

"Nice to meet you. I don't think Julia ever mentioned you before. I'm Julia's sister, Sarah."

"Okay then," Prejean said, his tone indicating that something had clicked in place. "Russell, let's go inside and talk to Navarro for a minute. There's something I wanted to run by both of you on the case."

"Yeah, sure. You and Julia catch up, and I'll see you inside," Russell said, and squeezed Sarah's hand.

"Nice night," Sarah said. She pulled a Marlboro Light cigarette from her purse and lit it, the glow from her lighter showing off her still pristine skin and tight jawline, despite her years of substance abuse. "Thanks for the chilly reception. I tried to tell you I was dating Russell when I called you yesterday, but you cut me off."

"When did this happen?"

"I met Russell at Ben's service, so we've been seeing each other for a couple of months. He asked me out six times before I said yes. I've never dated a guy as old as him, but I've never been treated better. He doesn't judge me for my past. And he respects the hell out of you, but you already know that."

"Russell's a good friend. I'm not sure if I'm comfortable with this."

"You don't have to worry about him hurting me. I'm a big girl. I get the sexist, womanizer vibe from him, but deep down, that's all bullshit. He's a sweetheart. He's so proud of my sobriety anniversary coming up, and he's going to take me to Traverse City for the weekend after the ceremony to celebrate. No worries, little sis. I'm not going to let him hurt me. I've told him every ugly detail about my past, and he hasn't run yet," Sarah said.

She smiled at Julia and looked jaded but hopeful, like a beaten-down dog at a shelter who finally got adopted by an owner who found the misfit animal the perfect fit for their family, warts and all. But the smile slowly faded from Sarah's face as a look of realization set in and her familiar mask of hardness settled back into its well-worn place. "I get it. You think I'm the one who's going to hurt Russell. Just like I hurt you. That was a long time ago. I thought we were past that."

"Russell's been a friend of mine for a long time. Sobriety is new to you."

"It's been almost two years."

"I think you should wait. I'm proud of what you're doing with your meetings and being a counselor, but I don't think you're ready for a relationship."

"Don't patronize me. You'd probably be fine with Russell dating someone. Just not a girl like me."

Sarah sank down on the front step of Julia's porch, reached for another cigarette, and kept her eyes level on the street. "You ever think about when we were kids?"

"I do. I don't like to talk about it, though."

"It's not good to keep stuff bottled inside. That time when we were all together in Sparrow, before Ben was taken and Mom and Dad ran off, what we had, it wasn't much, but it was something. Just enough to hold on to. Some days, I feel like if I just close my eyes for a second and open them back up, we'd be back there, all together again, like no time had passed. Maybe if I had a second chance to do it all over, I wouldn't screw up. Who knows? I could've turned out to be a girl like you with a normal life. Stupid, right?"

Sarah stubbed her cigarette out underneath the toe of her boot. "You want me to leave? I can't blame you if you did."

A stab of guilt struck Julia over her critical judgment of

her sister. Sarah had done some things to Julia that had crossed beyond even the brightest red line when she was using, including stealing from Julia and threatening Logan if Julia went to the police. But a sober Sarah had tried to save Julia's life three months earlier. Julia studied Sarah sitting alone on her front step, and felt an ache of pity for her sister.

"Come on inside. It's shaping up to be an interesting dinner."

Sarah gave Julia a wink. "Tell you what. If anything gets crazy, I've got your back."

"I believe you would." Julia looped her arm around Sarah's and the two made their way to the dining room, where everyone was already gathered at the table in front of Helen's lavish spread.

"Now that everyone is here, we have a feast. But there are a few rules first. There will be no talk of your case at the table with little ears listening," Helen said. "What I have made for you are pierogies, Polish red borscht, which is much more delicious than the Russian version, *golabki,* my cabbage stuffed with meat and rice, and breaded pork and potato dumplings. You adults behave, you get my *paczki* for dessert."

"What's that?" Sarah asked.

"Polish donuts. They're really good," Logan answered.

Julia got Will into his seat next to hers and pushed his chair up to the table. She motioned to Navarro, but Prejean grabbed the seat beside her before Navarro could reach it.

"Come on, buddy. How about I sit by you?" Navarro asked Logan.

"How do you know my little sister?" Sarah asked Prejean.

"I'm a cop. I met Julia down in New Orleans when she was green as could be. She was always feisty, though. I could tell she was going to be a good reporter, so I took her under my wing. She proved me right. But she didn't always have the best taste in men. An old boyfriend of Julia's was hassling her, and I had to chase him out of my fair city as soon as his plane touched down. Are you in journalism, too, Sarah?" Prejean asked.

"No, I'm a counselor at a rehab center. I'm a recovering addict. I've been sober for a while now, but I learned the hard way. I did some time down in Florida after getting popped on a couple of drug and aggravated assault charges. I almost got busted once on a prostitution collar, but that was a bogus charge. I woke up under a park bench in Tampa once, with my underwear around my ankles, and the cops thought I was turning tricks. I was just high as a kite and couldn't pull them back up after I relieved myself in the bushes."

Logan's eyes shot open wide and didn't blink.

"We are so moving on here," Julia said.

"Oh, geez. Sorry, Julia. I don't have kids, so things slip sometimes," Sarah said. "Russell knows everything about my past, and we're always encouraged to share in NA, so I got a little carried away. I promise, it won't happen again."

"What's 'NA'?" Logan asked.

"Narcotics Anonymous. It's for recovering drug users. You seem like a really good kid, so I'll give you a piece of advice. Never take drugs. They make you do crazy things and destroy your life."

"Sarah, please . . . ," Julia started, but Helen rushed in for the save.

"One more word in front of little boys about drugs or losing underwear under a park bench, the *paczki* will not be made. This is not a recovery meeting. It's a dinner table with children who are taking in every word of your colorful past. You are lucky you are Miss Julia's sister, or I would not be so nice."

"Sorry, I didn't mean to mess things up. Logan and Will, you've got a great mom. I've always looked up to her."

"It's okay," Julia said, and then tried to redirect what was turning into a train wreck of a dinner conversation. "Logan, tell us about your magic set."

"I am not a fan of magic," Helen said. "Magic can open the door a crack, just enough, to let the evil eye in."

"'The evil eye'?" Logan repeated "What's that?".

"And you gave me a hard time for talking smack in front of the kids," Sarah said.

"Pay no mind about the evil eye, Logan," Prejean said. "Magic isn't real. But if it's done right, magic makes the mind believe it's seeing something that is real. Magic is nothing more than an illusion done by a practiced hand."

"I will make my *paczki* now. You boys come into the kitchen with me and help. We let the adults have their conversation," Helen said.

"Did you find the student from Wayne State?" Julia asked Navarro.

He nodded his head subtly in Sarah's direction and shook his head.

"I get it. You can't talk to me because you're working an active case. Julia's okay because she's a part of it. I understand," Sarah said.

"Sarah's smart," Russell said. "And beautiful."

"Not smart, just experienced. Julia's always been the smart one, ever since we were kids. I've just spent enough time around cops that I picked up a few things. I'll get out of your hair. If Helen will have me, I'll help out in the kitchen. I'm taking my plate, though. This food is way too delicious not to finish."

Sarah still knew how to work the con, Julia thought, as she witnessed a slight smile rise from Helen over the review of her cooking.

"I have an extra apron. You join us."

Julia waited until half her dinner party exited into the kitchen and then jumped into her line of questioning.

"You didn't find the student from the college then. We've got to look harder," Julia told Navarro.

"We're looking plenty hard, Julia. And no, we haven't found him yet. We have his picture from his school ID. I'd like you to take a look at it." Navarro reached into the pocket of his jeans and slid the ID across the table toward Julia.

The man in the photo had dark hair, intense dark brown eyes, and a scar on his chin.

"I've never seen him before."

"Are you sure?" Navarro asked, and reached for his ringing cell phone in his pocket. He studied the number and gave a nod to Russell. "It's Jeb Wilson."

Navarro answered and listened for a few seconds before he responded, "You're positive? Okay. Make yourself available if we need you for anything else."

He hung up and stashed the phone back into his pocket.

"Russell and I interviewed a guy at Highland Park earlier who may have met the killer. Jeb Wilson looked at the picture of the student from Wayne State. Wilson claims it isn't the man he saw."

"The Voodoo King," Russell said.

Julia put her boys to sleep after her guests left and was huddled over her computer in her office, attempting one more search for the elusive Raven's Poe.

Navarro rapped on the open door with his knuckles and then sat down on the edge of Julia's desk.

"It's after midnight. How about you get some sleep and we'll get back to this in the morning. Come on. I promise I'll wake you up early. We have surveillance on the female English teacher."

"You and I both know it's not her. I can't afford to be wrong on this, Ray."

"*We* can't afford to be wrong on this. Off the record, I told Chief Washington the same thing. The killer is complex but precise. I don't see him changing the profile of his victim. Let's go, Gooden. We'll keep hunting in the morning. Your house alarm is set?"

"I activated it as soon as Sarah's and Russell's feet hit the porch."

"Good girl." Navarro grabbed Julia's hand and led her to the bedroom. She took off her blouse and jeans and slipped on a T-shirt and sat cross-legged on the end of her bed.

"You know I'm not a jealous man, but Prejean is territorial around you."

"You have nothing to worry about. Prejean and I are just friends. He thinks of me as his little sister."

"That's not the vibe I get from him."

"I promise you have nothing to worry about. Prejean has always been protective. He looked out for me once a long time ago, and I think he feels like he still needs to be my bodyguard."

"He mentioned something about stopping an old boyfriend of yours at the airport."

"I dated someone a few years before I met you. He was a doctor who was older than me. His name is Alex Tillerman. I broke it off with him because he started to get possessive and demanding, wanting to know where I was all the time."

"Did this Tillerman ever hit you?"

"No, nothing like that, but he got really possessive before I broke it off. One night, I had a late interview. I met my source at a coffee shop. The person I was meeting was a young male attorney. Tillerman followed me, saw me with the lawyer, and thought I was cheating on him. He caused a major scene and punched the lawyer in the face. It was humiliating and I felt terrible for the attorney. I found out Tillerman had a drug problem, and in hindsight, I think he was high at the time he beat up my source. I broke up with him that night. Tillerman wasn't used to being on the other side of rejection, so he wouldn't let go. He flew down to New Orleans after I moved there, but Prejean met him at the airport and scared him off."

"When was the last time you saw Tillerman?"

"Yesterday. I ran into him at a restaurant."

"You ran into him out of the blue?"

"Tillerman works at Harper University Hospital, so I've run into him before. I see where you're going with this. Tillerman is a loser and may still have a recreational drug problem, but I don't see him as a killer."

"I'm not ruling out anything when it comes to you and this case. Come on, beautiful. Get some sleep," Navarro said. He pulled the covers down for Julia and then patted her side of the bed. "I'm going to stay up for a while, just to be sure everything is okay."

"Nothing is okay. I know the next victim's still out there, Ray. I can feel it."

CHAPTER 16

Christy King chugged back a Red Bull and pulled on her ripped jeans under her size-two, perfectly conservative navy skirt she wore for her day job as a bookseller at Barnes & Noble on Warren Avenue downtown. She slunk down low in her old Volvo, trying to avoid being noticed by the few patrons she spotted heading into the Magic Stick on Woodward Avenue, where the indie/rock band she fronted, Raven's Poe, was playing in just five minutes.

She ripped a fingernail down to the quick, snagging it on the zipper of her black jeans, ignored the pain, and started working the buttons on her white shirt.

At thirty-one, Christy realized changing in her car made her just one step up from homeless, but she figured a quick change in the front seat of her Volvo was a better bet than trying to score a stall in the always jam-packed women's room.

The Magic Stick was a popular bar and live-music venue in the city, and she knew she was lucky as hell to have snagged the gig.

Christy scrambled with the straps of her red stiletto heels. She was cutting it close this time, but goddamn, it was worth it.

She could've come straight to the club after her shift at the bookstore, gotten a bite, and warmed up with the band, but instead drove the twenty minutes back home to see her six-year-old son, Clay. The five minutes she spent cuddling with him on the couch was the best part of her day. By far.

Right before she had hurried out of her house, Christy promised Clay they'd go to the movies after his soccer game tomorrow, but she secretly worried how she was going to fit it all in.

Juggling her life, and always feeling like she was coming up short, sucked big-time.

She looked over to the passenger seat and her duffel bag that was filled with what was left of her stage clothes, along with her notebook of lyrics and a lonely demo tape of her original songs. She always took the demo with her to her gigs in case some big producer might stumble into one of her shows.

As if.

Christy's good friend, guilt, wrapped an uncomfortable arm around her with a reminder of how she had hurried out the door before Clay could see her cry. In small, seemingly inconsequential—but huge—moments like these, Christy often wondered if she was a selfish idiot, trading time she could be spending with her son for chasing a dream, something she wanted for them both. But most nights, when she was alone in bed, or with her little boy sleeping by her side, a voice inside her head gave her a scolding reality check: That shit was likely never going to happen.

The paycheck from the bookstore was manageable, but she didn't want to live with her mom forever. And Clay's biological father was long out of the picture, a guy Christy dated for a couple of months, who once called her "perfection," until she broke the news that she was knocked up.

Christy unsnapped her bra and flung it into the duffel bag. The bag sat atop a few flyers she made announcing her new band's name, Raven's Poe, and their gig tonight, but she never found enough time to put any up, despite her effort.

Christy squinted when a bright beam from a set of headlights shone through her front windshield.

"Damn," Christy swore, and reached for her red satin camisole that she hurriedly pulled over her head. God, she hoped the driver didn't catch a glimpse of her chest. What there was to look at anyway. She could barely pull off a B cup in a padded bra, so if the driver was a guy and caught a look at her barely there breasts, it wouldn't be on his "top ten moments of his life" list.

The car passed by slowly, and Christy could make out the model, an old Buick, the kind her grandpa used to have and let her borrow every so often when she was in high school. That was until she tried to return it buzzed after a night of drinking and mistook his metal fence for the driveway.

Christy grabbed a black sheer blouse from her bag and kept half an eye on the Buick, which slowly drove past and then parked at a spot near the back of the building. No Beemers or Mercedes in the Magic Stick parking lot tonight, which meant each of the three band members in Raven's Poe would probably split a whopping ten bucks from the tip jar.

If they were lucky.

Christy began to sing the lyrics of her latest song, "Blue-Eyed Dreamer," one that was inspired by her major girl-nerd love of books and a favorite poem, "If," by Rudyard Kipling.

> *Dreams eat you alive if you let them*
> *But don't you know you'd die a bitter death with-*
> *out their ache*
> *Dark cloud over your head, baby girl*
> *Your soul bleeds for a lucky break.*

At least she'd get to sing one of her own songs tonight, an original tucked in between her covers of Amy Winehouse and Pink, two female artists she respected as singers and songwriters. Billy, the drummer and cofounder of the band, insisted she only got to sing one original song per gig because, "People want to hear the hits. Not some song they've never heard of, even if the lyrics are decent. I'll give you that."

Billy had caved last week and agreed to rename their band Raven's Poe. Score one for the struggling book nerd. Christy made a note to herself to update the band's website, since it still had their loser former name, Detroit Riot, posted on its homepage.

The Magic Stick's weekly-advertised live-music lineup had included her band's previous shitty name, so tonight was going to be Raven's Poe's big debut.

Yeah, drum roll to no one, please, Christy thought, and hurried out of the car, her duffel bag banging against her thigh as she ran in the stupid shoes to the back of the Magic Stick. Two minutes until they opened. Good thing she was a runner, something she would do tomorrow morning if she could haul her butt out of bed before Clay got up.

She shoved open the door of the bar and was greeted by the smell of beer, sweat, and fried chicken fingers and pounded ahead toward the stage.

"Where the hell have you been, Christy?" Billy asked. "We just got a gig tomorrow afternoon, playing a private party. You show up late like this, you're out of the band."

"You can't fire me. You think we booked this gig because of your drumming?" Christy asked. "I always get to our gigs in time."

"Barely. You need to figure out your home life, because you can't be cutting it close like this anymore."

"Heads-up. I can't make it tomorrow. My kid has a soccer

game. I need twenty-four hours' notice, remember? You're going to have to cancel."

"Then you owe me the two hundred we would've made. You need to make a decision whether you're in the band or you want to be a mommy."

"Shut it," Christy said as the stage lights came up. "Time to play. You ready? Let me show you how it's done."

When the lights hit her, Christy felt alive, a different, confident person who never, ever screwed up.

And she was about to give the audience one hell of a show.

Christy did her signature power-girl pose, hands on her hips with a sassy, defiant gaze as she stood in front of the microphone. Depending on the bar, sometimes the lights blinded her, but not tonight. Christy did a quick pan of the first row and caught a glimpse of a good-looking guy with sandy-blond hair in front of the crowd.

"Who says smart girls can't rule the world?" Christy roared. "We're Raven's Poe!"

She dropped her head down on her chest, raised her hand in a fist pump, and sang the first line of Amy Winehouse's "Back to Black" in her sultry, soulful voice.

The lyrics and the spell of the song caught her up and she took one more pan for the guy she had seen, always wanting to focus on someone in the crowd to fix her mood on.

But he was gone.

Damn. Another cute boy got away.

CHAPTER 17

In the dream, Julia could see a woman who looked like her, running alone on a trail with the sun rising in the distance. The jogger had blue eyes, long, dark hair, and she wore a T-shirt with Raven's Poe *on the front. A man was crouched behind a thick nest of trees just ahead of the jogger on the path. His face was hidden inside the hood of a gray sweatshirt, and he clutched the handle of a knife in his right hand.*

Julia tried to scream out her warning, but the words stayed trapped inside her as the killer jumped out from the trees and grabbed the woman while she tried to sprint past.

Julia felt the cool metal of the killer's knife against her own throat and she realized the runner she was trying to save was actually herself.

MMK dragged Julia backward toward the woods like a mountain lion that had just snatched a rabbit, bringing it back to its lair. But the Magic Man Killer stopped short when a little boy with jet-black hair and a red shirt ran down the path in their direction with his fist clenched defiantly over his head.

The boy, Julia realized, was her brother, Ben. He picked up a stone and threw it at the man.

"You can't stop me. Leave her alone!" Ben cried. His hand sprang back down to the ground, where he snatched up a large rock and threw it at the killer, striking him in the side of his head.

"Go on, black monster. I'm stronger than you! I always will be," Ben said.

"No, Ben! Run before he hurts you," Julia called out.

Ben turned his back as if he were distracted by a sound. When he turned around, the child standing before Julia was no longer Ben, but her son Logan.

"You better run, mister, or I'll make you disappear," Logan said. "I know magic."

The killer released his knife from Julia's neck and crept backward alone toward the woods.

"I'll be back. Make sure you write everything, Julia. Every single little detail," MMK said, and then ducked into the trees that seemed to swallow him whole.

A familiar, safe voice called out to Julia, a lifeline bringing her back up to the conscious world.

"Babe, you're okay. I've got you. You're having a bad dream."

Julia woke up, her heart pounding, and saw Navarro's barbed-wire tattoo and the rest of his arm wrapped protectively around her.

"What time is it?" Julia asked. She sat up quickly and looked at the clock. Seeing it was six AM, Julia jumped out of bed, pulled on a pair of shorts, and grabbed her cell phone.

"I slept too long."

"I was going to get you up. I came in last night after I checked in with the cop out front. I must've fallen asleep before I set the alarm on my phone."

Julia beat a path to the kitchen, where she already smelled

a dark roast brewing in the coffeepot. Helen was standing in the middle of the kitchen, stuffing pans, measuring spoons, and anything she could grab from the pantry into six large boxes that lined the floor.

"What are you doing?" Julia asked.

"Packing necessities for the apartment, where we have to go today."

"It's temporary, I promise. And you don't need to bring your kitchen supplies. Navarro told me the apartment is fully furnished. It's a corporate rental, so it's equipped with everything we'll need. All you need to do is pack a bag."

"I will not just pack a bag. Corporate place probably means it is tailored to bachelor men who don't know how to cook and need very little. If this family must be uprooted, at least we will eat well," Helen said, but then softened her tone when she studied the younger woman's face. "You're still troubled. I can tell. You think this woman the police are protecting isn't the right one, no?"

"Her profile doesn't match. But I've hit a wall. I can't find her."

"My grandmother used to tell me, 'Do not push the river, it will flow by itself.'"

"What does that mean?" Julia asked.

"If the answer is supposed to come, it will present itself to you."

"I'm not going to sit back and wait for something to happen."

"I told him to go back to bed." Navarro entered the kitchen with his arm around Logan's shoulder. "I hope that was okay. He didn't listen."

"I want to play with my magic set," Logan said, and rubbed his eyes. "Mom, you're going to give me that old tape recorder of yours, right? I was dreaming about a magic trick right before I woke up, and I need your recorder for it."

"It's in my desk. I'll get it. I want to check the news."

Julia returned to her office and her computer. She fumbled through her desk drawer, found the tape recorder, and pulled up her paper's homepage. The lead story was by a fellow reporter who did a ride-along with a cop patrolling the parks looking for MMK, so Julia realized her stall plan with Virginia had worked. Julia did a quick scroll through the other headlines, and froze the screen on a photo from the entertainment section of a dark-haired woman with blue eyes, fronting a band named Raven's Poe.

"Navarro! We found her."

Julia felt an adrenaline rush as she clicked on the picture, hoping to find a story that would include the lead singer's name, but all that had been posted on her paper's website was the photo and a one-sentence cutline, stating the band played at the Magic Stick the previous night.

"What do you got, Gooden?" Navarro asked, and shut Julia's office door behind him.

"Raven's Poe is a band. They played at the Magic Stick last night," Julia said while Navarro looked over her shoulder at the image on the screen.

"The Magic Stick is going to be closed this early, but one of our patrol guys likely knows the bar owner."

"I have an idea," Julia said, and hunted through the contacts on her phone until she found the name she was looking for, her paper's entertainment editor, Jack Roberts. She hit the call button and started to pray. "Come on, come on! Answer."

After six rings, a very rough voice came on the phone. "Hello? Hmm. Who is this?"

"Jack, it's Julia Gooden. I need a number, fast."

"Julia? It's six-fifteen in the bloody morning. This can't wait until I see you in the newsroom?"

"No. I'm not playing around. Someone's life is in danger. Do you know a group called Raven's Poe?"

"Never heard of them."

"Well, there's a picture of the band that ran in your section online."

"The Magic Stick has live bands on Thursdays. There wasn't much going on, so I sent a freelance photographer to cover whatever group was playing there last night."

"I need the name and number of the owner of the Magic Stick. Now, Jack."

Julia heard the sound of something crashing on the other end of the phone and then papers being rustled until Jack came back on the line.

"The owner's name is TJ. TJ Davison," Jack said amidst a yawn and then gave Julia the number. "Whatever you do, don't tell him I gave you his number. Is this about the Magic Man Killer?"

"Exactly. Got to go." Julia barely heard the dial tone before she plugged the number of the owner of the Magic Stick into her phone.

This time, the caller picked up on the third ring.

"I got him," Julia called out to Navarro, who was in the hallway on the phone. "Mr. Davison, this is Julia Gooden. I realize it's early, but please don't hang up. I'm a reporter. I don't know if you follow the news, but I'm covering the Magic Man Killer and I think the singer from Raven's Poe, who played at your club last night, is in danger. I realize this all probably sounds strange, but please believe me. I need to find her before the killer does."

"Shit. Hold on." Julia heard more fumbling on the other end of the phone until a slightly more awake TJ came back on. "You think Christy is in trouble? This guy's after her?"

"Yes. Christy what? What's her full name?"

"Christy King. She's a nice girl. Christy is cute and was real spunky onstage. She did a great show last night. The crowd loved her."

"Is Christy a runner?" Julia asked. She wrote down Christy King's name on the front cover of one of her reporter's notebooks and flashed it to Navarro.

"I hardly know her. It was her band's first time with us."

"How old is Christy? Does she have any kids? I'm guessing she's a single mom."

"Christy's early thirties, I'm guessing. And, yeah, I got the impression she's a single mom. She booked the gig through me and mentioned something about not always having a flexible schedule but that her band was usually available on Thursday, Friday, and Saturday nights."

"Thank you. This is helpful. I need every number you have for her, but her cell would be best. Do you have her home address?"

"That I don't have. Here's her cell, though. I hope she's okay."

Christy King took a weak sip of her Red Bull and looked at her puffy eyes in the rearview mirror of her Volvo. She and the rest of Raven's Poe had finished their last set just before midnight the night before, and sleeping in that morning had never seemed more tempting, but Christy hadn't run in a few days, and if she was going to sneak exercise into her insane schedule, this morning was do or die.

Welcome to her day off, a quick run, then home for breakfast with Clay, who had a day off from school, and then a movie with him after his soccer game. It was going to be their special time, and she'd be damned if she wasn't going to make her little boy feel like he was the most wonderful thing in the world.

Christy was exhausted out of her mind, but she was going to pull off a fabulous day for her kid, even if it killed her. Christy took another hit of her Red Bull and clicked through the radio stations, hoping she'd hear a kick-ass rock-and-roll song that would be motivation for her run. She listened to two seconds of a local news station, the news, something she rarely paid attention to these days, because with her schedule, who had time for it? Plus the news was always too depressing. Who wanted to hear about killings and death and the crazy shit coming out of Washington?

Christy gave up on the radio, got out of her Volvo, and began to stretch. Belmont Park, near her mom's house, was empty except for some old car she could barely see parked over in the second lot. She spotted a person next to the car and figured it was a fellow jogger. Christy didn't love being out on the trails alone so early, but she was smart and would stay on the main paths the whole way. Plus she had her trusty pepper spray in her waist pack, so she knew she'd be okay.

Her left hamstring muscle felt tender when she pulled her foot to the back of her thigh. God, a couple days without a run and her body was already atrophying. She thought about a new lyric for a song she was writing, "Last Girl for Battle," when she noticed the speck of the person she'd seen before grow closer. Now she could tell it was a man who was wearing what looked like a blue uniform. Maybe a park worker, she figured. She took a deep breath, ready to start, when she saw her cell phone sitting on the dashboard in her car.

Christy popped the locks to the Volvo and reached inside for her phone as it started to ring.

"Yeah, it's Christy," she answered, without looking at the caller ID, figuring it was her mom calling about Clay because no one else she knew would be up that early.

"Christy King?"

"That's right. If you're calling to tell me I just won a cruise to the Bahamas, I'm hanging up."

"No. My name is Julia Gooden. This is not a joke. You're in danger. I'm a journalist and I've been covering the Magic Man Killer stories."

"The what?"

"Please, you need to listen. He's been picking up female joggers in parks and killing them. I know this is going to sound crazy, but he sent me clues about his next victim, and I think you're it."

"Hold on. Did my drummer put you up to this? He's pulling some kind of prank because I couldn't play that gig this afternoon because of my kid."

"No. That's not what's happening. Look, you're right not to believe someone you've never met before who's calling you out of the blue. Believe me, I get stubborn and street smart. Your band is Raven's Poe, right? The killer sent me clues about the name of your band. I didn't know what it meant until I saw a picture of Raven's Poe playing at the Magic Stick last night on my newspaper's website. I told the bar owner what was going on and he gave me your number. The killer is targeting female runners who are in their thirties and single moms. Are you a runner?"

"Yes. I'm at Belmont Park in Royal Oak right now. I'm about to take a quick run before my kid wakes up. If this isn't some kind of joke, you're scaring me."

"You need to be scared. And you need to get out of there. I live in Rochester Hills, so I'm not that far out," Julia said. "She's at Belmont Park in Royal Oak."

"Who are you talking to?" Christy asked.

"A police officer. Are you alone?"

"Yes, except for one guy. He's wearing a uniform. He's walking in my direction. Now that I see him better, I'm thinking he's maybe a cop. His uniform is blue."

"You need to do exactly what I tell you. Get in your car, lock the door, and drive out of there as fast as you can," Julia said. "My cop friend is calling dispatch right now, so the police will be there soon."

"The car in the lot, it's pretty far away, but it doesn't look like a police car. It's old."

"A cop in uniform is going to be in a patrol car. And they usually work in pairs. He wouldn't be alone. Get out of there, Christy. Now!"

Christy's hand shook as she dove into the front seat. Her hand skittered across the side of the door as she saw the man in the blue uniform now running full tilt in her direction.

"Jesus, he's coming," Christy said.

"You can do this. Be calm. Lock the doors and get out of there."

Christy pounded the door lock, jammed the key in the ignition, and floored the gas just as the man entered her parking lot. She drove in the opposite direction and tried to get a good look at the man's face, but he was still too far out. She skidded as she looped around the length of the lot toward the park entrance and the second lot, where she saw the man's vehicle.

As she tore through the gate to the street, she swung a quick look into her rearview mirror at the car.

"Holy shit," Christy said as she realized the car was the old Buick she had seen at the Magic Stick last night.

CHAPTER 18

The Magic Man Killer's uniform stuck like Velcro to his body as sweat seemed to drip, drip, drip, from every pore, hermetically sealing his polyester blue pants and shirt to his skin. His eyes darted in a nervous pattern: rearview mirror, the road in front of him, and then a ticktock to the left and right to spot other cars, specifically the police, and then he started the round-robin all over again.

The sharp pitch of police sirens sounded in the distance, and he bit his lip, sinking his teeth down deep until he tasted blood. He pulled the Buick into the lot of a Meijer grocery store, parking next to a large minivan he hoped would work as a blocker to the street. He breathed out hard when a sheriff patrol car sped by with its lights flashing and then shot down the road.

He waited in the grocery store lot for a few more minutes, his thoughts screaming over his spectacularly failed attempt to snatch Christy King. He reached down to the cup holder and kneaded the baseball he had snatched from Ben Gooden's grave.

MMK then reached into his pants pocket and cursed out loud when he realized what he was looking for was gone: a small blue-velvet satchel that he was going to leave in Christy's hand after he killed her. It contained the clue for his next victim, a miniature skyscraper. Not an exact replica of a city landmark that held the true meaning, but he couldn't be too precise. He realized the satchel must've fallen out of his pocket when he raced back to his car after Christy got away.

Julia Gooden had to be the one who tipped the singer off. Christy wouldn't have torn out of the park like a screaming demon from hell otherwise.

Julia wasn't supposed to figure it out. His hints were just a little tease, after all. Raven's Poe was an obscure indie band, with no trail of breadcrumbs left behind on the Internet for Julia to connect. He had made sure of it before he left Julia the letter in the book.

When Christy ran in the park a few days ago, he followed her and spotted the flyers on the passenger seat of her car announcing her new band's name and the date of her appearance at the Magic Stick. Being the meticulous planner, he spent hours searching for any mention of Raven's Poe online, including her band's website, which still listed her group as Detroit Riot. He even went down to the Magic Stick to be sure Christy hadn't put up any of the flyers on the bulletin board by the bathrooms. But there was nothing about Raven's Poe. Anywhere.

So there was no way Julia should've made the connection.

But his girl was smarter than he'd thought.

The killer felt a stinging fury rise up inside him as he played through his ruined plan. Christy ran at the park every Friday morning, stupid thing, thinking it was okay to jog alone when the sun was barely up. What was wrong with these women anyway?

He knew his police uniform would've initially gained Christy's trust and later he would've reaped her appreciation when he warned her the police were closing in on the killer, who they believed was going to snatch his next victim in that very park. Christy's eyes would have shot open wide and she would've looked back at him with such gratitude for possibly saving her life. He might have reached for her hand to comfort her and suggest she should go on home to her son, purposely dropping that personal little factoid, and he'd watch in satisfaction as the first warning bell sounded in her head.

He'd smile at her then, and she'd think it was just a coincidence, her mind making it fit, since she had a child's booster seat in the back of her car.

When she started to ease up on her guard again, he'd tell her to be careful, and then drop another bombshell of a personal tidbit. He'd ask if she liked her job at the bookstore, or whether the rude customers who ignored her while she was ringing up their purchases annoyed her to no end.

When the realization and panic spread across Christy's face, that's when he'd grab the green-and-black knife from underneath his shirt and press it against her neck.

He always got an enormous erection when he stuffed the women in his trunk.

At least Christy King would've been famous in death instead of making barely more than minimum wage ringing up customers at Barnes & Noble and singing to drunks in bars.

God, he was sweating so much, he was sure he was going to spontaneously combust in the stupid Buick. He was positive Christy had seen his car in the park, and now the cops would be looking for his vehicle. If he could just get home and stick the Buick in his garage, he'd be okay. Even if the police had some way to trace every old Buick in the city of Detroit and the surrounding areas, he should be safe. His grandmother had given him the car, unofficially anyway, with no title transfer. When she went into the nursing home with dementia, he took the keys, and that was that. No cop would be looking hard for an eighty-one-year-old woman who didn't know her own name and spent her waking and sleeping hours in a diaper.

He had to get home. He started the Buick and took a quick right on Twelve Mile Road, deciding that he was better off on the side streets than on the highway, where the cops would spot him, easy.

He breathed out slowly and did a check of the speedometer. He was driving just one mile below the speed limit. He couldn't risk attracting attention to himself.

A black SUV flashed its lights behind him and the killer calculated his move, always a precise planner, and decided he'd rather give the cops chase than ever give in without a fight. A knife was his preferred weapon of choice, but he spared no details when it came to preparation. He reached down on the passenger floor for his duffel bag that contained his Smith & Wesson, but the SUV passed him in the left lane and tore up the road until it was out of sight.

The police were going to be scouring the parks for him now, if they weren't doing so already. He was going to have to change up his perfect plan. It was his canvas, his picture that he drew, the beauty and the destruction, all of it his creation.

He'd have to find a new hunting ground to snare his victims. But that would be easily worked through. MMK knew their routines, where they lived, when they left for work and got home, even where they shopped and their favorite Starbucks. He could still come up with a new face for each kill, representing someone who was close to Julia. For April Young, he had turned himself into the runner whose son Ben had died. For Heather Burns, he transformed into an old lady, just like Julia's housekeeper. And today, he was a cop, a link to her beat and the guy she was screwing.

Julia probably didn't even appreciate all his creativity and the excruciating hard work that went into it. But she would. They all came around eventually.

The Magic Man Killer kept his breathing tempered, in and out, in and out, until he reached his home. He pulled past his estranged wife's car, into their garage, and quickly closed the door.

His chest began to ache, and he wondered if he was having a heart attack. He was fit, in his early forties, and there was no way he'd let this fear beat him. As his heart beat triple time, he stripped his uniform off and stuffed it into a garbage can.

His new plan swirled in his head as he stood in the middle of the garage in his white underwear briefs. He'd tell his wife the car needed repairs, so she'd drive him to get a rental.

God, he was so furious . . . yet so, so proud of his Julia for locating and then warning Christy King before he could kill her. MMK pulled on a pair of gym shorts and a T-shirt from his duffel bag, quietly slipped back into the parked Buick, and called Julia, knowing he'd need to make it lickety-split quick.

"Julia Gooden," she answered.

"You weren't supposed to find Christy King. How did you do it?" MMK said as he let his rage simmer just below the surface of his voice.

"Because I'm smarter than you. So are the cops."

"No, no, no," MMK hissed. "Time-out, Julia. It's time for you to listen, not speak. The cops aren't even close to your brilliance. This time, with Christy King, I'm willing to forgive, only because it's you. But you broke our line of trust on this one. The clues I'll plant for my next victims, even my most bright and shiny girl, my Julia, won't be able to piece them together. Nothing is easy from here on out. Five. Four.

Three. Two. One. Five is a magical number for me. You are number five and that's all the time I have, five seconds, before my call is traced. Good-bye, Julia. Write my story for me."

The Magic Man Killer ended the call as he heard the sound of the door that connected the garage to the house unlock.

God, his wife was a nosy bitch.

He exhaled one more time and settled his expression on his face. The happy, normal guy was back in the house.

The door opened, and his mind crept back to one more thread of his new plan before he pushed it down until later.

He put on a real smile as he thought about Julia.

What he was going to do next would just kill her.

CHAPTER 19

"It's okay, Christy. You're safe. I'm pulling up to your house right now. Two police officers I know are here, too. I'm hanging up now, but I'll see you in a minute," Julia said, and jerked her car to a stop in front of Christy King's Royal Oak address just as she saw an incoming call from an unknown number.

Julia quickly dug into her bag for her cassette recorder and notebook when she heard MMK on the other end of the phone. She hit the play button and scribbled down what the killer said before he abruptly hung up.

Julia held tightly to her recorder and notebook and ran up Christy's path to catch up to Navarro and Russell, who were about to ascend the porch steps.

"MMK just called me. I recorded it," Julia said, and held out her cassette player to Navarro.

"What did he say?" Navarro asked.

"Listen for yourself. It's only a few minutes."

Julia hit the play button and the three huddled around her recorder, listening to the brief conversation.

"He's mad at you for saving Christy," Russell said. "And he likes the number five."

"MMK left behind clues in his first call. The number five probably means something," Navarro said.

"Okay, hold on," Julia said, and turned the number around in her head. "Maybe the number represents five victims. He killed April Young and Heather Burns. So that's two. Christy King slipped away, so maybe he's planning to kill two additional women, or maybe three, if he needs to make up for losing Christy, to get to five," Julia said.

"Or maybe he's just batshit nuts," Russell said.

"See if we can get a location for the call," Navarro said to Russell.

"It probably won't do any good," Julia said. "MMK knew just how long he could stay on the line without the cops being able to track him."

"Make the call, Russell."

Russell walked back down the path to the street to call into the station, leaving Ray and Julia alone.

"I'm going to need that tape, Julia, just like the last one," Navarro said.

"Only if I get a full transcript of both calls. I have my notes, but that's not enough."

"Fine, but we got this. You shouldn't be here. Washington is letting you in on the investigation, but she told me no interviews," Navarro said. "The Royal Oak PD are combing the park, and Russell and I are going to talk to Christy."

"Christy trusts me, and she's scared out of her mind right now. If you want any kind of answers from her, she'll be more willing to talk if I'm there."

"Just so we're clear on things, do you plan on writing a story about this?" Navarro asked.

"Yes. But I'm not going to use Christy's name. I'm not here to interview her, if that's what you're implying."

Russell joined his friends and shook his head. "Julia was right. MMK didn't stay on the line long enough for our guys to trace the number."

"Okay. You've got five minutes, Julia, and then I need you out. Chief Washington is on her way. It's not going to look good for any of us if you're hanging around when she shows up," Navarro said. "You made Washington a promise. She's fair, but she may pull your privileges on the case if she finds you here. Five minutes, Gooden. And I need the tape."

Julia popped the small cassette out of her tape recorder and handed it to Navarro.

"Let's go," Navarro said.

A woman who looked to Julia to be in her midsixties, with a dark brown bob and square-framed glasses, cracked open the door a few inches and peered with guarded scrutiny at the company on her front step.

"I'm guessing you're Julia," the woman said.

"Yes, I'm Julia Gooden."

"I'm Christy's mom, Ellen. You really think that man in the park was going to kill my daughter?"

"We have reason to believe that. I'm a detective with the Detroit PD and this is my partner," Navarro said, gesturing to Russell. "Can we come in?"

"All right, but my grandson is still sleeping. If Clay wakes up and scoots into the kitchen, I'll need everyone to keep a lid on your conversation until I can get him out of there."

Ellen led the three visitors to the kitchen, where Christy King sat at a round wooden table with her sneakers beating a fast rhythm on the brown-tiled floor beneath her.

"Christy, there are some people here to see you," Ellen said. "Two police officers, and this is the woman you told me about."

Christy jumped up from the table and threw her arms around Julia.

"Thank you. If you hadn't called, I don't want to think about what would've happened," Christy said.

"You don't need to thank me. I'm just glad you're all right."

"I realize you've just gone through something traumatic, but we need to ask you a few questions. Is that okay?" Navarro asked.

"I'll try. I'll be honest with you. I'm totally freaking out right now. If I didn't have to keep it together for my kid, I'm pretty sure I'd lose it."

"You're stronger than you think. Most people would've lost their cool and panicked back in the park, but you were smart and got out of there in time," Julia said.

Julia put her arm around Christy's shoulder and led her back to the table, where Julia took a seat next to her. "When we were talking on the phone, you said you thought you'd seen the car that was in the park before."

"I did. It was an old Buick. I think the color was gray or tan. I'm pretty sure I saw the same one in the parking lot of the Magic Stick last night. I was changing clothes for the gig in my car because I was late, and I think the guy driving the Buick might've seen me with my top off. Is that what this is all about?"

"No. We think he's probably been following you for a while," Navarro said. "Did you get a look at the car's license plate?"

"No. I just wanted to get out of there. I'm sorry."

"You're doing fine. Do you remember what the man in the park looked like? Maybe his hair color or build?" Navarro asked.

"Not really. He was far away."

"Julia said you told her the man started running toward you when you got in your car," Russell said. "So he was getting closer to you. Maybe you saw something. Take your time."

Christy grabbed a bottle of water on the table in front of her with a shaking hand and took a drink.

"Okay. The man was wearing a dark blue uniform. I told Julia this already. I figured he might have been a cop. But I didn't see a badge. God, I'm so sucking at this," she said, and then closed her eyes like she was trying to get a handle on the memory. "He was white, medium build, I think, and his hair was light brown. Or dirty blond maybe. Shit, I'm sorry."

"It's okay. Sometimes memories take a while to come. I'm going to show you two pictures. Do you recognize either of these women?" Navarro asked. He slid a picture of April Young and Heather Burns across the table.

"I've never seen them before. Who are these women?"

"We believe the man you saw in the park killed them. They were runners, too. Do you usually run in that park?" Navarro asked.

"It's the only place I run. I go there every Friday morning, early, before my son, Clay, wakes up, and sometimes during the week if I can fit it in. The park is five minutes away from my mother's house. I'm a single mom with a kid, a full-time job at a bookstore, and I sing in a band at night, at least whenever I can pick up a gig. There are better jogging trails, but since pretty much every minute of my life is accounted for these days, the park by my mom's is convenient."

"Have you run any marathons in Detroit or Oakland County?" Navarro asked.

"I did before I had Clay. But that was six years ago. Like I said, I only run a couple of times a week if I'm lucky, so I wouldn't be in any kind of shape to run a marathon even if I had time."

Navarro took a quick look at his watch and gave Julia a subtle nod.

"I'm going to be completely honest with you, Christy, I'm not supposed to be here. I just stopped by to be sure you're okay. The police need to finish interviewing you without me here. Navarro and Russell are friends of mine, so you're in good hands. Just so there are no surprises, I mentioned on the phone that I'm a reporter. I've been writing stories about the man you saw in the park."

"The Magic Man Killer. What a freak," Christy said.

"My editor is going to expect me to write something about what happened this morning, and I want to be sure you're okay with it. I won't use your name. Are you all right with me referring to you as a 'Royal Oak single mother in her thirties'?"

Christy looked down at her hands that were knotted into fists, and nodded her consent. "Sure, as long as you don't think your story is going to piss the guy off and make him come back for me or my kid."

"I wouldn't write anything if I did. Remember what I said. You can call me if you want to talk. Trauma finds a way to nest inside a person, so it's important to let it out."

Julia pushed back the natural fight in her to stay and let herself out of Christy's house. She pulled out her keys to get into her vehicle when a voice called out to her.

"Gooden, hold on," Navarro said.

"Don't you want me out of here before Chief Washington shows up?"

"It's nothing personal. You got a piece of paper? I want to show you something."

"Sure." Julia reached into her purse and pulled out one of her skinny, old school reporter's notebooks and a pencil, which Navarro took from her.

He drew a large circle at the bottom of a piece of paper.

"Russell and I were talking about this on the drive over. The big circle, that's Detroit. That's where the killer murdered April Young and Heather Burns. April Young lives and works in Hamtramck," Navarro said, and drew a small circle on the paper above Detroit with an *H* next to it. "But he picked her up in the RiverWalk in the city."

"I know this already."

"Hold on. The second victim, Heather Burns, works in Detroit, but the killer picked her up in Northville, that's half an hour northwest of the city," he said, and drew a third circle on the upper left hand of the page.

"I think I know where you're going with this. Christy King, she works in Detroit, but he tries to pick her up here in Royal Oak," Julia said, and pointed to a place on the page just above the large Detroit circle. "The parks are too spread out. His initial contact with the women wasn't in the parks. He met them somewhere else first."

"Exactly. There's something that links all these women and you. We just have to figure out what."

"You think the killer is a cop?" Julia asked.

"I'm not ruling anything out yet. I think my earlier theory that he's role-playing is right, and each role connects to you. The principal at the teacher's school said a man approached April Young at the RiverWalk and claimed he had a son named Ben who died."

"Ben is the connection. With Heather Burns, the killer likely wore a gray wig that was found in the women's room, so he was probably posing as an older woman."

"If the killer knows you, he likely knows Helen," Navarro said. "And whether the police uniform today was real or a costume, you cover the crime beat and you date a cop."

"If the role playing is true, MMK is taking a lot of intricate steps, more than I've ever seen before. But why?"

"MMK wants your attention and the notoriety," Navarro said. "That's why you and your boys need to be right next to me. The apartment downtown is all set. I can meet you at your house after work and drive everyone over."

"Thanks for the offer, but Logan has a basketball game tonight. Helen is going to meet me there with the kids and then we'll all go to the apartment from there. I've got to keep things as normal as possible for Logan and Will right now."

"I'll meet you at the game if I get out in time. I'm going back inside. Christy's son woke up and she needed to take a break to get him settled before we started back in. We're going to take her down to the station later if she's up to it to look at some pictures. See you later, beautiful."

Julia watched as Navarro returned to Christy's house and then snatched her ringing cell phone, in case it was MMK calling back for another round.

"Hi, Julia. It's Charlotte. Charlotte Fisher. Our kids play basketball together. I hope I'm not calling too early. Are we still on for a run today? We talked about getting together this Friday."

Julia did a quick pan of her watch as she calculated her next move.

"Sure, I'll go for a run with you. Are you familiar with Belmont Park in Royal Oak?" Julia asked.

"No, but I should be able to find it."

"Let's meet there in an hour and a half, if that works for you," Julia said, knowing if she arrived too early at the park, where Christy almost got nabbed, the cops would kick her out, since they would be treating it as an active crime scene.

"Sure. My ex has Steven for the weekend, so I'm flexible. See you soon."

A familiar Chevy Suburban pulled in front of Christy's house with a city patrol car behind it before Julia could make her escape. Washington exited the Suburban, looked up at the house, and then back to Julia.

"I was just leaving. Navarro and Russell are interviewing Christy. I just stopped by here to be sure Christy was okay. I know the rules. You'll want to know, MMK called me a few minutes ago. I recorded the conversation and gave Navarro the tape on the agreement that I'd get a written transcript from both calls," Julia said, and noticed the look of piqued interest over the mention of the call on the chief's face.

"Don't get too excited about the phone conversation. It was short and untraceable. Russell already checked. Essentially, all MMK said was that he was going to make the clues harder from here on out. And he was mad that Christy King was saved before he could kill her. He did mention the number five, so there could be some significance there. I'm thinking five could be the number of his intended victims."

"Thanks for turning over the tape. We'll get you a transcript of both calls. I heard you helped find the woman."

"Navarro was the one who found her," Julia bluffed, preferring to give Navarro the accolades for Christy's save. "I just caught a lucky break and reached the owner of the bar before he did."

"Nice work on both your parts. Just make sure my guys get partial credit. They've been busting their asses trying to find the killer. I'm assuming you're writing a story."

"Yes, but I'm not using Christy's name. Are you still thinking the killer could be a cop? You'll need to ask Christy, but from what she told me, it sounds like the man in the park was wearing a costume or some kind of outfit to make her think he was a police officer. Unless you've decided to equip your patrol unit with old Buicks, I'm guessing the man in the park wasn't one of yours."

"Don't write about the cop angle yet, Julia. I mean it. We don't need any leaks, especially about one of our own. Off the record?"

"Sure."

"We don't have any solid leads at this point that make us believe the killer is tied to law enforcement, or the military, for that matter. The only thing that points us in that direction is the theory of a former convict who was high at the time."

"Jeb Wilson."

"Is there anything you don't know? You're good at what

you do and you've never personally burned me or the department, but I understand that you and Navarro are seeing each other again. There are some things we don't tell the press or the public because it could jeopardize a case. He needs to be careful what he tells you. We're still in agreement about the limitations of your involvement in the investigation?"

"Yes, but in all due respect, Navarro is a pro and would never give me information if he thought it could jeopardize a case. I have lots of sources in the department, including you. And in case you forgot, the killer is reaching out to me and I'm the one filling you in."

"And that's one of the reasons I need you to be careful. The way I see it, you're looking at this more like you're writing a story than trying to take care of yourself. You've got two kids, Julia. You need to think about them before you put yourself in harm's way, chasing down this story."

"When you were first starting out on patrol, did anyone ever criticize you for 'putting yourself in harm's way' because you had young kids? Or how about when you made detective? Mothers aren't supposed to put themselves in danger, right, Beth?"

"I was doing my job."

"So am I. I can't help but wonder if you'd be giving me that same piece of advice if I were a man," Julia said.

Washington took off her sunglasses, looked Julia in the eye, and gave her a nod of shared understanding.

"Point taken. Good job on finding Christy," Washington said. She pointed at the patrol car parked behind her and then beckoned with a roll of her finger for the driver to get out.

Branch LaBeau exited, carrying a tray containing two extra large Dunkin' Donuts coffees.

"I know introductions aren't necessary," Washington said. "Although the bodies of the two victims were found inside

Detroit churches, Heather Burns and Christy King were running in suburban parks. LaBeau is the point person who'll be working with the various city PDs and the sheriff departments, specifically Oakland and Wayne counties right now. I'm hoping we're not going to have to expand the perimeter if we get more victims. That's not for attribution, but you can quote me on this, 'We're not trying to alarm citizens, and they should feel safe going about their daily activities, but we are asking women not to run alone in parks at this time.' Off the record, we'll be beefing up patrols in city and county parks with running trails."

"That's a lot of ground to cover. How are you going to patrol every single park with running trails in metro Detroit, not to mention Oakland and Wayne counties?" Julia asked.

"Teamwork. We've got twelve city PDs and sheriff departments partnering with us," LaBeau said. "We've pinpointed a list of all the running trails in Detroit and the counties in question, and the law enforcement agencies in those areas jumped on board to help."

"MMK is smart. Unless he wants to get caught, he's probably already changed his MO because of what just happened with Christy King," Julia said.

"Maybe, but we aren't going to take that chance. LaBeau, be sure Julia finds her way out of the neighborhood. I'm going inside."

LaBeau handed the boss a coffee from the container and then offered Julia the other cup.

"Thanks. But I'm not going to take yours."

"I'd have brought another if I knew you were going to be here. So, no offense, Julia, but boss's orders."

"I know, I'm leaving. Are you going inside?"

"No, I'm heading to Belmont Park with the other peons to see if the killer left anything behind. Detectives are the top dogs. Patrol, we're the B Team, but I don't mind. I had my chances to rise up to detective, but there's a freedom of working the streets. You can stay under the radar more," LaBeau said. He put the coffee tray on the top of Julia's hood and then opened her car door. "I hear you're with Navarro these days. Stand-up guy."

"I agree. How's your wife doing? Is she still at Henry Ford Hospital? Being a nurse, that's a calling in my book."

"She was just promoted to head nurse in the trauma ward. I married up. See you around, Gooden," LaBeau said. "You're not planning on trying to circle the block and then show back up here after I leave, right?"

"The thought never crossed my mind."

CHAPTER 20

Julia sped through the rear entrance of Royal Oak's Belmont Park, having returned home to change into her running gear and file her story on Christy King. She made a point to enter the park through the back lot, since she figured the residual cops playing clean up would likely be positioned at the front of the property. For Julia, back entrances to crime scenes were always the best bet and would, hopefully, at the very least, buy her a few minutes before she got booted out.

Julia estimated it would be a fast in-and-out for the police. Murder scene investigations could take days. But this was a different animal. Since Christy King fled the park hours earlier, the police, in Julia's estimation, had likely canvassed the surrounding residential neighborhood already and finished their door-to-door to see if anyone saw the man in the Buick or, better yet, a license plate. They would've also completed a thorough search of the park for anything the killer might have left behind, including scoping the trails, surrounding woods, and the two open parking-lot areas.

Julia checked her cell phone and played a voice mail from her editor, Virginia, who was calling with a fresh ration of grief over Julia's steadfast refusal to include Christy King's name in the story and the fact that she had e-mailed the story remotely instead of coming into the newsroom.

Her latest article on the Magic Man Killer detailed the roller coaster of events that had occurred in the last twenty-four hours: the killer's phone call that led Julia to Roseline's apartment; the note she found at John K. King Used & Rare Books; the discovery of Christy King, who Julia referred to as a Royal Oak single mother in her thirties, and finally, Christy's razor-thin escape.

Julia parked at the far side of the lot and did a quick inventory of the police cars by the entrance. Three vehicles were still at the scene, including a single Royal Oak police cruiser, a Detroit patrol vehicle, and a Nissan Sentra. Julia picked up a few familiar faces and moved toward the huddle of cops. The crew consisted of two unfamiliar faces who, Julia figured, were Royal Oak PD, LaBeau and his partner, and, most important, her strong ally, Prejean.

The officers seemed to move their heads collectively as one at Julia's approach, with LaBeau and Prejean breaking from the pack to meet her halfway.

"Hey, Julia. This isn't my call. But the boss told you not to come back here," LaBeau said.

"Beth asked me to leave Christy's house. And I did. This is a public park, which I'm guessing has recently been re-opened after your initial crime scene investigation. That means I have every right to be here. I won't get in your hair. I just came here to run."

Prejean gave Julia a wide smile and a wink. "She's got a point there."

LaBeau looked back at his partner and the two Royal Oak

officers, who were getting into their respective patrol cars, and made his decision.

"All right, Julia. You're not going to find anything here, but if you want to waste your time, have at it. The trails are open, but watch yourself on the unpaved parts. It rained late last night and the ground is still loose in some spots. I almost fell on my ass when we scoped out the trails a couple hours ago," he said. LaBeau then turned to Prejean. "My partner and I are going to head back to the station. Your call, but you can feel free to leave as well."

"I'll hang for a bit. I need to catch up with Julia about dinner plans," Prejean said.

"Right, I'm sure that'll be your topic of conversation. You want to brief Julia about what we found, have at it, as long as I don't catch heat for leaking anything to the media. It doesn't look good with the higher-ups. But you're on rental, so you don't need to worry about it."

"Down South, we're not so paranoid. We use the media, they use us. It's a functional relationship. Come on, Julia, let's take a walk."

Prejean put his hand on Julia's elbow and waited until they were halfway across the first parking lot until he spoke.

"You handled yourself well back there, girl. I was impressed."

"Did the cops find anything when they searched the park?"

"This isn't my case, so you should check with the chief or Navarro whether you can write about this. . . ."

"Okay, just for background then," Julia said. "Come on. You know you can trust me."

"Like LaBeau said, it rained last night. So they were able to pick up two distinct tire tracks in the dirt lot, one from Christy King's car in the rear entrance and one from the

Buick by the front entrance. They're working on getting a three-dimensional print from the Buick's tire tracks now."

"It's too bad Christy didn't get anything on the plate."

"We got something else. The way I figure what went down, the killer was surprised when Christy bolted out of the park. He realized she was onto him and that maybe you tipped her off. He knows the cops are about to show up, so he gets scared and sloppy. We found a small blue-velvet satchel on the ground next to the tracks where we believe the Buick was parked. The satchel wasn't wet from the rain, so by process of elimination, we figured the killer must have dropped it when he was hightailing it out of here."

"What was in the satchel?"

"A folded-up drawing of a red-and-turquoise heart."

"The Erzulie voodoo symbol."

"There was something else inside the satchel, a miniature building. It looked like a city skyscraper. It was gray and plastic and about six inches tall. From what LaBeau and the local cops said, it doesn't look like any specific building in Detroit."

"MMK called me after Christy escaped. He told me the clues were going to get harder, but I'm guessing you're right. He didn't mean to leave this one when he hightailed it out of here. The Magic Man Killer planned to leave the building clue behind in Christy King's hands after he killed her, as a clue about his next victim. Maybe the woman is an architect or works in a building downtown. You'd have to check, but the tallest buildings in Detroit, to my knowledge, are the Marriott, One Detroit Center, the Penobscot Building, probably the Renaissance Tower, and maybe the Guardian Building."

A bright yellow VW Bug with a plastic pink daisy on the dashboard, pulled into the parking lot and stopped next to Julia's car. Charlotte got out of the VW and gave Julia a wave.

"Is that your friend? She's a cutie. You should tell her what a great guy I am."

"Not a chance. Charlotte is a new acquaintance, and technically, you're still married."

Charlotte jogged over to the pair, but kept a watchful eye on the police cars that were pulling out of the park entrance.

"What's with all the cops?" Charlotte asked. "Should we go somewhere else?"

"There was an incident here this morning, but it's been resolved," Julia said.

"This is probably the safest place you could be right now. Every inch of this park has been thoroughly inspected by the fine boys in blue," Prejean answered. "Me included. I'd offer to accompany you ladies, but I didn't get the memo to bring along my running gear."

Prejean outstretched his hand to Charlotte, and Julia made the introductions.

"Are you a journalist, too?" Prejean asked.

"No way. I don't have the stomach for that. I'm a wedding florist."

"Working for high-maintenance brides sounds like it could be more stressful than police work," Prejean said.

"I love it. Weddings are usually one of the happiest days of a couple's lives, the groom's included," Charlotte said. "My wedding was wonderful. My marriage and divorce, not so much."

"So you're single?" Prejean asked.

"And we're taking a run now. See you later, Prejean."

"Tell you what. Just so Charlotte's comfortable with the police being here, I'll hang out for a bit until you're done. A woman almost got picked up here this morning, so you can't be too careful."

"Is this connected to the female runners who were killed?" Charlotte asked.

"It is, but the woman got away. And there's no way the guy who tried to nab her is coming back here anytime soon," Prejean said. He leaned back against Julia's car and folded his arms across his dark blue windbreaker. "Just consider me your bodyguard."

"I'm okay to run here, but if you're willing to stay, I won't say no," Charlotte said to Prejean.

"Don't worry. I'm armed and dangerous," Prejean said, and gave Charlotte a slow, easy smile.

Julia grabbed Charlotte by the arm, cutting off Prejean's play, and the two women exited the parking lot in the direction of the running trails.

"So you brought me here to look at the scene of the crime?" Charlotte asked, and fingered a silver Peace charm that hung on a thin chain around her neck.

"I'm sorry. I should've been completely honest with you. If you want to leave, I understand."

"As long as no deranged freak tries to grab me, I don't mind being here. I always thought it would be cool to be an investigative reporter, but I think I'd be too chicken. Do you ever get scared in your job?"

"No."

"Did anyone ever threaten you because you were writing an article about them they didn't like? You must have some crazy stories."

The faces of the top fifty murderers, rapists, pedophiles, white-collar criminals, and drug dealers who Julia had hostile, if not life-threatening, dealings with during the last fifteen years on her beat, flashed through her memory like cards being shuffled in a deck.

"I know how to handle myself."

"You don't like questions, I can tell," Charlotte said.

"I don't have a problem with questions, as long as I'm the one asking them."

"I make my clients do an icebreaker when I first meet them. I have the groom tell his bride-to-be something he's never told anyone else before. There are a few ground rules: nothing kinky, illegal, or a response that would upset their partner. You'd be surprised. Most couples go for it and the guy usually tells some sweet story about his childhood and then his girlfriend gets all mushy. I know it probably sounds ridiculous, but couples, especially the brides, get really uptight about weddings, and my little icebreaker helps bring down the stress level from the get-go. I know it makes my life easier. Now that you've dragged me to this creepy place, you've got to tell me something about yourself."

"I'm not one of your clients."

"See, you're avoiding opening up."

"You sound like my book editor. Okay. I've never been scared when I was working a story. There's an adrenaline rush that pushes everything else out of the way. But that's not why I became a reporter. I went into journalism because I wanted to give other people answers that I couldn't find for myself. My brother was abducted when we were kids. His case went unsolved for thirty years, but I helped find my brother's killer a few months ago."

"My God, Julia. That's so horrible."

Charlotte unclasped the Peace necklace around her neck and handed it to Julia. "I want you to have this. A friend of mine gave it to me when I was going through my divorce. Pass it on to a woman who needs it, once you find what you need."

"Thank you, but I'm fine. Really."

"After something like that happened? How can you ever be? Women need to look out for each other. Come on, lift up the hair."

Julia realized she wasn't going to be able to say no and let her new friend put the necklace on her.

"Maybe it will bring you good luck," Charlotte said. "Don't kill me on the trails. I get the feeling you're a hard-core runner. I'm a couple-of-miles, twice-a-week type of girl."

"I'll go at whatever pace you like. The cops combed the park and the trails already, but I'd still like to take a look, so slow is fine by me."

"I like your friend. I've never dated a cop," Charlotte said.

"Prejean is a good guy. Most cops are. I'm dating a police officer."

"I had a run-in with a cop a couple weeks ago. I was leaving a job in the city I picked up at the last minute, and I was in a hurry to get Steven from his dad's, because my ex is an ass and would've pitched a fit if I showed up thirty seconds late. I was speeding and got pulled over. The cop, he was a good-looking guy and asked me on a date. I would've said yes, but he was wearing a ring, so I told him I don't date married guys. He wound up letting me go without a ticket."

"Did you report him?"

"For what?"

"For using his badge to try and pick up a woman. If he was a Detroit cop, did you get his name?"

"I don't remember. I didn't feel like he was doing anything wrong. Even if he was out of bounds, I'm not a big fan of rocking the boat, especially with law enforcement."

"Your call, but I think he was in the wrong. Are you ready?" Julia asked, and pushed her way through the turnstile to the running trails.

The park was relatively small, just five acres, and Julia stuck to the main trail, which was bookended by a thick nestle of trees on either side. Julia figured these were easy spots for the killer to have hidden as he likely stalked Christy during her previous morning runs, while he patiently learned and mastered her routines.

Julia and Charlotte made two loops around the one-mile trail. The two women turned the corner to start the third mile, but stopped when they saw Prejean in the middle of the path, walking in their direction.

"We've got company. Thank God. You're killing me," Charlotte said to Julia. "Can we take a break? Just a minute breather. That way, you won't have to bring out the paddles to resuscitate me."

"We can stop."

Charlotte leaned up against the thick trunk of an eastern white pine, the needles from its branches splayed out like bony green fingers behind her.

"Did you change your mind about the run?" Charlotte asked Prejean.

"No, but I thought it would be a good idea to check on you ladies. I told you I'd be your bodyguard."

A patch of gray-black clouds slipped over the sun, and Prejean covered his eyes with a hand to look up at the darkening sky.

"It looks like another storm is coming. Never trust a weatherman. The forecast I saw this morning called for clear skies," Charlotte said.

Prejean continued to look up, unmoving with rapt intent, as if assessing the proximity of the pending storm.

"We missed something. Up there, Julia," Prejean said, and pointed up to a tall birch on the left of the path. "Right there, on one of the middle branches," Prejean said.

At first, Julia saw nothing, but then caught something swaying back and forth in the breeze.

Julia focused in on the object and realized it was a cloth doll, with long black hair and a blue dress. The doll was made of crude, coarse fabric, and two black X's were drawn where the eyes should have been. The doll had a noose around its neck and hung from a thin, peeling gray branch of the tree.

"What is that?" Charlotte asked.

"It looks like a voodoo doll to me," Prejean said.

"Holy shit," Charlotte said. "I'm never running with you again."

CHAPTER 21

The windshield wipers of Julia's SUV darted back and forth in front of her line of vision as the downpour from the storm continued.

Julia felt like every single pore of her body was water-logged. Charlotte had left the park after Prejean discovered the doll, but Julia had stayed behind and waited until Prejean climbed up the tree and retrieved it. Julia and Prejean got caught in the downpour a mile from the parking lot and were officially soaked to the bone from the unexpected storm by the time they reached their respective cars.

Julia blasted her heater on full throttle to help stop her shivering, but her wet running pants and shirt that stuck to her freezing-cold skin weren't helping matters. She ignored the steady drips of water from her hair and pulled off the I-75 exit to her paper.

Prejean promised he'd call with any updates, but without a peep from him in the last thirty minutes, Julia called Navarro.

"Tell me you have something," Julia asked through chattering teeth.

"Are you okay?"

"I'm fine. I got caught in the rain at the park, and I didn't have time to change. Did you get anything on the doll?"

"Nothing but dead ends. Just like everything else the killer left behind, there were no prints. I sent a picture to Roseline, and she said it wasn't one of hers."

"There's got to be a way to track it," Julia said. She pulled into the parking garage next to her paper and was surprised over her luck when she nabbed a coveted spot on the first floor.

"I spoke to LaBeau. He says our team and the Royal Oak cops combed over every inch of the park. LaBeau swears they were thorough, and he can't understand how they missed it."

"It's not like the doll had a neon light shining behind it. The woods there are pretty thick. I ran the path twice and didn't see it."

"Between us, this voodoo doll thing doesn't add up. I checked the weather forecast. It poured last night and didn't stop until five-thirty this morning. Christy King got to the park at six-fifteen. So even if the killer gets to the park before Christy, is he really going to go to all that trouble to scramble up a wet tree to leave the doll? Prejean brought the doll into the station and it was dry. The way I see it, the doll would've been at least damp from the water that was still on the tree."

"When I got to the park, the ground was damp. My sneakers were wet on the bottom."

"When were you there?"

"Ten-thirty. It was overcast all morning. But maybe the sun dried whatever water got on the doll."

"Just to be sure I have this straight, Prejean shows up unexpectedly on the trail during your run."

"Prejean was already at the park. It's not like he appeared out of thin air."

"But he's at the exact place on the path where the doll was found. Think about it. Prejean knows about voodoo. And he obviously likes you."

"If you're insinuating Prejean is the killer, to my knowledge, he doesn't drive a Buick. I'm going to run a story on the doll."

"Hold off. We're going back out to Mayberry Park and the Dequindre Cut path at the RiverWalk to see if we missed anything. I don't want the public searching parks for dolls in trees like it's some kind of scavenger hunt. Chief Washington agrees. I'll let you know if we find anything," Navarro said, and then turned to personal business. "I picked up the keys to the apartment. I'll meet you at Logan's game tonight, and we can all drive over together."

"Thanks. Logan will love that you're there. I'm not convinced Logan's buying my line about moving into the apartment short-term so we can do repairs on the house."

"He's a smart kid. Do me a favor, put on some dry clothes before you freeze to death."

Julia hung up with Navarro, grabbed her purse and a bag with a change of clothes, and headed to her paper. She got as far as the elevators when she heard the sports editor, Scott Baylor, call out to her from behind.

"What happened to you, Gooden? You look like a drowned ferret," Baylor said. "Are you okay?"

"Thanks for the compliment. And I'm fine," Julia answered. The elevator doors opened and the people getting inside began to shoot her glances, probably hoping she wouldn't be standing right next to them in the confined space as she drip-dried.

"You coming, Julia?" Baylor asked from inside the elevator as he stopped the doors from closing.

"Don't worry. I'll take the stairs," she said. Julia bounded up to the seventh floor, escaped into the ladies' room, and did her best to dry her hair with the cheap, generic brown paper towels in the dispenser and changed in the bathroom stall.

She did a quick inspection of herself in the mirror. Her hair was still damp and her nose was red from the cold, but at least she was out of her wet clothes.

Julia hoped she'd make it to her desk in peace, but she got only halfway across the newsroom when Virginia pounced from behind.

"Goddamn it, Julia. You need to answer my calls," Virginia said, but then paused when Julia turned around. "What happened? You look like shit."

"Thanks. I'm getting a lot of that today. I've got an update, but I can't write it until I get the green light from the Detroit PD. We won't get beat, I promise."

"I don't like to gamble, but what's the story?"

"The Louisiana cop I told you about, I was with him in the park where the woman was almost abducted and he found a voodoo doll strung up with a noose around its neck hanging from a tree. It's the same pattern. The doll had on a blue dress and black hair, just like the two victims."

"I don't feel good waiting on the story. I want you to call that woman who escaped from the park and get a few comments on the record from her. And I want to use her name."

"I'm not outing her. She's a victim and wants to remain anonymous. That's her choice and we need to honor that."

"Victim is a gray area here. Was she hurt?"

"No. But she could've been killed. I gave her my promise. She's got a kid and she's scared."

"The killer already knows who she is and probably where she lives, too. Why does she care about being identified? I don't want to get beat on this."

"Do you even hear yourself anymore, Virginia? I'm not doing it. You want to fire me, go ahead."

Julia knew her editor was right behind her, but she didn't

turn around. She made the familiar route to her desk and saw a bouquet of lavender roses sitting on top of it.

"That cop of yours has good taste," Virginia said.

Julia was surprised that Navarro would've had the time in the middle of the MMK case to send her flowers. She pulled out the attached card and read its message from the sender, not Navarro, but Alex Tillerman.

> *Julia!*
>   *It was great running into you at the restaurant the other night.*
>   *The ball is in your court. Give me a call.*
> *Alex*

Julia didn't think for a second that Tillerman was pining for her. His sudden renewed interest likely piqued because she hadn't reached out to him since their brief encounter. But still, Julia knew Navarro would want to rule him out as a suspect in the Magic Man killings. Julia picked up the bouquet and headed with it into the breakroom, where a group from the sports desk was gathered around a table watching the last inning of a baseball game that was playing on a TV mounted on the wall.

"Hey, nice posies," Scott Baylor called out.

"You like them? You can have them," Julia said. She opened up the top of the trash can and stuffed the bouquet inside.

"Man, don't let me get on your bad side, Gooden," Baylor said. "That was cold."

The parking lot of the gym where Logan was playing his basketball rec-league game was beyond packed. Julia hurried through the front door of the building and already heard the roar from the crowd echoing like a collective team-fight song booming down the hallway.

Julia did a quick glance at her watch and felt guilty for not making the start of Logan's game. She walked quickly by a table decorated with orange balloons and a banner that read: EARLY REGISTRATION FOR YOUR YOUNG ATHLETIC STARS!

She pushed her way through the gym doors and saw that Logan's team had the ball. Julia watched with pride as her son hustled down the court, not with an awkward gait like some of the boys, but with the fluid instinct of a natural athlete. She then scanned the crowd and spotted Helen and Will high up in the stands.

As Julia made her way to the bleachers, a burly man in the front row wearing the rival green team's jersey jumped to his feet and burst into a stadium chant when one of his players scored.

He gave a fist pump in the air. "The Cougars are sucking wind tonight."

The coach for Logan's team shot the man a look, and Julia moved in closer to put a muzzle on the beefy man's trash talk.

"Cut it out," Julia said. "It's just a game. These kids are nine years old. They don't need to be intimidated by parents on the sidelines."

"I'm guessing your kid plays for the Cougars," the man said. "You wouldn't be saying that if it was your son who scored the shot instead of mine. Your team sucks."

"Did you really just say that to me? You're ridiculous," Julia said.

"You think you're tough? I work at a prison."

"Which one?"

"The Detroit Detention Center."

"I'm a crime reporter, and I date a Detroit police detective. I've never seen you at the DDC before. What do you do there?"

The man looked out at the court as his swagger wilted. "I transfer prisoners."

"So you drive the bus. Those are little kids out there. Stop giving them a hard time."

"Sure. I guess I got a little out of hand. This is the play-offs. You know how it is," the man said.

"No, I don't." Julia said. She turned her back on the obnoxious man and weaved her way up the ascending rows of bleachers toward her family, but stopped and grabbed Charlotte's arm when she saw her friend on her feet and cheering when a boy on their children's team scored.

"Hey, Julia. I see you got out of the park in one piece," Charlotte said.

"I hope I didn't scare you off from running with me again. I'm sorry about all that earlier. If you want your necklace back, I don't blame you."

Charlotte leaned in and gave Julia a hug. "You keep the necklace. It's a definite no on the running, but drinks or play dates for our kids, most definitely. I hope you can make it to the Sugar House tonight. You owe me a drink for dragging me to that creepy park."

"Thanks, but I'll take a rain check. I see your friend with the dog isn't with you. If you don't mind the nosebleed section, why don't you sit with us?"

"Sure. I'd welcome the company. Before I forget, I picked up something you'll want," Charlotte said. She dug into her bag and handed Julia a bright orange piece of paper. "Does Logan play any other sports during the year?"

"Just baseball."

"Two sports, so you're going to want to sign him up for this. Parents here are crazy competitive, and the spots for the junior rec-league teams fill up literally in minutes. You'll need to be on your computer by six AM Friday to reserve a spot for tryouts. All you have to do is pay a hundred dollars up front when you register. It won't necessarily guarantee a place for Logan on the team, but he'll get one of the first slots for tryouts. That's big with the coaches around here. That way, they'll know the player is serious and the family, too. There's a lot of team fund-raisers and volunteer requirements, so we need all the parent support we can get."

"When did the parks department get so mired in making a buck?"

"Like I said, the competition between parents to get their kids on a good team is intense. If you sign up, there are perks for you, too. You'll get e-mails about special offers if you fill in your interests on the form."

"It sounds to me like Wayne County is profiting from overzealous, competitive parents. That would be a good story."

"This is a big deal for us. Sports are huge. And with the budget cuts in the public schools' athletic programs, county park teams are more important than ever. If you're angling to write a story about this, it could hurt the kids. I'm asking as a friend. Please don't do it."

"That's not my intent, but don't worry. Wayne County isn't my beat. Come on, let's grab a seat before there aren't any left."

The bleachers in the front and middle rows were completely filled and people had spilled into the narrow strip of stairs to watch the game. Julia pushed her way upward through the crowd until she reached Helen and Will in the very back and introduced Charlotte.

"Sorry I'm late," Julia said to Helen. She scooped up Will and put him in her lap. "It's been a crazy day. We'll leave straight from here to go to the apartment."

"No, we will need to switch cars so I can go back to the house. My Volvo is full up with the boys' things and your suitcase. I left my bag and kitchen supplies all packed up by the front door. We are not going to 'wing it' with dinner tonight in the bachelor pad."

"You must be a good cook. Some nights in our house, dinner is a bowl of cereal," Charlotte said.

"You joke, I hope," Helen said.

Julia's phone sounded in her purse and she looked at the incoming caller.

"I need to get this. It's Navarro."

"Always anxious to get the story. That is you. Give me the boy then. No police talk in front of Will or he won't be able to sleep tonight," Helen said.

"I agree," Charlotte said. "If you're going to talk about that freaky doll we saw in the park, please don't do it here. I'm the one who's going to be having nightmares. I can't burn that image out of my mind."

Julia passed Will back over to Helen and moved to the far end of the bleacher to take the call.

"Gooden, I'm running late. I'm just leaving Royal Oak, so I should be there in fifteen. The apartment is set, so we'll all leave from the gym after the game."

"There's one snag. Helen couldn't fit everything into her car, so I need to go back to the house."

"No, you won't. I'm closer to Rochester Hills than you are. I'll go to your house. Get settled into the apartment and I'll meet you there."

"If I don't tell you this enough, you're a godsend," Julia said. "Did you find any other dolls?"

"No, and to be honest, I'm not surprised. Either the killer changed up his pattern, or someone else planted the doll in Royal Oak. I'm going with the second theory."

"Listen, I should mention this. I don't think it's anything, but that doctor I ran into recently, he sent me flowers. I think his ego is bruised because I didn't call him. But I thought you'd want to know in light of the case. I don't picture Tillerman as the killer. We've lived in the same city for years, so the timing wouldn't make sense."

"I'm not going to discount anything. I'll run a background check on Tillerman. Tell Logan I'm sorry I missed his game, but I promise I'll be at the next one. Be careful, Gooden."

Julia returned to her seat just as the ref, Jeremiah Landry, blew his whistle for halftime, and the boys on the two teams scattered to separate ends of the court. Julia saw her opening to give Logan a hug and let him know she was rooting for him, but his coach pulled the teammates in a tight huddle in the corner of the gym.

"Where are they going?" Julia asked Charlotte as she noticed half the bleachers were emptying and the parents were exiting out the doors to the hallway and the parking lot outside.

"We tailgate on Fridays, before the games and at halftime. That's big around here. The parents cook up hot dogs and hamburgers. One guy Sophiah dated brought pate one time. Yeah, I know. Ridiculous."

"I'm going down to the court to try to talk to Logan," Julia told Helen. "I'll be right back."

Julia watched Logan's teammates scatter, a few of them now standing on the sidelines. She made her way back down to the court and noticed the loudmouthed prison bus driver reenter the gym and approach her with a renewed sense of confidence.

"You're still here," the DDC worker said. "You know, I was thinking, I didn't like your uppity tone from before."

"Mr. Montenegro, how are you this evening?"

Julia turned to see Jeremiah Landry. He was holding a basketball with his long fingers splayed across it. He held the ball across his chest and gave the male parent in front of him a warm but steely smile.

"Is everything all right here?" Jeremiah asked Julia.

"Nothing I can't handle."

"This lady here has an attitude," Montenegro said.

Landry kept his smile intact as he closed the space between himself and the other man.

"Mr. Montenegro, have you been drinking?" Landry asked.

"No way, man."

"That's good to hear. I wouldn't want to have to call 911 if a parent was being hassled or if a dad of one of our teammates has been drinking and got behind the wheel of a car with their kid after the game."

"Yeah. That would be a shame. See you around," Montenegro said, and quickly ended the conversation as he slunk back to his seat, losing himself inside the growing crowd of parents who were returning to see the second half of the game.

"Thanks," Julia said. "But you didn't need to do that."

"Defusing that guy with other parents is starting to become my nightly duty. I had to break up a near fistfight with him and another dad last week. I'm going to be in the parking lot after the game to be sure he doesn't get behind the wheel with his son. I smelled liquor on his breath."

"You're a real live Boy Scout," Julia said.

"Guilty as charged. I was an Eagle Scout. If you haven't gotten Logan involved in Scouting, you should. Kids learn good skills, and if Logan stays with it, he'd be eligible for scholarships down the road."

The end-of-the-halftime buzzer sounded and Jeremiah gave Julia a mock salute as he ran backward to his position on the floor.

Julia climbed back up the stands and plucked Will from Helen's lap, placing her youngest son right next to her as she squeezed his hand.

"These children, some of them play dirty," Helen whispered to Julia in a conspiratorial tone. "Look at that boy, he just shoved one of Logan's teammates who tried to make a shot."

Jeremiah, who'd witnessed the same incident as Helen, blew his whistle and called a foul on the boy.

"Our team is only ahead by two points. If this kid makes both shots, we'll lose."

"It's just a game," Julia said, but Charlotte didn't acknowledge and instead looked intently at the little boy at the foul line.

"Shit," Charlotte said as the ball bounced off the backboard, but then dropped through the net. "If he makes the next one, we're tied. We have to win this game or we won't make the play-offs."

Charlotte crossed her fingers on both hands and then jumped to her feet when the boy's shot smacked against the front of the rim and then bounced back down to the floor. The little boy took in the crowd over his failure and looked like he was about to cry.

"We won!" Charlotte said, and gave Julia a hug. "We'll do a tailgate in the parking lot for the play-offs. But we should celebrate now. You have to go to the Sugar House with me. One drink isn't going to kill you."

"I can't. We're doing some repairs on my house, and I'm moving my family into an apartment in the city while the work is being done."

"Ugh. Asshole alert," Charlotte said. She nodded her head in the direction of a dark-haired man who looked like he spent every off-hour in the gym. "That's my ex, Joe. He's picking up Steven. I better say good-bye to my kid and play buffer with King Dickhead."

Julia picked up Will and grabbed Helen's arm as she led her family down through the bleachers to the court.

"That woman, she uses bad language in front of children. But she seems okay. Except for all the hugging. I must go back to the house and pick up the rest of my bags. You take the boys and I will meet you there."

"No, you're all set. Navarro is going to the house."

"A chivalrous man Mr. Ray is. You go get Logan. I will take Will to the bathroom before we leave."

"I don't have to go," Will said.

"You will in five minutes. Trust me. Come on now."

Julia found Logan on the court throwing the ball back and forth to Charlotte's son as Charlotte and her ex exchanged heated words next to the boys.

"Where's Uncle Ray? Did he see me make that three-point shot?" Logan asked, and then looked back at his friend with a dead-serious expression. "My mom's boyfriend is a cop."

"Uncle Ray couldn't be here. He's working a big case, but he called me to be sure you knew he was rooting for you."

"Great game, kiddo," Charlotte said. "And, Julia, if you change your mind about a drink, call me. We'll be at the Sugar House."

The crowd began to filter out, and Julia heard the hard pounding of a basketball smacking down in a rapid *tat-tat-tat* on the court. Julia looked to see Jeremiah Landry dribbling to the top of the key and then taking a perfect shot that was all net.

"If this ref thing doesn't work out for you, I think you've got a shot in the NBA," Julia said.

"Thanks for the compliment, but I'm way too old. I had my glory days as a walk-on sophomore year at Oakland University. I started in junior college, but I quickly discovered the bench and I were going to be good friends all season when I started playing for the Golden Grizzlies."

"You'd be a good coach."

"Believe it or not, I'm a teacher. Or let me come clean. I'm a heck of a sub. I'm getting my master's degree. Without it, my full-time job prospects are minimal at best. I'm two courses away from my degree, and then I'll have to leave all this behind," Jeremiah said, and spread his hands wide. "Believe it or not, I enjoy being a ref. Since my classes are during the day, I had my choice of waiting tables or working as a night janitor. Being a ref was an easy choice. I like being around kids."

"What do you want to teach?" Julia asked.

"Middle school. English preferably, but social studies would be okay, too," Jeremiah said. "Middle school can be an awkward stage, but I look at it as a time when I could make a difference. Kids can be so mean."

"So can adults. I'm impressed, you always seem to keep your cool."

"It's a shame because most of the players follow the rules. It's their parents who don't. Logan here, he's a good kid," Jeremiah said, and bent down so he was the same height as Logan. "Do you play any other sports?"

"Just baseball, sir."

"Great. I'll likely see you in the spring, too. I'm an umpire for the Wayne County–rec baseball program, and I pick up shifts for Oakland County as well, if they get in a pinch. I assume you'll be playing for Wayne?"

"I'm not sure yet. It depends if the baseball parents are as nuts as the basketball ones."

"Sorry to break the news, but it's the same crowd. The competition is really over-the-top between parents here. Whose kid is the better player, which boy scored the most baskets or RBIs. Sports can be a petty, vicious animal if you let it, but you don't strike me as that type," Jeremiah said, and then turned to Logan. "Remember what I said about the follow-through on the jump shot. Do you want to try it again?"

Logan bent down in position when the sound of a door opening echoed in the nearly empty gym.

Julia looked over, figuring it was Helen, but instead saw a pretty blonde standing in the entrance.

"Are you ready, J? I don't want to be late," she asked.

"That's my lovely better half. I've got to go. We'll do some more practicing next time if you want, Logan. Have a good night."

"So the apartment is right next to Uncle Ray's, right? I like his place. Maybe we could move in there for good," Logan said from the backseat of Julia's vehicle.

Julia took a glance into her rearview mirror at Helen's slow progress in the parking lot and caught a glimpse of Will, whose eyes were half-mast, her little boy ready to fall asleep in her backseat.

Julia's cell phone rang on the dash and Julia grabbed it as soon as she saw Navarro's name flash across the screen.

"Are you okay?" Navarro asked.

"Of course. We're just leaving."

Over the phone, Julia heard the beeping of Navarro's car door opening and the sound of the wind blowing in the background.

"I'm at your house right now. Hold on a second, Gooden. . . ."

"What's going on?" Julia asked.

"There's an envelope on your doorstep."

"Come on, Navarro. What is it?"

"It's from the killer. He drew the heart symbol in the corner."

Julia heard a rustling of papers and then Navarro came back on the line.

"It's a piece of paper with just your name and the reference, Matthew 4:19."

"What does that mean?"

"It's from the Bible, from the book of Matthew."

"Are you sure?"

"I spent every Sunday up until I was eighteen going to Mass. I know the verse. Jesus tells his apostles, 'Follow me, and I will make you fishers of men.'"

"That has to tie into the building figurine MMK left behind in Royal Oak."

"There's the Fisher Building downtown, the next victim probably works there."

Julia pulled her car quickly back into a parking space and flashed her lights at Helen to do the same as a horrible realization surfaced.

"I don't think so. Jesus, Ray. I should've never taken her to that park. MMK's going after my friend Charlotte. Charlotte *Fisher.* This is all my fault. Charlotte's next."

CHAPTER 22

Charlotte Fisher followed the route to the Standby, their new meet-up place for cocktails. After the game, Charlotte had gone home to change and got a call from Sophiah, who insisted they go to the Standby because it had just been voted the hottest bar in Detroit. Charlotte really wanted to go to the Sugar House instead since she had met a man there two days earlier. At the time, Charlotte had proceeded with caution, since she got the vibe the man might not be single. The guy had left before Charlotte got the chance to verify his relationship status, so she was hoping she might run into him at the Sugar House again.

If he was married, hands off, but if he wasn't, it was open season. Charlotte didn't consider herself desperate for a man, but just lonely sometimes. Her divorce was a year behind her. Since then, she'd only gone on a handful of dates. The idea of companionship, instead of another lonely night binge-watching *The Walking Dead* after she put her son Steven to sleep, was a welcome one, if it happened.

Despite the prospect of possibly running into the man

again, Charlotte ultimately decided not to argue with Sophiah about wanting to go to the Sugar House because she didn't want to make waves.

The Standby was located in The BELT alleyway, which was once part of Detroit's garment district and had been transformed into a trendy hot spot known for its public-art displays. But more important, it had just been voted the number one bar in Detroit by a popular Wayne County single-mommy's Facebook group they belonged to, so queen Sophiah had insisted they change venues, because you never want to be "so yesterday."

Charlotte couldn't believe her luck when a car parked on Library Street scooted out in front of her. Charlotte quickly put on her blinker and nabbed the space. She shut off the engine, but stayed in her car as some old insecurities that she had never quite been able to overcome surfaced like a dark slick of oil over an otherwise pristine ocean.

Charlotte looked down at her hands and accepted the fact that she had become a follower. She knew the competitiveness among the parents about their kids' sports, grades, and extracurricular activities was getting out of hand. For her son Steven's sake, she should speak up. But if she didn't go along with the pack, she might run the risk of no longer being part of it.

That's why Charlotte liked Julia. Her new friend wasn't afraid to speak her mind and didn't care what people thought of her.

Charlotte got out of her car when a moment of clarity hit. Women, no matter what role they chose, would be judged. And the cruelest reviews would come from each other.

Two women about her age passed by and Charlotte lowered her head, not wanting to make eye contact, lest they start judging her, ranking her looks, clothes, and body on a scale of one to ten. Whether they critiqued Charlotte aloud or silently in their heads, it was all the same. Charlotte turned onto The BELT alleyway and knew she was just as guilty for picking apart other women's faults and vulnerabilities at times, probably in an attempt to prop up her own self.

At thirty-five, Charlotte had lived long enough to realize women could be each other's greatest soul sisters. But just as quickly, some could turn into ravenous vultures, ready to eat their own alive.

A painful memory surfaced that summed up everything she had become. Charlotte felt her throat tighten as she pictured the event so vividly, it was like she was a poor, unpopular misfit again, hoping to God someone would notice her for being anything other than a loser.

There she was again, eleven years old, on a class field trip to Lake Michigan. Right before the students boarded the school bus home, the boys began to chase the girls on the beach. Charlotte recalled the strange and wonderful sense of belonging she felt, running with the pack of fifth-grade girls, laughing amidst their collective squeals of protest. For once, Charlotte didn't feel stupid in the church hand-me-downs she wore, since her single mother couldn't afford much else on her Dollar Store cashier's paycheck.

That fleeting moment of childhood joy was snatched away by a female classmate looking for a chance to be cruel. The girl had grabbed Charlotte by the arm, her mouth a tight little bow as she told Charlotte she didn't need to run because no boys were chasing her.

She had stopped to find out if the girl was telling the truth. After standing for a minute like a statue, unmoving and unwanted in the sand, not one single boy had even attempted to chase her. In that moment, Charlotte could've disappeared, and no one would have even noticed.

Charlotte tried to take hollow comfort in the fact that she was part of the in crowd now. A cool girl.

And the boys always loved the cool girls the best.

Charlotte spotted the landmark of where she was supposed to wait for Sophiah: a giant white mural of a man's face on a distressed brick wall next to the bar. She was right on time, but, of course, her friend would be fashionably late. Charlotte thought about going inside, but she hated being alone as a single woman in a bar. She could pretend to watch what was on the TV or act like she was engrossed with something on her phone, but the entire time, she'd feel like she was being sized up as a woman wanting to get lucky or a desperate loser. She always admired the single women she saw reading a book on their Kindle while they were at a table for one, dining alone in a restaurant. Just a woman alone, with a book, and feeling no shame about it.

She felt silly, standing by herself waiting. She considered pulling the plug on her plans and instead calling Julia to see if she could bring over a bottle of wine or watch her boys while Julia unpacked in her new place. But Charlotte wasn't one to break plans. She'd have just one drink and then check in with Julia to see if she could help. That would be the right thing to do.

Charlotte lifted the lapels of her coat up around her neck and caught a sideways glance of a nice-looking, tall man with sandy-blond hair walking out of the bar.

The man turned in her direction and seemed to look through Charlotte, until his eyes focused on her face in vague recognition.

"Hi. I think I know you. Hold on, don't tell me. Your name is on the tip of my tongue. It's . . ."

"Charlotte."

"Charlotte. That's right. Sorry, I forgot. But I definitely remember your face. A face that lovely would be impossible to forget."

"I know who you are. And it sounds like you're trying to

flirt with me. Aren't you married?" Charlotte asked, and looked down at his empty ring finger for confirmation.

"I was. Wait. That's not exactly true. To be technically correct on the verb tense, I'm still married, but I'm going through a divorce. No need to bring out the tiny violins, we're both okay. What is it the celebrities say when they break up? 'We'll always be friends and have the greatest respect for each other'? I know. Major eye roll. But in my case, it's true. My ex and I got married too young and people change. I'm sorry. Too much information, right?"

Charlotte heard her cell phone chime and took a quick look at her incoming text message from Sophiah.

"Damn."

"Bad news?" the man asked.

"The friend I'm waiting for, she has a flat tire. She just called AAA. She's going to be late."

"Sorry, but her bad luck may be your good luck. The Standby is packed. There's a place around the corner, Vincent's, that has much better food and it's not going to cost you fifty dollars for a minuscule appetizer and a drink. I hear they've got a good band tonight. Tell you what. I'm willing to fall on the sword and have one more cocktail for a beautiful woman. How about you do me the honor to be your in-between guy while you wait for your friend? It's not like I'm a complete stranger."

"I'm not familiar with Vincent's, but thanks anyway."

"Come on. The night's young. I swear I'll keep my hands to myself and then deliver you right back to this spot when we're done. I promise I won't be the weird, creepy guy who spends the whole time talking about his ex. One drink. What do you say?"

A warm, engaging smile spread across his face and Charlotte made her decision. After all, it's not like it would kill her to have one drink with a handsome man.

"Okay. But just so you understand, I don't blow my girl-friends off, no matter how cute the guy is. One drink and then I'm back here, holding up the side of this bar until my friend shows up."

"I promise I'll return you back to this very spot before your carriage turns into a pumpkin."

"Where's Vincent's? It must be new."

"I think it's been open for about a month. *The Freep* reviewed it a couple of weeks ago and made it sound like the next big hot spot in Detroit. It's just a five-minute walk down Library to a side street. And Charlotte . . ."

"Yes?"

"I'm really glad I ran into you again."

Charlotte felt herself smiling as the man locked his arm around hers and led her toward the street.

"Sorry you're going through a divorce. If you need any pointers, mine was a year ago," Charlotte said.

"I knew you were a woman of vast knowledge. But I made a promise, and I'm not talking about my ex. I wish her well, but we'll leave it at that."

"You're a gentleman. I couldn't say the same thing about mine. But I don't want to be the creepy girl who talks trash about her ex the whole night."

"So we're both in competition now, trying not to horrify each other."

"Maybe we could teach a class to help the newly separated or recently divorced," Charlotte said. "We could call it 'The Top Ten Taboo Topics On A First Date.'"

"Our own survival guide to being newly single. I love it. Okay, so my top ten would have to include no talking about religion, politics, or why you're so screwed up because you think your mom didn't love you enough."

"That's a good start, but we also have to have no talking about health problems, medications you're on, and absolutely no talk about sex," Charlotte said. "No preferred positions, past experiences, and definitely no idle chat about deviant behavior. You know I had a date once—"

"You're about to violate one of our first-date commandments."

"This isn't a first date, but I see where you're going with this, so I'll shut it down. Where is Vincent's again? I feel like you're taking me to no-man's-land."

"It's just another few blocks. I think the owners of the bar wanted to be understated cool. It looks like a hole-in-the-wall from the outside, but I promise, it's urbane and hip and filled with beautiful people, if you like that sort of thing. I think you do."

The two hooked onto Library Street and walked down two blocks until they reached another alley.

"Charlotte, I need to confess something."

"Do I need to be scared here?"

"I hope not. I think you're lovely."

"Thank you. But just so there aren't any misconceptions, I'm going home to my own bed tonight. Alone."

"Of course," the man said, and leaned in so close, Charlotte was sure he was going to kiss her. "You need to get up early to go running."

Charlotte stopped and took a step back, trying to figure out how the man she barely knew had intimate knowledge about her personal schedule.

"How did you know that?"

"Because it's the weekend. You run at the RiverWalk every Saturday and Sunday mornings at seven. You usually park on the second floor of the Port Atwater Parking garage. Spot G-Four, Level Two, when you can get it. You're a creature of habit, Charlotte. That's not always a good thing."

Charlotte felt outside of her body and tried to keep her expression even, thinking, if she acted like everything was normal and played along, maybe she could get away.

"You must run at the RiverWalk the same time I do," Charlotte said, trying to retain her cool, but she heard a tremor in her voice. "You know, I should probably head back. There's another girl in our group who's supposed to meet us, and I don't want to leave her all alone. I totally forgot she was coming."

"Oh, Charlotte. You poor thing. I know you're lying. You're just not that smart. You're nice enough and very pretty, but you're like an unfinished paper doll with only half a brain."

The Magic Man Killer took a quick glance over his shoulder to the empty street, gave Charlotte a hard shove into the alleyway, and sealed his hand around her mouth.

Charlotte felt something sharp press against her spine and her scream got muffled against the killer's clamped fingers over her lips.

"You make bad decisions, Charlotte. You shouldn't go places with a man you barely know."

Charlotte started to cry as the killer pushed her forward, deeper into the alley. When her eyes adjusted to the growing darkness, Charlotte could make out the lines of a car parked at the end next to a Dumpster.

"It's your turn now, Charlotte," the man said, and began to whisper in her ear: " 'Hold me close and hold me fast . . . The magic spell you cast . . . ' "

The Magic Man Killer continued to hum the song, all the while pressing Charlotte farther and farther into the alleyway, until they reached the rear of the vehicle.

"I'm going to take my hand off your mouth now. If you scream, I'll kill you right here. Do you understand?"

Charlotte moaned when the Magic Man Killer pushed the knife harder against her back.

"I asked you a simple question. Do you understand?"

Charlotte nodded her head, her mind frantically trying to come up with an escape plan.

The Magic Man Killer released his hand from Charlotte's

mouth and then jerked both her arms behind her back. Charlotte felt pieces of hard plastic latch around her wrists and then fasten so tightly, it made her skin burn and started to cut off her circulation, causing pins and needles to shoot up her palms and fingertips.

"That hurts. Please!" Charlotte begged.

The man popped open the trunk, and Charlotte knew if she went inside, she'd never have a chance.

Charlotte felt completely helpless until her cell phone rang in her purse. Sophiah had to be at the bar, and when she didn't see Charlotte, she'd know something was wrong.

The killer grabbed Charlotte's bag from her shoulder and dug inside. He retrieved the phone and studied the incoming caller ID.

"Julia Gooden. Two minutes too late. I win this time," he said, and tossed the cell phone and Charlotte's bag to the ground.

"Why are you doing this?" Charlotte cried.

"For her. Everything is for her. And for me, too. She's going to make me famous," he said, and then pointed to the tight confines of the open trunk. "Come on. Get in. We're going to take a little ride."

CHAPTER 23

Julia pulled into the loading dock of the Sugar House and jerked her SUV to a stop. After she got her boys and Helen safely situated in the new apartment, she snuck out the front door while the patrol officer who was assigned to watch her family made a brief pit stop in the bathroom. She wasn't trying to give the officer a hard time, since she knew Navarro had laid down the hammer and dictated strict instructions to the officer to make sure Julia stayed put for the night.

But right now, that was something she surely couldn't do.

From experience, Julia knew the police had already gone to the bar, Charlotte's home, and were now trying to track down her last-known whereabouts through Charlotte's friends and family. Julia didn't know if she could do any more than the police had at this point, but she couldn't sit idly by in the apartment, knowing she was probably the reason Charlotte was in the crosshairs of MMK.

Julia felt something slippery and cold stir through her soul as she did a silent inventory of her faults and the mess that she had likely created. Julia accepted the fact that she was stubborn, and driven, and relentless, when it came to finding out the truth. It was a trait that served her well as a reporter, but she had let it trickle into her personal life, putting herself, and now her friend, at risk.

"Hey, lady. You can't park there," a man in a stained white apron said.

"It's an emergency. I'll be in and out. I doubt you're going to have any deliveries this time of night, so ten or fifteen minutes is all I need. Thank you for understanding."

Julia didn't wait for the man to respond and entered the employees-only back entrance of the bar, which she quickly discovered led directly into the kitchen. Julia hurried past a sauté cook who had two plump crab cakes sizzling in a giant pan, and made it to the door to the dining room when a large hand grabbed her by the elbow.

"Excuse me, miss, but you can't be in here," a man with a heavy beard and a chef's coat said.

"Sorry. My mistake. I was just taking a shortcut," Julia said, and followed a waiter into the dining room, which appeared to be at peak Friday-night capacity. Julia pushed her way to the front, where a thirty-something man, who looked like he should be on the cover of *GQ*, was tending bar.

"Excuse me," Julia yelled through the din. "I'm looking for somebody. Have you seen this woman? Her name is Charlotte Fisher. She's in trouble."

Julia shoved her phone in front of the bartender. On the screen was a picture of Charlotte that Julia had found on her friend's florist website.

The bartender barely gave it a glance and pulled a frozen martini glass out from a cooler. He then added a shot of vodka, a splash of vermouth, and a trickle of olive juice into a cocktail shaker. He lifted the shaker up, way above his head for what looked to Julia like dramatic effect, but Julia grabbed his wrist as hard as she could and wouldn't let go.

"I'm talking to you. A woman's in trouble."

"Then call the police. They were here about an hour ago, asking the same question. The other bartender called in sick, and I've got a line twenty people deep on both sides of the bar who want a drink."

Julia reached into her wallet and handed the bartender a fifty-dollar bill. "That should buy me two minutes. Have you seen this woman here tonight? Yes or no?"

The bartender took a brief look again at the picture of Charlotte and then went back to shaking his dirty martini and slid the liquid into the frosted glass.

"Yeah, I've seen her, but not tonight. She's a regular. I think the last time I saw her was a couple of nights ago with some other chick. The woman in the picture was nice. Her friend was a bitch, a dyed peroxide blonde with fake tits. But a lot of guys around here, they like that type."

"Are you sure she wasn't here tonight?"

"I can't be positive. But usually, she hangs out at the bar. You know I forgot to mention this to the cops. Your fifty probably helped, but the other night, she was here talking to a guy. It was Tuesday, so it was slow. I like to people-watch to kill the time."

"Who was the man?"

"I don't know. I'd never seen him in here before. He was older. I'd say early or midforties. Good-looking. But that describes three-quarters of the male customers who come here. We usually get a professional crowd."

"What did he look like?"

"Pretty boy in a suit, who looked like he had a manicure. Light brown hair, maybe. I remember he was hanging at the bar before he got a table and pulled out a pager. I haven't seen one of those things since high school. I gave him shit about it, and he said he needed the pager for his job. He said something about how he'd pay more attention to his pager than a text because he'd know it was important. Your two minutes is up. Do you want a drink?"

"No. If you see the woman in the picture, call me right away. I'll double what I just paid you," Julia said, and handed the bartender one of her business cards. "It doesn't matter how late it is."

"No problem. But with all due respect, you're kind of pushy."

"I know. It's a character flaw I can't seem to get rid of. What's your name?"

"Brad. Brad Jenkins."

"All right, Brad Jenkins. You have the chance to do the right thing if you see my friend or hear anything that gives you pause. If you decide that you're too busy and don't call me, trust me, I'll find out and come back for you. And you're not going to like that. Are we clear?"

"Crystal. Jesus, you're worse than the cops."

"Thanks for the compliment. Have a nice night."

Julia left the bartender to shake another cocktail and began to methodically comb through the space, eyeing each of the tables and patrons and finished her loop by doing a sweep of the ladies' and men's rooms before she decided the bar was a dead end.

Julia exited through the kitchen again, gave a small wave to the chef, and headed to her car, where she tried Charlotte's phone one more time.

When the call went directly to voice mail, Julia returned to the apartment, parking across from Navarro's high-rise. She looked at her watch. It was ten-thirty PM and Charlotte had already been missing for two hours.

Julia took a quick look over her shoulder as she ran across the street, buzzed herself inside the glass security door, and headed to the elevators when her cell phone rang.

"Where the hell are you?" Navarro asked.

"I'm on the way back up to the apartment. The patrol officer is still there with Helen and the boys."

"I know. I just called him. He said you slipped out when he was in the bathroom. What are you doing, Julia? The killer could be following you."

"No, MMK is with Charlotte. I know he's got her, Ray, and it's my fault. I led her to him when I took her on that trail. If anything happens to Charlotte, it's on me. My judgment sucks."

"Yeah, it's sucking right now, too. Don't go anywhere else by yourself. Got it? Stay on the line with me until you get inside the apartment."

"I went to the Sugar House. The bartender said he hadn't seen Charlotte there tonight."

"I know. The chief called the county parks commissioner to track down the name and number of her friend she was supposed to meet. It took longer than I thought, because that Sophiah you told me about, isn't her real name. We were finally able to track her by the name of her son, Jared Carpenter, from the roster of Logan's basketball team you gave me. Sophiah's real name is Margaret Needleman. She lives in Palmer Woods. We gave her a call and she said she and Charlotte were supposed to meet up at a different bar, the Standby, but when she got there, Charlotte was nowhere to be found."

"I'm going to the Standby now."

"No, you aren't. Russell and I were just there. None of the staff remember seeing her. But Russell and I spoke to a customer who thinks he might've seen Charlotte standing outside the club around eight-thirty. The witness said she was alone. Russell is working to get the credit card receipts to check names, in case the killer was inside before he grabbed her."

"The bartender at the Sugar House said Charlotte was

there a few nights ago talking to a man. The bartender didn't get the man's name, but he said the man had a pager. Hardly anyone uses pagers anymore."

"A few companies still make their employees have pagers. And paramedics and physicians use them, too."

Julia slipped the key into the lock of the apartment door and let herself inside, where she saw a young, grim-faced patrol officer sitting on a chair in the hallway.

"I'm in for the night. I didn't mean to get you in trouble," Julia said to the officer.

"He lets you out of his sight again, he'll know what trouble is. Give our officer a break and get some sleep."

"You should look at Alex Tillerman. There's no guarantee the man Charlotte met at the Sugar House was him, but Tillerman is a doctor, so he might use a pager. At the very least, we need to rule him out, like you said. I'm going to call him."

"Like hell you will. Stay put, Gooden, and don't you dare move."

CHAPTER 24

The Magic Man Killer watched the pieces of dust drift slowly down like dirty snowflakes in the dim, yellow light of his grandmother's old Victorian in the Woodbridge neighborhood of Detroit. He and his grandma Leticia first moved into the house with the pink-and-brown exterior after the two fled Louisiana, because, as she said the day they packed up and left, *"Son, we better get your ass high and dry out of this town before someone finds out what you did."*

The family, his uncles and his grandma, had circled tightly, protecting the peculiar boy who had grown into a nineteen-year-old man. The family Sunoco station in Plaquemine was sold to buy the Victorian, which was a few streets away from one of Leticia's older sisters who had moved to Michigan years earlier.

The Victorian had become their landing spot in their new city. He transferred colleges, and his grandma found their new place of worship, Ste. Anne de Detroit Catholic Church. Leticia was hesitant at first to share her voodoo with her grandson, because of what he had done to the girl in Plaquemine. But being alone and without many folks who shared their common, burning-bright, beautiful practice, she eventually drew him into the circle.

And the old Victorian had become their safe haven. Still, Leticia warned, even back then, you never practiced voodoo or black magic in the place where you lived.

"Too close to home."

The killer sat on the floor in the front parlor on a worn Oriental carpet amidst the filmy yellowed covers that he had placed over the furniture when his grandmother went into the nursing home a year earlier.

He remembered when they first moved into the house, his grandma held his face in both her hands in that very spot, and told him with a look of love and repulsion, *"Family do everything for family. But whatever dark business you got in your mind, don't you be bringing it around my house, boy."*

Her words turned into a perverse daisy chain of reminders that latched one on top of the other after each of his kills. He could do his planning and research in the shed of his own house, but murder must not be done on your own soil.

It would be like not honoring the Sabbath.

The broken rhythm of two short raps from a weakened fist sounded a floor below him, and he wished the thing he stuffed in the storage container in the basement would just die so she'd stop reminding him of his failure.

His second botched masterpiece this week.

The killer reached into his grandma's china cabinet and found Leticia's secret stash. Six black candles, a Virgin Mary and St. Peter prayer card, and a pink-and-turquoise heart he had handcrafted himself as a young teenager, the little sculpture a *veve* to Erzulie that looked crude but potent in his hand. He pulled out the final item, a powerful satchel of herbs his grandma had made up for a moment such as this.

He opened the bag and the mixed aroma from the herbs wafted out, emitting a strange combination of licorice, wet bark, citrus, and a bitter medicinal smell.

He carefully plucked out the herbs he wanted and studied them in the muddy light: calamus root to grant him control and domination over Julia or anyone who got in his way; aniseed, to increase his power; lemon verbena, to cause discord between Julia and her policeman lover.

And finally vervain and wormwood, two herbs he personally selected and added to the stash after his grandmother was institutionalized, because Leticia would never have allowed it. Vervain was used to conjure up evil spirits, demons, and even Satan himself. And wormwood, the most powerful of all to him, opened the door to make a pact with the Devil.

He formed a perfect circle with the candles and lit each one, letting the match burn down until it glowed bright at his fingertips. He didn't feel the pain when the flame reached his skin. Feeling to him in an otherwise suspended state was almost like catching a glimpse of a spirit from another world.

He got to work then, burning the incense, but more important, reestablishing a semblance of order that was recently lost. All the planning, all the painstaking research he had done, hadn't paid off in the long run in his last two attempts at a perfect sacrifice.

Julia had snatched away his hunting grounds of the parks, and now the police would undoubtedly continue to search for him there, as he had personally witnessed. That's why he had to deviate from his previous playground, but the spirits had made him creative, and it flowed like semen in his blood, a seed ready to give life to the ordinary.

He looked down at the candles and picked apart the mistakes that happened with Charlotte Fisher.

It was riskier this time, but it should've gone off perfectly. He had discovered Charlotte would be at the Standby after

Sophiah plastered the change of venue on all her social media accounts, including the stupid Facebook group the vapid girls belonged to, and the dutiful Charlotte reposted the update. So he went to the blond bitch friend's house and slashed her tire while she primped inside. He needed to be sure Charlotte would be alone.

He had scouted out the alley where he left the car ahead of time and arrived at the bar with just a few minutes to spare. It had to be a fast in and out. He couldn't risk being in the place long enough for anyone to notice, but the few minutes gave him enough time to be sure no familiar faces were inside. And as soon as he walked out, he had found her waiting outside, all alone and vulnerable. His new plan wasn't without risks. But it worked perfectly, and there was a certain thrill, almost a sexual satisfaction, of knowing he might get caught.

And then Charlotte acquiesced so easily, just like he knew she would.

The girl he had been stalking for weeks had absolutely no backbone.

The killer blew out the first candle and chanted a prayer offering to Erzulie. He knew the next part was going to be hard. It always was. But he knew rewards didn't come without pain.

He pulled out the green-and-black knife from his pocket, the one he had planned to use on Charlotte. But he had to abort his mission with her when he saw a cop car parked in front of the abandoned church, St. Ruth Holy Science Temple, in Hyde Park, the spot where he was going to work on Charlotte. He had taken a slow and steady right turn in his wife's sedan before he reached the church, so as not to draw attention to himself, and kept his eyes steady ahead on the road as he tried to figure out what to do now that his perfect plan had been completely upended.

So he had found himself here, where it all had started for him in Detroit. He had parked his wife's car in the garage that connected to the Victorian.

It all should've been so easy from there.

He had made Charlotte put on the dress and the silky black wig, and she didn't even fuss that much when he began to dance with her in front of his grandma's fireplace. But then his grandma's words had come back as if she were standing right in front of him, her spirit wagging a judgmental, disapproving finger in front of his face.

"Don't you be bringing it around my house, boy."

He was too close to home.

So he locked Charlotte into a musty old storage container that had been filled with sour-smelling clothes, batches of yellowed and curling photographs, and old copies of the *Times-Picayune* his grandma held on to from the Wednesday cooking section of the paper.

He took the tip of his knife then, stared deeply into the five remaining candles that burned on the floor, and jammed the blade into the center of his right palm. He heard a guttural moan come out of his chest as the pain registered, but then he fixed his concentration on the three drops of blood that oozed out of his fresh, throbbing cut. He held his hand out, palm down over the flames, as his blood dripped into the fire.

His crucifixion, his stigmata, his sacrifice, his practice for the final scene. All for clarity, and to receive a sign to show him what he should do next.

Another weak *tap, tap, tap* sounded from the basement, where the thing in the container was trying to make her presence known. But besides the spirits, it was just the two of them alone in the house. And he surely wasn't going to let Charlotte Fisher out until he got a sign of what he was supposed to do with her.

He closed his eyes and waited for the images to come, the bright spots of light, to flash in his head like exploding camera bulbs in a pitch-black room. For a second, he thought he saw a boy coming in and out of the folds of darkness. The boy was angry and shaking his fist as a warning. The child had dark eyes and a red shirt. The boy stared back at him, looking intense and powerful for a child that size. Before the boy disappeared, the killer thought he looked like Julia Gooden's son Logan.

He had taken care of the Ben boy, Julia's dead brother, with the mojo bag he had left on his gravestone. Regardless, no child's spirit, whether diluted or not, could be a match for him.

He closed his eyes tighter and saw the image of his first kill next. She was floating like a bloated white corpse in the bayou in Iberville Parish, where his uncles had dropped her with a large rock anchored around her waist with a rope.

He kept going, further down into the tunnel of his subconscious, a place that terrified but enthralled him, until he saw what was at the bottom.

What he was supposed to do next.

And there she was, Julia Gooden, in the blue dress, smiling at him, beckoning him to come down and join her.

Julia would be his next kill.

Sometimes the problems that seemed the hardest were actually the easiest to solve. People just made things difficult.

Despite his upended beautiful plans, sacrificing the woman in the basement at this point would pollute all that he had done. She was no longer pure.

He would just leave the thing in the container until she ran out of air.

From inside his duffel bag, the Magic Man Killer grabbed a piece of white gauze and wrapped a long strip of it around his self-inflicted wound. It throbbed and ached, but ultimately made him feel alive.

He grabbed the keys to his wife's car and turned off the light.

Julia Gooden was waiting for him.

CHAPTER 25

Julia woke with a start, still in her clothes from the night before. She found herself on the edge of the bed in the sterile master bedroom of the temporary apartment. Both of Will's knees were jammed against her back, and Logan was lying lengthwise across the mattress, with his pillow wedged against her feet at the bottom of the bed.

She walked softly out of the bedroom, but then beat a fast path down the hallway to the kitchen, where Navarro sat at a tall round table with a cup of coffee in front of him.

"I can't believe I fell asleep. Please tell me you have something," Julia said.

"We haven't found Charlotte yet. But one of our units found her purse in an alleyway a couple blocks off Library Street."

"If something happens to her, Ray, it's because of me."

"Don't start thinking the worst yet. Washington has our patrol guys doing a sweep of all the abandoned churches in the city, and her body hasn't been recovered."

"Maybe he's keeping her this time. He's changing his pattern because he almost got caught in Royal Oak. The killer knows Charlotte's routine and found out she was going to be at the bar last night, so he scoops her up there and plans to sacrifice her at a church he preselected, but when he gets there, he gets spooked because he sees a cop car," Julia said. "What did you find on Alex Tillerman?"

"One domestic battery arrest, but his soon-to-be ex-wife dropped the charges. Otherwise, he's clean. It looks like he spent a few years living down in Florida. We stopped by his house, but no one was there. The hospital said he's off today. He's worth questioning and I may need your help."

"Tillerman told me he's staying at a hotel. I can find him."

"Not without me there. I want you to stay put today. Russell and I are heading over to talk to Sophiah, or Margaret, or whatever she wants to call herself, and Prejean is going to tag along. I'll wait until the officer on the first shift shows up before I leave. After we meet up with Sophiah, depending on where that takes us, I want you to call Tillerman."

"What's Sophiah's address?"

"Not a chance."

"I'm not going to be waiting inside this apartment if there's even a remote possibility Charlotte is still alive. No cop is going to keep me in here. They can keep watch over Helen and the boys. And if you're worried about my safety, I'll be with you. Come on, Ray. If I have to beg, I will. Washington agreed I could be embedded in the investigation, as long as I fed her what I got from the killer."

Navarro sighed in frustration. "The address is 523 Gloucester Drive. She lives in Palmer Woods. At least I'll be able to keep my eye on you there."

Margaret, aka Sophiah with a silent *h* at the end, Needleman's house was a modest Tudor-style home complete with a cream-colored Cadillac Escalade parked in the driveway, with a brand-new tire on its left back wheel.

Julia pulled behind Navarro's Tahoe as Prejean, who was in the passenger seat, reached for her hand.

"This isn't your fault. I was with the Detroit cops in the park the entire morning yesterday. Unless the killer's a complete idiot, which I don't believe he is, he wouldn't go back to a place where he almost got caught. Which means he had his eye on Charlotte long before you took her running in Royal Oak."

"Then he knows Charlotte through me some other way," Julia said.

"Maybe. You know Charlotte, but you didn't know the other three women, April Young, Heather Burns, and Christy King."

"There's a common denominator that connects us. It's right there in front of me, but I can't see it."

Julia and Prejean caught up to Russell and Navarro, who were hovering around the Escalade in the driveway. Russell bent over to inspect the tire and then put his hand on the hood of the vehicle.

"The engine's still warm. Unless she went out for an early-morning coffee, Ms. Needleman just got home for the night."

Navarro led the group to the house and rapped hard with his knuckles three times on the front door as the sound of a small dog yipping frenetically echoed inside.

Sophiah opened up, wearing a full face of makeup, a pair of high heels, and a low-cut, loose-fitting dress that fell a few inches above her knees. She held the terrier Julia had previously seen housed in her purse. The dog let out a squeaky territorial growl from its throat when it saw the strangers on the front porch.

"Are you Margaret Needleman?" Navarro asked.

She gave Navarro and Prejean a quick once-over, but then her eyes turned into slits when she saw Julia.

"I go by Sophiah. What's going on here?"

"We spoke on the phone last night. We need to ask you a few more questions about your friend Charlotte Fisher," Navarro said.

"She hasn't shown up yet? Maybe Charlotte met somebody. I don't see what the big deal is."

"The big deal is that she was likely picked up by a killer," Prejean said.

"Are you serious? If you're cops, why is that woman from the basketball team here?" Sophiah asked, and pointed a long, manicured finger in Julia's direction.

"Julia's a reporter and she's been covering stories about a recent series of killings in the city. All the victims were female runners. The killer has been in contact with Julia," Navarro said. "May we come in?"

"You really think Charlotte is in trouble?"

"She may already be dead," Julia said. "We're running out of time, so you need to let us in. Now."

"Okay, okay. I just need to let Khloe out back. She's been cooped up in the house all night," Sophiah answered.

Sophiah led the group to a living room. It was decorated with white leather furniture and a giant framed photograph that held prime real estate in the center of the main wall. The picture was a shot of the backside of a long-haired blond woman's legs and torso in a short black dress.

"Is that you?" Russell asked.

"Yes. Dustin Murphy took the picture. He's a celebrity photographer and takes pictures of all the 'who's who' in Detroit. It cost me a thousand dollars for the shots, but it was so worth it. Do you gentlemen like it?" Sophiah asked the male cops.

"Are you serious? Charlotte is missing and you're honestly fishing for compliments right now?" Julia said.

"Julia's worried about her friend, as I'm sure you are, too," Navarro answered, trying not to inflame the situation so Sophiah wouldn't clam up. "Who knew about your plans with Charlotte last night?"

"Well, anyone who follows me on social media." Sophiah let her dog out the back door and then took a seat in the center of the leather couch. "Charlotte and I belong to a Facebook group. It's called 'Motor City Mommies.' It's a select group of single women with kids. We share information about the best bars and restaurants, cosmetic dermatologists, nail and hair salons, anything that's important. I got invited to join the group a year ago and Charlotte piggybacked on after me. The group just voted the Standby as the city's best new bar. I saw it and called Charlotte. We agreed to meet there instead of the Sugar House. I posted on my Instagram and Facebook accounts that Charlotte and I were going to be there last night at eight-thirty. I also posted it on the moms' Facebook page, too. Sometimes other women from the Facebook group show up. It's a good way to meet like-minded females with the same ideals. But no one else confirmed that they'd join us. So it was just going to be Charlotte and me."

"Is this Facebook group public?" Prejean asked.

"It's not private. Anyone can see the posts. I know that as a fact because one time, a couple girls showed up who hadn't been officially invited to join. It was awkward to say the least."

"So you were set to meet Charlotte last night, but out of the blue, your tire suddenly goes flat?" Julia asked.

"Yes. I don't know what you're implying, but that's exactly what happened. I left the basketball game and dropped Jared off at a friend's house, where he was going to have a sleepover. I came back home to change, and when I went back out to my car, the tire was flat. So I called AAA."

"Do you still have the tire?" Russell asked.

"It's in my garage."

"What time did you notice the tire was flat?" Navarro asked.

"I left the house at eight-thirty, the time I was supposed to meet Charlotte, but you never want to be right on time for something like that. It was dark, and I didn't see the tire at first, but when I tried to back out of the driveway, I heard this terrible thumping sound. I got out and saw the tire was flat. I was pissed because I thought it was going to ruin my night."

Navarro gave a subtle nod in the direction of Russell and Prejean.

"You mind if we have a look at the tire?" Russell asked.

"If you want to waste your time, feel free. My garage is open. Like I said, AAA came and fixed it, so I didn't get to the Standby until around nine-thirty. Charlotte wasn't there, so I thought she took off, but then I ran into some other friends at the bar, so it wasn't a total loss. We went to a few after-parties. I just got home," Sophiah said, and gave Navarro a smile as if that was something to be proud of.

"Did Charlotte mention anyone who might have been bothering her, or someone who asked her out recently? Maybe a man she met during one of your bar runs?" Navarro asked.

"They aren't bar runs. We're socially active. There's a big difference."

"Charlotte met someone, a man, a few nights ago at the Sugar House. Were you with her?"

"I was there. Sure. He was good-looking. Light brown hair, well dressed, and really intense."

"Did you get a name?"

"I can't remember. But he did mention he's a doctor."

Julia shot Navarro a quick glance of shared recognition. "Did he say anything about living in Florida?"

"Now that you mention it, yes. I think he said he used to live in Miami. He said he works at Harper University Hospital now. He seemed interested in Charlotte, but I don't know why she didn't jump on him. She told me later she thought she saw him take his wedding ring off when we first got there. Charlotte won't date married guys. I think that's admirable. If anything happened to her, it would just break my heart. She is so amazing," Sophiah answered, stringing out the last word.

"Was the man's name Alex Tillerman?" Navarro asked.

"It could've been. Honestly, when he seemed more interested in Charlotte, I stopped paying attention. I mean, his time wouldn't be worth my while. When you socialize as much as I do, you have to prioritize."

Julia grabbed her phone from her bag and punched Tillerman's name into Safari. The first hit was his bio page from the hospital, including his headshot.

"Is this the man you saw talking to Charlotte?" Julia asked.

"Yes. That's him. I'm sure of it. I remember the cleft in his chin. A good-looking doctor like that must make well into the six figures. Married or not married, Charlotte should've pounced."

Russell came back inside and hooked a finger at Navarro and Julia.

"Thank you for your time, Ms. Needleman. If you think of anything else, please give me a call," Navarro said, and handed Sophiah his card.

"I hope Charlotte's okay. I really do," Sophiah said. "We had plans tonight."

Russell led the way out of the house and to a path that

took them to an open side door of Sophiah's garage, where Prejean was bent down next to a tire that was leaning up against a concrete wall.

"The tire was slashed deliberately. It's as flat as a pancake, and the cut isn't on the tread," Prejean said, and pointed his index finger to the inside top wall of the tire. "There's a two-inch clean slice there. Someone wanted to be sure Charlotte was alone at the bar last night."

Prejean stood up to his full height and brushed the dirt from the garage floor off his hands.

"You're going to want to bring your crime scene guys down here to see if you can lift a print from the tire or the car, and you should canvass the street to see if any neighbors saw a suspicious person or vehicle hanging around last night," Prejean said.

"I've already got that covered. And we'll send Christy King a picture of Alex Tillerman to see if she can identify him," Navarro said.

"Alex Tillerman?" Prejean asked. "The guy I ran off in New Orleans who was bothering Julia?"

"Right, Julia's old boyfriend. He was popped once on a domestic, but the charge was dropped, and he met Charlotte at a bar two nights ago. He's looking good for this. Russell, make a call and see if any of the bar receipts from the Standby you pulled had Tillerman's name on them," Navarro said, and then turned to Julia. "Gooden, I don't want to risk having Tillerman make a run for it if he knows we're onto him. If he's still got Charlotte, we need to find him fast. I need you to call him and set up a time to meet. We'll be in a public space. Are you okay with that?"

"You're going to hang Julia out to try and grab Tillerman? I don't like it. Julia told me Tillerman used to have a drug problem," Prejean said.

"I'd never let anything happen to Julia. And we don't have

the time to wait around. Washington would agree. I'll brief her, but she already liked the idea of Julia baiting Tillerman when we suspected Charlotte might have run into him a few nights ago. Now we've got confirmation. Are you still good with this, Julia?"

"Tell me when and where. I'm ready to set a trap. One of the things about Tillerman that's not adding up to me, though, is the voodoo-occult angle," Julia said.

"Maybe he got into it after you broke up," Russell suggested. "We're looking for a connection between you and these women, and right now, this is a clear path."

"I want you to call Tillerman from my car. Put the call on speaker and tell him you'll meet at the Great Lakes coffeehouse on Woodward in thirty minutes," Navarro said. "I know the owner. He won't be happy missing the early-morning crowd, but we'll clear the place out and it will just be me, Russell, and Prejean posing as customers. I'll call Washington and suggest putting a couple other cops in the coffee shop, in case he tries to run. You sure you're okay with this?"

"Let's make the call," Julia said.

Navarro called Washington for the green light. After he explained the plan, he listened on the line and responded, "Are you sure, Chief? Yeah, send me the pictures."

Navarro hung up and addressed the group. "Washington did some more digging into Tillerman. Apparently, the domestic against his wife wasn't his first encounter with his beating up women. He had an incident in Miami with a nurse who was his girlfriend at the time. Same thing. He beat her up, but the girlfriend wouldn't press charges. The Miami cops told Washington the doctor got run out of the hospital down there, even though he wasn't charged, because of bad PR. One more thing. Washington saw the pictures of both the women in the initial reports. They both have dark hair and blue eyes."

"Tillerman's got a type," Prejean said. "From what Julia told me, he sounded like a sociopath, but why would Tillerman surface after so many years?"

"Maybe he thought Julia was the perfect girl who got away. His ex-wife and his girlfriend, who he beat on, look like Julia, and he's dressing up his victims now to look like her, too," Navarro said. "It's go time, Gooden."

Navarro got in the back of his Tahoe with Julia, and Prejean and Russell took the seats up front. "I'm going to put this on speaker. Russell and Prejean, not a word."

Julia listened to the phone ring and tried to create a script in her head of what she planned to say when Tillerman answered.

"This is Alex."

"It's Julia, Julia Gooden. I got your flowers," Julia answered, trying her best to sound engaged and actually happy to talk to him.

"I can't believe it. The one and only Julia Marie Gooden. I'm not trying to feed you a line, beautiful, but I never forgot about you."

Julia felt her cheeks get hot at the sound of Tillerman's voice, and his use of Navarro's personal term of endearment repulsed her and treaded on sacred ground. Navarro, sensing her discomfort, put his hand on Julia's shoulder and nodded his head, letting her know she was okay and needed to continue with the call.

"I hope you didn't take the flowers I sent you as being too forward. I've just been thinking about you nonstop since I saw you in the restaurant. You shouldn't make a man wait for you to call him. You were always a tease, Julia."

"How about we get together for coffee like you suggested. I'm pretty busy, but I could meet you this morning."

"I'm out right now looking at apartments, and I have to go back to the hospital. Why don't we meet for drinks tonight? How about we meet at the Sugar House, say, around seven-thirty? I want to hit the gym after work. I do triathlon training now. You know, I came in first at a recent meet. Not to brag, but I beat out guys who were half my age."

Julia made a fake gun with her thumb and forefinger, put it against her temple and pretended to pull the trigger.

"I can meet you in thirty minutes at Great Lakes Coffee on Woodward. Come on, Alex. Don't make me wait all day to see you. I've been thinking about you, too," Julia said, and rolled her eyes in disgust over her suggestion.

"Forceful little Julia Gooden. What a turn on. You know, you were pretty cold not letting me see you in New Orleans. Maybe you could make it up to me."

"Where are you staying?" Julia asked, knowing the police would want to search Tillerman's room, and she realized she was right when Navarro gave her a thumbs-up.

"The Marriott downtown. Room 323. What are you suggesting, Julia?"

"Just coffee for now. We'll see how it goes."

"You've been a very bad girl. You might need to be punished," Alex said. "Do you just want to meet at my hotel? From our conversation, I think that's what you really want."

"Thirty minutes and I'll meet you at the Great Lakes Coffee shop. Don't be late. I promise, you're never going to forget this day for the rest of your life."

Julia ended the call and then gave her cell phone the finger.

"You did good, Julia," Navarro said. "If Tillerman has Charlotte, we're going to find her."

"And then I'm going to beat the crap out of him," Prejean said.

CHAPTER 26

Julia sat at a table for two in the back of Great Lakes Coffee Roasting Company, a popular coffee shop located in a 130-year-old building on the corner of Woodward and Alexandrine in Midtown. The place had an open floor plan and distressed brick walls, environmentally conscious reclaimed wood from demolished homes in Hamtramck, and bookend chalkboards listing the latest coffee specials between shelves of wine and beer for the evening crowd.

Julia's carefully orchestrated position faced the street, with half a dozen cops who would run interference strategically placed between her and the door.

Julia wanted to get her encounter over as quickly as possible, but she also knew she had to play her role and not let emotions get the best of her if Tillerman was the killer. And especially if there was a slim chance Charlotte was still alive.

"Hey, Gooden. Don't beat this guy up before we get him in for questioning," Russell said. He was planted in a seat at the bar and gave Julia a big wink when she looked his way.

"I promise I'll be on my best behavior."

"We're all set, Julia," Washington said as she approached with Navarro. "Just so we're clear, you're still fine with this setup?"

"Thanks for asking, but I'm ready."

"That's the answer I want to hear. Calm and cool should be your mantra," Washington said. "I have a unit out on the street if Tillerman tries to run. But you need to check your worry about Charlotte and whatever past business you had with Tillerman if this is going to work. Tillerman has a history of domestic violence and we can't rule out that he's armed. I don't want to endanger my men, or you, if you can't keep your cool."

"I can handle this, Beth. Where's Prejean?"

"He wanted to help out canvassing the churches," Navarro answered. "That was his preference."

"It's better he's there, looking for Charlotte," Julia answered. "Beth, I want to be sure we still have a deal. I'm embedded one hundred percent in this case with the department, right? I'm hanging myself out for you. When you bring Tillerman in for questioning, I want to be there."

"No go, Gooden," Washington said. "You don't get to watch the interview."

"What if I refuse to meet Tillerman then? It seems to me I'm your bait with him and MMK, so I shouldn't have to bargain just to get access to the case."

"You wouldn't do that. Like the chief said, keep your emotions in check," Navarro interjected. "You need to be engaging when you first see Tillerman. We don't want him to suspect something's up and then he tries to run. I'll be sitting at a table in front. Don't make eye contact with me or any of the other officers. Once Tillerman walks in, smile, but stay seated. I don't want him to try to grab you when we make our move."

LaBeau, who was standing next to the front glass window

pretending to drink a coffee and looking at his phone, called out discreetly to Washington.

"Tillerman just parked across the street. He's getting out of his car now."

Navarro leaned in and whispered in Julia's ear, "I've got you."

Julia sat up as straight as she could in her chair and watched the entrance until the possessive man she had once dated, who'd possibly graduated to killing at least two women, strode into the coffee shop. Tillerman wore a pair of sunglasses, and took them off for dramatic effect when he spotted Julia.

"Julia Gooden," Tillerman said. He spread his arms out to embrace Julia, but when she stayed seated, he lifted up her hand and gave it a kiss. "Aren't you coy, but still lovely."

"It's good to see you, Alex."

"Are you sure you want to stay here? We could just go back to my hotel room and order room service. I think that's what you really want to do. Tell me, Julia. Tell me what I want to hear."

Julia forced herself to smile back as she saw Navarro move fluidly in their direction out of the corner of her eye.

She kept her focus on Tillerman as he edged in close, invading her space. He then spoke softly so no one could hear.

"You have a lot of making up for what you did to me in New Orleans, but I think you know that. You called me back, so I know you want it. But you're going to need to tell me you're sorry first. I want to hear it. Say you're sorry, Julia."

"Sure, I'll tell you whatever you want to hear," Julia said, and beckoned Tillerman closer as if she was going to whisper in his ear. "I'm sorry for nothing, asshole. Where's Charlotte?"

Tillerman had just enough time for an expression of surprise to register on his face when Navarro was on him. Navarro grabbed Tillerman's right arm with one hand and the back of Tillerman's hand with the other and easily slammed Tillerman against a brick wall. Tillerman, now prone and angry, like a vicious little dog being overpowered and emasculated by a mastiff, seethed as he tried to break free.

"What the hell is this?" Tillerman asked as Navarro started to frisk him.

"He's armed," Navarro said, and pulled a small handgun out of the rear waistband of Tillerman's pants.

The side of Tillerman's face was pushed up against the brick wall in Julia's direction, and she witnessed something dark and hateful pass across his eyes as they narrowed in focus on her. "You did this. Nobody embarrasses me. Nobody."

"Shut up. You say one more word, your head is going through the brick wall," Navarro said.

"I'm calling the cops," Tillerman said.

"We are the cops," Navarro answered.

Navarro snapped a pair of handcuffs over Tillerman's wrists as Russell, LaBeau, and Washington circled the suspect.

"I hear you like to rough up women. I have a problem with that. A big problem," Navarro said. "All I can say is that you're in a world of trouble."

CHAPTER 27

Navarro watched the suspect pace back and forth in short, angry steps in the precinct interview room as he studied Tillerman through the two-way mirror.

Navarro fixed his thoughts on the half-dozen photographs he had seen of Tillerman's estranged wife and ex-girlfriend, chronicled evidence of the vicious beatings Tillerman gave to the women. The pictures the Miami PD had shared included images of the doctor's former girlfriend with a black eye and a dislocated jaw—punishment she said Tillerman had inflicted on her because he thought she was cheating on him. The estranged wife's photos were just as bad. The woman had sustained severe lacerations on her face from a glass Tillerman had thrown at her and a deep purple bruise on her collarbone, where Tillerman had pressed his thumb down and left it there as he backed her against the wall and demanded to know why she had come home an hour late from work.

Navarro burned the images of the women in his head. What Tillerman had done to them would fuel him and help keep his edge when he grilled Tillerman in the box.

Tillerman sat down hard in the chair and sneered in Navarro's direction, the doctor having been arrested enough times to likely know he was being watched. Navarro studied Tillerman repeatedly clenching and unclenching his fists, and Navarro felt his own anger building inside him.

A weak man who abused women and took sadistic pleasure in belittling them through words or fists was the lowest form of life to Navarro. Not to mention the fact that the asshole stewing in the next room had once been overly possessive of his Julia, who had the smarts at a young age to leave Tillerman before things undoubtedly would've escalated.

Navarro didn't think holding on to anger was necessarily a bad thing when he interviewed a subject, as long as he could contain it and not go too far. He flashed to the look of humiliation on the women's faces in the photos. Part of Navarro wanted to throw Tillerman against the wall and beat him until he was nothing but pulp and bone, leaving Tillerman the one who was terrified and suffering this time.

But he knew a dark desire like that could be a dangerous and seductive drug. If acted on, it could turn him into a person like the monster he was trying to take down.

"I think it's safe to say Tillerman has some anger issues," Washington said as she entered the room with Russell.

"Is he on something? Even sitting, Tillerman can't keep still," Navarro said.

Tillerman's feet beat the floor in a rapid pace and his now-splayed fingers tapped incessantly on the interview table in front of him.

"Patrick and Villanova just got back from the Marriott. Our fine officers found a virtual pharmacy in Tillerman's hotel room," Russell said.

"Judge Palmer did us a huge favor and fast-tracked a no-knock warrant to search Tillerman's room. Tillerman has a permit for the gun, but even if we don't have enough right now to pin him for Charlotte and the two murdered joggers, not to mention an attempted murder and abduction charge for Christy King, we can hold him for drug possession."

"Patrick and Villanova found a couple of grams of cocaine and some Ecstasy inside a toothbrush travel holder, along with enough Percocet to kill an elephant in his toiletry bag," Russell said. "I wish I had one more present for you, but I went through the Standby's receipts again from last night, and there weren't any charges from Tillerman. I sent a photo of Tillerman to the waitresses and bartender who were working. One girl thought she might have seen him, but she said she couldn't be sure because the place was packed. And if it was him, he didn't stick around very long."

"Did you check to see if the Marriott had tapes of Tillerman coming and going last night?" Navarro asked.

"Patrick and Villanova are watching the tapes now," Russell said.

"All right. I want you to go in there with shock and awe, I just got an update on the crew doing the surveillance on the churches, and there's still no sign of Charlotte Fisher. Tillerman's a doctor and obviously smart. I don't want him to lawyer up, so hit him with the fact that we know he was with Charlotte a few days ago at the other bar," Washington said.

"No problem. We've got this covered, Chief," Navarro said.

Navarro and Russell entered the interview room, with Russell taking a seat directly across from Tillerman. Ray remained standing on purpose, to show a position of dominance.

"This is an outrage, an absolute insult," Tillerman said. He started to stand up, but Navarro put a hand on his shoulder and pushed him back down in his seat. "Get your hands off me. Do you have any idea who I am?"

"An asshole?" Russell asked.

"I'm a physician. Is that too much for your tiny cop brains to comprehend? I get it. Julia knows you from her beat and she set me up. That bitch. She's going to pay for this."

"Let me make myself clear. If you threaten Julia, I'll personally make sure you'll never walk again," Navarro said.

"So, Alex Tillerman, M.D., we already know you're no choirboy. You've been arrested twice for domestic assault, and we found your drug stash in your room," Russell said. "Your head is sweatier than a fat guy who decided to take up jogging, and the way you're moving, I'm guessing you did a couple of lines of coke before your meet-up with Julia this morning."

"I'm going to sue your ass. You searched my room illegally."

"We got a no-knock warrant," Navarro said.

"The search of your room was completely by the book. We have a witness who can place you at the Standby last night," Russell bluffed. "Where's Charlotte Fisher?"

"Who's Charlotte Fisher? What the hell are you talking about?"

"We have multiple people who saw you with Charlotte three nights ago at the Sugar House. You met her, she fit your type, and you picked her up last night outside the Standby. Did you kill her the same way you murdered April Young and Heather Burns?" Navarro asked. "Things aren't looking good for you, Tillerman. We've got two dead women and one missing who was seen with you, not to mention the bookseller you stalked and then tried to pick up in Royal Oak. I have a question I've been trying to figure out. Why do you dress the women up to look like Julia? Was she the one who got away and needed to be punished?"

Tillerman swatted away a drop of sweat from his forehead and retracted back from the table. "I don't know what kind of lies Julia fed you about me to try and jam me up with whatever happened to these women, but I don't know what you're talking about. I'm innocent."

Navarro pulled a picture of Charlotte out from a manila envelope tucked underneath his arm and pushed it across the table in front of Tillerman. "Don't bother trying to tell me you don't know her."

Tillerman studied the picture and then steepled his fingers together and pressed them to his lips. "Okay, I saw her. She was cute. I talked to her at the bar of the Sugar House a couple nights ago. That was it. I was going to buy her a drink, but I could tell she wanted me to chase after her, and that's not something I do. She went back to her table with her friends, and I didn't follow her. I don't run after women, and she was maybe a seven on a scale of one to ten. Small up top, so she lost points for that. Don't look at me that way," Tillerman told Navarro. "You're a man. You can't tell me you don't do the exact same thing. We all do. I left and went to another bar. I never saw that girl again."

"Where were you at eight-thirty last night?" Navarro asked.

"I have a question for you. Why is that bitch Julia trying to connect me to this? She should be the one in here for giving false information to the police, not me."

"Last warning. You call Julia that word one more time, and your face is going through the window. Do we have an understanding? You think I was rough on you before in the coffee shop, but that was me playing nice," Navarro said.

"All right," Tillerman said as he backed down. "I was at the Standby last night, but only for a few minutes. I was there maybe around seven-thirty or eight. I'd need to check my phone. I was planning to hang at the Standby for a while, but I got a text from a woman I met the night before. I met her back at the Sugar House and then we went to my hotel room. She was there all night until three. I never let the sluts stay over until morning."

"I need the name and number of the woman you were with last night," Navarro said, and shoved a notebook and pen across the table to Tillerman.

"If you're trying to pin me for the murders of those women, call the hospital where I work. Anthony Dejardin is the hospital administrator. He'll tell you when I was working."

"I'm sure old Anthony can't wait for us to call him. Another public relations nightmare for a hospital that made the mistake of having a drugged-up woman beater and killer on its payroll," Russell said.

"I didn't kill anybody. Those are lies Julia made up. I don't know why she's doing this to me."

"If all your convenient alibis work out, explain this. Why were you at the coffee shop this morning with a gun?" Navarro asked. "Did you plan on using it on Julia? Maybe you wanted to beat her, like your other women, for walking away and embarrassing you when she dumped you and then didn't respond quick enough to your overtures when you saw her again. You don't seem like the type of guy who takes rejection well. I saw the photos of how you roughed up your wife and ex-girlfriend."

"Those were lies told by hysterical women who came to their senses. If you talked to the cops in Miami, they already told you that my ex-girlfriend dropped the charges. Same thing with the cops in Wyandotte, where I used to live. My ex-wife rescinded her bogus accusations against me, too. There was no case and no threat to my physician's license, and you better not turn this into an issue for me now. I carry a gun because Detroit is a crime-infested shithole. If you knew how to do your job, I wouldn't need a weapon."

"Since you hate Detroit so much, let me do you a favor. I'll make a call to your employer to let them know you're high on something right now," Navarro said. "I'm also guessing Harper University Hospital doesn't know about your previous arrests."

"I wasn't convicted, and those charges were dropped," Tillerman said. "Those were witch hunts, just like this is. You make an issue with my employer, I'll see you in court."

"Why did you want to meet Julia?" Russell asked. "Were you hoping you two would hook up?"

"Sure. That's not a crime. I'm newly single. And I wanted her to apologize for what she did to me. She's the only woman who ever got away with treating me like a dog. I saw her in the restaurant. She looked good and wasn't wearing a ring anymore, so I wanted to score. Plus she treated me like shit, so I was going to make her pay for it in the bedroom. I wasn't looking for a relationship. I'd screw her blue, enjoy some rough sex, and then I'd tell her to get the hell out. That's all I wanted. That bitch is going to regret this."

"Last chance. You say one more word about Julia, you're going to be the one who's in regret," Navarro said.

Tillerman studied Navarro and then nodded his head as if he finally understood.

"Ah, I get it. You and Julia have a thing going. Nice," he said, and then banged his fists together like he was simulating two people having sex. "Does she still do that thing with her tongue? You can thank me. I taught her that."

"That's it," Navarro said. He lunged at Tillerman and yanked him up by the collar from his chair.

"Easy, Ray," Russell said. "Are you always such an idiot, Tillerman, or is it just the drugs?"

Washington entered the room, and with just one powerful movement of her finger, she made Navarro drop Tillerman back down to his chair.

"I'm sorry, Chief," Navarro said. "I didn't mean to lose my cool."

"Navarro, Russell, come with me," Washington said, and led the two officers into the hallway.

"Patrick and Villanova just got through looking at the video security footage from the Marriott. Right now, it looks like Tillerman's story is checking out. He was on the tape leaving the hotel lobby at seven PM, and then again later entering the hotel and going up in an elevator with a woman who wasn't Charlotte at eight forty-five last night. The woman was seen again on the tape, leaving the hotel at around three-fifteen AM, and then Tillerman isn't seen again on the footage until nine AM when he left the hotel this morning."

"We still need to check his alibis for the April Young and Heather Burns murders," Navarro said.

"Already done. Corporal Smith just got off the phone with Harper University Hospital. The administrator confirmed Tillerman was working on both those mornings when the female joggers were picked up," Washington said. "Apparently, Julia called the hospital right before we did and got the same information. I don't want her to get ahead of us on the investigation, Ray. If she tips someone off before we can get to them and they clam up, that could hurt the case."

"I understand. And Julia realizes that. She wouldn't do anything to jeopardize the investigation. Since you wouldn't let her be part of the interview, knowing Julia, she probably wanted to keep searching for the suspect if she ruled out Tillerman. I can talk to her, but I can't tell Julia what to do," Navarro said.

"All right. We can hold Tillerman on the drugs, but we can't charge him for being a misogynist ass," Washington said.

"I want to jam him up on the drug charges then. It would be his first drug possession conviction, so the judge would likely suspend his sentence to probation. But a couple of nights in the Detroit Detention Center might make him think twice about hitting a woman again," Navarro said. "We've still got nothing on Charlotte."

"We look back at the case and we figure out how all those women are connected to Julia. Now go break the news to your little friend," Washington said, and motioned toward the two-way mirror and Tillerman.

"I want a lawyer. Now," Tillerman said to Navarro and Russell as they went in for round two.

"Your choice. We're still verifying your alibis. But you've got a problem that's not going away. We found drugs in your hotel room. The Ecstasy alone will cost you up to ten years in jail and a fifteen-thousand-dollar fine," Navarro said.

"Those drugs weren't mine. I was holding them for a friend, the girl I was with last night."

"You may have a medical degree, but you're not smart. I can't tell you how many low-life druggies have fed me that line," Navarro said. He got up from his chair to leave, but turned back around at the last minute to face Tillerman. "You should've listened to Doug Prejean and never bothered Julia again when he confronted you in New Orleans."

"Who the hell is Doug Prejean?" Tillerman asked.

"Don't play dumb with me. Prejean is the NOLA cop who met you at the airport when you tried to harass Julia after you tracked her down in New Orleans. Prejean said he scared you straight. If that didn't stop you, this better. I'm going to be watching you from here on out. If you bother Julia or any other woman ever again, you're going to have to deal with me."

"I'm freakin' shaking in my shoes right now," Tillerman said, trying to feign bravado, but he scooted his chair back a few inches away from Navarro. "I don't know who this Prejean person is, but you better check your sources. I was going to fly down to see Julia, but I never got on the plane. I called Julia and told her about my plan, but then I got a message from her telling me if I showed up, she'd call the cops. I knew Julia was covering the crime beat, and she said in her message that she told a police friend I was harassing her. Let me make myself clear. I never hit Julia. Not once. I thought about it, but I never did. I didn't want to deal with any police problems, because I'm a doctor, so I never got on the plane. That Prejean person, he lied to you."

CHAPTER 28

Julia entered the Wayne County parks-and-rec gym on Grandville Avenue, the place where she was to meet Charlotte's ex-husband, Joe Perkins.

The clipped sound of Julia's heels against the cement floor echoed down the long, empty hallway. She passed by the table still decorated with orange balloons and flyers announcing the opportunities for early junior rec tryouts in exchange for a wad of cash, and heard the thump of a single basketball hitting the hardwood floor of the court as she neared the gym.

"Hey, Julia."

She turned to see the ref, Jeremiah Landry, walking in her direction. "What are you doing here? There aren't any scheduled games today, just open gym. Is Logan going to play? I'm here to pick up my paycheck, but I can stick around if you'd like me to work with him. Your boy's got talent."

"Thanks for the offer, but I'm solo this time. I'm here to talk to a parent," Julia said. She kept her poker face intact, since the Detroit PD had pressed her not to reveal anything about Charlotte's disappearance.

"Is it Steven's dad? He's in the gym. Steven's shooting around. Usually, it's only his mom here. The dad shows up once in a while for games. I was glad to see him with his son. That kid lights up when his father is around."

"I was in the area and Logan had something of Steven's he needed to return, so I told Mr. Perkins I'd drop it off," Julia lied.

"I'm glad I had the chance to run into you again. I just swung by to clean out my locker and get my last check. I got a student teacher job at Davison. It's K through eight, so it's an elementary-slash-middle school. I'll be helping out with sixth-grade English. I'm not exactly sure how much actual teaching I'll be doing, as opposed to passing out tests and doing grunt work for the real instructor, but I'm excited. It's funny, this being my last time here. There were days I hated pulling into the parking lot. I could do without most of the parents, present company excluded, but now that I know I'm leaving, I feel kind of sentimental. I'll miss the kids. Most of them anyway. Please give Logan my best. He's a really nice boy and he has some mad burgeoning basketball skills."

"I'll let Logan know and congratulations. The school is lucky to have you."

"There are times in life when you have to work a crappy job just to pay the bills, and if you're lucky, you meet a few people who treat you with respect instead of like you're below them because of the job you're doing. You fall into the category. Take care of yourself, Julia. And watch out for those obnoxious parents," Jeremiah said, and whistled cheerfully as he exited the building with his jacket slung over his shoulder.

Julia continued on into the gym, where Charlotte's husband, Joe, was sitting on the front bleacher while Steven played in the far court. Joe's eyes were bloodshot and he was wearing a wrinkled shirt that looked like he had fished it out from being long-lost for years between sofa cushions.

"Mr. Perkins, thank you for agreeing to meet with me," Julia said, and outstretched her hand. "I can't tell you how sorry I am."

Joe ran a hand through the stubble of a fresh beard and looked on while Steven made a layup. "I haven't been able to tell my boy about what happened to his mom. I know I'm going to have to. But just look at him. He's a regular, sweet kid whose biggest problem in the world right now is that his parents split. It's going to crush him. Steven and Charlotte were really close. I want to believe she's okay, but deep down, I know she's not coming back."

Julia took a seat next to Joe and watched the probable last few hours of a boy's innocence play on in front of her. "I've been a reporter for fifteen years and have some personal experience in a missing person's case. I'll be honest with you. In this circumstance, it doesn't look good. But, if there's no body, there's always a chance. That's what you hold on to."

"I don't want the press coming for me. I got cleared by the cops, but they always look at the husband or the ex first. If you need to check my alibi, I went bowling with Steven last night after the game and then we went out for pizza. I've got a list of a dozen people who saw us."

"Like I told you over the phone, I'm not trying to connect you to Charlotte's disappearance. The police probably already asked you this, but did Charlotte mention anything about a person who might have bothered her, or maybe someone she started dating or was interested in?"

"Charlotte didn't tell me about her love life. That would've been awkward."

Perkins shifted his gaze away from Julia and looked down at the ground, his body language telling Julia he wasn't telling her the full truth.

"If you know something, it could mean the difference between Charlotte coming home or not. Is there something you should tell me, Mr. Perkins?"

Joe Perkins gave Julia a side, furtive glance and then looked back to the floor. "I feel like a real shit about this, but I looked at some of Charlotte's texts a few nights ago on her phone. She dropped Steven off at my house and went up to his bedroom to help him unpack. Her purse was on the table. I don't know why I did it. It was my idea to get divorced. I was seeing someone on the side, but still, I didn't like the idea of Charlotte dating. I wanted to know if she was, so I went through her text messages."

"I won't judge you. But the clock is ticking. What did you find?"

"Charlotte is friends with this idiot woman I can't stand. Charlotte texted the woman about being pulled over by a police officer she thought was hot. She said the cop asked her out."

"Charlotte mentioned something about this to me. Did she say what the cop's name was?"

"No. But Charlotte texted her friend that she gave the creep her number because she felt intimidated by him, like if she didn't, things weren't going to go well. That's when she came downstairs and caught me with her phone. We got into it. I told her she was stupid and naïve, and the sleazebag probably pulled her over because he saw a pretty woman driving alone and made up some bogus story to pull her over. I don't know if it's true or if she was trying to make me jealous, but she mentioned she was thinking about going out with him. I figured it was a dig because I cheated on her, so I responded in true asshole fashion."

"Do you remember when Charlotte said this happened, the cop pulling her over?"

"I do. Only because a buddy of mine was thinking about giving me a ticket to the Tigers game, so it was exactly two weeks ago Saturday. Charlotte picked up a last-minute wedding job, since the regular florist was sick, and she made me watch Steven because she couldn't find anyone else. I was pissed because I wanted to go to the game. That makes me sound like an asshole now, doesn't it? Anyway, she got back home around two in the afternoon, I think."

"Did Charlotte say where the cop pulled her over?"

"Okay, yeah, I remember now, because it wasn't in a great part of town. Third Street in the Cass Corridor, a block away from the homeless shelter. I'm pretty sure that's what she told me."

Julia took the off-ramp from I-75 into the city toward the Cass Corridor, a once-seedy area of Detroit that was becoming gentrified and reclassified as part of Midtown, the new moniker, in part, an effort to shed the neighborhood's past reputation. While the Cass Corridor was becoming more hip and less 'hood, there were still drug dealers and pockets of crime that had burrowed deeply into footholds that refused to leave.

Anxious to find out if the cops had anything new, Julia placed a call to Prejean after her call to Navarro went to voice mail.

"Well, friend, I'm guessing you already know Tillerman is no longer the lead suspect, since you beat the Detroit cops on verifying his alibi," Prejean answered. "Well done, girl. Where you at?"

"I'm heading over to the Cass Corridor to check a lead near Third Street and the homeless shelter. Apparently, Charlotte was pulled over by a cop there a few weeks ago. I wanted to check with Navarro to find out who usually patrols the area, but since I couldn't reach him, I'm going to take a swing by there myself."

"I've got some time on my hands with my feet on Russell's desk. Hang tight once you get there."

Julia cruised past Third Man Records on Canfield Street,

the place founded by musician Jack White of the White Stripes, which was a combination record store and performance-and-recording studio.

As Julia drove deeper into the Cass Corridor toward Third Street, the trendy restaurants and bars disappeared, and the old, tarnished part of the neighborhood that still hadn't died surfaced. Julia stopped at a light and didn't make eye contact with a heavily tattooed, skinny white man in a Sex Pistols T-Shirt, who was leaning against a boarded-up building. He was smoking a cigarette and looking like he was in desperate need of a fresh fix.

The light changed, and Julia wondered if this was the spot where the cop stopped Charlotte.

Julia did a slow cruise down the block, ignoring the driver behind her who leaned on his horn, and then pulled her car to a fast stop when she saw the rear of a patrol car poking out from a side street.

Julia hugged close to the side of the building that connected to the corner of the dead-end street and did a quick pan of the scene. Parked in back of the patrol car was an older silver Honda with weathered, peeling paint and a broken bumper that was hanging on to the vehicle by four thick overlapping strips of gray duct tape.

Both vehicles were unoccupied.

Across from the Honda, the faint cry of a woman's voice sounded from inside a boarded-up building with the sign VITO'S RESTAURANT hanging above the door in tarnished red and gold, like a reminder of its possible glory days.

"Please. I don't want to do this."

The front door of Vito's was locked with a dead bolt, so Julia ran around to the back of the abandoned restaurant and came to a lot that consisted of ragged open space, overgrown with tangled weeds and a chain-link fence, with a pit bull snarling on the other side.

"You can't take my car. That's all I got."

Julia moved to the back door of Vito's, which was open a few inches, and peered inside to a large room that appeared to be a kitchen.

A cop in a patrol uniform, with his hands on his hips, faced away from Julia.

In front of him was a pretty young black woman whose fingers were knotted together as if in prayer. She was backed up against an industrial-sized commercial dishwasher with racks filled with dirty dishes. At the end of the dishwasher's counter lay a few loose pieces of cutlery, including a long, two-tined carving fork at the edge of the stainless-steel surface.

"What we have here is a problem. And what you need to do now is figure out the best solution. You have an expired license, no insurance, and your car isn't registered. What do you think we should do about this?" the patrol officer said, and looked closely at the woman's license in his hand. "Nadine. That's your name? It's real pretty, just like you."

"Please, I'm begging you. I got a job I need to get to."

"I ran you through the system. You've got two prior drug convictions. I'm offering you a way out. No one is going to believe a former druggie with a record. What you need to realize is that I'm doing you a real big favor here. Now it's your choice. Which way do you want to go?"

"I don't do drugs anymore. I've been clean for a year."

"Nice try, but I don't believe you, and neither will any other cop. You know why I asked you to come in here?"

"Please don't do this to me, sir."

"The way I look at how this could go, you have two choices. We can impound your car and send you to jail. Or you have an alternative, like none of this ever happened. Your choice. What do you want to do?"

"Jesus, please." The woman was thin with large dark eyes

that filled up as the officer put his hands on her shoulders. "Okay. I'll do what you want."

The patrolman pushed the woman down to her knees, and as he reached for his zipper, he shot a quick glance at the door, revealing his face to Julia.

"Who's out there?" Officer Branch LaBeau called, and turned away from the young woman. He instinctively put his hand near the holster of his gun, which was secured on his duty belt; sensing someone was just outside, watching.

Julia reached for her phone to call 911, but it was too late. The young black woman, seeing her opening, jumped to her feet, scrambled across the length of the room, and pushed the door to the outside wide open. The woman brushed by Julia in her escape and ran until she disappeared around the corner of the building.

LaBeau stepped back in surprise when he saw Julia, but kept his hand latched on the grip of his weapon.

"What are you doing here?" LaBeau asked. He smiled at Julia like everything was completely normal and walked purposefully in her direction.

"Let me ask you the same question," Julia said.

"I'm working."

"No, you're not. You pulled that woman over, just like Charlotte Fisher. You lay in wait to pick up single young women driving alone. With Charlotte, you probably didn't solicit her for sex, but you harassed her. You had her license number and address, so you followed her. If we go back to the station and run a search, I'm betting you also pulled over April Young, Heather Burns, and Christy King. Am I right, LaBeau?"

LaBeau's smile remained intact as he closed the space between them. "You shouldn't have come here, Julia."

Julia reached for her phone, but LaBeau grabbed Julia's hand and pulled her into the building.

"This is a problem, Julia. A big problem. I like you. I really do. But this is not how this was supposed to happen."

Julia tried to fight off LaBeau, but he spun her around and shoved her against the wall, pinning her against the dirty surface with a meaty arm and then pressing the barrel of his gun against the back of her head.

"It's a dangerous job, your beat. Sometimes you wind up in places that you shouldn't. You come down here, chasing a story, and walk into some criminal's drug den, and you get popped. Just. Like. That," LaBeau said, leaning so close to Julia, she could feel his breath on her cheek.

"Not going to happen. Drop the gun and get on the ground. Now."

Julia stood stock-still when she heard Prejean's voice.

LaBeau turned Julia around, his arm still wrapped around her neck and his weapon now pointing at her temple as the two faced Prejean.

"I'm not going down for this. I swear," LaBeau said. "This is a mistake."

LaBeau began to back up with Julia, dragging her through the kitchen to an open doorway that led to another section of the restaurant.

"You're a cop. You're trained to do the right thing. It's in your blood. Let Julia go and we'll talk it out together," Prejean said. "Just you and me. You're a young guy. You got a lot of life left in you."

LaBeau kept backing up until Julia could see the counter of the kitchen's dishwasher immediately to her left. She did a quick mental map of the room in her head, trying to remember where everything was in reverse, and glided her hand below her until she felt the surface of the stainless steel.

"Drop it, LaBeau. We'll figure it out. I saw the young woman running out of here. You pull her over, bring her back here out of sight? She does you a favor and you don't give her a ticket or send her to jail. There are two sides to every story. Remember? Innocent until proven guilty. You let Julia go, and you tell us where Charlotte Fisher is, you got the power. It puts you in the negotiation seat."

"My life is over."

Julia ran her hand over the cool metal of the dishwasher, willing that what she thought she saw lying at the end of the counter earlier was really there.

"We've got units from the Detroit PD pulling in any minute. I called them when I saw your black-and-white parked in the alley. You want to go down like this in front of your fellow officers?"

LaBeau continued to drag Julia backward, now halfway to the end of the industrial dishwasher, until Julia's fingers slid across the rough handle of the carving fork. She prayed LaBeau wouldn't see her as she plucked it from the counter and slid it down to her side.

Prejean's jaw set tight, obviously picking up on Julia's move, but his eyes stayed on LaBeau, not giving her away.

"You got family, LaBeau? A wife and kids?"

"I know what you're trying to do. My wife is a bitch. I don't care what she thinks of me. Those women, they were nobodies. They didn't matter. It wasn't hurting anybody with what I did. The classy ones, I never made them go back here. Not once. You've got this wrong."

"We can talk about this later, the women you killed. You had the cops on a chase."

The sound of police sirens wailed down the alleyway and LaBeau lowered his gun for a second as he took a quick look at the door to the street.

Julia gripped the handle of the carving fork with all her might, reared her hand up, and then jabbed the two-tiered prongs of rusted metal deep into LaBeau's upper thigh.

LaBeau howled and spun around with his gun as Julia

dove under the space below the dishwasher. She scrambled behind a thick metal storage bin as a shot rang out and the bullet pierced through the wall behind her, just inches above her head.

"Drop your weapon. Now."

Navarro's voice hung in the room as Julia crawled backward.

"I'm not going out like this."

"Don't do it," Navarro said.

A second shot exploded in the kitchen, and Julia curled herself into a ball.

"Shit," Navarro said. "Julia, are you hurt?"

"No. I'm fine."

"Hold on a second," Navarro said.

"There's nobody else here. The room is clear," Prejean said. "It's over."

Julia crept up from her place of protection and looked at the scene. Russell was at the door, while Prejean and Navarro were bent over LaBeau, who was lying on the floor. LaBeau's feet were splayed awkwardly under him, and his own gun was inside his mouth as a stain of red gushed from the back of his skull.

CHAPTER 29

Julia sat in the hard metal chair in the police interview room and drummed her fingers impatiently on the desk in front of her. After LaBeau's suicide at the abandoned restaurant in the Cass Corridor, she was taken to the Detroit PD. She had been questioned extensively for the past hour on what LaBeau said, but more so, on what he didn't say, about staking his claim as the Magic Man Killer.

The interview room door swung open and Navarro entered with a bottle of water, which he handed to Julia.

"Almost done, Julia. Washington wants to talk to you. Your account of events matches up with Prejean's."

"So Prejean is saying that LaBeau didn't actually confess to the killings."

"Well, Prejean said LaBeau didn't deny it."

"The department can't wrap this thing up with a pretty bow. What did you find at LaBeau's house?"

Navarro gave an almost indiscernible head nod in the direction of what Julia knew was the two-way mirror as Washington entered the room and handed Navarro a piece of paper.

"Another address we need to check. I just called the sheriff's department in Montcalm County. LaBeau's wife said he had a cabin up there," Washington said.

"So that means you didn't find anything to connect LaBeau to the Magic Man Killer at his house here in Detroit. Did LaBeau write any tickets to April Young, Heather Burns, or Christy King? That's circumstantial, but still, it's a solid connection if LaBeau made contact with all three women. Come on, Beth, you said I was embedded in the story. I almost got killed an hour ago, so I'd like the courtesy of some answers."

"Navarro spoke to Christy. Go ahead. You can tell Julia, but it's off the record for now."

"Christy said she was pulled over by a cop in the city a few months ago for running a red light, but she said it was dark and she couldn't be sure if the officer who pulled her over matched the photo we showed her of LaBeau," Navarro said. "She said the officer didn't hit on her."

"But we can't rule out that it wasn't LaBeau. He pulls her over, sees that Christy is his type, and he gets her address from her license," Washington said.

"What about the two victims?" Julia asked.

"LaBeau never wrote a ticket to April Young or Heather Burns. But he still could've pulled them over, looked at their licenses, gotten the information he needed, and let them go without a citation. We're questioning their family members to see if either victim mentioned anything about being stopped and possibly harassed by a police officer," Washington said. "This is turning into a public relations nightmare. LaBeau was a cop. The fact alone that he was targeting women and offering a pass on a ticket or an arrest for sex or their phone number is not going to go over well. With the past chief's incarceration, this department's reputation has barely made its way out of the Dumpster fire it was in. And now we've got this."

"LaBeau doesn't represent the entire department," Julia said. "And you found out what he was doing."

"You found out," Washington answered.

"What about the voodoo angle?" Julia asked.

"Branch grew up in the South and moved here when he was a teenager. His wife wasn't aware of him practicing any kind of black magic, but we got some names of his relatives, and Russell is trying to track them down."

"Were there ever any complaints lodged against LaBeau?" Julia asked.

"Off the record?" Washington asked.

"Your call. The press is going to start digging around about this," Julia said. "I'd be completely transparent if I were you. Otherwise, it looks like you've got something to hide."

Washington looked up to the ceiling and shook her head. "This was before my time as chief, but there was a complaint filed against LaBeau by a woman he pulled over who was drunk. She claimed he tried to come on to her, but his dash cam was off, so it was her word against his. IA investigated, and it turned out the woman had a history of suing people, trying to make a quick buck, and Internal Affairs cleared him. Are you absolutely sure that LaBeau didn't admit to killing those women?"

"I'm positive. LaBeau said something about not 'going down for this,' and it 'was a mistake.' There could be a lot of different interpretations for what he meant."

"The mistake could be his own admission that what he did was wrong," Washington said.

"Or that he was being wrongfully accused as the killer," Julia added. "Pinning LaBeau is a quick and dirty way to wrap up the case. But what if you're wrong? Do you honestly think the killings are going to stop?"

"I've got a press conference to go to. If you get a call . . ."

"If I hear from the Magic Man Killer, you'll be the first to know. If LaBeau didn't do it, then the real killer wouldn't want someone else to take credit for his work. If you're straight up with the press and public that you're looking at LaBeau as a suspect in the murders, I think it would piss off the real killer. He'd call me, and then you'd have your answer."

"If it's not LaBeau, we'll see if the devil wants to come out and play. Julia, you're free to go. Time for me to face the jackals."

"Whether it was LaBeau or not, we still haven't found Charlotte," Julia said.

"No body, we keep looking for her, no matter what," Navarro said. "I'll walk you to your car, Julia."

Navarro steered Julia to the back exit to avoid the media that were gathering in front of the precinct. Julia felt an odd sense of not being with her regular crew, since she and Navarro bypassed the press and arrived at the outdoor parking lot and her SUV a block away from the station.

"Washington wants the killer to be LaBeau," Julia said.

"Not necessarily. It would solve one problem, but create another one for the department. She'll do the right thing. Until we confirm LaBeau is MMK, I want you to stay at the apartment. Washington is pulling the surveillance detail off you and your family, so you need to stay close. I need you to do one more thing for me."

"What is it?"

"I don't want you to be alone with Prejean until we wrap things up."

"Prejean just saved my life."

"I don't trust him. Tillerman said Prejean's story about meeting him at the New Orleans airport wasn't true."

"Tillerman is a liar. Why would you take his word over Prejean's?"

"Right now, anything that pertains to you, I need to look at. Corporal Smith has a connection in the New Orleans PD. I asked him to give the cop a call. It was unofficial, so it wouldn't come back to Prejean. I asked Smith to make out like he was just curious about what kind of officer Prejean is, since he wants a job here in Detroit."

"You ran a background check on my friend?"

"It wasn't a background check. Too many things about Prejean aren't adding up to me. The NOLA cop said about two months ago, Prejean and his partner got a call on a domestic. Prejean shot and killed the common-law husband, because he said the suspect pulled a gun. The woman who got beat up claimed Prejean planted the weapon *after* he shot the guy."

"Prejean is a good cop. He wouldn't do that."

"His partner vouched for him, and IA cleared Prejean of any wrongdoing. He kept his badge, but there's still a cloud around him. That's why I think he wants a transfer to Detroit. I think he also could've planted the voodoo doll at the park. Whether he's the killer or not, he wanted to make out like he was still helpful to the investigation. Things aren't good at home, and if he gets good points on the MMK case, he slides into a job in Detroit."

"If you're liking Prejean for the killer, then explain to me how would he be able to scout out the victims' every move before their murders if he was in Louisiana?"

"He could've done it while he was on leave during the IA investigation. He was sidelined when April Young was killed, and he wasn't on duty the day Heather Burns was murdered."

"Come on, Ray. That's a stretch. I don't like what you're doing here."

"If you're mad at me for looking into Prejean, I'm sorry. But I have to check him out. If he didn't do anything, then I stand corrected. My mistake. But I have to be sure you're okay."

"If you and Prejean don't like each other, that's one thing. But if you're accusing him of being the killer, you're wrong," Julia said. She got into her vehicle and slammed the door. "I'm heading back to the apartment to see my kids."

"If the Magic Man Killer is still out there and he sees the press conference about LaBeau potentially being the killer, he might want to make a showboat move. Stay put at the apartment and I'll try to get there as soon as I can. I'm not trying to be a jerk about your friend. I'm just trying to look out for you and your boys."

"I know, Ray," Julia conceded.

"So we're good?"

"Of course."

"All right," Navarro said, sounding relieved. "Don't let your guard down."

He leaned in through the open window, gave Julia a quick kiss, and then rapped his knuckles on top of her car. "I mean it, Gooden. That paranoia that you've carried around with you since you were a kid? This time, it's okay to hold on to it tight."

Julia sat on the floor in the living room of the temporary apartment. She had her shoes off and each little boy sitting by her side. Will was engrossed in playing a smashup derby battle with two of his miniature figurines, Spider-Man and one of his archenemies, Venom, while Logan, whose black magician hat was perched on top of his head, practiced shuffling a deck of cards.

Julia ran a finger over the silver Peace locket around her neck, the one Charlotte had given her, and realized the crucial first twenty-four hours of her friend being missing were coming to a fast close. The ticktock of the inevitable likelihood that Charlotte would be found alive was now a pipe dream at best.

"We are out of butter, and I need to pick up some groceries at the store," Helen said. Helen was wearing her coat, a blue scarf was draped over her hair and tied at her neck, and she clutched her purse at her side. "I go out now and take the boys so you have a few minutes. You look tired, Miss Julia. Little boys will come with me. Ah, I see the extreme excitement from the children who won't even look at me when I offer to take them out for some fresh air. Fine. Bribery then. We stop at the ice cream parlor first."

"I want to go with Helen," Will said. He jumped up with his toys still clutched in his hands and gave his mother a kiss on her cheek. "Sorry, Mamma."

"It's okay, sweet boy. You didn't do anything wrong. But Helen doesn't need to cook."

"Of course I cook. A new place, we need some normalcy. It's good for you, good for the children, and, especially, good for me. I've been stuck all day in this apartment with the policeman standing guard. Now we are free. One hour or so, we will be back. Come on, boys, get your coats. We give your mother some time to rest."

"I don't want to go. I left my tape recorder in Uncle Ray's apartment. I have an idea for a magic trick I want to try," Logan said.

"Logan can stay with me. Helen, I need to talk to you about something. In private."

Julia pulled Helen into the hallway and away from curious ears.

"The police think the officer who committed suicide is the killer they've been investigating. But there's still a chance he's not. I don't think you or the boys are in danger. I believe the killer's only interest is in me. If you insist on going out, keep Will as close to you as possible. Never let him out of your sight. And if anything happens, or anything gives you pause, no matter how small, you need to make me a promise."

"I know. I call you or Mr. Ray. My life spent with you must require that I keep you both on my speed dial. What a world."

Julia helped Will put on his coat and kept a guarded watch as Helen and Julia's youngest son made it to the elevator. She then affixed the dead bolt and the lock on the door handle and returned to the living room, where Logan had his deck of cards fanned out across the floor.

"I need the tape recorder in Uncle Ray's place."

"We'll get it, but I want to talk to you about something first. I'm not trying to scare you, but it's a good reminder. If anything ever happened to me, who would you call?"

"Uncle Ray."

"Good. Tell me his number again."

Julia waited until Logan recited Navarro's personal cell phone.

"Now can I get the recorder? I want to do a ventriloquist trick."

"I'm going to make a work call in the bedroom. It's to my editor, and the details aren't for little boys to hear."

"Time-out, Mom. How about you let me go to Uncle Ray's for a couple minutes? You can take me over and then I can find the tape recorder and practice my trick until you're done. I'll lock the door. I swear, I won't let anyone in. I promise."

" 'Time-out'?" Julia asked. "What's that all about?"

"Sorry, I wasn't trying to be disrespectful. All the kids on my basketball team say it. Come on, Mom. Let me go to Uncle Ray's. I won't do anything stupid. I swear."

"I don't know," Julia said, and analyzed the situation in her head. She'd given Virginia only a brief lowdown of what happened with LaBeau back at the abandoned restaurant in

Cass Corridor, and she knew she'd need to get into some graphic details that she didn't want Logan to hear.

"Five minutes. And you keep the door locked. Swear to me, Logan. The only person you would open the door to would be Uncle Ray, or Helen, or me."

"I promise, Mom."

"I don't love this, but come on."

At the front door, Julia peered out the keyhole and unfastened the locks when she saw the hallway was empty. She let herself and Logan into Navarro's apartment with her spare key, scooted Logan inside, and clicked the dead bolt in place.

"I'm going to check the apartment first before I leave you alone in here."

"You mean like look in closets and under beds? Can I help?"

"You practice your trick. Mom will handle it."

Julia scoured every potential hiding place in the apartment, and when she was satisfied, she took a seat next to Logan on Navarro's couch and grabbed his hand.

"I'm going next door and I'm going to lock the door behind me. What are the rules?"

"I know. I don't open the door for anyone. Do we need a secret code if something happens?"

"Nothing is going to happen."

"Things always happen, Mom. I got it. If one of us is in trouble, we bang hard on the wall, kind of like Morse code. Two times, like this," Logan said, and pounded his little fist against the common wall between the two apartments. "And then we call Uncle Ray."

"Like I said, nothing is going to happen. But if it did, you'd call Uncle Ray and wouldn't leave this apartment even if you knew I needed help. Promise me."

"Okay. I promise."

"Practice your trick and I'll be back in a few minutes. No trying to eavesdrop on my conversation with my editor by putting your ear against the wall. I know your ways, little boy."

Julia kissed the top of Logan's shiny black hair and let herself out. She locked the door to Navarro's unit and returned to their apartment to call her editor.

The doorbell buzzed as soon as she reached the living room, the unfamiliar chime making Julia jump.

Julia tried to walk soundlessly, her feet treading lightly across the carpet until she reached the peephole and a view of the common hallway of the eleventh floor.

Prejean stood on the other side of the door.

"Julia, are you there? It's Prejean. Is everything okay? I heard that you were here."

Navarro's warning hung in Julia's head, but then she flashed to an image of her old friend coming to her rescue, gun in hand, when LaBeau was about to kill her.

"Hold on," Julia said. She grabbed her cell phone in case her gut was wrong and opened the door up a few inches so the protective chain was still in place.

"Washington told me she pulled the plug on your cop babysitter. I figured that was a bad move until she can figure out whether LaBeau is her man. I heard you left the station, so I wanted to come by before I left, to be sure you were okay."

"I'm fine."

"Are you going to let me in? Some hospitality you Midwesterners have. Shoot, I got perps who treat me better than this."

"I'm sorry, but let's catch up later."

"Is someone in there with you?"

"No, I promise."

"I don't believe it. Back up. I'm going to break down the door."

"No. Don't do that. I'm fine."

Julia watched as Prejean reached for his weapon, preparing for a showdown.

"Okay. Hold on," Julia said. She unlatched the security chain and opened the door for Prejean to come inside.

He kept his weapon leveled as he entered the apartment and pushed Julia behind him.

"Prejean, I'm alone. I'm not being held against my will. Without a security detail, I'm just being cautious."

"Well, that's good, but you don't need to be that way with me," Prejean said. He secured the gun back in his holster and locked the door behind them. "I'm heading back to New Orleans pretty soon. It looks like the case is wrapping up. I'd like to stay and try to find Charlotte, but my supervisor doesn't want me to be on loan any longer. Are you sure you're okay, girl? You look kind of funny."

"You weren't at the coffee shop when the police set up Tillerman. Why was that?"

"Because I was looking for Charlotte. You know I always got your back, but you had a fleet of cops around you. I wouldn't have let you go there if I didn't think you'd be safe."

"Tillerman told Navarro the story about you meeting him at the airport was a lie, that he didn't even fly down to New Orleans after I called and warned him not to come."

"Well, darlin', that boy is the one who's lying. I met him there at the Delta Terminal, and he got on a plane back home. Why's Navarro trying to cause trouble with you and me? This is where this is coming from, right? You can tell him, I'm not after his girl."

Prejean took a step toward Julia and she backed up, down the length of the hallway into the living room.

"When we were in the park in Royal Oak, did you plant that voodoo doll in the tree?"

"What are you talking about, and why are you moving

away from me? You know who I am. Navarro's been putting poison in your mind about me, like sewage in the water killing the fish."

Prejean grabbed Julia's arm and drew her to him. "Don't believe what people say about me. I care about you more than you know. What happened with you and LaBeau today, you must still be shaken up."

Prejean wrapped his arms around Julia and tried to hug her, but she pushed him away and reached for her phone in her pocket, ready to call Navarro.

Prejean took a step back and a look of hurt spread across his face.

"I don't know what you think is happening, or what my intentions are, but you're wrong on all counts. I didn't lie, and I didn't plant evidence. And you and me, we're just friends. Or at least, I thought we were."

"I want you to leave, Prejean."

"I planned to stay with you until Navarro was done at work, because I was worried when I heard Washington pulled the detail off. But if that's how you want to play it, I'll be going now. You take care of yourself and get your mind right."

Prejean left, slamming the door behind him, leaving Julia alone in the apartment to face a sudden onslaught of guilt over her accusations. She thought about following Prejean, but ultimately she knew she had to listen to Navarro. Julia waited until she heard the *ting* of the elevator arriving on their floor, and then went to the living room to call Virginia.

Julia reached into her bag for her reporter's notebook, which included the latest summary she had jotted down and planned to share with her editor to update her on the case. Julia laid the notebook on the coffee table, sat down on the sofa, and pulled out six pieces of paper that she had folded and stuffed inside the notebook: the transcript of her two calls with MMK that the police provided upon her insistence after she turned over the actual recordings to Navarro and his team. The police had also included the initials of each speaker immediately following their respective quotes.

She did a quick study of the transcript from the first call when she was in the parking lot with Logan after his game. She re-read the words the Magic Man Killer had said to her in his smooth, emotionless tone and the clues MMK had planted about "finding the dark magic in Detroit" and the *Alice in Wonderland* references that led her to Roseline.

She began to review the rest of the transcript that chronicled her conversation with MMK during his second call after she and Navarro saved Christy King in the park.

Julia ran her index finger underneath each sentence as she read.

> *"You weren't supposed to find Christy King. How did you do it?"* MMK
>
> *"Because I'm smarter than you. So are the cops."* JG
>
> *"No, no, no. Time-out, Julia. It's time for you to listen, not speak."* MMK

Julia's index finger stopped abruptly under the phrase "time-out."

The two words seemed to hang in the air like a fast-descending sickle. "Time-out" was the exact same phrase Logan had just used, and his reference to the expression made something finally click into place.

Julia grabbed her phone and then hurriedly searched her contacts until she found the number for the director of the Wayne County Parks Department, Matthew Morales.

Julia felt her heart racing so fast, she tempered her breathing to try and make it beat in a natural rhythm until Morales answered.

"It's Julia Gooden," she said in a rush.

"Julia, it's after hours and I was just leaving for the day. We had a late staff meeting tonight and I'm heading home."

"This is an emergency. I need to find out if three women had their children in sports teams through your parks-and-rec department."

"I'm sorry. Your boss, Virginia, is a personal friend, but if this is for a story, it's going to have to wait. Call me tomorrow."

"No. Get on your computer and search the names April Young, Heather Burns, and Christy King. Do it, Morales. Two of those women I mentioned are dead, and a fourth woman is missing. I think their connection is through Wayne County sports teams. The missing woman, Charlotte Fisher, has a son who plays in a parks-and-rec basketball team."

"Is this about the serial murders of the female joggers you've been writing about?"

"That's exactly what this is. Just get on your computer. Please."

"Okay, okay."

Julia could hear a door close on the other end of the phone, followed by movement in the background. She waited the longest four minutes of her life until Morales finally came back on.

"Okay, Heather Burns's daughter, Carly, was on a senior girls' Wayne County soccer team. April Young's boy played on our peewee baseball league, and Christy King's son, Clay, is on a junior soccer league for ages eight and under."

Julia's mind spun back to the blue dress MMK made his victims wear and the time she had worn her own version. She had put on the blue dress for Navarro's police awards banquet, which had tied into the initial theory that MMK could be a cop. Her correlation to the dress had been stuck on that single event. But Julia now realized she had first stopped to watch Logan play on an All-Stars Little League game on his final day of baseball camp during the summer before she met up with Navarro for the awards banquet.

"Hold on one second," Julia said.

She pulled out the orange flyer from the parks-and-rec department from her bag, the one for early registration for the kids and the opportunity for parents to get discounts, and studied it for the first time.

The top part of the form was information about the child and the teams they were interested in, but the bottom half of the form was for the parents to fill out about themselves, including their gender and age. There was also a check box of sporting activities parents participated in, and one of the options was running. Underneath each selection, the parents could include information about which current parks they frequented for the activities they checked off.

"The orange flyers the parks department is giving out for early youth sports registration and perks for parents who sign up, who has access to those?" Julia asked.

"Plenty of people. Those forms are in at least twenty gyms. We also have them posted in every park we have in the county, and people can fill them out and leave them in drop boxes. All that information is input into our computer system."

Julia's eyes stayed on the orange form, and she realized MMK likely did his initial vetting of his victims through the form, and for those who fit the profile, he could easily see where the women ran if they filled out that line on the form.

"Thanks for your help, but you're going to need to be accessible to the police and me tonight. We're going to need to comb through your records," Julia said. "I think someone who works for Wayne County Parks and Rec is the Magic Man Killer."

Julia hung up with a startled Morales and then called Navarro, feeling a burn of frustration when her call went straight to voice mail.

"I found the connection," Julia said as she left a message. "All the women—April Young, Heather Burns, Christy King, Charlotte Fisher, and me—all our children play youth sports through the county-rec league. I'm sure someone who works for the Wayne County Parks and Rec Department is the killer. I'll explain more when I see you. I'm heading to the station now with Logan."

Julia ended the call, left a note for Helen, and grabbed her bag. She left the apartment, ready to retrieve Logan, and turned around to lock the door. But the key froze in her hand when she felt the sharp edge of a knife wedge itself against the side of her neck.

"Hello, Julia. We're going back inside now."

The person behind Julia gave her a hard shove into the apartment. Once Julia got inside, she felt the knife move away from her neck.

She spun around to see the referee from Logan's basketball games, Jeremiah Landry.

"I've got something of yours," Jeremiah said. He reached inside his sweatshirt pocket and retrieved a baseball. "You left it at your brother's grave. That was a strange thing to do. But we're both strange, aren't we? You haven't been running in a while. I always enjoyed watching you run. It was a thing of grace."

"Get out of here," Julia said as her eyes swept across the sterile apartment for anything she could use as a weapon.

"That's not going to happen. I came for you. It's all for you. A man like me, most of the time, we're invisible," Jeremiah said, but this time, his voice sounded different, with a brush of a Southern accent.

Julia began to hit Navarro's number on her phone again, but stopped when Jeremiah raised up his thick green-and-black knife and pointed it at her chest.

"Don't do it, or I'll cut you before I planned."

Julia dropped her phone back into her purse, knowing she needed to buy time. "Why me? Why are you doing this?"

"The first time I saw you, I was subbing at a Little League summer camp game, umping behind home plate. You were wearing the blue dress. You looked so lovely and came to my defense. A true warrior, you are. One of the bitches, those women, the parents who live and die for their stupid kids' games, started yelling at a call I made. You told her off. You never saw my face behind my umpire mask, I'm guessing. Either that, or I was simply forgettable. I started following you after that. When I saw Logan's name on the basketball team roster, I switched schedules with another ref so I could work his games, and I made myself into a nice guy for you when we talked, the type of man I thought you'd like. None of the things I told you about myself were true. But I think you liked that version of me, Julia. I really do."

Julia looked at the blade of the knife Jeremiah clutched in his hand and prayed that Logan would remain in Navarro's place if he heard a struggle.

"You have no idea how much work I did to prepare for this moment. You and me, we're just the same, exact halves that make a whole. After I started following you, I saw your interview on TV and I knew our meeting, our relationship, was preordained. You never cared about your brother, did you? It was all a charade, an act, we put on, behaving like we're supposed to in the real world. You didn't show any emotion when the reporter asked about how your brother's murder made you feel. Not one single ounce of emotion."

"Don't talk about my brother. I'm nothing like you. Where's Charlotte?"

"In a basement. I stuffed her in a container," Jeremiah said. "She's probably dead by now. The cops were at the church where I planned to take her, so I had to find a safe place real quick. But then I realized it was too close to home. You don't mess with the darkness where you live."

"You found your victims through the parks. You saw the mothers in the stands watching their children play the games you worked. And you tracked them through the registration forms."

"That's right. But you didn't figure it out in time. With Charlotte, I knew that one was going to hurt you. The registration forms were a big help to me in my planning. If the women ticked the right age box and indicated they were runners, I'd go to their kids' games and find them. It was painstaking work to get the right women. They didn't have to look just like you, but they had to have your body type. I could fix the rest. I followed them and knew their patterns. Enough talk now. It's time for our dance. I've been waiting a long time for this moment."

Jeremiah reached inside a duffel bag, which hung by his side, and pulled out a blue dress.

Julia looked to the front door, but Jeremiah's body blocked its route. She knew she could try to escape from the patio, but she was eleven stories up with nothing but concrete below her.

"Here's your dress," Jeremiah said. "Don't worry. It will fit. I know what you're thinking. We don't have any music, but I thought of everything."

"You're crazy," Julia said, and refused to take the dress Jeremiah held out to her.

"'Hold me close and hold me fast,'" Jeremiah began to sing. "'The magic spell you cast . . .'"

Julia ran as fast as she could to the living room and banged her fist twice against the common wall that connected to Navarro's apartment, praying her little boy would keep his promise and call Navarro without coming in to save her.

"Help! Please, someone!" Julia screamed.

Jeremiah raced after her into the room. His face remained

eerily calm as he grabbed her around the waist and pressed the blade of his knife against her neck.

"Say you love me, Julia."

"The cops are on the way."

"No, they aren't. I followed you here. I follow you everywhere. I saw the blond-haired cop leave. He's gone. It's just you and me now, where we were always supposed to be. Put the dress on. Don't tease me and make me wait any longer. It's almost time."

CHAPTER 30

Logan looked at the framed picture on the living-room coffee table of his mother and Uncle Ray, who wasn't really his uncle, but he'd been calling him that since he could remember. He thought it was weird when parents made kids call people who weren't relatives "auntie" or "uncle," just to make it seem like you had to like the person because they were now part of your family.

But Logan liked Navarro. A lot. Some days more than his own dad, who, up until he died, had spent more time at his law practice than with his kids, even skipping out on family events on the weekends just so he could work.

Plus his dad wasn't nice to his mom sometimes.

The jerk.

His dad had done some bad things before he died, and Logan just couldn't bring himself to forgive his father for them yet. Or for dying. Kids needed their dads, even if they weren't very good ones.

Logan was sure of one thing. His uncle Ray was brave, just like he was. Logan picked up a copy of something called

Police magazine, which lay next to the framed picture, and thought maybe he'd be a cop one day, or a lawyer who didn't neglect his family. Either career path was good, just as long as he could take down the bad guys, like he had done one time in the woods when he tried to save his mother and little brother.

He was small, but he still had a heart of a lion, he thought. Logan thumbed through the magazine that had boring stuff about guns and some weird article titled "Beware Armchair SWAT Commanders," and looked at his reflection in the hallway mirror.

Uncle Ray was a big man who looked like some muscular movie guy who wore camouflage and jumped into hostile territory out of a helicopter to rescue an entire village.

Now that was cool.

Logan posed and flexed in the mirror, trying hard to make a muscle, but all he saw were two puny kid's arms in the reflection.

Man, he had some work to do. He'd ask his uncle Ray if he could go with him to his gym sometime. Maybe they could be lifting buddies.

His mom had gotten a lot better about letting him do things in the last year. She'd been so paranoid before, always worried something was going to happen to him or to Will.

It's not like bad stuff happened every minute.

Boom! Boom!

Logan jumped backward when he heard two sharp bangs on the common wall in front of him, and then his mother's voice screaming for help.

Logan's first instinct, just like it had been that time in the woods, was to run to save his mom. But he had to be smart. Logan realized the person with his mom must be the killer he had read about online in the stories he wasn't supposed to see.

MMK had his mother.

Logan raced into Navarro's bedroom, where Logan was pretty sure he had seen a landline.

"Dear God, please!" Logan whispered as the call went through to Uncle Ray.

Navarro grabbed his leather jacket and keys from his desk at the precinct, ready to drive to LaBeau's cabin. He nabbed his cell phone from the top of his desk and saw he had a voice message. He was about to play it when Sheila, the receptionist, poked her head in the doorway of the detective unit.

"Ray, you're going to want to take this one. There's a woman here. She's real upset. She thinks her husband might be the Magic Man Killer. She went into a shed I guess he has in the back of their house, because she said he's been acting weird lately. The woman found a closet with blue dresses and black wigs, and a treasure trove of creepy stories written by Julia Gooden, and some videotaped interview she did with CNN."

"We got him. What's the husband's name?"

"Jeremiah Landry. The chief is with the woman now. Washington already put an APB out on Landry."

Navarro felt his cell phone buzz in his hand and did a quick look at the number. "Hold on. Tell Washington I'll be right there. Something's up. I'm getting a call from my own apartment."

"God, please, I'll do anything, I swear, just let Uncle Ray answer," Logan begged as the phone continued to ring. If Navarro didn't pick up, Logan knew what he'd have to do. He'd scour the kitchen, find a knife, and burst into the apartment to rescue his mother.

"It's Ray Navarro. Who's this?"

"Uncle Ray, it's Logan! Someone's got my mom. I think

it's the killer. I heard my mom scream for help. They're in the apartment next door. I'm in your place. You've got to get here right now!" Logan cried, racing to get the words out.

"I'm coming. I'm five minutes out. Stay calm, Logan. It's going to be fine," Navarro said.

Logan could hear movement, like Navarro was running, and then he heard his mother's boyfriend shout to send units to his building, the eleventh floor, apartment 11C.

"Five minutes is too long. We need to get my mom now or he's going to kill her. I know it. I'm going in there to stop him," Logan said.

"No, you're not. Your mother wouldn't want you to do that. She's smart and she'll be okay until I get there. You stay on the phone with me."

Logan felt hot tears run down his face and he ran into the kitchen to get a knife.

His tape recorder was sitting on the counter. He stopped his pursuit and grabbed the little recorder, clutching it tightly in his small hand.

Logan knew what he was going to do.

He'd use magic to save his mother.

"I've got an idea," Logan said as he heard Navarro start his car in the background. "I'm going to plug a cord into my tape recorder and connect it to the phone. I need you to yell as loud as you can when I tell you. You're going to say, 'Stop! Police! We have the place surrounded!' You need to sound really mean when you say it."

"Come on, Logan. It's going to be all right."

"No, it's not. You need to do this for my mom. I mean it, Uncle Ray. I won't let anything happen to her. We need to record your voice. Right now!"

"All right. Tell me when."

Logan's fingers remained steady while he plugged the cord into the tape recorder and then the other piece into the bottom slot of the wireless phone.

"When I say 'go,' count to ten first in your head before you start talking. One Mississippi, two Mississippi . . . and then yell as loud as you can. Okay?"

"All right."

"Go!" Logan said.

Logan hit the record button, silently mouthed the numbers until he reached ten, and then Navarro came in on cue.

"Stop! Police! We have the place surrounded!" Navarro yelled.

Julia pulled the blue dress over her head, knowing she had to keep Jeremiah away from Logan. She was sure Logan called Navarro, but the longer the police took to arrive, the more urgency Logan would feel to rescue his mother personally. Even though Logan gave her his promise. A knot of fear grew inside Julia, and she willed her little boy not to come into the apartment.

Jeremiah stroked the length of Julia's hair with his hand. He then leaned in close and inhaled her scent.

He reached into the duffel bag and retrieved two black candles, which he lit and placed on the floor. "Open your hand. This will hurt, but it will be worth it."

"No, I won't do it."

"You will. If you don't, after I kill you, I'll find your boy and do the same thing to him. Just a drop, Julia, that's all. Just enough to let them know you're here."

Julia tried to pull away, but Jeremiah grabbed her hand and pried her fist open. He took the tip of the blade from his knife and slipped it across her index finger in one fast, deep slice. Julia bit her lip as hard as she could to stop herself from crying out, because she knew Logan would try to save her if he heard his mom in distress.

Jeremiah squeezed the fresh cut, and Julia suppressed a scream. He turned her hand over and placed her injured finger over one of the black candles. His eyes seemed to grow bigger in delight as he looked on at Julia's drops of blood falling into the flame.

"My turn," Jeremiah said. "It's a prelude for what's to come next for both of us." He took the black-and-green knife and repeated the gruesome ritual with his own left index finger and let the blood from his cut drip down into the second black candle.

"Dance with me, Julia. We're so close to it now."

Jeremiah grabbed Julia's arm and pulled her to him. She reared her strong runner's leg back and kicked him as hard as she could, but Jeremiah wouldn't let go.

"You're spoiling it! You're not supposed to spoil it. You need a lesson in who's in control, my bright and shiny girl."

Jeremiah threw Julia to the ground. She scrambled to get up, but he was already on top of her, pinning her body down with his hips. He threw the knife onto the floor, away from Julia's grasp, and wrapped both his hands around her throat.

And then he began to squeeze.

"You are going to listen to me and do as I say."

Julia pounded her feet against the floor and grabbed at Jeremiah's hands, trying to pry them off her neck, all the while struggling to breathe, as if she were underwater drowning, struggling to hold on to that very last breath until she could resurface back to the top of the water.

The room began to lose color, fading to black and white. And then all began to disappear behind a light, filmy cloud as Julia started to lose consciousness. A vision of something red, like a crimson drop on a white rose, flashed by. She looked out to the patio, where she thought, in her mind's eye, she saw a flicker of a little boy in a red shirt, with dark, shiny hair, standing on the other side, with his hand pressed against the glass.

Logan crouched down on Navarro's patio with the tape recorder clutched tightly in his hand. He looked at the dead air of space that separated Navarro's terrace from the one that belonged to the temporary apartment and had no idea if his plan would work.

It was desperation time. But he had to try.

Logan leaned over the railing as far as he could toward the apartment's patio, hit the play button, and then aimed the little recorder in the direction of a brown mat outside the other terrace's sliding glass door, tossing it underhand. He watched the tape recorder sail through the air and felt as though he were trying to land an impossible three-point shot on the basketball court right before the final buzzer sounded.

Logan crossed his fingers as the tape recorder hit its mark and landed on the mat.

"Three. Two. One," Logan counted backward.

"Stop! Police! We have the place surrounded!" Navarro's voice boomed from the recorder.

Logan spotted Navarro's Chevy Tahoe pull to a stop in front of the apartment.

They were running out of time, Logan realized. He ran into the kitchen, pulled out a steak knife from a rack, and ran as fast as he could to save his mother.

Julia began to choke and gasp for air when Jeremiah Landry released his grip from her throat.

The Magic Man Killer got up quickly and looked, to Julia, at first like a shadow unattached to a body as she watched him snatch up his knife and run to the patio door.

Julia willed herself not to pass out and climbed back up to her feet. She couldn't lose this moment, the only chance she would have to escape, and turned around to the door when it banged open.

Julia looked on in horror at Logan, who stood on the other side, brandishing a knife.

"No, baby!" She tried to run to his side, but the cool,

sharp edge of Jeremiah Landry's knife pressed against the base of her throat.

"Let my mom go," Logan said. He held out his own knife in front of him, strong, unflinching, and steady, like a small, mighty child warrior, refusing to give in to defeat.

"Logan. A coming-of-age ritual we both will share. I saw my mother's fresh kill. But you'll do me even one better. You get to watch your mother's murder. I would've liked to have seen that."

"No!" Logan cried. Logan started to run into the room when a large arm shot around the side of the doorway and yanked him out of sight.

Julia watched the veins of Jeremiah's arms stand out as he tightened the grip of his knife around her neck.

Navarro shot a quick look inside the room from behind the door, and then moved into the apartment slowly, with his gun trained at the Magic Man Killer.

"This is not a recording this time. Drop your weapon. Now."

"It's you. Of course it is. It's predestined, all of this. Demons versus angels. I see who you are. Our famous final scene for the girl. But Julia's empty. Just like me. You're out."

"Drop the knife," Navarro said. "Gooden, don't move."

"I got a real good sense about people. You've got darkness licking like flames around your soul. That taste will make you greater than you've ever dreamed."

The shrill peal of police sirens sounded their warning in the background and caused Jeremiah to turn his head toward the patio for a split second.

"This is not how we're supposed to end, Julia."

A shot rang out from Navarro's gun, striking Jeremiah on the left side of his skull, the point farthest away from Julia.

The knife that had been embedded against Julia's throat fell away as the Magic Man Killer collapsed on the floor.

Jeremiah Landry, the parks-and-rec referee nobody paid

much attention to, who so easily blended in with his mask he wore in the real world, and the demon who killed at least two women, while hiding in plain sight, was finally dead.

"Are you okay, Julia?"

"I'm fine," she answered, and ran into the hallway, where Logan was standing just outside the apartment door, still clutching the knife in his hand. Julia grabbed her son and hugged him so tightly, she thought both of them might break.

"Thank you, baby," Julia told Logan. "But don't ever do that again."

CHAPTER 31

The street in front of Jeremiah Landry's house was jammed with police cars. Julia found the only available spot, which blocked a neighbor's driveway, but there was no time for polite rules of parking etiquette.

Her finger that Landry had sliced was self-wrapped with a couple of her kids' *Star Wars* Band-Aids, and her neck where Jeremiah had choked her still hurt, but she refused to seek medical attention. After she made sure Logan was okay, and secured him with Helen and Will in Navarro's apartment, she didn't listen to Ray's strongly worded advice and drove across town to try and find Charlotte.

It was evening, but Julia could make out Chief Washington, who stood in front of the property, a seemingly normal ranch home with a cheerful welcome mat and two potted plants filled with orange and yellow chrysanthemums on the stoop.

Sitting on the top step next to Washington was a blond woman, who had the frozen death stare Julia recognized from witnessing people on her beat who had just found out a terrible tragedy had befallen a loved one. In this case, the woman, who Julia recognized as Jeremiah Landry's wife from briefly seeing her at the parks-and-rec gym, wore the familiar mask of disbelief and horror because she found out the man she thought she knew was pure evil.

Washington did a double take on Julia and walked the length of the front yard in her direction.

"Are you okay?" the chief asked. "You were right to have doubts about LaBeau. I should've kept the detail on you and your family."

"I'm fine. Did you find Charlotte? I'm sure Jeremiah Landry has her here. He said he stuffed her in some kind of container in a basement."

"We're searching the house. We looked through his shed already. Are you sure Landry said he had Charlotte in a basement?"

"I'm positive."

"Then he lied to you. There's no basement here. There's an attic, though, and we're searching it now."

"Then this isn't the place. Charlotte has to be somewhere else. Does Jeremiah have any other properties?"

"Landry's wife says this is it. She said she left last night for a work conference and got back early. Landry knew the house was going to be empty, so he probably hid Charlotte here. Navarro's on the way over. I'm going to need you to go to the station to give a statement on what happened at the apartment."

"Navarro killed Jeremiah Landry because he had a knife to my throat. It would save you a lot of paperwork if you'd just leave it at that."

"The case is over, Julia. Go home. I'm not letting you inside the house. Your kids need you."

"I made sure my kids were okay before I came here," Julia

said, and a thin red thread of annoyance clung to her tone. "I'm throwing out a wild guess here, but I'm betting you forgot that I've had a hell of a day. I'm not going anywhere. And the case isn't over until you find Charlotte."

"If you won't leave, then you stay on public property, which is the street. You're not going into the house. Let us do our jobs. I appreciate what you've done on MMK and I'm glad you're safe. Honestly, I am. But we'll take it from here. Come on, Julia. Like you said, you've had a hell of a day. Go home. Trust me and my department to do our jobs without an assist from you."

Washington retreated into the house, and Julia felt a burn of frustration and dread, knowing the clock was ticking down to zero.

"Julia, girl. You gave us a scare."

A sandy-haired man approached from the side of the ranch home, and Julia looked through the darkness to see Prejean.

"I'm so glad to see you. I'm sorry about how I acted at the apartment," Julia said.

"It's okay, but if you accuse me of being a liar and planting evidence again, I might not forgive so quick. Come here, sweetheart."

Prejean gave Julia a hug, and this time, Julia didn't pull away.

"I was completely out of line. I apologize."

"I understand. If I take my pride out of the equation, Navarro was just trying to protect you as best he could. In a lot of ways, I fit the killer's profile. You and me, we're good. But I know that's not why you're here. There's no sign of Charlotte in the house yet."

"I heard," Julia said. She shot a quick glance at Landry's wife, who was still sitting on the front step.

"Can you play interference for me with the chief? I'm frozen out of the investigation and Beth won't let me inside, but I want to ask the wife a few questions. This isn't for a story. I'm sure Jeremiah has Charlotte hidden somewhere else."

"It's possible, but we still need to check out the house, and I'm sure the Detroit cops already talked to the wife. Whatever MMK said when you were back in the apartment, he could've been playing with you. Go on now. I'll cozy up to Washington for a bit. You take care of your business."

"I owe you," Julia said, and then called out to Jeremiah's wife. "Excuse me, Mrs. Landry. I need to talk to you."

The blond woman turned around, and Julia beckoned Landry's wife in her direction.

"I'm sorry to bother you at this time. I realize you've just heard some terrible things about your husband, but there's a woman who's still missing."

"Are you a cop?"

"No, but the missing woman is my friend. You and your husband didn't have any other properties?"

"I already told the police. This is the only place we own. We've lived here for seven years and rented an apartment in Midtown before that."

"Is there any other place your husband might have considered home? Maybe a house where he lived before you two got together?"

"Well, there's his grandmother Leticia's place, but he hated that old house. Leticia has a Victorian over in the Woodbridge neighborhood. He lived there for a little while when they first moved here from Louisiana. Leticia's in a home now, so the place is empty."

"Does the house have a basement?"

"I don't know. Wait . . . I think it might. I remember Jeremiah saying something one time about Leticia needing help because she had a water leak in her basement, so, yeah, I guess it does. Why?"

"Do you have a spare key and an address?"

"I don't know," Landry's wife said, and looked back with suspicion at Julia.

"A police officer will be with me. I'm going to be honest with you here. Your husband did some horrific things, but you might have the chance to do some good."

"I never thought in a million years Jeremiah would be capable of doing something like this. Is there a chance this missing woman could be alive?"

"It's possible."

"Okay. I'll be right back."

Julia took a quick look into the beehive of Landry's place, staying far enough away from the cops' direct line of vision. She saw Prejean engrossed in conversation with Washington, and then Landry's wife came back out and approached Julia on the path with her head down.

"Here's the key to Leticia's place and the address."

Navarro's Chevy Tahoe pulled to the curb and Julia ran to the vehicle, positioning herself in front of Ray's door before he could get out.

He slid down the window, and Julia spotted Russell in the passenger seat.

"Charlotte isn't here. I think she could be at Jeremiah's grandmother's house. We have to go there right now," Julia said. "Jeremiah said he put Charlotte in some kind of container in a basement. There's no basement here. The cops are wasting their time. I have an address for the grandmother's place."

"Gooden . . ." Navarro started to say, but Julia had already thrown open the door to the backseat and climbed inside.

"Trust me on this one. Please. Just drive."

Navarro hung up with the chief and the trio drove through the historic Woodbridge neighborhood, passing by the former Eighth Precinct Police Station on Grand River Avenue and lines of homes dating back to the Victorian era, until they arrived at the address Jeremiah's wife had supplied.

The home was a worn pink-and-brown Victorian that looked to Julia like a faded gingerbread cookie.

"Washington is sending over a unit to help search the place," Navarro said. "They still haven't found Charlotte, but they did locate a notebook in Jeremiah Landry's shed where he kept a detailed list of all the surveillance he did on his victims. He's been tracking Charlotte for the past few weeks. So whatever we find here, Landry was already stalking Charlotte before you took her running in the park."

"In other words, it won't be your fault, Julia," Russell said.

"Stop talking in the past tense about Charlotte until we know for sure."

The three exited the vehicle and Navarro grabbed two flashlights from his trunk and threw one to Russell.

"Julia said Landry has Charlotte locked in a container," Navarro said.

"Do you have tools? You're not going to be able to shoot the lock off if there's a chance there's a live body inside," Russell said.

Navarro reached into a tool kit in the back of his SUV and retrieved a set of lock picks, a screwdriver, and a small hammer, and stuffed them into a duffel bag. "Let's go."

Navarro led the way into the house, flicking on a light in the entryway.

"At least we've got power," Russell said.

The three moved to a small front room with an old brick fireplace and filmy, ivory-colored dust cloths that partly covered up pieces of furniture in the dank space that was thick with dead air. Above the fireplace was a mantel filled with figurines and prayer cards of Catholic saints.

"I'll take the back of the house and, Russell, you and Julia search the front."

"These old places, the basements are usually connected to the kitchen. I'm betting the basement is in the back of the house. I'm going with you," Julia said.

Julia tried to take the lead, but Navarro moved ahead of her.

"I found something, Ray, by the fireplace," Russell called out. "It looks like a woman's silver bracelet. It's got a charm on it. Hold on. Let me put on my glasses. Okay. There's a word inscribed on it. It says 'Peace.'"

Julia reached up to the matching necklace Charlotte had given her. "She's here. The bracelet belongs to Charlotte."

Navarro pushed forward, down a long, narrow hallway, ducking in the short space, until he reached a door and threw it open. He flicked his hand over a light switch, and Julia peered over his shoulder, seeing a set of wooden stairs descending below.

"This is it. We found the basement," Navarro called out to his partner.

"Charlotte? Charlotte Fisher. It's Julia Gooden."

Julia ran down the stairs after Navarro, and the tiny seed of hope that had started to blossom dissipated when she saw the contents of the basement, a hodgepodge of boxes, containers, mannequins with women's clothing, and stacks of old newspapers, all crammed throughout the space. The search wouldn't be as easy as she had hoped.

A dim single yellow bulb provided the only light in the room. Navarro reached for his flashlight and panned the packed basement in a slow and steady sweep. The beam streamed past cobwebs and boxes until it lit up an old gray trunk with a thick padlock.

"Did Landry say a container or a trunk?" Navarro asked.

"I think he said a container. But this could be it."

Navarro bent down over the trunk and did a quick inspection with the flashlight. He then gave a light rap on the side of the trunk with his fist.

"It's solid. Russell, I think we've got her," Navarro yelled. "There are finger imprints on the dust on the front and the sides, where Landry probably opened and closed the trunk."

"A black-and-white unit just showed up. We'll be right down," Russell called out.

"Hold the light for me, Julia, right over the lock," Navarro said. He reached into the duffel bag and pulled out the small hammer, holding the top of the lock in one hand and the hammer in the other.

Navarro gave one hard rap on the side of the lock. When it didn't pop, he did the same with the opposite side, and the lock snapped open.

"Step back, Julia," Navarro said.

The top of the old trunk squeaked as he pulled it open.

Julia moved forward, still holding the flashlight, and pointed the beam of light inside.

Charlotte Fisher, barefoot and wearing the blue dress, was crammed into the trunk. Her legs were curled in a C shape underneath her, and her face was pale and waxy, but Julia was sure she saw her friend's eyelids flutter when she moved the light across her face.

"I said back up, Julia!" Navarro ordered.

He reached inside the trunk and stuck his middle and index fingers against the side of Charlotte's neck.

"It's weak, but she's got a pulse," Navarro said. He dove his hands underneath Charlotte and pulled her limp body out. "Call for a paramedic, Russell. Now."

CHAPTER 32

Julia held a Styrofoam cup filled with hot water and a tea bag between her hands, as she waited in the hospital visiting area, hoping to see Charlotte.

The events of the previous night now seemed like a blur.

She had returned her family back to the safety of their home in Rochester Hills after Charlotte was found. She and Logan had talked for hours. The two of them sat on the floor by his bed, discussing what had happened in the apartment, his bravery, and his future career aspirations of becoming a policeman, a district attorney, or a professional magician.

A doctor who looked familiar to Julia exited her friend's room, along with Charlotte's son and ex-husband, Joe Perkins.

Julia watched on as Perkins put his arm around his child and the two headed to the elevator, a private moment Julia didn't want to disturb.

The doctor walked in Julia's direction and his profile became clear, prompting a flashback to when her estranged husband had been treated at the same hospital.

"Julia Gooden. I'd say it's nice to see you again, but under the circumstances, I don't think that would be quite appropriate," Dr. Brian Whitcomb said, and extended his hand. "I hope you and your family are doing well. I understand you're here to see Charlotte."

"Yes, she's a friend of mine. How is she doing?"

"Charlotte is in stable condition. Under the circumstances, she's extremely lucky to be alive. Still, your friend underwent a horrible ordeal, both physically and mentally. But Charlotte said she would like to see you."

Dr. Whitcomb turned to leave but stopped to address Julia one last time.

"I don't mean this in a negative way, but in the greatest respect to you, Julia, I hope I don't see you at the hospital again anytime soon."

"No offense on my end either, but the feeling is mutual."

Julia entered Charlotte's room and stood witness to the ghost of the pretty, vivacious woman Charlotte had been just a day before. Charlotte lay in her hospital bed staring up at the ceiling, unblinking, looking ashen and wan, with two thick half-moon dark circles under her eyes.

"Charlotte, it's Julia."

Julia sat down by the side of Charlotte's bed and reached for her hand. "I'm here. I'm so sorry about what happened. I know it might not seem like it now, but you're going to be okay."

Charlotte continued to look up at the ceiling, not making eye contact, but gave Julia's hand a weak squeeze.

"You're a survivor. Don't forget that. Your son needs you," Julia said. She felt wooden and struggled for the right words to say, but then recalled Jeremiah Landry's assessment of her, that she was just like him, a shell, unable to feel or express emotion.

"When you're ready, you should talk to somebody, a therapist or counselor. They can help you. I waited years to seek counseling myself, and that was a mistake. I told you about what happened to my brother. For a long time, I pushed my feelings way down deep, and it screwed me up. Keeping everything bottled inside can destroy you a little bit each day. If you want to talk about what happened, I'll be here for you, too."

Julia ran her fingers over the Peace necklace Charlotte had given her and unclasped it.

"I want you to have this," Julia said. She opened up her friend's hand and tucked the necklace inside Charlotte's palm. "Just like you told me, hold on to it and then pass it on to someone else when you've found what you need."

Charlotte looked to Julia for the first time and started to weep.

"It was so dark in there," Charlotte said. "It felt like I was buried alive."

"You're okay," Julia said, and put her arms around her friend. "I'll make sure of it."

Julia reached her Rochester Hills house, never feeling happier to be home in her entire life. Navarro's Chevy Tahoe was parked out front and Julia noticed the SALE PENDING sign was no longer on her front lawn.

She expected her two little boys to come running, but instead, the house was quiet, except for Helen, who was busy in her beloved kitchen, rearranging her pots and pans and unpacking the mounds of boxes she had brought with her to the temporary apartment.

"You are back. How is your friend?" Helen asked.

"Traumatized, but I think she's going to be okay," Julia said. She looked out the kitchen window over the sink to her backyard where Logan, Will, and Navarro were shooting hoops.

"I have some news I don't think you're going to like," Helen said. "The Realtor stopped by."

"I saw a message from her this morning, but I haven't had a chance to listen to it."

"The family that was going to buy the house, the father's job offer fell through. So they pulled out. I'm sorry. I know you were looking forward to moving closer to the city. We will not move to the other place now, no?"

Julia looked on as Navarro picked up Will and put him on his shoulders so her little boy could reach the basket.

"That house might not be a good fit for us after all."

"So we stay here?" Helen said.

"Yes. For now."

"Thank heavens. I am tired of having to box up my kitchen. This place, although you have some bad memories from the past, the good ones you create in the present are all that matter. Your friend, Mr. Ray, he is good with the boys. I see you completely happy for once, Miss Julia. You go out and see your boys. The tall one, too."

The fall leaves that had strewn across her backyard and desperately needed to be raked crackled under her feet as Julia watched Navarro pretend to miss a block and allowed Logan to run by him and score.

"Hey, Mom, want to play with us?" Logan asked while Navarro gave him a high five for his scoring shot.

"How about a rain check. I hate to break up your game, but I need to borrow your uncle Ray for a minute."

"We'll play later," Navarro promised. "I'll be ready to take another beating from you two then."

Julia's rule was never to talk shop in front of her boys and waited until the glass screen door to the deck closed behind Logan and Will.

"How was the hospital?" Navarro asked.

"It will take time, but I think Charlotte is going to be okay."

"I've got to be honest with you, Gooden. I didn't think

that was going to be a good outcome last night. I've seen my share of dead kids who hid in car trunks and suffocated. And they were in a bigger space."

"How come you think Charlotte survived?"

"That trunk Landry put her in was ancient. It was pretty beat-up and there were a couple decent-sized holes in the back that Landry probably didn't know were there. Charlotte was lucky."

"So, Detective, it was an unexpected surprise finding you here when I pulled in."

"You said I had an open invitation on the weekend."

"That you do. How long do we have you for?"

"I filled out most of the paperwork for the LaBeau and Landry cases, and Russell said he'd do the rest. He was asking about a double date with your sister and us. I told him I'd have to run that by you first."

"That's still a union I can't understand, but they seem happy, so I won't judge. I've got some news. The sale on my house fell through."

"I'm sorry. I know you were excited about moving closer to the city."

"Maybe everything is working out for the best. We may actually stay here or look for a bigger place."

"The house you wanted to buy seemed plenty big to me, but that's coming from a guy who lives in a one-bedroom apartment."

"About that. Maybe we'd like to have you around more often."

"Are you serious, Julia?"

"I'd need to talk to the kids, but it feels right. Is that something you'd want to do?"

"I'd love it more than anything. You're absolutely sure about this?"

"A hundred percent. We could look for a place together as

a family in the city. A fresh start, unless you want to stay here."

"The department doesn't have residency requirements, so I don't have to live in the city limits. But there's one thing. I'd want to make it right by you and Logan and Will."

Julia looked on at the gentle giant in front of her, the man she had lived with and loved as a younger woman, and the man who had stayed her loyal friend after they broke up. Navarro had always been the one person who had never let her down. Or left her side.

Julia was certain of one thing. Helen was right. With Ray and her boys, Julia was happier than she'd ever been.

Navarro lifted Julia up and kissed her. Julia closed her eyes, thinking this was one of the moments, the beautiful ones, a life ahead being created on a cold October Michigan morning in a backyard where bad memories that had once lingered were now gone.

"I'm going to make you so happy, Julia," Navarro said. "You and your boys."

"You already do. We have all the time in the world to figure things out. By the way, Helen comes along with the package deal with the Gooden family."

Navarro gave Julia his perfect smile. "She'll keep me in line, and we'll all eat well. It's going to be a beautiful life. I promise."

Julia jogged in place, waiting for her date who zipped out of the garage in his orange two-wheeler. She waved back at the bay window to Will and Navarro and started to sprint to catch up with Logan, who was almost halfway up the block already for their run/bike ride.

"Stay in the bike lane," Julia said as she kept pace next to her son.

"You're on the road, not the sidewalk."

"Consider me your buffer." Julia looked away from the road ahead, and the potential dangers that she once was sure were always lurking.

Instead, she took in the image of her oldest son, his dark hair shining in the sun like liquid black gold.

"Come on, Julia. We've got twenty whole dollars to spend today. I earned the money by mowing Mr. Cole's lawn. I lied and told him I was twelve. If he knew I was only nine, he'd think I was too little to work hard. We're going to have a great day for once, kid. I promise. I'm going to make everything good for you."

The voice of her brother from long ago echoed in her head, and she reached inside her waist pack for the baseball Jeremiah Landry had taken from Ben's grave.

The ache for her brother was still there. It would always be. But she knew the pain that she still felt wasn't going to kill her.

She'd learned if you held a bad memory too tightly, you could squeeze out the beauty that was once part of it, too.

"Hey, kiddo. I need to make a pit stop," Julia told Logan, who was making it a point to ride a few feet ahead of his mother, like a sheepdog tending its flock.

"If you want to go to the cemetery, it's okay. I'll go with you."

Logan leaned his orange bike against the wrought-iron fence of the Sunset Hills Cemetery and mother and son walked silently past the tidy rows of gravestones until they reached the back lot, where Benjamin Gooden Jr., a little boy whose biggest dreams had been to see the New York Yankees reach the World Series and to keep his little sister safe, was laid to rest.

Julia carefully took the baseball out and placed it by her brother's grave. She felt the tears come, and this time, she didn't try and hide them from the outside world.

"You know, you remind me a lot of my brother. He was brave and loyal, just like you."

"Are you crying, Mom? You never cry."

Julia smiled at her little boy and recalled Roseline telling her she needed to let her brother go, that it was time for him to pass, but part of him would always be watching out for her. Whether that was true or not, Julia knew what she had to do.

"You saved my life back at the apartment. I wouldn't be here if you hadn't been so smart and courageous. Thank you for protecting me."

Logan smiled his crooked smile, the same one Julia had seen her brother give her as he raced in front of her on the boardwalk so many years ago, always looking behind him to be sure she was safe.

The flapping of what sounded like a thousand wings beating in unison startled Julia, and she looked on to a grove of trees in the woods behind the back row of gravestones. She reached for Logan's hand as a flock of blackbirds shot up from the branches and then scattered across the sky, flying back and forth in what seemed like a random, uneven pattern, until they conjoined in perfect formation, instinctively knowing the way to go.

Julia watched on until the blackbirds flew to the farthest point on the horizon, looking like a tiny dot, until they disappeared out of sight.

"They're flying away for the winter, but they always come back," Logan said. "They never leave for good."

Julia and Logan returned to the house, where Logan immediately ran to the backyard to play basketball.

Julia went inside where she was greeted by Helen, who put her index finger up to her thin lips and motioned her head to the living room, where Julia could see Navarro on the sofa with Will laying on his chest, both of them fast asleep.

"I don't think Ray has really slept in three days," Julia whispered. "Logan is in the backyard. I'm going into my office to do some writing."

Julia savored the moment and looked on at the life she had now, one created from the ashes that learned how to burn bright again.

Inside her office, Julia opened an e-mail from her book editor, asking how things were going with the revision of her manuscript.

This time, she was ready.

She opened up the file and started a new Chapter 1.

Thirty years ago, my brother, Ben, was kidnapped from the room we shared. He meant everything to me.

This is his story.

And my story, too.